SECOND CHANCE WORKPLACE

ROMANCE COLLECTION

JUST BAE

CONTENTS

JESSIE

AMY

D r. Jack Reynold lost his mind and university hospital's research assistant, Amy Taylor was smart to send him away when he approached her after what had transpired the day before. Thoughts of what had gone right and wrong had dawned heavily on her; Jack's fingertips plucked her puffy pregnant nipples as she jerked his cock almost causing the doctor to ejaculate on her desk. They almost made out and didn't only because Amy was called on the PA system to the first floor.

She's eight months pregnant and her verbally-abusive cocky boyfriend, Frank Ramsey works at the city's best hospital down the road. Amy and Frank have had problems since she became pregnant and Frank often leaves her for days telling her he's away for work. Amy's not innocent either; she's crossed the line with a few guys, flirting her curves and teasing but she hasn't been totally unfaithful. When she has the baby, she just wants to leave Frank.

―――――

The sensual encounter came into play that night, when Jack Reynold was in bed with his wife of fifteen years, Kate. She reached over and Jack woke up.

"Come closer, honey."

Jack came and began fondling Kate's breasts. *He really wanted her but now that she's seeing a woman as well, she wasn't his.* Jack's cock rose and Kate lifted her nightie for him to put it in her. Their ooohs and ahhhs could be heard throughout the dawn and after forty-five minutes, Jack was at the end of the bed, feeling unclean for having sex with his wife.

"You okay, honey?" Kate said, lighting up a cigarette.

"Yeah, just have a headache."

"Come here. Let me make it feel better."

Jack laid back as Kate massaged his head. They fell back to sleep until it was time for Jack to leave for work.

―――――

Jack stumbled through another day, his mind searched for reasons why's he still with his wife. He never had thoughts about another woman until that episode with Amy. He knows that he and Kate are only together for the sake of their son Mark.

Kate started seeing one of her friends, Marlene while they were working at SmithKline and Beecham. Jack was away in Dubai for a month for a doctor's conference and Kate blamed his absence for her transgression.

Jack came home from work and took a breath before stepping inside. Mark was on the sofa, stretched out reading the book, *The Odyssey.*

"Hey, son, where's your mother?"

"She's outside, Dad," he said waving in the direction of the back.

Kate was hanging out the laundry.

"Hey, Kate."

"Jack?" Kate said jumping.

"I'm sorry. I startled you. I've been thinking—"

"Thinking about what, sweetheart?"

"About going out for dinner tonight. Just me and you. I think Mark will be okay for a few hours."

"Where?"

"Margaret's." *He overheard Amy Taylor talking about Margaret's to her colleagues at work.*

"So—you want to take me to Margaret's? What's that for?"

"Just want to spend some quality time with you—"

"I see—all right, then. Did you make the reservations yet?"

"No, I haven't."

"Well, if we want to eat tonight, I'd call them right away."

———

Nine o'clock was the earliest time and Jack took it. "Be a gentleman," he said as he put on his best suit seeing he hadn't shaven in weeks. Between the long hours at work, his son's soccer practices and Kate's rendezvous with her lover Marlene, Jack's probably violated his hospital's grooming protocols. *Yet, Amy likes it,* his brain remarked replaying the scene at the lab. Jack sighed forcing the memory to go away as he showered.

When he came out of the bathroom, Kate was there, arms crossed. "Out, Dr. Reynolds, my turn," she said pushing Jack out of the way.

"Okay, okay."

———

When they are ready to leave, they go to Mark who's playing with his Nintendo Switch in the living room.

"Son, your mother and I are heading out for dinner. I trust you won't burn the house down while we're gone." Jack said looking in the mirror. "How do I look?"

"Nice, Dad."

"Hey, put that Gameboy down and read another chapter?" Kate said.

"Mom, it's not a Gameboy. It's called—"

"Whatever it's called. Please, son, make sure you finish your reading before going to bed. We will be back late."

"Ok, Mom."

"There's some leftovers in the fridge. Just heat it up in the microwave. Okay, Mark?"

"Yes, Mom."

Kate kissed Mark on the forehead while Jack's already by the door with his coat on and glancing at the clock.

"Bye, Mom, bye, Dad!"

"Bye," Kate tossed her handbag over her shoulder and stepped outside.

"Bye, son," Jack said, "In bed by ten-ish, all right? And make sure the door's locked."

"Okay, Dad."

———

This is the first time in five years that Kate and Jack went out to dinner. Kate walked ahead of Jack as he hurried to open the car door for her but doesn't manage to do so in time. Kate got in and Jack sighed, "Can I be a gentleman for once?"

"You move too slow? Just hurry before we're late."

During the drive, Jack spent time trying to remember exactly how to go out on a date. They arrive at Margaret's and are led to their seats.

"May I take your coats?" The waiter said pulling out the chairs for them.

"Here and thank you," Jack said, slipping off his and Kate took off hers.

"Thank you!"

"You're welcome."

"Well, isn't this nice," Kate said looking around.

"Yes, it is," Jack choked, trying his hardest not to look at a woman in front of his table. *Oh my God! That's Amy Taylor! Look at those breasts coming out of her dress.* Jack hurried to open the menu almost reading every word.

"Sorry, ma'am," a man said plopping down in the seat behind Kate. It was the guy who came with Amy and Jack didn't recognize him. He looked harder and saw the hospital ID around his neck with the words, **"Frank Ramsey - Orthopaedic Surgeon"** written in bold caps on top. *What the hell is Amy doing with that foot butcher?*

"No problem—so," Kate said turning to Jack, "Did you have a good day at work? Anything new?"

"Nothing special. How about you?"

"If the house looked the same as it did when you left this morning, then you know how my day went." *Kate was bored to death working from home. She started writing contemporary romance novels three years ago and a few made the USA Today's Bestseller's list.*

At the table across them, Amy's date was blabbering about something, and Jack couldn't help but notice her looking at him every few seconds. He put his elbow on the table and rested his head in his hand so that he might do the same. *God, she's beautiful.* He began daydreaming about Kate and Dr. What's-His-Name vanishing, their tables come together and Jack and Amy start making love on top of them.

"Jack!" Jack flinched and looked at Kate. "What are

you looking at? Do I have something on my face?" Kate took out her mirror to look.

"Nothing. Just something about work. That's all."

The waiter came over to take their order after Amy and the butcher ordered first. Jack looked again seeing Amy smiling at him. The butcher snapped his fingers, getting her attention.

"Is there something on this menu that Margaret's known for, honey?" Jack said turning his eyes from Amy.

"If there was, I'd expect they'd mark it in red on the menu you were just memorizing—so you tell me?"

"Oh, I'm sorry. It's been a while since I've been out on a date."

"Well, get it together, Jack. This is my time, honey. Not the lab rats or the girl in the red dress with the big boobs."

"Honey, what are you talking about?"

"Jack, please let's just have a good time, okay?"

"Okay, honey."

"We'll have…," Kate started saying to the waiter.

———

They ate, and Jack continued staring at Amy's breasts during the course of the meal. Kate noticed but didn't say anything else.

"Would you like dessert, sweetheart?"

"What time is it, Jack?"

Feels like it must be nearing midnight, Jack grumbled checking his watch, "A quarter after ten."

"No, it's all right, honey."

Suddenly, Amy stood up and started walking out with the butcher. He trailed behind her trying to pull her back. Jack then got up and told Kate he was going to the restroom.

"Ok, honey! Don't get lost."

"I won't. I'll be right back." Jack kissed Kate and headed in the bathroom's direction checking behind him to see if she was looking. Then, he snuck out spotting the surgeon and Amy's arguing.

"I don't *want* to go with you," Jack overheard Amy yelling.

"We go out to dinner and now you're not going back with me? For God's sake, I'm the father of your child."

Amy paces back and forward. "Not tonight! Leave me the hell alone!"

"Oh, now, we're playing like kids at school? Just get the hell in the car."

"No!"

The surgeon grabbed Amy and tried dragging her into the car. Amy swung her handbag and hit him in the face. The surgeon stumbled back and Jack ran to her rescue.

"You okay, ma'am?" Jack said seeing the surgeon on the ground.

"I'm okay, Jack. Please leave."

"I'm not going anywhere."

"You hit on a pregnant woman and you think you're a tough guy, huh?"

Jack hit the man with his cane and Amy tried pulling Jack back.

"Stop it, Jack!"

The surgeon covered himself and Jack grabbed Amy's arm. Amy flinched and said, "Don't touch me, Jack."

"Amy, please—"

"Just leave me the fuck alone!" Amy gathered her things and marched back inside Margaret's.

———

Jack came back in and walked right by Amy who was at the mirror fixing herself. Jack's wife, Kate was sitting at the bar having a Scotch.

"Oh, you're finally back," she said. "I thought you left me. Somebody said you were fighting outside over a woman."

"Well, that's fake news!"

"Well, baby. I need you to tell you something." Kate leaned in feeling tipsy.

"What honey?"

"Sweetheart, I paid the bill so you can—"

"What?"

"Marlene's here to have a few more drinks with me."

"What the fuck? You're on a date with me, remember?"

"Jack, please not tonight. Marlene's right outside."

"Sweetheart, I told you to keep that bitch out of our lives."

"When you left me to go to Dubai to learn about taking out people's organs, I needed some attention. Remember?" Kate grabbed Jack's hand and he pulled away. "It will only be for a little while. I'll be home soon."

"Pardon me, pardon me," a woman said from behind Jack. She had on a black dress and walked right in front of him sliding onto the stool beside Kate. "Right on time, darling." Kate kissed her and put her arm around her.

"Would've been early if I could've gotten away from a minute sooner," Marlene said staring at Jack. " Oh, hi, Jack."

"Oh, Lord! You again…"

"I know, I know—don't listen to Mr. Grumpy," Kate said. "Good *night*, sweetheart. I'll see you when I get in."

"Kate, you're so fucking wrong?"

"I said I'll see you when I get home, sweetheart."

Jack walked out and thought that Amy had left but she didn't.

———

Two days later, Jack spotted Amy Taylor walking down the university's first-floor corridor and stopped her.

"Good morning, Amy. Will you be available to assist me in a study later this evening?" Jack asked *feeling a trickle of hope that maybe, against all reason, Amy will agree. That perhaps, afterward, she'll want to talk. They can grab a coffee and sort everything out. He can then apologize for his behavior, and explain his situation with Kate, and she will understand that his marriage is nonexistent except on paper.*

"I, I don't—"

"I'll be the guinea pig this time. I could definitely use you for this one."

"I—I don't know, Jack. You know the other night—" Amy stuttered.

"Forget about the other night. Are you free?"

"I am but not until after 8."

"Ok, I'll meet you at the lab—let's say around nine?"

"Ok."

———

Jack went back to his office to devise a plan on how he'll have to sneak out if Mark isn't asleep. Over the last few days, he's seen his wife only twice. She's been hanging out with Marlene in the evenings and coming home right before it's time for Mark to go to school and Jack to work.

Jack dragged through the rest of the day anticipating what happiness he can get from coming home. When he arrived, he found Mark on the couch finishing *The Odyssey*. Jack talked about his son's favorite parts and how to tackle his book report.

At eight, Mark went upstairs and twenty minutes later, Jack left.

———

Jack drove to the hospital dreaming about what happened inside that room, letting the memories soothe him until when he arrived. Once he arrived, he found Dr. Rothschild in the lab instead of Amy.

"What are you—"

"I know Jack this is odd but Amy Taylor had to excuse herself this evening. She said she wasn't feeling well."

"Oh my! I hope she's going to be okay." Jack cursed under his breath.

"She'll be fine," Dr. Rothschild said bending down to wrap an Ace bandage around his ankle.

"There, that's enough," he said feeling pain.

"Would you like a magazine to take your mind off of pressure?"

"Thanks but no, thank you."

"All right. You're ready to go," Dr. Rothschild said as she left the room to turn on the machines.

"Now, Jack. You'll be put in a sort of a dream in order for us to examine actually how the mind reacts to pleasure. It's okay to express yourself," Dr. Rothschild said in the speaker in Jack's room.

"Okay, Doctor."

"Just relax. It'll only take a few minutes."

Jack lies back and tilts his head to look at the door that Amy stepped through, that night, looking ridiculous yet adorable with her wires and electrodes and oversized robe. Jack's right leg bends unconsciously and his heel presses into the hospital bed make pain creep further up his leg. He takes a few breaths and stretches it out again, then squeezes his eyes shut and reconstructs his fantasy. Amy's fingers run an inch below his navel before she removes her hand entirely. His sigh fades when she peels off her robe, treating him to the incomparable sight of her nakedness. Jack might reach for her, but she'd grab his hands. "No, no," his dream scolds him, "This is for you. Just relax." His left hand twists in the sheets, while his right plucks open his robe uncovering his cock. He uses three fingers—the best he can do to simulate. The look on Amy's face makes his cock stretch longer. Amy's first jerk is tentative and he tightens her grip with his left hand. She catches on quickly, and he's soon bucking up to meet her rhythm. His bad leg is bending, pain winding through the pleasure. Jack can't focus on stretching it back out as Amy increases the pace, can only try to push the pain away. His apex is approaching, Jack's so close and his back is arching and Amy's name is coming out his tongue—then his foot slips, wrenching his ankle on the hospital sheets. Pain swallows pleasure and Jack bolts upright. He grips his lower leg with both hands, unable to do anything to help.

Suddenly, the door opens and Mrs. Rothschild comes in. "Oh my, are you okay?"

"No, I'm not."

"Let me try turning up the frequency. The machine has been acting a little weird these days."

"No, I'm done. Get these damned wires off me," Jack said turning to the mirror. "Go find yourself another guinea pig, Dr. Rothschild!"

"My God, Jack! Calm down." Dr. Rothschild said as she removed the electrodes. "I think we've gotten some of the data that we need. That's the thing—even if it doesn't go as expected, there's still a sample of a result."

"What the hell are you saying?"

"I'll need you to come back for one more session at a later to complete the results."

"I'm done with this, Doctor."

"Jack, calm down, you were doing okay. What were you feeling as the machine stabilized?"

"Nothing. Are we done here, doctor?"

"Yes, Jack. You may leave. Thanks for coming."

"Never fucking again," Jack said as he rushed out the door.

CHAPTER TWO

"Amy, just so you know, there's a flying pig in the bathroom."

Amy blinks away from the page she's been staring at for at least ten minutes, "What did you say, Dr. Rothschild?"

"I wanted to make sure you hadn't gone catatonic. What's going on with you?

"Frank and I, you know."

"Must have been a helluva a reason to ditch Dr. Reynolds?"

"Well, let's just say it wasn't what I expected when I got home." Amy blushed.

"Girl, you are such a wreck."

"I know." Amy reached over to grab her coffee mug.

"Well, make sure you get some rest. The baby doesn't need to have its mother stressing out.

"Ok."

"Don't worry about anything. Frank will put a ring on that finger one of these days," Dr. Rothschild said walking away.

"I hope not," Amy murmured.

"I heard that young lady," Dr. Rothschild said surprising Amy.

———

Amy's baby daddy, Frank has been out of town for work for the last week and Amy since bailing out on Jack's research has been dodging him. She spotted him once walking down the corridor and hid behind a patient's room.

When she went back to her desk, she scribbled notes on one of her doctor's requests, recalling the scene when she left the restroom and saw the woman who came to meet with Jack's wife. Amy couldn't understand why Jack's wife would be with her, minutes after having dinner with him.

Amy just can't figure it out and for the rest of the days before Christmas break, kept away from that lab room. She knew better than to go there but a new fantasy sprang up; she and Jack sitting cheek-to-cheek in Margaret's bar and later ended up having sex in the restroom. Amy gasped out Jack's name as she came over and over again.

"No! No! not again," Amy said getting up throughout the day and washing her privates in the bathroom.

———

Amy is still hamstrung over Jack but it's been now ten days since the lab episode. At dinner after a long day of returning from his travels, Amy's fiancé Frank said, "Amy? I need to talk to you about something."

Amy stared at her plate hoping for the worse. "Yes, what is it, sweetheart?"

"I'm thinking about spending the holidays with my old man before the baby comes."

"Oh, okay. Have a nice time."

"Won't you come along?" Frank said. "I'd hate to tell you but you'll have to buy your plane ticket. You know we're pinching pennies for the baby."

"No, no. Doctor's orders that us pregnant women don't fly. I'll stay put right here."

"Baby, you're only two months pregnant. You shouldn't be alone for Christmas?"

"I'll be fine, don't worry. Go see Papa and give him my regards."

"I don't want you sitting at home by yourself reading *A Christmas Carol* over and over," Frank said making Amy chuckle. "Are they still having the Christmas party at the university this year?"

"Yes, honey."

"Oh, that's fantastic! I'm sure you'll have lots of fun." Frank said being sarcastic as usual. "Who knows? You might even meet some new people there."

"I've already met all the people I work with." Amy recognized his sarcasm but didn't feel like arguing.

"Really? Everybody on the whole campus? I doubt that."

"Sweetheart, go see Papa and let me manage this *being-at home-alone-Christmas-thing* myself. Love you."

"Love you too."

———

On the morning of Frank's departure, he and Amy loaded his luggage into the Uber and Frank left for the airport. Amy stayed behind and readied herself for the Christmas Party swearing to herself over and over that if Jack's there with his wife, she'll kill herself.

Tables were cleared from the middle of the university's cafeteria and red and green streamers were taped to the walls. Someone brought in a radio and set it to playing Christmas tunes that are nearly drowned out by attendees' conversations. Amy went straight for a punch bowl and poured herself a cup. The burn of alcohol makes her nauseous. She cradled the cup to her midsection and commenced looking around, trying to project an aura of poise.

As the evening goes on, Amy managed to hold a conversation or two with co-workers she was close with. In between chats, she sipped her drink finding the punch has somehow increased in alcohol. The fruit juice almost went up to her nose when she spotted Mr. Jack standing a few feet inside the cafeteria, with his suit and cane, and without Kate.

Amy can hardly believe what she's seeing. *Jack without his wife?* Powered by alcohol and indignation, Amy finished her drink and marched across the cafeteria to good ole Jack.

"Merry Christmas, Jack!"

"Thanks, Merry Christmas to you as well!"

Amy kicks herself for not thinking of something to say before she walked over here. "Your son Mark, did he find *The Odyssey?*"

"Oh yes, he finished reading it last week."

"Did he like it?"

"Very much. His favorite character was Ulysses."

Amy deeply wished she had another drink to hide behind as memories of Exam Room Five fill her unwilling mind.

"It's quite a good story. You wouldn't expect a kid from Generation Z to like something so old. Hey, who's knows? He might read *The Aeneid* next, but perhaps that would be a bit more advanced."

"Mark could benefit from the challenge."

"Oh, Mark is such a sweet boy. I remember when he came to the library," Amy slurred knowing she's talking too much.

"Thank you, he is. I don't know from whom he gets it from."

"I do."

Jack raises his eyebrows as Amy tries to figure out who said that because it couldn't possibly have been her.

"Let's dance?" Amy said steering away from the conversation.

"What did you say?"

"I said let's dance. Come on, it's Christmas."

Jack knows Amy is drunk. "I don't really—I don't dance. Can't." He lifted his cane a few inches and then let it drop.

"I think you can," Amy reached out her right hand to Jack's elbow and led him through the crowd and over to the radio.

Her hand trailed down to his and wrapped around it, lifting them up to shoulder height. Her left covered his on the cane, and she set a simple swaying rhythm that Jack falls into easily. Jack stares at her like Amy's some kind of magical being, and she can only bite her lip to temper a blinding smile. *This feels right, she knows it. No matter how wrong it is, it's still right.*

"I didn't think you'd speak to me after what I did," Jack said.

"What do you mean?"

"I scared you. I'm so sorry."

Amy shook her head, "You didn't scare me. Or, well, I was already scared. You didn't help, but you did... um, help." She closed her eyes briefly in an attempt to clear some of the haze. "You helped me not be in a position to be scared anymore."

"Regardless, I don't know what came over me."

So soon the song is ending and Jack steps away. Everything in Amy begs her not to let this become another memory she'll fantasize about. Once again, her heart takes control and words come out of her mouth, "Take me home, Jack."

"Amy..."

"I'm tired, Jack. I want to go home, I took an Uber here. I'm wasted and don't want to go alone."

"Come on, I'll drive you."

———

Both ignore the stares that follow them as they exit the cafeteria and walk to Jack's car. Amy's heart thuds as Jack opened the passenger door for her and she sits in. Her mind demanded to know what Amy thinks she's doing, but she has no answer for it. She just sat there and tried not to stare at Jack for more than three seconds at a time while she gave him directions. Jack Reynold's such a mystery to her, for all that she feels like she knows him so well. "May I ask what happened to your leg?" Amy sighed, "I mean, um, it's fine if you don't want to talk about it."

"I was drafted in '04," Jack said, his eyes fixed on the road. "So, I went to basic training, and…well, then…"

"An accident?"

"No. No, there wasn't an accident. I got a call from my wife and she told me she was pregnant. At that moment… nothing else mattered. The only thing that mattered was that I came straight home. My father abandoned me when I was little. I couldn't—I could never do that to my son. *Nothing* would make me do that. Even if it meant…so, I left the office where soldiers took calls from outside, and kept walking, and didn't stop until a jeep ran over my foot."

"Oh my God, Jack!"

"I was discharged in hours, of course. Most of the bones healed, but not all. Now you know." He glanced over at her.

"Well, Mark has his father. Turn here, it's the second house on the right."

Jack parked and then opened the passenger door for Amy. They walked to her house and Amy's feeling woozy. "At Margaret's, was the woman you were with, your wife?"

"Yes."

"But—I saw her with someone else."

"Well, yeah. Kate's lover means more to her than I do."

Amy stopped watching Jack languish. Her mind is blank when she stepped forward and wrapped her hand around the back of Jack's head. His mouth landed on hers.

The kiss was only for a moment, then Jack pulled away. "I'm sorry," he gasped.

Amy can hardly hear him through the blood pounding in her veins. Jack's lips are parted and wet, and all Amy does is smile.

"I'm not sorry," Amy said, closing the distance between them.

Amy clung to Jack's head and shoulder as the heat roared through her, stroking her tongue over his and scraping his lower lip with her teeth when he retreats. A growl rolled from his throat into her mouth and Jack kissed her harder. Amy's nails dig deep into his scalp and coat causing them to stumble. Her back hit the wall beside the front door.

"Wow!"

"I'm yours," Amy said, her voice low and desperate, "You know that, don't you?"

"I do."

Amy moaned and her leg has loosely hooked itself over Jack's and she pressed up against him in a way she's only done in her most fevered fantasies. She'd rather die than stop, realizing with something between elation and panic that they don't have to. Her boyfriend, Frank is likely halfway to Maine right now and the house is empty. Amy can pull Jack inside and finally take what she wanted for a long time.

She wanted to get to the door first, and can't make herself loosen her grip on Jack. She managed to inch closer to it, but then he ducked his head and started sucking on her neck. Her arm dropped and elbow hit the doorbell, sending a chime through the empty row home. A second later, lights came on inside.

"Christ!" Amy hollered and shoved Jack away.

Jack blinked, looking up at the windows, "Who's that?"

"Bloody Frank, I thought he was gone!" Amy said.

"Damn it," Jack moved back, but Amy grabbed his hand and pulled him closer.

"There's a hotel. Hollytree, on Stanmore. Meet me there tomorrow night at ten o'clock."

"Are you sure?"

"I am. Now, hurry."

"I'll be there." He stole one last kiss, then spun around, scooped his cane off the ground, and hurried to his car.

Amy put her hand over her mouth and grabbed her key and opened the door, Frank was dressed in a house-coat standing on the stairs.

"Amy, there you are, sweetheart. Would you believe it? There was engine trouble on the plane, so my flight was canceled until tomorrow. Hey, why did you ring the doorbell?"

"My elbow slipped, good night," Amy said bolting up the stairs and into the bathroom.

Oh my God! she whispered sitting on the toilet. *I almost got caught. Shit!*

Jack dragged his feet through the extra shift he took at the hospital, lost in a haze, unable to come to terms what would happen tonight. He called Mark to tell him that he would be home soon and asked where his mother was. Mark told him that she wasn't there and Jack told him to do his homework.

The day's end comes, and Jack comes home finding Mark sitting on the sofa as he enters. "Hello, son."

"Hi, Dad."

Jack hung up his coat and look at Mark. For the first time in weeks, he doesn't have a book in his hands. Instead, he's rigid and hunched over, looking at the carpet. "Is something wrong, son?"

Mark looked up. "Mom didn't come home today. She always does, after school. Where is she? I'm hungry."

Jack crossed the room and put his hand on Mark's

shoulder. "It'll be okay, son. She'll be here soon." he said, "Just... just wait here one minute. I'll be right back."

Jack went to their bedroom and checked the closet and the drawers. There was a complete absence of anything belonging to her. Jack looked around and spotted a corner of something white tucked beneath the pillow on the bed. He pulled out a piece of paper. *"I'm not coming back. Take care of Mark."* It's all Jack needed to hear and it wasn't something he hadn't been expecting. He folded the paper and walked back downstairs to Mark. He put his arm around his son and said, "Mark, your mother's not coming home."

"Why?"

Jack took out the letter from his pocket. "Your mother wrote this. You can read it if you like. I can tell she was unhappy here and needs to find her own way."

"Without us?"

Jack squeezed his son as tight as he can. "So it would seem, son. But, I'll never leave you, Mark. You'll always have me. I promise."

Mark sobbed and is shaken, curling up against his father. Jack nearly felt a measure of peace as he comforted his son.

———

Jack cooked Mark supper, and afterward put him to bed like he hasn't since Mark hit double digits. Stretched out,

Jack read aloud from *The Aeneid*, thinking of Amy. He looked at the clock seeing it's near ten.

"Keep reading Dad," Mark said.

Mark cried, and Jack cradled him until the boy finally fell asleep.

Jack slowly got up from the bed and close the door behind him. He stood for a few moments in the dark hallway, wavering between staying and heading out the front door. Jack ultimately grabbed his coat and car keys and headed out.

———

It's not until Jack's parked that he realizes he has no idea what room Amy is in. He got out and stood beneath one of the parking lot's lamps, staring at two rows of hotel doors. In luck, a curtain twitched aside, and one of the doors opened. Amy walked out onto the upper deck and Jack spotted her. "May I come up?"

Jack thought Amy nodded before she went back inside. He climbed a flight of stairs and followed the lights leading to her hotel room. Jack went inside seeing Amy standing with her arms over her stomach.

"I meant to—" he stuttered wanting to say, "call." Instead, Jack continued, "My wife just left me."

"What?"

"She's gone along with her clothes."

"Did she take your son?"

"No, no, she-ah. No, Mark's home asleep."

"I'm so sorry."

Jack blinked and truly looked at Amy for the first time since entering the room. She looked back at him, leaving only pure empathy.

"She fucking left him," Jack said, as his eyes began tearing. Amy pulls him inside and sat him on the creaky mattress.

"I'm so sorry, Jack."

"I thought you said you weren't sorry."

"I did, and I'm not. That's my dilemma."

"I don't want you to be. Not for any of this."

Jack leans on Amy's shoulder looks up at her. "Tell me what to do, Amy. I'm so lost."

"Well, go home and be with your son. He's had his world fall apart and he needs you."

Jack nodded.

"Call me up when you're ready, Jack."

"What about you?"

"I'll be sitting here alone with a child soon."

"What are you saying?"

"Yes, that's why I'm here with you tonight. Frank left me for some huzzy at the hospital. They're transferring to Singapore at the end of the month. What a deadbeat?"

"I'm so sorry."

"Don't be. I'll be okay."

Their faces are close, and Jack wanted to kiss her, but he limited himself to pressing his lips on her cheek. He lingered there as Amy's arms tighten around him. When he pulled away, she released him.

"Let me drive you home?"

"All right."

Amy gathered her things and canceled her reservation for the night.

—————

Jack can't stop looking at Amy as they drive to her place. When they pull up in front of her house, he couldn't resist the urge to reach for her hand and bring it to his lips. He kisses her fingers and began sucking the tips. But Amy pulled her hand back, instead of kissing and licking Jack's.

"This is for you, sweetheart until later," Amy said moving her tongue up and down each finger. Her eyes stay fixed on him and she said, "Later."

"Later."

She got out of the car and walked to her house. Jack didn't block until she was inside. He pulled off, happy that they didn't make another mistake.

CHAPTER FOUR

The next few weeks go by without Jack's wife Kate coming by at least to check on Mark. Her lawyer sent the divorce papers in the mall making Jack grieve inside. He signed them and days later, their marriage was dissolved. To take his mind off the pain, he spent more time with Mark, going out to dinner when he got off and buying Mark whatever he wanted.

Amy went into labor and Jack heard about it in the middle of a patient's checkup. He wanted to ring up Amy to find out how she was doing but doesn't. He just walk to where Amy's normally stationed to just say hi to her fill-in.

That evening, Jack gave in and told himself he would sit down with Mark to discuss him seeing another woman.

"Who?" Mark asked after his father opened the discussion at dinner.

"Do you remember I told you about the woman at the hospital's library?"

"The one who told you about *The Odyssey*?"

"Yes."

"Oh, yeah, she's nice."

"You think so?"

"Yeah, so, you want to take her out, huh? Wasn't she pregnant?"

"Yes, she was. She had the baby and now is at home resting. I hope this doesn't make make you feel uncomfortable."

"Well, I won't know unless you do it."

"Fair enough, so."

———

Amy called Jack at work a week after her delivery and told him to come by after work. Jack felt like a teenager again, the first time he came inside her home withstanding the looks and questioning faces of her neighbors wondering about *Amy Taylor and Mr. Frank Ramsey*.

Amy said, "Good night!" to her babysitter as she grabbed Jack's arm and marched with him out the front door.

And that was the first of a few dates, all scheduled while Amy was on her first month of maternity leave.

A month into their courtship, Jack found himself in a jewelry store in town, inspecting the best ring his budget would allow. A little voice crawled around the back of his mind whispering, *you think Amy would marry me.* Jack doesn't listen and buys the ring. It lives in his suit pocket and the small velvet box becomes dusty during each date. He almost crushed it when Amy suggested for their next date that they go to Margaret's.

"Really? You want to go there?"

"I'm sure we'll be fine. We don't expect Frank or what's her name to be there. Do we?"

"No."

———

And indeed, they enjoyed one of the best dinners Jack can remember before venturing to the bar. He wondered if he should be uncomfortable, but the memory of Kate with Marlene withered away as he watched Amy sip from a glass of wine. Her gaze lit on him only to jump away, and he noticed her cheeks slowly turned a shade not far distant from her drink.

"I feel as if I've missed the joke," he said.

"Not so," she said with her chin almost touching her chest.

Jack leaned in closer. "What then?"

Amy leaned in closer until they're almost cheek-to-cheek. "I had this fantasy about us, being here... then going into the restroom together and, um..."

Jack saw his cock rising and tried patting it down, "I see." Images race through his mind of Amy's dress hiked up over her hips, her hands holding his shoulders while he grabs her thighs and pounds into her. She screamed "Jack, Jack" every ten seconds.

"Anyway, we're not doing that. Just a thought. I'm still recovering, you know."

"Oh, we're not."

"Not unless we——"

"No, until we are——" Amy stopped talking and so did Jack. Her face is unreadable as she looked at him, but Jack found his fingers wandering into his pocket anyway while his heart hammered in his chest.

"Amy?"

"Yes?"

"I love you. I'll never love anyone the way I do with you. I know it hasn't been long, and nothing has to change right away, we can carry on like this as long as you like, but..." Jack opened the box and held it up. "Please tell me you'll marry me."

Amy only stared at him. Then, her head went up and down. "I will."

"You will?"

"Yes."

"Oh, my God!"

Somewhere far away, the bar's patrons applaud and the bartender announced, "Free champagne for the happy newlywed, and glasses all around!"

Amy and Jack broke apart to smile to the bartender and anyone who came up to pat their backs and wish them the best.

Jack gently wipes a tear away with his thumb. "Thank you. I love you."

"I love you too, Jack," Amy said. They kissed again before having another few drinks and leaving the restaurant.

———

Jack dropped Amy off but declined to go inside. On the drive home, he envisioned the way he'll break the news to Mark tomorrow, hoping he'll take it well.

He climbed in bed, letting Amy's wonderful fantasy play out in his mind. A few tugs and Jack sat up groaning. He then masturbated saying her name until he finally became tired.

CHAPTER FIVE

A my's postpartum period was over and she and Jack started going over each other houses daily but never had sex. This evening, Jack told Amy he'll cook dinner before they head out to their clinical appointment with Dr. Rothschild.

Amy convinced Jack to go back for the second part of his experiment, telling him that she had volunteered after Dr. Rothschild had contacted her. Dr. Rothschild explained that she was seeking to explore differences between a coupling who is close to marrying and have one child from a previous relationship. The condition was that both parties never had sex prior. *How convenient!* Dr. Rothschild gave her a date and time and they ultimately both agreed to participate.

Amy was on the couch while Mark was reading.

"That dragon kind of came out of nowhere," Mark said to Amy closing the book.

"I think they wanted Beowulf to go out with a bang."

Amy loved to continue discussing this with Mark, but found her eyes constantly roaming to the clock. It was getting late and their appointment was scheduled for 11 PM. She looked over in Jack's direction seeing him washing dishes. Mark had started yawning and finally told them he's going to bed.

"See ya!" Amy said.

"See ya! Thanks, Amy."

"You bet."

Amy sat upright, hearing Mark leave the bathroom to his bedroom. "I think we're all clear," she whispered grinning.

"Ok, I'm ready. I hope this goes better than the last time," Jack said.

"I'm sure it will, sweetheart."

"It was so weird being in that chair so sucked into subspace."

"Hmm, it sounds freaky."

"Well, it was, especially for an old man like myself."

"You're not old, Jack. Stop it!"

As they went to the closet, Jack grabbed both of their coats and put on Amy's first.

———

Amy hummed along on the way to the hospital texting her babysitter to make sure her newborn was okay. Her hand and Jack's found each other in the car's dark interior, drifting and lacing each other's tightly.

Within thirty minutes, they arrived at Exam Room Five in the university's clinical studies wing. It was difficult for them to keep their eyes off each other as they got undressed. Once they put on their robes, Dr. Rothschild came out and greeted them. "Jack, whatever you do. Let Amy have satisfaction first, please," Dr. Rothschild said handing them their electrodes, condoms, and earpieces.

"Ok, Dr. Rothschild. But I'm warning you she's the curviest woman I've ever been with."

"Jack, you'll be fine. Just keep that in mind."

"Jack, you listen to the doctor, okay?"

"Haha, very funny!"

———

Dr. Rothschild went on to tell the couple that she was monitoring the signals but couldn't actually see the experiment. It was the hospital's policy. They signed off on the final waiver and Dr. Rothschild left telling them to relax and have fun.

Jack sat at the end of the bed in a blue bathrobe twitched aside exposing his injured ankle. Amy opened the bag she'd brought from home and pulled out a towel, wrapping it around his lower leg. She then took a medium-sized collar and buckled it over the towel. "There," she said, "No rough stuff buddy."

"Who says no?"

Amy stood up and brought her hands down to the belt of her robe. "I did. Now watch me undress," Amy said as she untied the belt and let her robe slip down off her shoulders.

"Oh my! Those curves."

Amy's body was curvier now that she had the baby. Her breasts were milky and she felt vindicated. At this moment, all she thought about was her baby daddy Frank complaining about how curvy she was but he was long gone.

"Meanwhile, you can put your hands underneath and see what you can find that's wet."

"Is this part of the experiment?"

"Mic-check—I hear you guys in there," Dr. Rothschild said in the earpieces.

"Can we have some privacy, Doctor?" Jack said.

"Yes, Jack. You already do. I won't see what's happening. Now continue on."

Amy's robe hit the floor and she didn't wait for another second to let her hands dive inside Jack's robe, rubbing his chest and downward. "Oh my, Jack! What do you have here, buddy?"

Jack's hands met Amy's thighs and ran up over her hips to her waist, gently tugging until Amy straddled him. Once on top, Jack sucked her nipples, causing her to moan 'Jack 'as the breastmilk flooded his mouth. "I've done something right if I hear you say that."

Amy giggled, "And I know what makes that thing down there so hard."

Jack chuckled, "And what's that?"

Amy wrapped her hand around the back of his neck while the other went to his cock. One jerk made Jack hiss as his eyelids fluttered.

"God, Amy," he gasped leaning up to kiss her, managing to avoid the electrodes as he continued sucking her breast filling his mouth with milk. Amy continued jerking and Jack felt he was about to ejaculate.

"Jack, do something that'll raise your heart rate a little," Jack heard Dr. Rothschild say in his earpiece. Amy heard it as well.

"But, Doctor…"

"Do it now before the meter goes too low."

"Fuck me now, Jack. Suck the milk out of my titties," Amy begged, "Oh, Jack!"

Amy rose on her knees high enough to position Jack where she needed him. She lowered, breathing through the pressure of him entering. She's been thinking about this all day and can't wait any longer.

Jack's hands slid down to her curvy ass and he squeezed.

"That's it, right there, Jack," Amy moaned. She closed her eyes again and laid her head in the hollow between Jack's shoulder and neck as she surrendered to the plea-sure. She started off slow but soon sped up until her head rocked back. Jack's mouth descended on her neck, seeking out her G spots. The pleasure crested through Amy, leaving her gasping for more.

When her heartbeat slows, Dr. Rothschild, said in

their earpieces, "Amy, I need you to raise your heart rate?"

"Ok, Doc."

"Oh God, Jack! Fuck me, fuck me." Her muscles tighten as Jack stroked harder.

"Fuck me faster, faster…ah, ah, ah, Oh my God!!!!!!!" Amy said knowing Dr. Rothschild was likely listening in on them. She gazed in the mirrored glass as Jack kept thrusting. "Oh, he's so wonderful, Doctor," she gasped. Jack's eyes were shut, his hands were holding Amy steady for his erratic thrusts, which Amy matched by tightening her grip on his ass. "Yes, yes, oh God! That's it, Jack. Right there, right there."

"Ah- Amy!" Jack squeezed Amy, squirming. Unfortunately, he was the one who came first.

"Jack, why's your heart rate going down? Please raise it," Dr. Rothschild said through the earpiece.

"He came, Doctor. Jack broke the rules."

"Shit, shit, shit! I'm sorry, Doctor. I told you those curves…"

"Experiment's over. We'll have to go off the data we have. Thanks a lot, Jack."

———

Amy eased off Jack and soon Dr. Rothschild appeared to help them unplug. Amy unbuckled the collars from Jack's leg and unwrapped the towel before gently lowering his leg to the floor.

"Did we actually contribute something to science, Dr. Rothschild?" Jack said visibly embarrassed.

"I'd say, "Yes, Jack." The full readings were almost in. I think we have enough data to go off of though. I wouldn't be surprised if these were published in next month's journal. Anonymously, of course."

"How exciting!" Amy said hugging Jack.

"You are good for each other. Best of wishes to you in your upcoming marriage!"

"Thank you, Doctor."

"I'm sure there are couples around the world who wish they had your bond. Though I don't know how many would do a test like you. It seems like a one-in-a-million odds."

"Yeah, Doctor. I have to train good ole Jack here how to maneuver these curves of mine."

"Thanks for participating, guys and see you around," Dr. Rothschild said walking out of the room.

Amy and Jack finished dressing and returned to their car. She grabbed Jack's hand and presses the back of it to her cheek as they drive home through the night.

"Those curves got me," Jack said turning on the radio.

"I know. You ain't the first one to say that."

CAMERON JAMES

CHAPTER ONE

An empty restaurant in the morning had always been Makayla's favorite place to conduct an in-person interview. She was friends with the owner so she was allowed to work there while kitchen staff was preparing for the day.

Makayla sat across the table from a sophisticated older gentleman. They had coffee and a few pastries, which were alongside her papers and laptop.

"How does it feel to be the most hated man in New York City, Mr. James?" Makayla started off in a cheeky tone, which was more serious.

Cameron couldn't help but laugh. "Is that what I am? I thought that title was reserved for criminals?"

"Well, according to the media, it's you."

"Aren't you part of that same media?" he asked.

"I'm just the one who writes the story."

"Hopefully you won't write a hatchet piece about my

character."

"That all depends," Makayla replied. "If you give me anything, I'll do it. If not, the article could be a positive spin for you."

"So you're a typical member of the so-called fake media, it seems."

"If you thought so, then why did you agree to this interview?"

"You have a pretty face. Looking at you is a good way to start my morning off."

Makayla sharpened her gaze. "That was kind of sexist, but anyway. Tell me a little bit about yourself."

"I'm a regular guy with expensive taste. But I'm not the story. You want to know about the sex club."

"Yeah, let's start there."

Cameron collected his thoughts.

"The club itself was not my doing. The first establishment was a high-end place in Manhattan, where socialites and the rich can go to fulfill their darkest fantasies in privacy, of course. The owner is a woman in her late forties who inherited from her rich grandfather and wanted to do something meaningful with her money. That's why she opened the bondage club. A place where people can go without being judged. I won't go into specific details, but she was my submissive. She later hired me to be a dom at the club."

There was a brief pause as Cameron took a drink and gathered his thoughts.

He continued, "After a while, I was bored of Manhattan. You see, I've always been one who does not stay in one spot for long. My sub understood this. And when I told her I was coming to New York City, she told me that she had real estate out here. She was interested in creating a franchise of bondage clubs, so she asked me if I'd be interested."

"Why would this kind woman ask you to open a bondage club for her?" Makayla asked sarcastically.

"Because I have experience with running businesses. And the woman trusts me. Also, I have the option to leave whenever I want. Someone will take my place when I'm long gone."

"This doesn't sound like you're motivated entirely by money," Makayla noted. "It sounds like there's more to it."

"Correct. It's not about money. It's about providing a chance for like-minded people to explore. Anyone with a dark fantasy. fetish, kink, BDSM; whatever the hell you want to call it. We provide that platform to consenting adults."

"But critics say that you provide a platform for abuse."

"And who are these critics?" Cameron scoffed. "What the hell do they know?"

"Well, they are a certain segment of this New York's population, along with a few local politicians and members of the media."

"All I can say is that we've gotten the necessary permits. It's our right to open this establishment. Adults have the right to explore what desires they have legally."

"But critics would say that your wealthy 'friend' had bribed certain officials to get those permits."

Cameron smiled. "I wouldn't know anything about that."

"Of course not," Makayla said.

"Look, in all honesty, the reason I'm doing this interview is because I'm well aware that my club has generated some negative publicity. I think that's too bad. I really do. We aren't the deviants that people say we are. We have doctors, lawyers, small business owners, church goers, you name it."

"So you actually care about your image. And the image of your club?"

"That's why I'm here. I don't like to see our clients being vilified for doing what they enjoy."

Makayla nodded. "Very well. Tell me more about your place then…"

* * *

"It's a small two-story building that's newly renovated. It's a bit classy and we have rooms for just about everything."

"Define everything."

"Everything meaning rooms for bondage, whips, spankings, pegging, voyeurism, and group sex. You name it and we got it."

Makayla gave a slow uncomfortable nod. "I see."

"Does this bother you."

"Not at all."

"You seem uneasy about this," Cameron noted.

"Please, I've covered a lot of things in this city."

"Including sex?"

"No. This is my first story with sex as the focal point."

Cameron rubbed his chin. "Writing about sex is much different than covering politics or the local stuff. It's a lot more exciting, isn't it?"

"I try to approach each story the same way. With a fair and open mind."

"Do you normally do all your interviews like this? Face to face in an empty restaurant."

"It depends," Makayla replied. "If I'm interviewing a local politician, I would go to their office. Then I'd write the story at home."

"That sounds about right," Cameron said. "Send me a message and we'll continue this interview at my club. I'll give you a personal tour."

Cameron got up prepared to leave and Makayla looked peeved.

"You know, I don't really have to do this. My editor is pushing for this story."

"I think you'll want to," Cameron replied.

"And why is that?"

"Because you've already gotten this far. And I think this is something that you'll want to pursue."

With that, Cameron got up and left. The only thing Makayla could do was wonder if she had just wasted her time.

CHAPTER TWO

B eing a journalist was in Makayla Turner's blood. Her mother was a news anchor, and father was a segment producer for another local network. They met at a party and the rest was history.

It was an easy decision for Makayla to pursue the family trade. At the dinner table each night, all she heard about was her parents talking about news segments they were putting together at work.

With that sort of background, it was inevitable that Makayla showed up at the club days later, at an early hour. It was much nicer than she had expected, located on a quiet side street on the outskirt of downtown. The exterior of the building looked bland, but that was to avoid unwanted attention.

Inside, there was a receptionist and a spacious lounge. Whoever did the interior design had good taste, Makayla thought.

The receptionist gave Makayla the directions to Mr. James's office. She went alone, nervous, wondering if she would see anything obscene on the way. But to her surprise, there was nothing. Most doors were closed and no one was around except for staff.

It wasn't hard to find Cameron's office. The door was open and she saw Mr. James behind the desk, typing. The duo made eye contact and Cameron closed his laptop.

"The office look doesn't suit you," Makayla said jokingly.

"Which is why I'm not the corporate type. But someone has to do it and I'm the unfortunate one."

Cameron stood and went to Makayla.

"Aren't we going to do a sit-down interview?"

"I think it's best if I give you a tour. That way, you can see exactly what I'm talking about. You can take notes on the way."

"Sounds good."

"I hope you remembered that recorders aren't allowed. It's company policy."

Makayla reached in her purse and took out a notepad. "I remembered."

"Excellent. Let's begin."

CHAPTER THREE

Mr. Cameron James and Makayla casually made small talk while walking down the hall. Cameron reached for the key and opened the door to the guests' reception area. When he turned the lights on, the space was revealed. It was small by most club standards, but had a comfortable and vibrant feel to it. Yet there was a darkness to it, the gothic kind. Overall, Makayla was impressed.

"Nice," she observed.

"It's amazing what good designers can do. It takes a special talent."

"What about your talents? You're a professional dom, right? Have you always had those sets of skills?"

"No," Cameron replied after a moment of thought. "No one is a perfect from the start. Believe it or not, it takes practice, and experience. But even then, one's instincts are most important. Not anyone can do it."

"When did you start? How did it happen?"

"In college with a girlfriend. I dated a girl who had dom/sub fantasies, which she learned about from her father's dirty magazines. Her father had a large stash of them in the shed and this woman used to secretly read them after school. Once we became a couple, she had asked me to try it with her."

"Were you any good?" Makayla asked.

"Terrible. I was the worst. I thought everything was about the pain threshold but it was not."

Makayla took notes.

"I'm assuming that particular relationship didn't last very long."

"Not really. Pain is a delicate thing."

"So how did you learn the proper way?"

"Several years later, I went to a bondage club near my parents' home. I didn't know what the hell I was doing there. I just wanted to see what it was all about and quickly realized that I couldn't sub for a dominatrix. That wasn't me. I need to be in control. I have to be the one giving orders."

Makayla took more notes.

"So who taught you how to be a dom?"

"A dominatrix who worked there," Cameron said. "I waited outside the club at three in the morning looking like a creep. I was young but I wanted to learn. I guess the woman saw something in me, and decided to be my mentor. She taught me everything over the months to come. Little by little, she poured her knowledge in me.

She taught me the psychology of it all and since she was getting older, I suppose she wanted to pass her knowledge onto me."

Makayla nodded.

"Obviously, this knowledge served its purpose."

"I happily run a successful BDSM club. I was groomed well."

"Why do some enjoy this so much?" Makayla asked. "For the average person, can you explain the appeal of domination and submission?"

"I would explain it like this: Why do married couples love their spouses? Why do people have hobbies? Why do people have goals in life?"

"So you're saying, it's something that people naturally have inside of them."

"In a way," Cameron replied. "I can't explain why some women crave to be submissives. But in my experience, there are those with great careers who want nothing more than to be called 'sluts' while on their knees. In privacy, of course."

"Many would call it sexual abuse."

"And sometimes it is. But we don't do that here. We take every precaution to ensure that everything is consensual. We don't tolerate abuse."

"Many community leaders say that your sexual practices do contribute to abuse. They say that your club provides an haven for abusers and sadists to legally hurt people. How what you respond to that?"

"Fake news. They're totally wrong."

Makayla nodded again.

"Mr. James, could you be more specific in how you ensure content in your establishment?"

"Makayla, we screen very carefully. I'm a great judge of character. And what you're eluding to is actually bias towards our lifestyle. If it's abuse, then it's not allowed. Unless, of course, the person wants to be abused."

There was a slight smile on Cameron's face, which made Makayla a little uncomfortable.

"And how do you respond to the allegations that your club is misogynistic towards women?"

"How so?"

"You keep women tied up, don't you? There have been reports of group encounters and so forth, with women being on the rough end of things."

"First of all, women that come here want to be tied up and restrained," Cameron said. "Secondly, there are men who also want to be restrained. Men and women both enjoy bondage. In a place like this, there are no traditional gender roles. A man could be in charge, or he could be submissive. The same goes for women. We have plenty of dominant women who proudly enslave submissive men."

Makayla furiously took more notes.

"I see."

"Why don't you come and have a look?"

She raised her eyebrow. "I'm already here. I think I've seen enough today."

"I mean won't you come through at night, when the

real action is happening. You'll have so much to write about. And your writing will be authentic because you'll have actually witnessed it firsthand."

"I can't."

"You can't, or you won't?"

Makayla crossed her arms to stop the interview. "Look, I'm here to write a story. Please don't be an ass."

"Don't forget, you arranged this so-called interview. You chose to come here today."

"Okay, you're right. But that doesn't mean I want to see, whatever it is you or your freaks are doing here."

"There's your problem…"

"What?"

"You want to write an article about a sex club, and after everything we've discussed, you still have no idea what happens here. That's not the sign of a good journalist, is it?"

Makayla crossed her arms even tighter knowing Cameron had a valid point.

"Suppose I came to watch," she said. "How would that work?"

"Well, the way our club works is, you can do whatever you want, with whomever you want, in any room."

"And I can just stand back and observe?"

"Observe, participate, whatever you want."

"Watching sounds just fine with me," she said. "You provide masks to the people who request it, right?"

"Yes. But there is a condition for wearing a face mask."

Makayla sighed. "Which is?"

"In this club, we expect our guests to be open and honest. However, that is not always possible since many of our members prefer their identities to be concealed. Which is why we provide masks."

"So what's the condition?"

"If you wear a mask, you have to be naked."

"You're out of your damn mind if you think I'm getting naked in front of you."

"That's the rule."

"I get the feeling that you're trying to take advantage of me. You've been eyeing me since the moment we met."

"Rules are rules," Cameron explained. "If you want to remain clothed, you have to show your face. If you want a mask, then you have to be naked."

Makayla shook her head. "I can't be seen in a place like this."

"That's a sentiment shared by a good number of our members."

"Really? What percent would you estimate?"

"Probably about a third wear the mask. Those people include doctors, lawyers, accountants, teachers, and even some of the church-going zealots who oppose this place."

It wasn't a very surprising comment to Makayla. In her line of work, she knew that hypocrites were everywhere, especially when it came to sex.

"Well, the answer is no. But if you ever make an

exception, I'd be happy to observe, masked and fully dressed."

"That's too bad," Cameron said half-shrugging. "I would love you to accept my invitation."

"And see me naked, right?"

"You could always keep your clothes on. But of course, you'd have to show your face."

"That's never going to happen. Ever."

"I understand, so think about it. You're a beautiful young woman with so much potential. Why not give it a try? There will be a lot of other people like you here. If you don't like it, then leave. But at least try. You'll be able to capture the essence of the story you desperately wish to write."

There was a confidence in Cameron's voice, like he knew what he was talking about. And of course, Cameron did.

That night. Makayla sat in front of her MacBook and typed much of the article. She was determined to make the most comprehensive and journalistic piece she had ever written. It was her ticket to getting it in the mainstream news outlets or that she hoped.

So far, she had written about Cameron's beginnings and his unexpected journey to adult entertainment. Then she wrote about America's secret obsession with BDSM. Afterward, she described Cameron's club in her limited scope and how she thought the operation ran.

No matter how much she wrote, the article still felt incomplete. The details felt missing. The real life stories. The interactions. In Makayla's past articles, she had a meticulous approach to research. She prided herself on having a high journalistic standard and prided herself even more on telling the stories of Black people.

When it came to the dom/sub lifestyle, Makayla didn't know much.

What she needed was the inside scoop; to get up-close and personal, just like she always had before.

The question Makayla then asked herself was, was she able to handle the lewdness of such a setting?

Yes, she was proud of her figure and worked hard to keep herself in good shape. Besides Cameron, who would ever know? In a weird way, the whole ordeal seemed kind of arousing resembling a secret taboo to help further her career.

* * *

The next morning. Makayla waited in a room of the club, where the receptionist had directed her to go.

She marveled at the place. It was simple, yet there was an elegance to it. There weren't any soft chairs inside and it definitely wasn't a place for relaxation.

The room had a hard edge to it. And that was affirmed by the array of sex toys and devices. There was an assortment of blindfolds, whips, cuffs, and chains. There were also tables and seats which were designed to restrain a person.

"Here you are," Cameron said, entering the room.

Makayla turned. "You're a very persuasive man."

"I'll take that as a compliment."

"Look, I've thought a lot about your offer, and, I think you're right. The article I'm working on is some of the best stuff I've ever written, but it feels like something's missing."

"Incomplete, huh?" Cameron slowly nodded. "I knew you'd return. You're a smart woman. People like you always strive for the best."

"And I always have succeeded when doing so."

"Now onto the big question: Masked or unmasked?"

"Masked," Makayla said without hesitation.

Cameron smiled, "Good choice. Frankly, I had no idea which decision you were going to make."

"Now are you glad you'll be seeing me naked?" Makayla asked sarcastically.

"I've seen plenty of women in my time. Yet, I find you amusing."

"Why?"

"A stuck-up, well-educated journalist naked in my sex club. What's not to find amusing about that?"

Makayla rolled her eyes. "Let's get to the point. How is this going to work?"

Cameron walked further inside. He looked around, admiring the different devices on display.

"New members are required to fill out a questionaire. We want to know the specific preferences of the member, that way, we can cater to them. We make sure that each new member has everything needed, and leaves satisfied."

"Sure," Makayla shrugged. "I can't promise that I'll give truthful answers though."

"Take off your clothes. Then I'll take you to my office."

Makayla crossed her arms. "You must be out of your damn mind."

"Well, you've clearly thought about this. You've already made the decision to get undressed in my establishment."

"Yes, but with a mask."

"Being naked in a room full of people can be a terrifying thing - mask or not. It's not something that can be easily done. You'll need some practice, Makayla."

Makayla sighed, "You're a con man, you know that?"

"Maybe or maybe not?"

"If it wasn't for this…"

Cameron cut her off mid-sentence. "Remember it's your choice…"

"Shut up!"

* * *

Makayla put down her bag and began undressing while Cameron watched without a hint of expression. She took care in removing each article of clothing. Once removed, she folded her clothes neatly and placed it on the table.

She briefly paused when she was down to her bra and panties, standing barefoot. Her feet cold from the tile. She sighed again as she reached back to unclasp her bra. She tossed her bra onto the table and the same with her panties.

She stood naked in front of Cameron James. Her breasts were perky and upturned. Her arms were thin, but Makayla had the legs of a track star. She was also shaven between the legs.

However, Makayla was brave in doing this. She was proud of her body and her pose showed it.

"Not bad," Cameron said casually.

Makayla knew it was part of his game to get to her. Everything was part of his game.

"I'm sorry to disappoint," she replied.

"Nothing is disappointing about you. Now onto the next step."

Cameron went to the wall and removed a black collar with silver spikes on it. There was a leash attached to it.

"What's that?"

"A collar. Now hold still."

"What are going to do with that?"

Cameron stepped forward, directly in front of Makayla. He then placed the collar around Makayla's neck and tightened it. Cameron took a few steps back and tugged on the leash.

"Follow me, my dear."

"Oh my God! No…no…"

"Shush! You must crawl before you walk."

* * *

Cameron exited the room with Makayla naked stepping into the halls with a collar around her neck. She prayed that no one would see them.

Those wishes soon ended as they passed by a female staffer and two other men, who were part of the cleaning crew. The woman had a nonchalant attitude about Makayla's appearance. But the men had smirks on their faces feeling it was a wonderful way to start their morning.

Makayla tried ignoring them as they walked down the hall.

Moments later, they entered an office and Cameron locked the door. He pulled Makayla and had her sit in front of the desk, where several papers had been placed, along with a pen.

It was at that moment when Makayla realized that Cameron had anticipated this whole thing all along. From her stripping down, to the collar, to now these papers. *This cunning son of a bitch.*

Makayla sat and stared at the papers as Cameron stood at the window.

"Those are the papers for our new members," he said. "Consent forms, legal liabilities, and so forth. There's usually another paper to cover fees, but obviously we won't be needing that. Your first time will be free."

"How nice of you!"

"I'd like you to sign those documents. And I'd like you to fill out the questionaire. No one will read it except for me."

"Fine."

* * *

The questions on the form were very straight forward. Each was blunt and directly to the point. The form inquired about a new member's sexual history and preferences; everything from orientation, curiosities, number of past partners, fantasies, desires, and so forth...

Makayla felt embarrassed knowing that Cameron would be holding this information on her. She was tempted to write a few bullshit answers but she filled it out truthfully. Makayla admitted that she only had six sex partners in her life and wrote a few brief answers about her likes and interests. She also stated that she was curious about women and about giving oral sex. Lastly, she mentioned that she had an interest in group settings and multiple partners.

Then Makayla signed the NDA and consent forms and placed the pen neatly on top.

"Done," she said.

"And your reward."

Cameron opened his desk drawer and lifted a gold mask. It was very elegant and sensual. It had adjustable straps and small holes for seeing. The mouth area was uncovered which Makayla thought was perfect for giving oral sex.

"May I put it on you?" Cameron asked politely.

"I—I," Makayla stuttered.

"I won't bite."

* * *

Cameron put a mirror on the desk and Makayla viewed her topless reflection with the collar around her neck. She felt so dirty as she shook her head.

Then, Cameron stood behind her and put the gold mask on her, tightening the straps. Makayla noted how bizarre it looked.

While still behind Makayla, Cameron reached down and felt her vagina.

"What are you…" Makayla said as she panted.

"Stay still…"

Makayla flinched at first but after a few seconds of arousal, she gave herself to Cameron's fingers. His fingers touched her so intimately and Makayla knew it was the hand of a pro. All she could do was stay still, moan and look at herself pant in the mirror.

Minutes later, she came falling frontward on Cameron's desk.

"Saturday night," Cameron said, kissing her hair. "We begin at 9 pm. And we close at 1 am. I expect to see you."

"I'll be there," Makayla grunted softly.

Cameron untied the mask and collar and Makayla breathed a sigh of relief.

* * *

The entire time while driving, Makayla kept reminding herself that everything she was doing was for the story.

She repeated it over and over: *This is for the story. This is for my career. This is for the public.* This is not for me.

Yet, the possibility of craving more kept her in suspense.

Once Makayla arrived home, she opened her laptop and typed more details about today's experience in general.

CHAPTER FIVE

Saturday Night

Cameron's club was lively and you could feel the sexual excitement in the air.

Makayla entered through the back entrance, not wanting to be seen, much like several others. She put her head down hoping that no one would recognize her.

Others proudly came through the front door. To her surprise, she saw many couples there, looking to have a great time, pushing the edges of their relationships. Makayla knew she wanted to interview them later.

Firstly, she went directly to Cameron's office, as she had been instructed.

It was 8:55 pm.

She entered and shut the door feeling like a secret

agent sneaking around. Cameron was sitting behind the desk in a sharp suit.

"You need to relax," he said, standing up to greet her with a hug anda kiss on the cheek.

"I am relaxed. I keep telling myself that this is for the story."

"What are you hoping to get out of this?" Cameron asked. "What's your goal for tonight?"

"Learning about the lifestyle. I want to see what draws people to a place like this. You know, learn the psychology behind it all."

"Good," he replied. "Now take your clothes off."

"Well that was blunt."

Cameron checked his watch. "The show has already started. Why wait?"

"I guess I have no excuse."

With that, Makayla undressed. It wasn't awkward like before. She stacked her clothes on the chair then left her shoes on the floor.

Cameron looked over her. He could act dismissive all he wanted, but his eyes revealed how much he lusted after Makayla.

It was time.

He got her mask and told Makayla to stand still. He stood behind her, then he put the mask on her.

Cameron then led her to the office mirror and once again, Makayla saw her reflection. It was erotic, yet terrifying. Sexy but scary. Her nerves reappeared and she knew exactly what was about to happen. *Oh God, did I make a mistake? Can I still back out?*

Cameron suddenly opened the door to the hallway.

"After you," he said. "I think our members are going to be pleasantly surprised by the sight of your beauty."

Oh, God! What have I agreed to?

* * *

The floor felt cold and Makayla's nipples had erected. She tried walking with her shoulders broad and her back straight, looking confident.

By her estimate, there were at least fifty people in the main area. Half of them were sharply dressed for the sophisticated environment while others were naked, wearing gold masks. It was a surreal sight as the nudity seemed so casual in the club. No one appeared to be fazed by it.

In the background, was deep house music playing which blended perfectly with the sexually-charged atmosphere. Most of the members were middle aged and professionals just as Cameron had described. And it made sense too, given that membership costed thousands of dollars.

"Is this what you expected?" Cameron asked.

"I had no idea what to expect."

"Here's your chance to explore," he said. "If you'll excuse me, I have some things to do. I'll check on you later. Will you be okay?"

Makayla looked around the room. "I'll be fine."

"Go on and explore," Cameron said, rubbing Makayla's shoulders.

Upon that, he left and Makayla was left alone naked in her gold mask.

* * *

Makayla walked around the club and observed feeling as if she was walking in a dream. People had their lust proudly on display but not in a lewd or lascivious manner. Things were classy and primal, yet controlled.

Makayla roamed and watched how the members interact. A few guys made offers to her for sex. She declined. A few women had made offers to her and she declined them, too.

A group of people had left the club area and went to a private room. That intrigued Makayla. Whatever they were going to do, it was going to be fascinating. And she had to watch it. All for her story, of course.

* * *

She followed the group to the room and was in luck, the door was left open. It was her perfect chance to be a voyeur into the world of BDSM.

Makayla slyly moved to the door and her jaw nearly dropped by what she saw. Two women were blindfolded and bound, with their wrists tied to the top bedpost.

Their men were on top of them, pounding away. Other guys stood by the blindfolded and bound women, with their cocks in their mouths getting sucked.

"A beautiful sight, isn't it?" Cameron came back asking from behind.

Makayla kept her eyes forward.

"It'll definitely give me a lot to write about. That's for sure."

He wrapped his arms around Makayla's back. "I've read your questionnaire. I know what you're interested in. When we first met, I already had an impression on you. I knew you are an intelligent woman, who's open sexually, but is still unfulfilled in many ways."

"What's your point?" Makayla sighed, eyes still on the orgy.

"My club can fulfill your desires. You want firsthand experience for your article? Here's your chance. Do you want gratification? Be my guest."

Makayla continued watching. "You know that will never happen. I'm not that type of girl."

Cameron put his fingers on her gold mask. "Don't forget what you're wearing. No one will ever know. It's our secret. Here, you can explore everything. Just think about it."

"You're a real fucking asshole."

"Why? Because I'm making your pussy wet? Or are you wet because of what you're staring at?"

Makayla turned back. "How do you know I'm wet?"

"I understand women. And I can smell your cunt."

Cameron reached below and put his fingers on Makayla's pussy confirming his suspicions. Her pussy was dripping and Makayla couldn't deny it.

"You know you're an ass," Makayla said defensively.

He pulled his hand away. "Let me know when you're interested. Remember, this is for you, not me."

As Cameron attempted to walk away, Makayla grabbed him by the wrist.

"Wait," she said, before pausing. "You swear no one will ever find out?"

He smiled. "You've signed the non-disclosure forms, right? There's your answer. Secrets are safe within these walls. That's part of my job. Keeping people's secrets."

"What would happen if... you know..."

"Leave everything to me. You're in good hands, Makayla."

Cameron snapped his fingers and a female employee of the club approached him. He told the employee exactly what he wanted and Makayla's eyes widened.

CHAPTER SIX

Not only was Makayla naked and masked, but her wrists had been locked together in shackles. There was a light chain attached to the shackles, which Cameron used to lead her around the club area.

Heads turned when Cameron paraded Makayla around the club. People wanted to know who the beautiful woman was. But of course, that was a secret those people could never know.

As Makayla was being led around, Cameron had pointed to a number of members. Signaling them to follow. Cameron had picked two women and three men to follow. Some naked and masked, some were dressed with their faces showing.

Then Makayla was led to a private room followed by the selected individuals.

Makayla's pulse was pounding. She was no fool. And

she wasn't naive either. She knew exactly what was going to happen: Cameron had arranged for Makayla's first lesbian experience, along with her first group encounter.

Once they were all inside, Cameron escorted Makayla to lay on the bed and tied her shackled wrists above her head, to the bedpost.

The guests were quick to opine:

"What a lovely gift, Cameron," a man said. "You have a talent for getting the best pieces of ass."

"She's so beautiful," a lady added.

"I can't wait to fuck her," a man chimed in.

"I want to know what she tastes like," another woman added.

The most shocking thing was, although one of the men was naked and masked, Makayla was able to recognize his voice. It was a city councilman who had publicly opposed the opening of Cameron's sex club.

Suddenly, Makayla's mind went back to journalism mode wondering if Cameron knew the man was a local politician. *Of course he did. Cameron knew everything. That's probably why the man was chosen to be here.*

"This is a precious woman," Cameron said to the group. "It's her first time here and her first time playing with bondage. She's a bondage virgin. Let's make this memorable."

Cameron gestured to the two women in the room. One was naked and masked, the other was dressed (and she quickly got undress). Both were sexy and gorgeous. And both were much older than Makayla.

When they were ready, the women approached Makayla's bound body. Each woman bent down and gave Makayla a sensual kiss on the lips. The kind which said, 'You're going to enjoy this.'

Each woman then again pressed their lips softly against Makayla's, then harder. Then there were wet, tongue kisses. It was Makayla's first lesbian kiss. It was glorious and fulfilling. More than she could have ever expected.

The women rubbed and fondled Makayla. They rubbed her smooth skin and breasts. They then flicked Makayla's nipples, pinched them, then sucked them.

"Oh, ah, oh, yes…" Makayla moaned as both of her nipples were being sucked simultaneously.

Then the women played with Makayla's pussy while they were sucking her nipples. It was clear that they were experts, and knew exactly what to do.

"Oh, yes…" Makayla moaned and groaned.

One of the women moved down and began licking Makayla's pussy, making her gasp.

"Oh god, Oh God..." Makayla panted.

This was a long time fantasy of Makayla's, and once it did happen. After that time, Makayla wished she could have experienced it again and now this woman's mouth lived up to the hype.

Makayla's body tensed. The other woman kept fondling her breasts and took turns sucking on each nipple. Makayla was stimulated everywhere.

She closed her eyes and enjoyed the feeling. She tried

to forget about the men watching her. But then again, maybe it helped arouse her. Maybe the exhibitionist side of her (if there was one) fueled her first girls' encounter.

Whatever the case, it felt amazing.

"Fuck, I'm coming…" Makayla yelled unable to control herself. She came, having her most powerful orgasm ever.

When it subsided, the women stopped what they were doing, and looked down at their feast. Makayla was laying in a state of bliss.

"Did you enjoy that?" Cameron asked.

Makayla stretched her legs. "Yes."

"I figured you would. That was the first step. You have much to experience and we're going to help you."

"Oh, I thought…"

"Don't think, my dear. Relax."

* * *

Cameron signaled two of the men, who were dressed. After receiving the signal, the men got naked, revealing their already hard cocks. They knew exactly what they were about to do and looked forward to enjoying each second of it.

The men walked towards Makayla. Not to her body. But to her face. The men were near middle age, and were fairly good-looking. Cameron and the masked man simply stood back and watched. Th ladies continued rubbing Makayla, touching her breasts and legs.

As the men stood near Makayla, it was obvious what was going to happen. Makayla had already revealed her love for giving oral sex in the questionaire that she had filled out. And that information was being used to push her boundaries.

The men got on the bed, on their knees, and got very close to each side of Makayla's face. They guided their cocks to her mouth. The fact that the mask didn't cover the mouth area came in perfect use. Makayla was able to open her jaw and accept the first cock in her mouth. She sucked for a while. Then she turned her head to suck the other man's cock.

During the oral process, the two men groaned:

"What a mouth."

"Cameron, you found a real keeper. She's a perfect angel."

"Where did you find this woman?"

"She needs to be tied up here forever. This mouth is born to suck."

Instead of feeling degrading, Makayla actually felt proud of herself. With her true identity a secret, she could do whatever she wanted, without fear. She could explore whatever she wanted. The only person who knew that she was 'Makayla the journalist,' was Cameron.

She continued sucking each of their cocks. Taking turns for each of them. Making sure everything was done equally for both men. Her neck was becoming sore from the constant head bobbing. Her body remained still since her hands were bound above her head.

The women continued fondling Makayla's breasts and pussy. Their mouths returned to action. Makayla was being pleasured all over. Her groans were muffled by the cocks sharing her mouth.

"God this woman can suck," a man groaned.

Once again, Makayla felt a sense of pride that her oral skills were being well received. She continued to suck, lick, and kiss each guy's cock. She made sure that each man was equally satisfied, with her head turning back and forth to suck both off.

"Now for the final step," Cameron said, before the men could come.

Cameron signaled the masked man who stood by the wall. He was the local politician.

Deep down, Makayla wondered if the politician knew that she was a journalist. The question lingered as the masked politician positioned himself between Makayla's toned legs. In Makayla's mind, the answer was 'no.'

The politician probably didn't know, she thought. Because there was no way a person of power like him would have knowingly fucked a journalist in a dodgy sex club. He would have been petrified that the little secret would be reported, and that he would be exposed. At least that was Makayla's analysis during the moment.

The masked politician guided his cock between Makayla's labia. Then he pushed and entered. Makayla gasped.

"Fuck…"

The men got up and stood beside the bed as the

women continued rubbing Makayla's breasts and sucking her nipples. It was the encounter of Makayla's wildest fantasy. Only it was more intense than she could have imagined. Nastier. Most lust-filled.

*** *** ***

This was a real life gang bang, and Makayla, the brave local journalist, was the star of the show. The politician began to pound her pussy. It was bizarre being ravished by a naked man in a gold mask, especially as other people in the room watched. But it was beyond pleasurable. It was a sensation Makayla had never felt before.

With her hands bound, she felt powerless. She could do nothing as the female hands and mouths played with her breasts. And she could do nothing as the man on top fucked her.

And she liked it that way. Makayla's body began to tense and her arms pulled the restraints tightly.

"Oh my god!" she yelled. "My pussy... my pussy..."

"Are you close to coming?" Cameron asked.

"Yes... yes..."

"Relax. Let it happen. Don't struggle against the restraints. Just relax. Enjoy your new role. You are the submissive tonight."

As always, Cameron was right. The female orgasm was mostly mental and required relaxation. The moment

Makayla let go and stopped struggling against the bondage, the orgasm came.

"Oh my God! Fuck, oh fuck…" Makayla screamed.

It was Makayla's second one. Her senses had reached a peak. She screamed and cried as her body shivered from coming.

After her orgasm, the politician pulled his cock out of her and masturbated until he came all over her stomach. It was a wet mess. He got up and paced the room, needing to clear his mind after the intense session.

CHAPTER SEVEN

akayla was left in a shivering state. All she felt was bliss. She now felt comfortable with the restraints on her wrists. Nothing seemed to matter anymore. She was beyond satisfied.

However, the night wasn't over yet. Another man climbed on top of her. He was still hard from oral sex, and from watching Makayla getting fucked. He needed a turn. And he got it. He guided his cock to Makayla's pussy. Then he thrust.

"Oh, fuck. You're so big…" Makayla grunted.

Makayla was being fucked again and wondered if she could actually reach another orgasm. Two orgasms were doable. But three? She was about to find out if her body was capable of such a thing.

Her body rocked as the man on top began fucking her wildly. The other women continued playing with her breasts. One of them reached down and played with

Makayla's clit as she was being ravished. It was at that moment which Makayla knew her third orgasm would be possible. It would be the first time in her life that she was ever multi-orgasmic.

It was all so much for her delicate senses. It was the night of many first-times. Each sexual experience was more intense than the next.

A third orgasm was impending, but it didn't happen. So close. The man fucking her had pulled out and came all over Makayla's chest, leaving another mess further upward.

The man got up, only to be replaced by another. He got on top of Makayla, as the women held Makayla's legs and pussy open. The man gave a thrust and entered Makayla's pussy. It was the third and final guy who would be fucking her that night.

The women continued fondling her breasts, kissing her mouth, and playing with her pussy. While she was being thoroughly ravished, Makayla kept her eyes on Cameron, who simply stood back and watched the gang bang of the respectable journalist. He admired her for her courage.

EPILOGUE

Two weeks later

Makayla was naked in front of her laptop. She typed away in Cameron's office. The article was complete. She had written extensively about the club and the people who attended. Identities concealed, of course, but she told the stories of people who secretly confided in her for the article.

She had described the nature of the club and the sex acts involved. The goal was to write something that would get people talking. And hopefully, if she was lucky, land a higher position in the world of journalism.

The article was entitled: ***Gold Mask Fantasies***

There was a lot riding on it and Makayla felt confident about her work. She emailed the article to her editor and let out a sigh of relief.

Cameron smiled, "Congratulations. You've done it."

"I'm proud of what I've written. I think it's great."

"Are you ever going to let me read it?"

Makayla winked, "I never show my work to anyone before publication, except for the people I work with."

"Shame. I guess I'll have to wait."

"I've written good things about the place. You'll enjoy it."

"Then I have a present for you."

Cameron reached in his drawer and took out a collar with a leash attached to it. It was a customized collar made just for Makayla. It was a black strap with the letters S-L-U-T in silver letters.

When Makayla saw the letters, she smiled, wanting to laugh.

He went to where naked Makayla was sitting, then he put it on her neck, tightening it just the right amount. He held the leash tightly in his hand, ready to pull at any moment. Ready to control her body.

"You look beautiful," he said.

"I'm sure you think so."

"It's the truth. I'd like you to wear it tonight. I'm sure people will be amused seeing it."

"You love humiliating me."

"Only because you love being humiliated. One of these days, I'd love to see you at my club without the mask."

"We're a long way from that happening," she replied.

"Okay. But what happens now?"

Makayla gave a playful expression. "Well, you've

helped me so much. It's only fair that I repay you. Can I suck your dick?"

"Of course."

She undid his pants and freed his cock. That's when Cameron exerted his power and pulled the leash which was attached to the collar. Makayla's face was pulled forward, directly in front of Cameron's long cock. Another pull, and her face was pressed against it.

Makayla opened her mouth and licked it. She pressed her lips against it. Then took it inside her mouth and sucked away. She orally made love to it in a passionate way. Her head bobbed as Cameron pulled the leash, signally her to gag on it.

And Makayla obeyed. She took it deep down her throat and gagged like she was ordered.

It was sexual domination at its finest. Makayla being naked, collared, and deep throating the Boss. For reasons unknown, it gave Makayla pleasure to be his plaything. She was done trying to figure it out. All she knew was that it felt good.

The End

BULL

There's no guidebook on how to cope with falling in love with your best lady friend, and certainly none on how to cope with falling in love with the person who is happily involved with your long-time boss and bud from schooldays. Take Bull's word for it, he's Googled it, and the only results that have come back were a few cheap romance novels on Amazon. The greatest tragedy of Bull's life is some cheap plot device for a bored housewife fantasy-fodder. Those books were geared toward women, but Bull doubted that it was Serena's fantasy for him to pound on her door at midnight to confess his feelings for her while her boyfriend, the fire chief at his station, Randy stood behind her.

But when Serena had taken on the task of writing an article about the history of the fire station, she and Bull spent a lot of time together; more than usual. She needed his help and he was glad to assist. What he hadn't known was the fact that it would make him fall for her despite knowing her for years.

When Bull's alone, the guilt eats him alive. Bull's jealous, but not envious. To say Bull's jealously implies that he would like to take Randy's place is not what he wants. Randy is right for Serena and Bull loves seeing them together. Bull isn't sure what he wants other than a miracle that Serena one day falls in his lap.

Let's face it, whoever wrote that it was better to have loved and lost than not loved at all, was a liar. Lord Tennyson? He's obviously never felt, unrequited love. Sure, there are times when wanting Serena feels really good, but like all good highs, they come crashing down eventually. The warm glow of having Serena slide her feet into his lap under the blanket when they're snuggled up is irresistible. She'd lay across his broad body, her head on his chest, her pretty fingernails scratching lightly at his scalp, whispering, "I love you, Big Bull" in his hair, and then lean up to kiss him.

———

For years, Bull lived on a hard line between wishing Serena wanted him and wishing he'd never met the woman. He can't unlearn her quirks or program himself not to respond to them. His eyes watched Serena's shine in the fire station's front window, and Bull's heart skipped a beat only to sink hundreds of times. Her cheeks are puffed with air, as she tries not to scream at the fire stations' database that just won't work like it's programmed to, and Bull just giggled. He knew that call to him to just fix it on his day off was coming but Bull also needed to run the other way, because he didn't want her to turn in her office chair to face him. He envisioned Serena holding his face, calling him her hero while planting wet kisses on his forehead. All-day, every day Bull's high on affection crashes when he hits the pillow at night.

CHAPTER EIGHT

ull went into monk mode when he and Serena
were called to do an interview for one of the
local rescuers for a house fire they put out a few
weeks ago. Serena was always in touch with the local TV
station, and they proposed for the station to interview the
hero at their location. The two were the first ones to
arrive and were waiting for the rescuer to come. Bull
walked over to Serena holding out his arms and Serena
tilted her head and planted her palms on his chest. She
slowly used them to smoothen the fabric of Bull's navy
blue uniform. "There you go, Bull. You look like a million
bucks," Serena said placing her hands on her hips. Her
eyes crinkled as she bounced up and down. "You always
look so handsome! I love a firefighter especially in
uniform!" she whispered. Bull grinned weakly as Serena
caressed his stubbled cheek after planting a long kiss
there.

"Thank you, ma'am."

"You're welcome," Serena said wincing at the lipstick stain she left.

"Go on and sit, Bull. I need to clean something off your face before we get started."

Serena wiped off her lipstick and then for some odd reason, took out some powder and blew it on his face, like it was the final touch to make Bull's face perfect. "You're chipper today," Bull said dusting the leftover powder off his pants.

Serena hummed absently as she put away her make-up kit. "Oh, Bull. You're a close friend. Is there anything I can't hide from you?" she sighed whimsically as she sat down next to him, her skirt parachuting before falling in perfect over her legs.

"Not a thing," Bull jested in an accent that sounded British. "What's on your mind, Rena?"

Serena looked down and smiled. "Aren't things just perfect right now? I think about how it was when Randy and I first started living together, barely had enough money to make a meal, and how different everything today. It feels like everything is perfect." Serena's lamenting, looking happy, but conflicted. "So is it the right time to start a family?"

Fuck! Bull's heart rate dropped like the final nail in his coffin, the sickening snap of the rope that's around his neck, the execution shot that rang out. He felt like he was going to cry. "Rena—" Bull stuttered, lost for words.

Serena's eyes widen. "Oh no! No Bull, I'm not pregnant! I'm not!" she said. "It's just one of those talks Randy and I been having lately. I always thought I wouldn't be ready to have kids until I was at least thirty-five, but it just seems like if there's a perfect time, then it's now." Serena frowned when she saw Bull wasn't even looking at her. His gaze was fixed on the floor, trying not to spin out of control. "It sounds stupid, right? I should just wait a little longer, right?"

"I think you should do what you feel is right. I know it sounds cheesy, but if your heart's telling you that's what you want, then go for it. If you're having second thoughts, give it some time. There's still so much more to life."

Serena smiled and embraced him, running her hands over his broad back and shoulders. "Thank you, Bull. I can always count on you to make me feel better," she whispered in his ear.

Bull didn't feel up to doing the interview as the word "heartbreak" was written all over his face but did so anyway.

CHAPTER NINE

Bull made it through the interview but barely made it out of the news studio and into his car before collapsing against the steering wheel, gasping for air. He was having a panic attack and cried catching his reflection in the rearview mirror, looking awful, like a bully who punched him in the face. Then, Big Bull had banged on the steering wheel.

His sighs were guttural and his throat felt raw from the emotional outpour. He didn't realize he'd been talking, until his phone blipped and Siri told him "I'm sorry, I didn't catch that." Bull sniffled and pushed his hand against his forehead, feeling hot and sweaty. His fingers trembled as he considered the interruption. "S-Siri," he stuttered.

Blip-Blip: "Yes, Bull?"

"Call Dustin," Bull hiccuped.

Blip-Blip: "Calling Dustin."

"Bull, what's up?" Dustin's voice crackled through the speakerphone. Bull tried to catch his breath. "Bull man, are you okay?"

"D-Dustin I need you to come get me. Take me home. Take me home. Just take me home, Dustin."

"God! Bull, Bull, calm down. Slow down. Where are you? Are you still at the studio?"

"Yes—Yes. Please, just—I need you to get down here—"

Dustin cut him off.

"I know—I know you need me to come take you home. Bull, you're freaking me out. Are you in trouble? What the hell's going on?"

"I'm okay. Just can't drive. It's been a long day," Bull said barely getting that much out, feeling his gut lurch.

"Alright. Alright. I'm on my way. Just hang tight. Don't kill yourself. It'll be okay. I'll be there in a few minutes. Now, tell me what happened—" Dustin tried to get Bull to stay on the phone but Bull hung up.

———

Bull was shivering and too agitated when Dustin came. During the ride, Bull didn't answer any of Dustin's questions; crying quietly with his forehead against the window.

When they got back to their apartment complex, Dustin ran around the side of the car and opened the door. He wrapped his arm around Bull's big shoulders and led him up the stairs. Once inside, Dustin lowered

Bull onto the couch. "Bull, are you okay? What the hell happened out there?"

Bull tried talking but quickly hyperventilated and wept. When he finally stopped, his breath came out shaky. "I don't know—" Bull said. He knew he couldn't tell Dustin what was making him freak out. "I'm fine. Just exhausted, man," Bull said.

"You had a panic attack, Bull. You're not okay, man."

"I'm fine, Dusty," Bull said setting his face inside his palms. "I'm just freaking drained, too much going on at once."

"Get some sleep. Maybe being on camera made you nervous. How'd it go?" Dustin said.

"I don't even remember," Bull snickered. "I just know I've never been so damn scared in my life."

"No worries, bud. It's a first time for everything."

Bull walked to his bedroom without saying another word and closed the door. He let his face sink against the limp, worn-out pillow that he rested his head on every night for the last few years. It wasn't long before his heavy eyelids can't peel open anymore and he fell into a deep dreamless sleep.

———

When Bull's eyes opened again, it's because he can feel the singeing hallway light pouring in onto the back of his eyelids. His door was cracked slightly and he heard Dustin's soft voice muttering. Bull tried honing in and focused his attention on what Dustin was saying and who he was talking to.

"What do you mean what kind of panic attack? Like full-blown, can't breathe, crying, shaking, fucking panic attack, Randy!" Dustin whispered into the phone. Bull tried to get a look at Dustin through the sliver into the hallway, but he heard his fingers curl around the door frame. He quickly saw Dustin peeking his head in and Bull quickly closed his eyes and pretended he's still asleep.

"No, he didn't have to go to the hospital. He calmed down by the time I got there, but he didn't tell me what happened." There was a pause and Bull assumed Randy was asking more questions. "Yeah man, he just said he was exhausted. That's all he kept saying." Dustin sighed leaning his hand against his forehead while against the wall outside of Bull's bedroom. "I mean what else can it mean? He's been working so hard. I think he's burnt out, man." Dustin muttered against the receiver.

Bull sighed knowing Dustin was clueless about how in love with Serena he is.

"I mean yeah I think Bull needs some time off. Yeah, just tell me what Matt and Nolan say. Yeah, I'll let him know. I'll tell you what he says. We'll make this work, Randy." There's a long pause and then Dustin spoke again, "No, no, Randy, stop. Stop it, Randy this isn't your fault. We've all been working really hard, I think it's just a testament of how important it is for us to check in with one another other. Randy, it's okay, it's going to be okay, I'm sure he isn't mad at you."

Bull was too caught up in his own reprimands that he didn't hear Dustin end his conversation with Randy until his bedroom door creaked and the hallway light flooded the room. "Bull? Bull, are you awake?" Dustin whispered as he came halfway into the room.

Bull stirred and stretched, pretending to have just woken up. "Dustin?" Bull asked as though his mind wasn't clear. He sat up slowly and reached for the lamp, turning it on.

Dustin walked in and sat on the foot of Bull's bed, folding his arms over his knees and looking over to Bull. "Hey man," Dustin said softly, "Are you feeling any better?"

"Yeah, a little." Bull said.

Dustin nodded. He was never good at beating around the bush. "I talked to Randy. He thinks maybe it would be a good idea if you took a little time off, to recharge you know? He's just worried about you,"

"Yeah. I guess that would be best. I don't think I'll need too long," Bull said.

"Take as long as you need, Bull. It's going to be okay. We've all been here before. Don't work yourself up this hard." Bull reached over to Dustin and put his hand on his shoulder.

"Thanks, Dustin." Bull pulled his hand off before he would begin sobbing and spilling his guts. He smiled at Dustin feeling the effort of every muscle it took to do so.

CHAPTER TEN

ull took three days off but needed to get back to
the fire station. His EMTs, Matt and Nolan were
capable but without his lead, they'd be out of
employment. Rather, the entire fire station needed him
and Bull didn't want to let anyone down.

Bull moved slowly through his work, a stack of paperwork sat in his corner of the small station office. He
scarcely talked to anyone on his first day back and when
he got off, he dodged his roommate's attempt to hang out
at the local bar. He went to bed, curled into the covers
and fell asleep. His dreams lately had often begun with
Serena's belly growing with Randy's child.

Serena didn't mention her relationship with Randy
again when Bull saw her after days of avoiding her. Bull
had been avoiding any attempt of seeing her, sparsely
texting back, and politely turning down her lunch invites.
Serena realized what was going on and her face grew

sadder. Bull hated doing this to her, but his heart ached more.

Bull told himself it would only going to get worse especially when there may be a kid involved. He doesn't want to show up to their child's birthday parties and graduations like a shadow in the background, grimacing with heartbreak at Serena and Randy's family portraits.

———

Two weeks passed and Bull and Serena barely spoke beyond work stuff. They went out a few times for a few meetings but it was cordial. Bull knew if he kept this pouting up much longer he might ultimately lose her as a friend.

He'll miss her smile and pleasant humming around the office but he never asked what if it was his fault for leaving Serena in the first place. There was a time where they were nearly a couple, but when Randy became fire chief, things changed after that.

Bull tried to slip out of the fire station unnoticed, but Serena who was working late caught up to him. "Bull!" Serena said grabbing the sleeve of his hoodie with her delicate little fingers. She looked worried as she looked up, her eyes were gleaming. "You're headed back home already? I'm done with my article on the station and the guys and I were going to go out and grab some sushi at that karaoke bar down the road. I was hoping you'd come along?"

Bull wished he could say yes, wished he could agree to go along and have a good time. He wished he could strut semi-buzzed onto the stage and belt out some classic rock & roll while Serena looked on laughing fondly under the rose-colored lights because it was so easy to get addicted to having her look at you that way. Bull smiled weakly before tilting his head, he tried to look as remorseful as possible. "I would, but I'm just really tired. Raincheck?"

"Oh yeah, get some rest then," Serena said, letting go of his sleeve. Before Bull can smile and make for the door, Serena wrapped her arms around his waist and pulled him into a tight hug, balling the back of his sweatshirt into her fists, she rested her face against his chest and sighed, "I've missed you, Bull."

Bull felt the backs of his eyes stinging, so he closed them as he rested his lips against the top of Serena's head, smelling her shampoo and felt suffocated. "Yeah, I've just been exhausted. So much going on..." Bull muttered against her hair and Serena squeezed him tighter, practically trying to bury herself in his chest. "It's not going to be forever, Rena, I promise." Bull felt Serena squeeze him a little tighter before she pulled off him gasping. She put on her brave face and patted his shoulder. "I won't ever forget, Bull. Don't you ever either?"

"I won't, Rena," Bull said walking off.

CHAPTER ELEVEN

When Bull made it home, he went online to browse for places to take a quick getaway. He browsed looking for anything in the wilderness so he could have solitude. He didn't want to be around a bunch of couples asking what brought him there. "Maybe a cabin in the mountains but the prices are pretty damn steep," Bull said spiraling tirelessly further down the rabbit hole of clicking link after link.

After Bull came upon a list of jobs about National Forests, he hit something that piqued his interest; a site about fire lookouts, spending roughly three months at a time during forest fire season posted at lookout stations. What ended up interesting Bull was the focus of being able to cope with solitude the position stressed in bold letters. The lookout was expected to live deep in the woods only allowing him to go into town ever so often.

While it was tempting, Bull exited the website, realizing that the whole idea of dropping everything to live alone in the forest and watch out for forest fires, seemed too lofty and difficult to explain to the others. Bull closed his laptop and laid back. The ceiling widened out bare white above him and if he stared at it long enough, its popcorn bubbling texture would pop out as pictures his mind would create, resembling constellations. Bull fell asleep dreaming about being on a wrap-around porch of a cabin, looking up at the stars with Serena.

———

As the week went on, Bull started considering the whole idea of leaving town. Serena begged him to come have lunch with her, reminding him how much she missed her confidant displaying some urgency of their last real conversation. However, Bull during his free time found himself on some dot gov site looking through maps and forms about fire lookout positions across Northern California.

He found what he's looking for on the border of California and Oregon, sitting on the edge was a small mining town. It sounded completely insane and if Bull can register early enough, he'd be okay. But his heart sank when he realized the application submission was nearing to the deadline.

How would Randy feel about Bull leaving? Only Bull knew best but believed Randy would be more than happy to hold his position for him until he got back. However, Bull was thinking about not coming back. What he needed to do next was tell his Captain or at least drop little hints that he's thinking about taking an extended leave of absence. He talked with his EMTs Dustin and Ray, and anyone else who would listen about wanting to get out to be around nature, go camping or similar. He became less secretive about his research, leaving tabs in the open on his computer when he took bathroom breaks. He wanted to soften the blow as much as possible for his friends and colleagues.

———

The day Bull had broken the news to Randy, he got a real taste for how ridiculous the proposal sounded. He stood in front of Randy, watching him shake his head. "I don't know Bull…I don't get it. My best firefighter wants to go up to God-damn Oregon for three months…to see if trees catch on fire?"

Bull frowned and Randy tried to find some common ground, "Just, help me understand where this is coming from Bull? You've never mentioned wanting to do anything like this." Randy leaned back in his chair and pushed his hair back, out of his face, his eyes glowed with the blue light of his computer screen.

"I love being here with you. I love the station, Randy. I love my work," Bull said. "We've been putting out fires and saving people's lives for more than ten years now, and it's good, but I need to see who I am outside of this." Bull began sobbing. His voice became scratchy.

Randy pressed the heels of his palms hard against his eyes, trying to hold back the well of tears pressing at his eyelids. "I knew something was wrong. I just thought we could get through it together," Randy said.

Bull's breath hitched and he put out his arms as he walked around Randy's desk. Randy stood up to meet him and Bull pulled him into a long hug, resting his face against Randy's chest. Randy's body is so naturally solid and comforting, making Bull feel all the more guilty. Randy noticed a problem in Bull that he can't diagnose and he wanted so badly to fix for him but to do so he would have to separate himself from Serena and the station. Bull knew he could never ask that of Randy.

"It won't be long, Randy. It'll be for three months and I'll be back. Hopefully, I'll come back stronger. I want to be a better person," Bull said.

"What if you don't come back though? What if you're out there and you decide you can't do this anymore?" Randy said, "That's what this is about right, making peace with yourself?" Randy thought this was about Bull questioning if he wanted to keep being a firefighter, that that's what Bull has to let make Randy think. He couldn't tell Randy the truth.

"I'm going to come back. No matter what, okay? We're best friends and firefighters, that will never change," Bull said rubbing Randy's back. Randy squeezed him a little tighter and nodded.

———

They told the others together and Dustin was supportive of Bull's decision. He recalled to Bull how critical his mental health was after spending time away in France on a retreat. Dustin told Bull spending some time around nature will really turn his attitude around and help him clear his head. Meanwhile, Randy tried to extend this sense of positivity in the face of a grave situation to his girlfriend, Serena, who seemed all but depressed these days.

Serena knew the rift between her and Bull was growing deeper by the day. Now, knowing that he's going to be away for three months would feel like he's just drilled a canyon between them. Serena spent strenuous hours these past weeks pursuing Bull, trying to get her best friend back, reeling in a line she worried she had cast too far. Suddenly, it's beginning to feel impossible. Serena determined that it might be in her best interest to stop trying, and maybe if she just walked the other way, Bull will come back better. It's been emotionally draining, as she started to see Bull even less than before and what's worse is Bull didn't even seem to notice the difference.

It was like Bull bounced back now that his plans are known. He waxed on happily to Ray and Dustin about the application process, about how kind and sharp his new boss appeared to be. Bull emailed the park warden, telling him that he was not particularly interested in having to take hikers to his tower on tours. "You're looking to be posted in the Hardy Tower, then," Bull's new boss, Park Warden Bradshaw said on the phone in a thick midwestern accent that seemed misplaced. After hanging up, Bull told his current EMT Ray that the Hardy Tower was an isolated place, harder for hikers to access so he'd have some peace and tranquillity. Bull also told Ray that because of this, the connection between them might be limited until he can get to in town.

"No problem, bud. We'll see you soon." Ray said.

Bull jumped when he heard something slam against the table behind them. Bull barely caught Serena's blurry form marching fast from where she sat at the main table in the center of the fire station. Bull tried calling after her but she was too fast, going to the back room and slamming the door behind her. Ray looked to Bull, and Bull just shrugged even though he's sure why Serena stormed off.

CHAPTER TWELVE

ull bit the bullet and jogged to the room. Serena immediately turned away when Bull opened the door, his knuckles pressed against her lips as she fought the urge to cry, trying to pretend she hadn't wanted Bull to come. "Go away, Bull, I'm fine," she choked out as Bull closed the door behind him, sealing them off from the rest of the station. Bull pulled her into his big arms, rubbing the space between her shoulders to soothe her. "Why are you ghosting on me like this? You're leaving in a few days and you've been talking to everyone about it but me. You didn't even tell me anything was wrong, you didn't tell me why you are so depressed," Serena cried into Bull's chest.

"I haven't really told anyone specifically what's wrong with me and it's hard as heck to describe."

"You didn't even try me!" Serena said with her hands flat on his broad chest, taking a deep breath and thinking about what she's saying. "I'm being stupid and selfish, right? But you're going through something and I'm doing something to make you feel like you can't talk to me. Now, I'm making it worse by asking you about it right?"

"No. No, it's me. You're right. I've been dealing with this alone and it's not fair to you. I just didn't know how to express my feelings to you because—" Bull said feeling his resolve starting to crumble as Serena looked up at him with her big blue eyes reddened with tears, while her lip was trembling.

"I feel so unfixable. I know how much it stresses you out to have problems you can't solve and that's what I felt like and I just didn't want to let you down."

Serena took Bull's face in her hands, the aroma of sweetly lotion. She then pressed his forehead to hers. "You've never let me down, Bull. You could never let me down."

Bull felt the warm ghost of Serena's breath against his lips and if he closed his eyes, he'd imagine hers moving against his.

Bull then took a step back and Serena's fingers were still tangled in his scruffy face. He tried swallowing down the words before they left him but they come out in a sigh too fast for him to catch. "I love you, Rena." Bull's mind was short-circuited.

"I love you too, Bull," she said. "You'll always be my best friend in this life." Those words lifted him sky high and dropped him onto unforgiving concrete in a matter of seconds. "Please don't shut me out anymore. Even if I can't help you, please let me be there. Please just don't stop talking to me."

"Okay." As an afterthought, he adds "It may take a while, but I'll call you when I can. I'll be back and it'll all be better. I promise. It will."

Serena nodded solemnly, looking puzzled.

Bull decided five days later to leave on a Wednesday, and the fire station planned on closing for a few hours to see him off. He stopped by the station early to make his peace, to say his goodbyes. Ray was the one who was the most light-hearted about the whole situation, he embraced Bull short and sweet like he'd be back in a week. Dustin's embrace lasted a little longer, with a firm pat on the back in there and a wish for luck. It was hard for Bull to look into Randy's eyes who was looking disappointed but sadly at him. Randy told Bull that things will be kept in order while he's away, that they'll let the lovelies around the neighborhood know he's taking a vacation.

Serena held Bull for a long time right in front of everyone. Dustin and Randy both awed from the side-lines, it's so touching and heartbreaking to watch these two besties part ways for now. That's what they looked like to everyone else, a couple of kindred spirits that will suffer by their separation. But Serena will survive, she will have Randy to keep her strong while Bull figures things out. Bull breathed in and lamented his need to exhale, wishing he could hold the smell of Serena's shampoo inside of him until he returned. Bull felt her warmth, as his hands clutched the back of her hoodie like he was desperate to die.

"Stay gold!" Bull said leaving out the station.

———

The drive up was a long one, taking roughly eleven hours. Bull opted to drive for some odd reason, not sure if he'd be up to the task of managing being packed into a security post while a bunch of tourists roamed the forest.

When he finally arrived at Oregon's border with California, the autumn sun just begun to settle to bed beneath the blanket of the tree-lines. It was five in the afternoon and Bull staggered into the foyer of a cabin where he'd be stationed for this week's orientation. He was greeted by the park's warden, Mr. Bradshaw, a short fella with a large brown mustache and lines all around his eyes. "You're just made it in time for supper! When we're done, go and mingle for a bit with the others before sunset. You'll be good to go by tomorrow afternoon. Is that all square to you?"

Bull nodded and was ushered into the dining room where several other new lookouts were already seated around an oval table. He waved and introduced himself after taking a seat next to a woman in her forties, with dark brown hair and bangs. She quickly introduced herself as Deborah Sikes, and Deb for short, shaking Bull's hands.

"Deb here has been a lookout for us for the past three years," Bradshaw pointed out as he sat at the head of the table, "You could say she's a veteran." Deb touched her chest feigning flattery. "She's stationed at Mulle Hill this season so she'll be close to you, Mr. Kramer," Bradshaw said pointing to Bull with his spoon. "You're very lucky to have her close by. Deb will be able to quickly answer any of your questions and concerns."

Deb nodded, "Just a walkie-talkie away, so if you have any issues or just need someone to chat with, I'm all ears. It can get a bit boring at times."

"Thanks. I'll be sure to do that," Bull said dryly, making a polite attempt at eating but he didn't find most of it appetizing. He gave up on the soup and focused on the chicken breast and sautéed green beans.

"You're going to be eating a lot of these type of apocalypse foods for the next three months, shit in cans with shelf lives until the year 3050."

Everyone laughed.

"I like to give my recruits a good home-cooked meal before starting to remind them of home!"

Bull tried savoring the chicken a little longer, enjoying its seasoning. After a few servings, he sat back and listened as the rest of the table swap stories about where they came from and how they all got there. Bull kept his story simple, making it about wanting time away from the city. After a few questions mainly from Deb, Bull was ready to get up and leave.

Bradshaw got up first and brought back a blueberry cobbler with vanilla ice cream for dessert. Bull kindly excused himself, feigning a headache.

"Sorry, Bull. The long drive in the heat probably did it," Bradshaw said leading Bull down the hall into one of the several guest rooms in the large cabin. There was a bunk bed and cot across the room from it. "Rangers Dave and Ted will be joining you here later in the week, they'll probably take whatever bed you don't," Bradshaw said.

"No problem. Thanks, Bradshaw."

Once Bradshaw left, Bull put down his duffle bag and settled onto the cot across from the bunk bed. He kicked off his shoes and jeans and rolled over, facing the wall that the bed is standing parallel to. His eyes traced the swirling patterns in the wood grain of the panels until they began to sag and minutes later, Bull fell into a deep sleep.

CHAPTER FOURTEEN

Bull woke up the next morning to find that his meal at dinner last night was a farce, Bradshaw's pancakes were making the rounds and everyone seemed to like them. Bradshaw told the rangers about how they were going to take a hike to a remote clearing in the forest and then depart on separate helicopters to their stations for orientation. Bull nodded to most of it and Bradshaw patted him on the shoulder after he finished giving instructions.

Deb asked Bull if he felt better and Bull almost asked her what she's talking about. "Much better," he said and Deb told him to stay hydrated.

"Lots of folks complain of headaches during their first few weeks. Withdrawal, I think, from all the technology." Deborah hummed, taking a sip of her coffee, closing her eyes and relishing in the bitterness of the blend. "You worked at a fire station right, Bull?"

Bull's face twisted a bit at that as he mumbled, "Yeah. You might be right" hoping it will end the conversation.

"Well, Bull. You'll have all the serenity one could ask for once you get out in the bush."

"I hope so," Bull said right before Park Warden Bradshaw came to gather the recruits to be escorted to different helipads. Bradshaw deferred half the recruits to one location that had left before sunrise. Bull ended up in the same helicopter as Deb. In the back of his mind, he wanted to yell *God damn!*

———

The helicopter ride was tense and Bull's jaw felt tight and uncomfortable as he tries dodging the eyes of the others, as he tried not to get sucked into their conversations. He looked out the window and saw the rolling cliff sides covered in nothing. He felt small, like a mosquito flying over a black hole. For close to an hour, Bradshaw kept talking and Bull just wanted to tell him to shut up.

They reached the lookout tower that Ranger Dave is scheduled to be posted at. There was a little outhouse overlooking a large expanse of forest and a lake close by. It was a prime tourist spot, the kind of place that Bull was looking to avoid. The group took a hike up the hillside and all clamber up the soggy wooden stairs and into the small space of the tower. The room was surrounded on three sides by countertops, on one side there was a bulletin board with maps, photos, and an old calendar. In the center was a table with a circular, movable map fixed to it.

"This," Bradshaw announced tapping the top of the topographical map, "is the Osborne Fire Finder. Invented in 1840 by Sir Francis Ronald in London to combat fires." Bradshaw told them so proudly that it was as he created it. "Re-imagined in the 20's by William Osborne, hence the name." Bradshaw rested his hand on the rectangular window posed on one side of the map. "You line this window up with the fire through the window, look through and find where it intersects with the compass and graduated ring on the map," he instructed while pointing to each piece on the device. "This is how you find the coordinates of a forest fire, this is how you get the information you need to call in a report of one." Bradshaw's face became serious then, "This is how you save lives."

The solemn nature of understanding the equipment loosened its hold on the throats of the rangers when Bradshaw turned their practice using the fire finder into a game. He placed sticky tabs on the window of the look-out tower, signifying where the smoke or actual fire would be visible and had the rangers take turns determining the coordinates of the "fire." It took Bull a few tries to get it right. Bradshaw stood by and offered a series of hints, urging Bull with chants of "Warmer....warmer....oh... colder...warmer" and jumping excitedly when Bull had found the right location. In the end, naturally, Deb was named the reigning champ. She insisted on not playing because it would be unfair to the newbies, but Bradshaw had insisted that it would be good for them to see an expert in action.

Once the game petered out, Bradshaw escorted Dave around his station, droning on about food supplies, gas-powered stoves, and routes into town. Bull found himself gazing out the window in the lookout area, sucking in the details of the forest that seems so far below them. His eyes trailed up from the blanket of emerald pines to the bright blue sky above and in the distance, he saw vultures circling over something dead on a patch of land far off from where they were, and is idly amazed at how easily, how quickly they could find their prey.

———

The day moved faster with the basic training squared away in the first cabin. As the rest of the team moved from one lookout tower to the next, each ranger was given the rundown on how to proceed day-to-day and how to establish contact with Bradshaw and ask for help. As helpful as Bradshaw tried to be, Bull didn't deny that the job required a lot of self-sufficiency from the get-go. Once Bradshaw finished explaining the ins and outs of the look-out tower, the remaining rangers found them-selves back in the helicopter. Bradshaw made it clear that once you're dropped off, you're expected to mill about through the rest of your day, fending for yourself and moving forward from that point on.

Bull was the last in the group to be discharged. He, Bradshaw, and their pilot arrived at the Hardy lookout tower in the early part of the evening. The sun began to hang low in the sky, glowing orange along the tree lines where Bull's new home overlooked. The view was stunning, thick crowds of evergreens as far as eyes could see. It was a lot less untouched land where he was stationed, hardly any place for tourists to camp out safely. The long expanse of dipping valleys and branches stretched high along the rifts are all so untamed, uncharted by man. It was sobering and remote. Bull then was startled back to his senses when Bradshaw unrolled a map and set it down against the countertop, pointing to their area.

"You're pretty far off from town, son, further than the others. I'm afraid it's going to take a lot more effort and planning to get you into town than a couple days hike. There's a good chance you'll have to call in for a dispatch every other week, so you've got to plan your excursions accordingly." Bradshaw said looking sternly into Bull's eyes.

Bull nodded. "I'll make sure to call you up ahead of time to set something up." Bull said, and Bradshaw smiled, patting Bull on the shoulder. "Oh, hang on a second!" Bull reached into his bag and pulled out an envelope to pass to Bradshaw. "Since I won't be able to make it into town for a while, do you mind dropping that off at the post office for me when you can? It's just a letter letting my people know I made it here okay."

"I got you. I'll be sure to send this out tomorrow," Bradshaw said, tucking the envelope into his back pocket.

"Hey, Bull."

"What's up?"

"Do you have a wife or girlfriend back in Cali?"

"There's someone I left behind. God knows if I'll ever have her."

"Well, I think Deb has the hots for you if that doesn't work out."

"I know."

The men laughed and Bradshaw left Bull to himself, his helicopter disappeared over the horizon. Bull sat out on the porch of his tower, bundled up in his a coat he's hardly ever needed back in L.A. The chill bite right through his clothes. The stars slowly began to manifest, freckling the pitch-black sky above him, so radiantly that it took Bull's breath away. He never saw so many stars at once and never seen them so bright. It reminded him of the first time Bull saw snow when he and Serena did training in New Hampshire. It was a reminder of how far from home he is, far from everything he knows, including Serena.

CHAPTER FIFTEEN

Bull didn't let himself think about why he was here, only that he's here now, and that there's a job to be done when he woke up in the morning. He sighed in a way that manifested into a swirling fog in front of his face, the dancing ghost of all his anxieties, dissipated before his eyes. Bull knew that he couldn't just lay there, cold wood against his back, stargazing forever. His bones popped as he stood and trudged over to the screen door, letting it creak and slam behind him. He shrugged his coat off and choked out a sob that wrenched itself from his chest so painfully that he clutched himself.

Everything began to hurt the same way it had when Bull had caved in on himself in the parking lot of the studio, just after Serena had broken his heart so bad that he had to run all the way out here to getaway. He felt stupid for coming all the way out here and not having the self-control to contain his feelings. Even now as Bull clutched his pillow smelling already of trees and dust, he longed for the ability to wrap his arms around Serena and bury himself in the scent of her shampoo. He longed for her proximity, even as it kills him from the inside out. He held himself tight but still felt cold, his chest is heavy like an anchor is on top of it even though he's lying curled on his side. Bull struggled to keep his sobbing quiet when it occurred that he could damn well scream his lungs out and no one would hear him.

Clenching his fists around his pillow, Bull tried screaming as loud as he could. It took some effort to get past the initial fear of disturbing the peace but he worked himself up to a loud growl, a guttural noise of pain. It didn't make him feel any better. It felt like empty air leaving him, his lungs no less full of the sorrow that was drowning him. Bull wanted to kill himself. He wanted to distract himself from the pain he feels contorting inside. He could just throw a punch against the wall or just break something. He got up and started working himself up almost ready to do something awful. Then someone yelled:

"Hey? Bull? You in there?"

Bull stopped in his tracks, forgetting his thoughts for a moment. He got up and yanked open the door. It was the face that he long desired.

"Serena?" he gaped. "What in Lord's heavens are you doing out here?"

"I made a choice to join you," she said, her voice wavered so much that it sparked hope in Bull's mind. "I don't know if it's the right one but I'm here. For you, Bull, I'm in love with you."

Bull barely heard anything she said because he thought he was dreaming, his ears were ringing and it was only when Serena stepped forward to kiss him that he realized it was not.

JESSIE

Derek recognized Jessie's soft, clean perfume the moment she entered any room. He'd know it was her, blindfolded, every single time simply from how her scent danced around him every time she breezed through. He'd bet his life on it.

It made it damn near impossible to make it through his workday, considering they shared a cubicle wall.

"Well, the badge scanner is on the fritz again," Jessie Morrison announced as she strode straight into Derek's cube and dropped off two cups of coffee on his desk. She peeled off her knit cap, completely oblivious as the motion sent little droplets of melted snow sprinkling onto Derek's desk papers before picking up her cup and taking a hasty sip. "That's the third time this week!"

Derek spun in his office chair to face her, eyeing her from beneath his heavy brows. "I didn't realize you were keeping track."

Jessie shrugged. "I'm not trying to. It's just obvious and annoying, and therefore, I remember. It was fine Monday, it happened Tuesday and Wednesday, and it worked fine again yesterday. Now today it's-"

"Back on the fritz," Derek finished for her.

Jessie cocked her hip to the side and rolled her eyes as she whipped off her gray scarf. "Yes," she said with a sigh.

"I'm sorry?" Derek offered, giving Jessie a sheepish look before reaching for his coffee. He took a sip and grimaced as he swallowed. "Jesus, what the hell is this?"

"It's coffee," Jessie replied, furrowing her brow at him. "Obviously."

"I know it's coffee, but where the hell did you get it?"

Jessie blinked. "The new place that opened right downstairs."

"It's open? I didn't know that." Behind him, Derek turned to see the notification that pinged on his computer, sitting the coffee cup back down on his desk. "Oh, shit, meeting in the conference room in five." He reached for his tablet and shoved a pen into the chest pocket.

"Mmm," Jessie grumbled, picking up her latte and pursing her lips at Derek as she backed out of his cube to head into her own. "And good morning to you, too, Mr. Grumpy."

* * *

Derek closed his eyes and hitched a quiet breath at

her words, silently blessing the cube wall separating their workspaces for the little privacy it gave him. Moments like these brought him back to just why being Jessie's co-worker made getting through his day feel like a Sisyphean trial.

For the last two years, he'd worked with Jessie, sometimes sharing projects and lab testing but always right next door as her cube neighbor. Ever since Jessie joined the firm that spring day, he'd been... slightly obsessed. And the worst part of it all was that Derek was one-hundred percent certain Jessie did not see him in the same light.

Derek spent the entire design status meeting spinning his pen around his first and fourth fingers, sending into a little helicopter propeller motion - something his coworkers had long learned to ignore. Derek claimed it helped him concentrate, but what exactly he was concentrating on was far from work.

Jessie.

He was stuck on her, no matter what he did to break free of it, though he was the first to admit he did little to fight it. It was all too easy to let his thoughts spiral, and it seemed to getting worse with each passing week, ever since the company party back in June. Their engineering firm had rented a yacht from Green Bay as a company outing and had taken the staff on a scenic city skyline ride along the Hudson and East Rivers. The skies had been clear, the summer sunset was bright, the music pounding, and the bar open. And like the rest of their coworkers,

Derek and Jessie had downed a few drinks over the three-hour dinner cruise, loosening their lips just enough for Derek to have learned all about Jessie's new boyfriend.

Well, that had been a joy.

And ever since, the obsession - which, prior to that day, had been a minor interest - had flared to life like gas on a flame. Derek didn't know what made him feel so angry hearing about Rick or Rob or whatever his name was, but it made his stomach sour and made his heart pound uncomfortably.

———

The trip was over. Everyone said their goodbyes and left for home, but something inside Derek had never really left that boat's bar. The vinyl stool he'd sat on beside Jessie the whole time they'd amusedly watched their drunken colleagues make fools of themselves on the dance floor became something else entirely in Derek's mind - a prison of his own making: the dreaded Friend Zone.

Months passed and here they were, just weeks from Christmas, and Derek was still stuck on that damn yacht, watching Jessie leave.

"What do you think, Derek?" Terrence asked from across the conference room table, one dark brow crooked in question, snatching Derek from his memories. "Will the new chassis design have room for the additional circuitry?"

Derek cleared his throat, buying time, trying to recall what the hell they might have been talking about. He took a shot and replied with a nod, "Yes, I think we could accommodate that change."

"You think or you know?" Terrence pressed. "We don't want to go to production and have a real estate issue on our hands," he added, steepling his fingers beneath his chin. "Why don't you connect with Morrison on this one and have her create a 3-D prototype of the new chassis, so we can be sure?"

Sucking in a breath at the mention of Jessie's name, Derek tamped down his excitement at having a reason to pull her onto his current project, making even more of an excuse to spend time with her. Feigning nonchalance, Derek shrugged. "Yeah, okay."

"Good," Terrence said with a nod, satisfied. "That should be it for now. I'll schedule a follow up with the team for one week from today; that should be enough time for you to get with Morrison and get what we need."

I wish, Derek thought wryly.

"Shouldn't be a problem," he replied aloud, keeping his thoughts to himself as he gathered his tablet and slid his glasses back into his pocket, along with his spare pen.

Derek's heartbeat was erratic as he loped back to his desk, his six-foot-three body leaving him feeling a bit awkward and strange in his own skin. He needed to get his thoughts under control before talking to Jessie. He peeled off the main hallway toward the men's room to use the bathroom and just chill for a second; practically salivating over the chance of working with Jessie hours at a time the following week.

I need to get a grip on- his thought was briskly interrupted as he turned the corner and crashed directly into a sweet-smelling wall of Jessie, knocking her into the gray cube right as the collision sent Derek's tablet slipping from his grip directly onto the toes of his shoes.

"Hey!" Jessie called, surprise thick in her voice right as at the same time Derek howled beneath his breath, "Ouch, Jesus!"

"What the hell, Derek?" Jessie asked, staring at him wide eyed as she rubbed her shoulder. "You practically ran me over."

"Shit, sorry, sorry," Derek said as he clamored to pick up his tablet and kneeled to rub at the top of his left shoe. "I... think I broke my toe." He was busy pressing down on his throbbing baby toe when Jessie's hearty laugh had him tipping his chin back up to her in disbelief. "What's so funny?" he mumbled, the pain in his toe subsiding as he stared at the dimple on her right cheek.

Jessie sighed, squatting down to be nearly eye-level. "Oh, Derek," Jessie shook her head, her hazel eyes dancing with humor, "there's no way you broke your toe through the leather of your shoes."

Derek blinked, realizing the pain was now completely gone. He looked down at his foot and felt the heat creep up his neck toward his hairline. "No, I guess that's not likely."

"Nope," Jessie agreed, shaking her head back and forth slowly. She reached over to pat Derek's right shoulder. "Come on, Ferdinand, let's get you up."

Derek stood, tucking his tablet beneath his arm. "Ferdinand?"

"You know, Ferdinand the Bull, the children's story?"

He chuckled, "No, I must've missed that one."

"Well, let's get you to your desk and you can sit and smell the flowers for a few minutes and mind that toe of yours."

Derek didn't know what the hell she was talking about, but it didn't matter because Jessie still had her hand on his bicep, gently leading him back toward their cubicles. Her hand felt warm even through the thin cotton of his dress shirt, his top button suddenly feeling way too constricting even though it was unbuttoned. And was that a bead of sweat rolling between his shoulder blades?

"Here we go, Jansen," Jessie announced as she gently shoved him into his cube, motioning toward his chair. "Have a seat and perhaps you can distract yourself from the pain of your toe by asking me if I'm okay, considering the bull in a china shop move you just pulled."

He was an idiot. An absolute grade-A idiot.

"Oh, Jessie, I'm so sorry," Derek began, eyes wide. "I was rushing to the bathroom after the meeting and wasn't paying attention. Did I hurt you? Are you okay?"

Jessie giggled again, crossing her arms over her chest. "Of course I'm okay, you blubbering fool," she replied, rolling her eyes playfully. "I'm not quite as delicate as china."

Derek swallowed, images of Jessie in delicate lace, delicate positions, her delicate skin marked by him... they flooding his mind at the most inappropriate moments in all of time and space. "No, of course you're not." It was a weak, unconvincing reply, but he'd managed it.

"Of course I'm not," Jessie echoed. "Now that's done with, let's get some Thai for lunch later."

Jessie pulled her cell phone from her back pocket and unlocked it, opening up the app to get an order placed for later. "I've been craving spring rolls."

The side of Derek's lip lifted in a hint of a smile, his heart rate finally settling into something resembling normalcy. "Only you could crave spring rolls. You don't even get the fried ones."

Jessie lifted her brow. "Well, some of us eat things that are green and some of us survive on 'swill' and negativity."

Derek felt his lips twitch again as he watched the mirth in her eyes. "You'll get my negativity in full force next week when I'm constantly dissatisfied with the 3D prototype of our new design you make me."

"Really?" Jessie's voice rose an octave as her eyes lit up. "I love prototyping!"

Derek nodded. "I know, but don't thank me. It was all Terrence. We need to be sure the new design's circuitry will fit in the chassis without having to change dimensions."

Nodding, Jessie agreed. "Makes sense. I'm sure I can find time to work on that, along with my other projects."

Jessie snapped her head when the sound of her desk phone rang on the other side of the cube. "Shoot, I'm expecting a call from a vendor. Let me grab that," she said, distractedly dropping her cell down on Derek's desk as she shot over to her cubicle.

———

Just as she stepped away, Jessie's cell phone pinged, an alert lighting up her lock screen. Derek didn't mean to look, but since the phone was just inches from his face, it was hard for his eyes not to notice Fish's obvious icon - one he recognized from his own lukewarm on-and-off experiences with the same dating app.

Since when was Jessie on a dating app? What happened to Rick or Rob, or the guy from the summer? And why the hell did Derek not know Jessie was single again? And why was he staring at her phone screen, memorizing her screen name - "A.A.Bev" - and reading notification that some dude named Jeremy wanted to connect with her?

Derek did not like this guy called Jeremy.

But Derek had an idea.

A very, very bad idea. An idea that could help him get the one thing he'd wanted for the last six months: Jessie finally seeing him as someone other than a co-worker or friend. Derek wanted out of the Friend Zone.

He ached to know what every inch of her skin felt like. Derek wanted to memorize the shape of her body with his hands. He yearned to recognize the taste of her tongue, the way he recognized her scent in the air. He was desperate for her to see him in a new light - not as her crabby, awkward colleague, but as a man worthy of her affection.

Maybe, someday, a man even worthy of her love.

"Desperate times and all," Derek murmured, emblazoning Jessie's screen name in his memory for after work.

He had a new profile to make.

CHAPTER TWO

The next day

"I don't get him, Paige," Jessie said, shaking her head as she chewed and swallowed her last bite of her burger. "Sometimes it's like he's two different people."

Paige took a swig of her beer and set it down, her face stone-cold serious. "Wait. Are we talking about Derek? Again?"

Jessie shrugged. "Yeah. So?"

"So you spend an awful lot of your time thinking about the guy."

"Well, he's strange. It's like… he's a mystery I'm trying to figure out."

A single, dark brow arched over Paige's right eye. "Uh, huh? Right."

Jessie grabbed her beer bottle and brought it to her lips, shaking her head. "No, no. I don't think I do."

"Oh, really? Then why do we spend every dinner discussing him for at least forty percent of our time together?"

"We don't," Jessie scoffed.

"We do," Paige stated. "I think he sounds a little strange, but mostly he sounds… I don't know… nice?"

"Ha," Jessie said, cocking her head. "Derek is anything but nice. He's constantly in a sour mood, all worked up and mumbling to himself. And the other half of the time, he's quiet and barely speaks a word to me. I'm lucky to get a gruff nod those days."

It was quiet momentarily before Paige gently placed her hand on Jessie's and asked, "So, why do you hang out with him?"

"I… don't know," Jessie shrugged. "Sometimes I think he's lonely. Sometimes I think he's shy and needs someone to help break the ice. And when he comes out of his gloomy shell, he's actually hilarious, and he... "Jessie felt a smile tug at her lips. "He makes me laugh."

"And you're sure you maybe don't like him? Just a little?" Paige pressed, smiling at her best friend across the table.

"He's just not my type," Jessie answered, shaking her head.

"Okay, I'll bite," Paige grinned. "What exactly is your type these days, Morrison? Last I knew, you were pretty into tall, tan, and handsome. Does this Derek not fit that bill?"

Jessie felt her cheeks blush. "I think I need someone more…" she sighed, shaking her head again. "I don't know. Just someone more into me. Like, who I am as a person."

"You deserve that," Paige agreed. "I just don't know why you think he's not into you. I mean, you know you're pretty hot. You run nine miles a week, and you're fit as hell. You're a mechanical engineer who likes to fix cars in your spare time. Let's face it - you're any dude's wet dream."

Jessie's flush darkened further. "Thanks, Paige, that's sweet of you to say, but I'm clearly not his type."

"Aha!" Paige exclaimed, her eyes glinting with glee. "I knew it. You like him!"

"I do not!"

"You just keep telling yourself that, sister," Paige said, bringing her beer back to her lips and tossing back what was left of the bottle.

* * *

An hour later, Jessie was home, flopped down on her couch in her cozy flannel PJs, opening up her Fish app.

She'd never tried a dating app before, but when she'd heard about this one, she figured she'd try it. After she and James had parted ways two months ago, their summer romance as short-lived as the season itself, Jessie had wondered if she'd ever find "the one."

Between work and a scarce group of mutual friends still in the city after getting jobs and moving on after grad school, Jessie didn't have a ton of outlets in which to meet new people. A dating app had seemed like a good idea. But after almost a month on the site, Jessie hadn't found over three or four profiles that piqued her curiosity, and each of them had turned out to be of little interest once she had a couple of brief interchanges online.

Jessie sighed as she scrolled through the profiles of the people who'd shown interest in connecting with her, seeing the same images she'd seen for weeks until a picture she didn't recognize caught her eye.

The photo was in low light, barely more than a silhouette of a man who seemed quite tall and broad against a back-lit background. She couldn't tell if his hair was short or pulled back, but by the wisps in shadow near his neck, Jessie thought maybe it was back in a man-bun kind of thing. She couldn't decipher much about his appearance other than he was big. Built. And completely shirtless.

She swallowed, her mouth suddenly flooding with saliva as her heart raced. Jessie never reacted to profile pictures like this.

With an eager finger, she swiped right on Hank Johnson.

———

Derek's phone pinged from the pillow beside his head, and his tense body reacted to the sound with a startled jerk. "Shit!"

He palmed his phone in his hand, and his pulse pounded in his throat when he saw the sound was a notification from Fish.

"It worked," he breathed, looking at the message alerting him that an A.A. Bev had swiped right on him, too. "Okay, okay," he muttered to himself, scrambling to set up and lean against his headboard, "stay cool."

His right hand shook as he tapped Jessie's profile - the little green dot showing she was active online - and began composing a message. It took about forty seconds for him to decide to go with Hi.

Immediately, his phone pinged with her reply.

> Hello.

> How are you?

Derek cursed under his breath at his ineptitude. Why couldn't he sound intriguing instead of like a high schooler?

> I'm fine and you?

Derek took a deep breath. This wasn't him; this was Hank - and Hank could do all the things Derek wasn't brave enough, cool enough, confident enough, or comfortable enough to ever do. Exhaling slowly and willing his pounding heart to settle down, Derek replied.

> Better now.

His phone was quiet for a full minute, sending Derek's

blood pressure skyrocketing once again, before Jessie's reply came through.

> That's bold of you.

> Why pretend like I didn't want you to contact me when I've been sitting here thinking about you for an hour?

Derek hit send on the message and cringed, squinting his eyes down, wondering if he'd just killed all possibility of hope with this absurd plan. After another agonizing minute, a reply appeared on his screen.

> And what exactly did you like about my profile?

> Besides your pic, you mean?

Derek wondered if this was flirting. If it was, he was simultaneously in awe over the tingling feeling deep in his gut - more like a flock of geese than butterflies - and hating how his palms were sweating and how he felt almost lightheaded.

> Don't judge a book by its cover and all that.

He huffed a laugh. Fuck it, he thought to himself. Hank Johnson had something to say about that.

> Didn't you?

> What was it about me that caught your attention?

> I'm sure it wasn't my obvious good looks.

> Your pic was a little... mysterious.

> And you like that?

> OK. I'll answer honestly.

> I liked your chest.

> Your turn.

Derek inhaled.

> I like your smile.

> Your mouth.

Again, Derek waited, not breathing, not moving an inch. Was he being a vile pervert? Would he scare Jessie away and ruin any chance he had of ever finding himself closer to her? Finally, after a full eighty-four seconds (he counted), Jessie's reply pinged his phone.

> Tell me more about yourself, mysterious Hank.

A grin stretched wide across his face, and Derek settled back onto his headboard, finally feeling like he'd been granted some permission for which he'd never truly asked. He started typing line after line, little snippets about himself - all true - just things he never had the guts to share in his real life.

He told Jessie that Hank was an only child and grew up independently. His parents divorced when he was young, and shortly after, his father died in a car accident. He told her he worked in insurance and traveled a lot, which he definitely did not, but he hoped the white lie would steer Jessie away from asking too much about his profession. He admitted he was often lonely and spent a disproportionate amount of his time at the gym simply because he had nothing better to do - and no one to do it with.

Jessie shared things about herself in return, and Derek was surprised to realize most of what she messaged him were things he already knew about her from their real-life interaction at work over the last couple of years. He'd known from a casual conversation that Jessie, too, was an only child. But Derek hadn't known she was a product of an unfortunate youth spent in orphanages and foster homes until she became emancipated at age seventeen.

The thought of sweet, smart, lively Jessie spending all those years alone and suffering made something deep within his ribcage ache, made his heart race with bursts of anger toward the injustice of it all. His fingers whipped across his phone screen, and for a moment, he didn't know if it was Hank or Derek typing a reply.

> You're not alone.

> Neither are you.

Jessie's reply came moments later, along with a picture of what he knew had to be her hand in her lap, palm upturned in silent question as if waiting for him to hold it.

Derek groaned.

There was no other word for it - a sound from deep in the back of his throat filled with longing, need, relief and heartbreak all at once.

His fingers ached to slide against hers and touch that warm, soft skin he felt through his dress shirt that morning. He squeezed his palm into a fist, wishing to feel something other than empty air and his bones and tendons.

He wanted to prove how much he wanted her, how amazing she'd made him feel with those three simple words. And though he'd started this whole thing as brave Hank, all Derek desperately wanted was to give something of himself, something that would make Jessie feel safe and wanted, the way the picture of her hand had made him feel.

> Can I send you a picture?

> Yes!

Derek smiled at her timid reply. He was certain she expected a dick pic to come through the app at any moment. Instead, he searched on his phone and sent a zoomed-in image of the near-touching hands of Michelangelo's Creation of Adam painting, hoping it conveyed what he was trying to communicate.

> Oh!

When Jessie replied, Derek wasn't sure he'd been successful. Her single word left him scrambling, trying to backtrack and return to the easy chat and banter from before.

> Sorry if that was too much; it just made me think of that.

> Anyway, never mind.

> No! Sorry, no, it wasn't too much.

> It was beautiful.

Like you, Derek thought.

> Glad you liked it.

> So I need to ask you something.

> Okay…

> It's really deep and personal, fair warning.

> Okay…

> What does A.A. stand for?

> LOL!

> Oh my gosh, you really had me nervous there.

> Well, your boy Hank wants to know who he just held hands with.

> That's a lot for a first date, you know.

> First date? You're cute.

Derek blushed as he replied, pushing again to see if Jessie would reveal her name.

> And you're only initials.

> Tell me your name, pretty girl.

> You know already.

Fuck.

Where did Derek screw up? How had Jessie figured him out so quickly? He was so, so dead. Derek sat with his phone in his right hand, his left angrily shoving stray locks of hair that had fallen out of the tie-back at the top of his head. He started sweating again, his hand finally settling over the thin seam of his lips as he stared at the phone and waited for whatever horrible thing was coming next.

But it never came.

Instead, another message appeared after an interminably long moment.

> My name is Jessie. I use the initials to keep some semblance of privacy.

Derek's hand dropped from his mouth as he huffed out an enormous sigh, his body sagging and his eyes closing in utter relief.

> Jessie.

> I like it. Little sunshine.

> I don't know about that…

> I do.

> I'm already happier in the last hour chatting with you than I've been in months.

> Maybe years.

> That's… another wow!

> Send me another picture of yourself.

> Not your hands.

> Wow me!

> If you're a good boy, maybe I will…

Goddamn, if that didn't make Derek's cock hard. She was killing him slowly. Just the thought of Jessie even considering sending him another picture was almost more than Derek could handle.

* * *

Derek had spent months fantasizing about how he could get Jessie to ever talk to him like this, to see him differently, and here he was mere hours after creating his alter ego, and it was perfect. He bit the corner of his lip, debating whether he should reply with the thought that just came to mind. Would it scare her off once and for all? Or could Hank Johnson help show her just what Derek was capable of?

Jessie was perfect. His plan, though far from perfect and poorly crafted in its planning phase, was working with the engineering precision he was accustomed to. Somehow, he'd figure it out. He'd think about it and come up with a way to tell Jessie the truth and make it right.

Some day, he'd fall to his knees and beg her forgiveness. She'd wrap her arms around his shoulders as he pressed the side of his face to her stomach, engulfing him in her light, righting his sins, making him holy and whole.

But for now, Derek needed to make Jessie see. He needed to keep her in the dark for just a while longer.

He needed to bring this Hank to life.

> I can be very, very good.

> Let me show you...Derek's phone pinged from the pillow beside his head, and his tense body reacted to the sound with a startled jerk. "Shit!"

He palmed his phone in his hand, and his pulse pounded in his throat when he saw the sound was a notification from Fish.

"It worked," he breathed, looking at the message alerting him that an A.A. Bev had swiped right on him, too. "Okay, okay," he muttered to himself, scrambling to sit up and lean against his headboard, "stay cool."

His right hand shook as he tapped Jessie's profile - the little green dot showing she was active online - and began composing a message. It took about forty seconds for him to decide to go with *Hi.*

Immediately, his phone pinged with her reply.

> Hello.

> How are you?

Derek cursed under his breath at his ineptitude. Why couldn't he sound intriguing instead of like a high schooler?

> I'm fine and you?

Derek took a deep breath. This wasn't him; this was Hank - and Hank could do all the things Derek wasn't brave enough, cool enough, confident enough, or comfortable enough to ever do. Exhaling slowly and willing his pounding heart to settle down, Derek replied.

> Better now.

His phone was quiet for a full minute, sending Derek's blood pressure skyrocketing once again before Jessie's reply came through.

> That's bold of you.

> Why pretend I didn't want you to contact me when I've been sitting here thinking about you for an hour?

Derek hit send on the message and cringed, squinting his eyes, wondering if he'd just killed all possibility of hope with this absurd plan. After another agonizing minute, a reply appeared on his screen.

> And what exactly did you like about my profile?

> Besides your pic, you mean?

Derek wondered if this was flirting. If it was, he was simultaneously in awe over the tingling feeling deep in his gut - more like a flock of geese than butterflies - and hating how his palms were sweating and how he felt almost lightheaded.

> Don't judge a book by its cover and all that.

He huffed a laugh. Fuck it, he thought to himself. Hank Johnson had something to say about that.

> Didn't you?

> What was it about me that caught your attention?

> I'm sure it wasn't my obvious good looks.

> Your pic was a little... mysterious.
> And you like that?
> OK. I'll answer honestly.
> I liked your chest.
> Your turn.
Derek inhaled.
> I like your smile.
> Your mouth.

Again, Derek waited, not breathing, not moving an inch. Was he being a vile pervert? Would he scare Jessie away and ruin any chance he had of ever finding himself closer to her? Finally, after a full eighty-four seconds (he counted), Jessie's reply pinged his phone.

> Tell me more about yourself, mysterious Hank.

A grin stretched wide across his face, and Derek settled back onto his headboard, finally feeling like he'd been granted some permission for which he'd never truly asked. He started typing line after line, little snippets about himself - all true - just things he never had the guts to share in his real life.

He told Jessie that Hank was an only child and grew up independently. His parents divorced when he was young, and shortly after, his father died in a car accident. He told her he worked in insurance and traveled a lot, which he most definitely did not, but he hoped the white lie would steer Jessie away from asking too much about his profession. He admitted he was often lonely and spent a disproportionate amount of his time at the gym simply because he had nothing better to do - and no one to do it with.

Jessie shared things about herself in return, and Derek was surprised to realize most of what she messaged him were things he already knew about her from their real-life interaction at work over the last couple of years. He'd known from a casual conversation that Jessie, too, was an only child. But Derek hadn't known she was a product of an unfortunate youth spent in orphanages and foster homes until she became emancipated at age seventeen.

The thought of sweet, smart, lively Jessie spending all those years alone and suffering made something deep within his ribcage ache, made his heart race with bursts of anger toward the injustice of it all. His fingers whipped across his phone screen, and for a moment, he didn't know if it was Hank or Derek typing a reply.

> You're not alone.

> Neither are you.

Jessie's reply came moments later, along with a picture of what he knew had to be her hand in her lap, palm upturned in silent question as if waiting for him to hold it.

Derek groaned.

There was no other word for it - a sound from deep in the back of his throat filled with longing, need, relief, and heartbreak all at once.

His fingers ached to slide against hers and touch that warm, soft skin he felt through his dress shirt that morning. He squeezed his palm into a fist, wishing to feel something other than empty air and his bones and tendons.

He wanted to prove how much he wanted her, how amazing she'd made him feel with those three simple words. And though he'd started this whole thing as brave Hank, all Derek desperately wanted was to give something of himself, something that would make Jessie feel safe and wanted, the way the picture of her hand had made him feel.

> Can I send you a picture?

> Yes!

Derek smiled at her timid reply. He was certain she expected a dick pic to come through the app at any moment. Instead, he searched on his phone and sent a zoomed-in image of the near-touching hands of Michelangelo's Creation of Adam painting, hoping it conveyed what he was trying to communicate.

> Oh!

When Jessie replied, Derek wasn't sure he'd been successful. Her single word left him scrambling, trying to backtrack and return to the easy chat and banter from before.

> Sorry if that was too much; it made me think of that.

> Anyway, never mind.

> No! Sorry, no, it wasn't too much.

> It was beautiful.

Like you, Derek thought.

> Glad you liked it.

> So I need to ask you something.

> Okay…

> It's really deep and personal, fair warning.

> Okay…

> What does A.A. stand for?

> LOL!

> Oh my gosh, you really had me nervous there.

> Well, your boy Hank wants to know who he just held hands with.

> That's a lot for a first date, you know.

> First date? You're cute.

Derek blushed as he replied, pushing again to see if Jessie would reveal her name.

> And you're only initials.

> Tell me your name, pretty girl.

> You know already.

Fuck.

Where did Derek screw up? How had Jessie figured him out so quickly? He was so, so dead. Derek sat with his phone in his right hand, his left angrily shoving stray locks of hair that had fallen out of the tie-back at the top of his head. He started sweating again, his hand finally settling over the thin seam of his lips as he stared at the phone and waited for whatever horrible thing was coming next.

But it never came.

Instead, another message appeared after an interminably long moment.

> My name is Jessie. I use the initials to keep some semblance of privacy.

Derek's hand dropped from his mouth as he huffed out an enormous sigh, his body sagging and his eyes closing in utter relief.

> Jessie.

> I like it. Little sunshine.

> I don't know about that…

> I do.

> I'm already happier in the last hour chatting with you than I've been in months.

> Maybe years.

> That's… another wow!

> Send me another picture of yourself.

> Not your hands.

> Wow me!

> If you're a good boy, maybe I will…

Goddamn, if that didn't make Derek's cock hard. She was killing him slowly. Just the thought of Jessie even considering sending him another picture was almost more than Derek could handle.

****

Derek had spent months fantasizing about how he could get Jessie to ever talk to him like this, to see him differently, and here he was mere hours after creating his alter ego, and it was perfect. He bit the corner of his lip, debating whether he should reply with the thought that just came to mind. Would it scare her off once and for all? Or could Hank Johnson help show her just what Derek was capable of?

Jessie was perfect. His plan, though far from perfect and poorly crafted in its planning phase, was working with the engineering precision he was accustomed to. Somehow, he'd figure it out. He'd think about it and devise a way to tell Jessie the truth and make it right.

Some day, he'd fall to his knees and beg her forgiveness. She'd wrap her arms around his shoulders as he pressed the side of his face to her stomach, engulfing him in her light, righting his sins, making him holy and whole.

But for now, Derek needed to make Jessie see. He needed to keep her in the dark for just a while longer.

He needed to bring this Hank to life.

> I can be very, very good.

> Let me show you...

CHAPTER THREE

Jessie stared at her phone, her jaw hanging open in disbelief. At dinner earlier, she'd been resigned to probably spending the rest of her life alone. She'd already Googled cats up for adoption at the local shelter because she'd been fairly convinced after her talk with Paige that she'd be one of those career women who eventually turned into an old cat lady. And that was okay.

Mostly.

Despite the deep ache she felt at the thought of it, Jessie knew she'd rather be alone than with the wrong guy. Her last few boyfriends had all but ruined Jessie's concept of healthy relationships and love… between Dennis cheating on her this summer and the Compulsive Liar Liam before him, she was just tired of feeling cheap and used.

What she wanted - what she dreamed about when she let her mind wander to that magical imagined future where she had a loving husband, a cozy home, maybe a kid or two running around - was someone who would simply stand by her side. When she was feeling small, Dream Husband would bolster her. When she felt lost in the dark, he'd be right there, a shadow beside her.

Dream Husband would care about her deeply intense, obvious, and unashamed of his passion.

And he'd simply know her.

So though she'd been reluctant to set up a profile on Fish, she figured at least she could put herself out there in a controlled environment and really decide if she was interested in pursuing anyone after giving herself time and space for thoughtful consideration.

There was absolutely no thoughtful consideration happening right now.

> Let me show you...

Jesus, Jessie told herself that it's hot in here.

Jessie pawed at her shirt and started undoing the buttons, stripping down to her white tank top. She was flushed from her chest upward; she wouldn't be surprised if the ends of her hair were blushing too.

Not after the way this man was talking to her.

This Hank was completely unfiltered in his conversation, but Jessie felt like every word he shared was brutally honest. It's like he had no pretense; he didn't tip-toe around her feelings or say things she thought he thought she wanted to hear. He seemed intense and decisive; a man who knew what he wanted, and was not shy to ask for it. And Jessie felt he wanted her.

Jessie felt wanted.

And that was maybe the sexiest thing of all about Hank.

So with only the tiniest reservation from the part of her brain who watched and questioned what the hell Jessie thought she was doing engaging in this kind of talk with a virtual stranger, she typed her reply.

> **Show me.**

> **Whatever you want to show me.**

She dug her teeth into her bottom lip and waited.

What came through next on the app wasn't at all what Jessie expected. She'd been bracing herself for a picture of him, maybe something a little risky. Hell, maybe something a LOT dirty. Either way, when she'd told him he could show her, she kind of thought he'd show her… something.

Her cell phone screen lit up with a zoomed-in image of a man's large hands palming the globe of a woman's rear, the material of a tiny white thong threading between the pointer and finger of his right hand in a strangely possessive, gentle caress.

"Oh," Jessie gasped, the shock of it all - the image, the boldness of him having sent it, the surprise of it not being a tasteless shove of the camera down his pants - leaving her a puddle of speechless drool. The picture he'd sent was so honest it made Jessie feel like she could spare to let her guard down a little more, too.

She exhaled slowly as she typed a reply.

> **Well, that was not what I was expecting.**

Hank's reply came back immediately.

> I want to know you.

> What you like, what turns you on.

> And then you'll know the things I'm thinking about doing with you.

Jessie shot up from the couch, dropping her phone on the table behind her.

"Holy shit," she muttered on her way to the kitchen to get herself a tall glass of water. Freezing cold, to be precise, because she felt like she would spontaneously combust at any moment. She needed to hydrate, to cool down, to… to… something for God's sake, besides stripping naked and jumping into a cold shower.

Jessie filled her glass and gulped it down, but her hasty, shaking hand sent a small dribble of water down her chin. The spill slid down her neck, a tiny cold pool settling at the notch of her collarbone.

"Damn it," she mumbled, reaching for a paper towel to clean up her sloppiness, but as she moved, the droplets slid from her collarbone straight beneath the top seam of her tank top, the chilly liquid coming to a stop on the flesh of her left tit. As she stared down at the damp spot seeping through her top, her nipples stiffened into strained peaks, pressed angrily against her tank top.

Slowly, Jessie set the glass back down on the counter. Her heart smacked against her rib cage, wild and wicked with the crazy idea that just flitted into her brain. She pivoted on her heel and walked back to the living room in a daze, her breath coming in rapid puffs, the heat of each exhale ghosting over the damp trail of water still on her neck. A shiver rolled through her body at the stark contrast between the chilly wet spot on her bosom and her warm, damp of breath.

Retrieving her phone, Jessie sat down on the couch and opened up her camera app, switching it to the front facing lens.

"I can't believe I'm about to do this," she huffed, digging her top teeth into her bottom lip, steeling her nerve.

Jessie aimed the lens down to catch the bottom of her chin, making the angle such that her neck and chest were visible on the screen, the lamplight caught the wetness lingering along the column of her neck; her left nipple clearly showing her arousal beneath her shirt. She took the picture and quickly edited it to be black and white to match the style of photo Hank had sent her, then attached it to her chat window and pressed send before she could change her mind.

Though Jessie knew the picture, he'd sent was a public domain photo of some sort, she wondered if he would realize the image she'd shared was of herself and not an internet photo. Jessie's emotions waffled between hoping he'd immediately guess the photo was of her own body and praying to any deity that would listen that he'd never suspect her to take such a brazen action mere hours after connecting with him, for all intents and purposes, a virtual stranger.

Time moved in slow motion as Jessie waited for

Hank's reaction. In reality, the man's reply came within seconds, and with it, a rush of desire coiled deep in her belly, an electric thrill running along her spine as she read his words.

> You're even more amazing than I imagined.

Jessie's eyelids slipped closed, her breath leaving her body in a relieved exhale. Her reaction made her realize she'd secretly been hoping he'd know it was a selfie - that he'd intuitively recognize her form - that he'd know her.

She typed a reply, again biting her lip to fight the wild grin tugging at her lips.

> **Quite the compliment, Hank.**

> Only the truth, Jessie.

Warmth flooded her chest, and Jessie couldn't feel the wet spot on her shirt anymore. It was probably long gone, turned to steamy vapors minutes ago. As she stared down at her phone, her eye drifted and caught the timestamp at the top of the screen and she groaned.

———

It was well after midnight. How had hours passed already? Jessie was loathe to end their chat. She had an irrational fear that she was Cinderella in this scenario, about to run off after the ball, her prince lost once the magic of the moment had passed. But the morning would come quickly, and she and Derek had agreed to meet at seven to go over the schematics and the redesigned circuit board for their project.

Sighing, Jessie tapped the keys to start her reluctant goodbye.

> I hate to leave, but I think I need to go to bed.

> You definitely need to go to bed...

> ... with me.

Jessie giggled as the grin she'd been fighting broke free.

> I walked right into that one, didn't I?

> You kind of did.

Still smiling, Jessie tried again.

> But I really need to get some sleep.

Derek's reply came instantly, making her smile.

> Sleep tight.

> I'll find you here again.

She ran her right pinkie along her bottom lip. Sorry to walk away from this… whatever this was. Finally, Jessie tapped out one last message.

> Promise?

> Only the truth from me, Jessie.

> Good night!

> Good night, Hank!

———

Logging out of the app, Jessie stood and went to the kitchen to close up for the night, retrieving her discarded flannel PJ shirt along the way. She headed toward her bedroom, the chill in the apartment suddenly more intense with every passing moment away from her online chat, with every step deeper toward the dark bedroom at the end of the hall. She flipped on the lights and grabbed an extra blanket for the foot of her bed before popping into her bathroom to brush her teeth and wash her face.

By the time she slid beneath her cool sheets, Jessie was already regretting the bold moves she'd made in the last hour.

What nice, upstanding girl behaved so wantonly? Hank seemed like a brave, bad boy, but if this part of her was what he wanted, what would happen when he finally met her? The real her? The no-nonsense, independent mechanical engineer who worked so hard to make a name for herself... the young woman who'd been hurt too many times to count... the parts of her that, despite her effort to hide them, were lonely and shy and sometimes insecure?

Hank had stated nothing but truth...

But what was Jessie's truth? Had this... strange desire always been inside of her, waiting to be kindled awake?

Jessie sighed and turned on her side, curling around her knees to stay warm. She bunched the blankets beneath her chin and closed her eyes, forcing her racing thoughts to soothe themselves. In her memory, she saw Hank's words on her phone screen, wishing her goodnight.

Sleep tight.

Suddenly, Jessie felt heated again.

CHAPTER FOUR

Derek Jansen didn't know what the hell he was doing.

He'd risen well before dawn and spent an unreasonable amount of time sitting at the edge of his bed, head resting on his hands, wondering why in hell he'd thought creating a fake profile was a good idea.

He groaned, rubbing the sleep from his eyes and wondering just how he was going to manage getting through the day working side-by-side with Jessie. If he thought being in her company before all this was a little jarring, Derek couldn't imagine how he could be productive now when, in the back of his mind, he'd be seeing the picture Jessie sent him last night. And damn, receiving it from her had near about killed him.

That long, sleek column of her neck with… was it sweat, water? Derek didn't know what had gotten Jessie wet, but he hoped to holy hell it had to do with him.

Or, well, Hank.

"Shit," Derek breathed. He stood and made his way toward the bathroom, shuffling along with about as much enthusiasm as a man to the guillotine. He was well and truly fucked, and he'd no one to blame but himself for his harebrained idea.

Standing under the spray of the shower, hot water dripping down the length of his hair and across his chest, Derek's conscience switched from waving caution flags to displaying neon red signs flashing 'abort!' This situation was a disaster waiting to happen - part of him knew that before he'd ever opened that damn app.

He rinsed the last of the conditioner out of his hair and turned off the tap, using the flat of his palms to sluice the water off his skin. He shoved open the shower curtain and stepped out onto the mat, standing in the steam like a giant version of a boy lost. Derek grabbed his towel and dried off before swiping his hand to clear the steam from the mirror.

Derek stared at his reflection, feeling remorse bubble up from the depths of his soul. He braced his arms on either side of the sink and leaned closer. His dark eyes roamed over his face and lingered on the protruding ears his wet hair no longer hid. Derek always hated them, along with his distinguished nose. The small freckles smattering his face didn't do him any favors with the girls growing up, either, and Derek knew that now, even at twenty-nine, there was a part of him that still felt like the awkward, oafish, too-big teenager he'd been.

The self-doubt that plagued him back then sure stuck around. Derek did his best to hide it by keeping to himself and maintaining a low-profile. At work, he was serious and extremely competent, known among the team of fellow electrical engineers to keep his nose to the grindstone and get the job done with precision and efficiency. He was polite, but not overly animated. In fact, the lukewarm camaraderie Derek had developed with Jessie over the last year was probably his only genuine relationship, beside those of pure professional courtesy among his colleagues.

And outside of work? Well, it was much of the same. Besides his near-daily visits to the gym, Derek had little on his calendar. He wasn't a social man.

He tried, and for a while, when his college friends were still in the city, he'd attempted to have some sort of life outside of his job. But within a few years, they'd all grown tired of the city life and had each moved on to different adventures - Lana high-tailed it to sunny San Diego. Hugo took a cross-country road trip four years ago and decided never to come back. Three weeks after that, Penny finally caved to her pining over Hugo and followed him out west.

The staffs at the gym and his favorite coffee shop were probably the only people who actually saw Derek regularly, besides the occasional weekend train trip to visit his mother out on Long Island.

Besides Jessie, of course.

Jessie, who continued to talk to him cheerfully every

day, even when he was a surly ass. Jessie, who grabbed an extra coffee for him when she made a stop for herself. Jessie, who never failed to ask him to pick up lunch with her at least twice a week, even though half the time he just complained about her food choices.

Jessie… who smiled at him despite his inability to emerge from behind the irritable mask he wore; his enigmatic persona, a helmet he'd designed a long time ago to shield himself from his own dark, spiraling thoughts about his self-worth.

Jessie… who trusted him with her friendship and who was trusting Hank with something more of herself, something for which Derek would slay another man if he took such a gift of hers for granted.

He clenched his jaw and lifted his chin, his decision made.

His voice gruff from lack of sleep and hours of contemplation, Derek directed his words to the reflection in the glass, a command and a doctrine: "I know what I have to do."

* * *

An hour later, in the design lab at the office, Derek sat across from Jessie, trying really, really hard to focus. He'd known this morning would be a challenge, and that was before he'd decided he had to come clean about what he'd done on Fish. His mind was a jumble of clashing thoughts and desires. He ached to make Jessie happy, to reveal himself as the man she'd opened up to the night before. And yet, he dreaded making the confession he was one-hundred percent certain would push her away from both Hank and him for good.

"Derek? Earth to Derek."

Derek blinked and shot a glance at Jessie, her voice startling him out of his obsessive deliberation. He cleared his throat. "Sorry," he said, running his right hand through his hair with a sharp tug. "I didn't sleep well last night."

"Oh," Jessie said, her voice sounding peculiarly strained. "I'm sorry."

The obvious flush that crawled across Jessie's cheeks caught Derek's eye and he couldn't help but wonder what it was she was thinking about that brought on the reaction. Could it have anything to do with the chat she'd had with Hank?

Derek's brain lost the fight to mind his own damn business as he blurted out, "How did you sleep?"

Jessie's lips worked for a moment, her eyes widening in surprise. "Um, well," she replied, then cleared her throat. "Really well." Her cheeks pinked further.

"That's...nice." Derek swallowed and clenched his jaw tight. Do not say another damn word, Jansen.

"Yes," Jessie agreed, her nod and overly bright smile somehow off from Derek's perspective. "Very nice." She cleared her throat and placed the tip of her pointer finger on the printed schematic unfurled on the table between them. "So what I was asking about before..."

Derek did his best to concentrate on the questions at hand, not Jessie's lips or the long column of her neck he'd seen in a completely new light on his phone screen the night before. It was very… hard.

And so was he. And this was work, and he wasn't in middle school anymore and this was just bad.

Minutes passed, and Derek grunted monosyllabic replies to Jessie's questions, running through every concept he'd had to memorize in engineering school from Ohm's Law onward just to get his body under control.

———

Finally, as Jessie announced she had the information she needed to start working on the revised prototype, Derek's head shot up, finally risking a glance directly at her again.

"So," she was saying, "maybe I'll see you later? The whole mechanical team is having a staff meeting in about ten minutes and I really need to pee," she said with a cheeky grin, completely oblivious to the painful distraction he'd been fighting for the last fifteen minutes.

"Sure, yeah," he said before darting his eyes to the door behind him, making sure the hallway outside was quiet. It was now or never. As he turned back to face her, Jessie was just grabbing the last of her supplies and making a beeline for the door.

"Jessie, wait!"

She stopped immediately, about-facing with wide eyes and pinked cheeks, her breath coming quickly.

Derek's thoughts swirled incessantly, the questions coming at a relentless pace: why did it look like she was… aroused? For God's sake, could he not control his damn hormones for three minutes to confess his sins?

"Um, Jessie." His voice was a deep rumble, his intended words getting lost in the depth of her eyes and the soft, quickened breaths she took.

"Yes?" she whispered.

"I need to… uh," he shook his head with a sigh, "tell you…" Derek looked down at his shoes, squeezing his eyes tight.

Jessie took a step closer and Jessie's black ballet flats entered his view. "Tell me what, Derek?"

"Tell you…" his voice wavered, the words coming out in an unbidden sing-song, he sucks in another lungful of air before exhaling in a mad rush as he says, "I really liked that new sandwich place on Adams we tried last week."

A deep crease formed between Jessie's brows, yet she gave him a gentle, curious smile. "Okay," she said slowly, dragging out the word, "that's good to know…?"

"We should pick up from there today," Derek said, nodding once, doing his damndest to sound normal.

On the inside, his neon 'abort' signs malfunctioned, flickering as if possessed, then exploded.

"Sure, Derek," Jessie said with a chuckle. "I'll find you after my staff meeting." She started walking backwards out the conference room door, keeping her smiling eyes on Derek. "You know how we mechanical engineers can just drone on and on…"

It took a moment before Derek realized she was joking with him. Jessie just made a joke. And he just failed in the one thing he was supposed to accomplish today.

"Haha, right," Derek barked out an over-enthusiastic laugh, attempting to make up for his obviously strange behavior and clear distraction. "Okay, yeah, see you when you're done," he said with another nod.

———

Jessie left and Derek turned his back on the doorway, staring at the empty room, his face flushing with heated frustration. He was so angry with himself - not only for not telling Jessie the truth like he'd resolved to do - but also for his moronic behavior.

Could he be more of an idiot?

Anger coursed through his veins and Derek swiped his pen and notebook off the table onto the floor, scattering his supplies all over the industrial carpet. He hated when these childlike tantrums took hold of him, but Derek had learned long ago that trying to keep them contained would only lead to a bigger, more massive blowup later.

He sank down onto a chair and hung his head in his hands, breathing deeply. He wanted to get better; be better. He wanted to be a better man for Jessie, but the years of self-doubt and his absolute debilitating lack of confidence left him feeling stunted half the time.

It was a miracle he'd ever even had a girlfriend, though his relationships in the past had been few and fleeting. He'd racked up a little more experience with women simply by casual dating once he'd become more ingrained in the professional world - one-night stands here and there with consenting women who seemed to simply be looking to scratch an itch - just like he'd been.

But ever since he'd come to know Jessie… interest in going to a bar to chat up a potential partner had dissolved, leaving Derek celibate by default.

And that sure as hell didn't help him mitigate the testosterone tantrums.

The regular visits to the gym helped quell that pent-up energy, and Derek knew the main reason he was so jacked beneath his work clothes was the fact that he was getting no action whatsoever. Zero. Zippo. Zilch.

But Hank…

Derek sucked in a breath as the thought crossed his mind. It was so very wrong, but Derek recognized the truth of it: Hank had already had more action in a two-hour online chat than Derek had had in nearly a year.

Maybe Derek could learn a little from Hank, for just one more night. After that, he'd come clean with Jessie, deal with the fallout, beg her forgiveness, and pray for the chance to show her all Hank had taught him about himself.

Looking behind him to make sure no one else was around, Derek took an extra moment alone in the confer-ence room to open up Fish and send another bold message to Jessie... something he'd been thinking about all morning.

> I didn't know I was lonely until I saw your face.

He pressed send and quickly pocketed his phone, his heart hammering in his chest at the risk of potentially being caught by anyone waltzing into the room, or even Jessie herself. Guilt welled up to match the thrumming of his pulse, and Derek felt conflicted all over again. It was like suddenly developing a split personality and he wasn't at all comfortable with the jumbled emotions of both him and Hank - a monster of his own making - fighting for dominance.

Derek sighed.

Well, he thought, the damage is already done.

One more night of this facade couldn't make that much of a difference, could it?

* * *

Derek was panicking. He'd heard nothing from Jessie all day, not even a reply to the lame "hello" he sent thirty minutes earlier when he finally got back to his place. He obsessively refreshed the window on his phone, looking for the little icon next to her name to turn green. He'd already gone to the gym right after work and lifted for an hour before doing a five-mile run, just to force himself to stick to his routine and be patient. When he'd gotten home, he'd made himself put his phone on the charger without logging into the app while he took a shower. He'd changed into a pair of low-slung flannels and gotten himself a huge glass of water before finally - finally! - letting himself sign in to Hank's profile.

But still no Jessie.

Had she figured out the ruse? Did she suspect him after his odd behavior at work today? Had she... found someone on the app she simply liked better?

A bubble of jealousy curled beneath his ribs, and Derek had to fight to distract himself enough from bashing his fist into his dresser mirror. That wouldn't accomplish anything. No, he could channel his intensity and be productive at the same time. He had to believe Jessie would be online soon, and Hank had the imperative task of wooing her with sexual imagery. So Derek got to work.

He knew exactly the kind of thing he wanted to send next. He just had to find the right photo to convey it. A brief keyword search resulted in a slew of black and white images, and almost immediately Derek's eyes caught something perfect.

"Here we go," he spoke beneath his breath to his empty room, his fingers tapping the phone screen to save the gif so he could message it to Jessie through the app.

The image in place, he added a second image, this one simply type-set words from a Neruda poem he'd read in college:

> In one kiss, you'll know all I haven't said.

Derek sent the images and tossed his phone on his nightstand, forcing himself to walk away. If Jessie didn't reply, her message of disinterest would be heard loud and clear. He'd distract himself with a sandwich and pray that when he came back in his room to check the phone, there'd be a message from her.

His long legs had him almost out the bedroom door when his phone pinged. He didn't even have to look at the alert. Just like he could smell Jessie's sweet perfume the minute she entered a room, Derek had already seemed to develop a sixth sense for her in other ways. He knew with every fiber of his being she was online and had just messaged him back.

He dove for his phone and flopped back down on his bed, feeling like at long last, his night was getting started. As he unlocked his screen and read Jessie's message, the thought crossed Derek's mind that maybe it was his life finally getting launched.

T ime moved in slow motion for Jessie. She'd watched the clock all day, counting seconds until she could slip out of work and get to her Thursday night kickboxing class. She'd hoped the activity would knock the arousal right out of her, but all that sweating and kicking and power left her hornier than she'd been all day.

And that was saying something.

Because when her meeting ended right before lunch, Jessie had checked her phone and to see an alert icon on her Fish app, and she'd made the fatal mistake of checking it from her cube right then rather than waiting until she was home and in private.

Hank had messaged her.

> I never knew I was lonely until I saw your face.
Oh, my God!

Jessie's throat had felt thick, pressure welling behind

her eyes. She'd had no idea what she could possibly say in reply. She could have told Hank the truth, that his words were making her feel things she'd given up hope of ever experiencing: feeling desired, cherished… simply wanted. Her cheeks had flushed with heat as she'd swiped a knuckle beneath her right eye to catch the moisture pooled there. She'd been reaching for a tissue when Derek's deep baritone startled her.

"Knock, knock," Derek had announced.

Jessie had turned to see his hulking frame draped along the entrance of her cubicle. It was almost comical the way he took up so much space, his body broad and long yet somehow still lithe as he'd leaned against the cube wall.

"Hey," she said, her voice sounding thick. She'd sniffled and blew her nose quickly, using the tissue to mask her face.

Derek's countenance changed when he'd gotten a look at her face. His jaw clenched and his eyes had narrowed as he stared at her in silence for a beat too long. "You okay?" he'd asked, and his voice was so soft that Jessie felt further burning in her nose as more tears threatened to spill.

"Fine," she'd lied, "just allergies."

Derek stared at her from the entryway a few seconds longer before he'd finally said, "You hungry? Want lunch?"

Jessie had sniffled again and gave him a look that could only be interpreted as what do you think ?

"Ah," Derek said, lips twitching, "You do. Of course you do." He'd tapped a drumbeat to the top of her cubicle wall and gave Jessie a goofy smile. "Silly question."

Despite herself, Jessie had laughed. "You should know better by now."

"Hmm," Derek had agreed with a nod, his expression indecipherable. His dark gaze softened, his shoulders dropped, and it looked like his hulking body melted a little as he'd stood in hushed silence. It looked for a moment like he'd had something more to say, but changed his mind. Finally, Derek flattened his lips into a modest smile. "I'll meet you by the elevator in ten," he'd announced before spinning around and loping down the corridor to the lobby.

Confused by the sudden flutter of attraction deep in her belly, Jessie had shot him a gentle grin and told him she'd be ready to leave in a few minutes.

—

As soon as he was out of sight, Jessie had spun in her desk chair and stared at her reflection in her darkened computer screen. With the backs of both hands, she angrily swiped the apples of her cheeks, frustrated by her indiscriminate desires. How could she have been swooning over Hank's message in one moment, then two seconds later be feeling the hots for Derek?

Especially after she'd lied through her teeth when

Paige had called her out on it the night before. Especially when those old, unrequited feelings were a waste of her time.

———

Derek was… difficult. And he'd failed to pick up on her subtle interest for nearly two years, so it was just sheer madness to think anything would change. Hell, if she truly believed Derek would ever pay attention to her as much as whatever project they were working on, she'd never have had to resort to joining Fish.

But he was grumpy seventy percent of the time, and enigmatic the other thirty, and Jessie had given up months ago trying to figure him out. They were work friends… buddies… and that was the end of that.

———

Jessie had stood, giving a slight shake of her head to clear her thoughts before pulling her purse up onto her desk, desperately in need of a quick touch-up on her smudged makeup. As she had finger-combed her hair with one hand and shoved her cosmetic case back in her bag with the other, her phone had vibrated with a message from the app.

Jessie had bitten her lip and unlocked her phone, her heart battering her ribcage. She hadn't even processed what he'd sent a few minutes earlier. The man was going to be the end of her and she hadn't even seen his face!

She'd stared at the screen, her freshly fixed makeup about to be ruined again.

> In one kiss you'll know all I haven't said.

It hadn't been just those nine words Hank sent that stirred her. He'd attached a gif. Jessie's eyes followed the black-and-white image of a woman with her head tilted back, the long line of her neck catching the light in profile. From off the screen, the shadowed shape of a man's face appeared, leaning in to press a sensual kiss to her throat. The pixels shifted and slid, repeating themselves on an endless loop of…*fuck*.

Her knees had gone weak, and Jessie had just enough functioning brain cells to comprehend the fact that swooning was real as she slid into her chair, the wheels rolling her backward a few inches with the uncontrolled motion.

That was not what she'd expected to hear from Hank.

Sure, the man she'd chatted with the night before had been bold and sexy as hell, but she'd never have thought he could also sweep her off her feet - literally with words.

Jessie had stared at the message, her pulse pounding along the column of her neck, her gut tingling as she re-read the line she recognized from a Pablo Neruda poem.

"Jesus Christ," she'd breathed, her voice a mere whisper.

She'd immediately texted Paige asking her best friend to meet at their favorite bar at seven that night. Jessie had needed to spill her guts and have someone remind her it was impossible to fall in love with a man she'd never seen, never spoken to, and knew virtually nothing about.

She also knew she could count on Paige to bring up Derek, which would in turn force her Jessie to deny, deny, deny any interest in her co-worker. And maybe, if she kept repeating the lie enough times, she'd even convince herself it was true.

* * *

"I mean," Jessie had huffed, waving her hands in the air in front of her face as she poured her soul out to her best friend, "my reaction cannot be normal!"

Sitting on the barstool beside her at The Falcon, Paige had finished the last of her wine and exhaled slowly. "Probably not," she'd agreed with a shrug. "But stranger things have been known to happen, you know."

"Bullshit," Jessie had snapped, slamming her empty gin and tonic tumbler onto the slick wood of the bar. Lowering her voice, she'd added, "What could possibly be more strange than wanting to drop my pants for some dude I've never even met?"

"Haven't you ever heard of all those people who fell for each other back in the day just from writing each other love letters?"

Jessie had responded by shoving her phone in front of Paige's face. "These are not love letters!"

Paige had simply smiled and shook her head. "Of

course they are, silly. Erotica can be just as romantic as, say… poetry." Her eyes had lost focus as Paige tilted her head in consideration. "It's kind of like visual poetry in a way. Paige reached her hand out and placed her palm on top of Jessie's. "Look, I'm just saying, if it makes you happy, don't fight it." Jessie had squirmed and pulled her hand away, but Paige's fingers gripped tighter and held her steady. "I mean it, Jessie. Embrace what you love. And if what you're loving right now is a hot dude who texts you porn, then I'm all for it - you win."

Jessie had chuckled. Only Paige could deliver a serious sex-related sermon. "I win?"

"Hell yes, you win." Paige had grinned as she lifted her hand to get the bartender's attention. "Barkeeper, we're going to need another round over here!"

* * *

By the time got home from the bar, it was well after nine. As Jessie stripped out of her work clothes, she realized with all the excitement and surprises of the day that she never messaged Hank back.

"Shit," she mumbled as the pearl button on the neck of her sweater caught her hair as she whipped it up and over her head. Guilt-ridden, slightly intoxicated, and still horny as hell, Jessie flung off her bra and tossed on an oversized sweatshirt before bypassing the couch and jumping straight onto her bed.

She grabbed her phone - fully charged courtesy of

the bar, thank you - and opened up Fish. A pang of disappointment whisked through her belly when she saw no new messages from Hank, since the ones that had nearly turned her into a mere puddle of goo before lunch. It was a miracle she'd made it to the lobby to meet Derek, and an absolute revelation that she'd made it through their quick shared meal of soup and sandwiches at the corner deli without jumping his bones. Jessie wouldn't have been able to say if it was because of Derek's own mysterious appeal or just her wicked desire for Hank after he'd sent those stimulating messages, but the need was real, and her thirst remained utterly unclenched.

———

The app opened, and she quickly typed a greeting to Hank, praying the little dot by his name would turn green, showing he was online.

> Hi, so sorry. It's been a crazy day.

Paige's pep-talk had given her the courage to go for it (and the three G & T's she'd downed hadn't hurt, either), and Jessie was on a mission.

A sin mission.

Before she could talk herself out of what she wanted to do - and Paige had said she shouldn't be ashamed to go for what she wanted, after all - a reply appeared on Jessie's screen.

> There you are.

Jessie exhaled deeply, the anxiety of the day ebbing as her lungs emptied. Another message from Hank followed.

> I was worried I scared you away.

This is what she wanted. She could do this.

She gave him a single word in reply.

> **Never.**

The chat window remained still for a minute, and Jessie wondered if maybe it was her turn to fret over having said the wrong thing or having scared him away with her forwardness.

> Don't make promises you can't keep.

Her front teeth bit down into the pillow of her bottom lip as her pulse sped up. The moment of truth had arrived. With a deep breath, Jessie murmured, "Here we go," beneath her breath and started to type.

> **I'm pretty sure that I'm so turned on right now.**

> **There's not much you could tell me that would chase me away.**

> **Last night you said you would show me how good you were...**

Jessie grimaced down at the phone as soon as she hit send, feeling a little uncomfortable with the promiscuous directive she'd just given. But, damn, if it worked... if Hank followed her train of thought and wanted this with her... it could be so good. He was good. She knew it. And she knew he could make her feel it, even across their two corners of space and time in this city.

His reply pinged on her phone. Jessie's jaw slid open

as she read it.

> I want my hands on you, my mouth on you.

Oh...

> **Where would you touch me?**

The messaging app remained silent again, and Jessie was certain she'd mucked it up now. Derek aka Hank obviously was a flirt, but maybe this wasn't exactly what he'd been looking for. Maybe he wanted to find a nice girl on the dating app, not some crazy, touch-starved, almost-drunk woman who was clearly initiating phone sex.

> Are we really doing this?

Jessie whimpered, rolling her eyes at herself. Her fingers shook a little as she typed her reply and muttered, "God help me, but hell yes."

> **YES!**

Hank's reply was instant, as if he'd had his thoughts queued and ready to go.

> I'd touch your hand.

> Lace my fingers with yours,

> Feel the pulse at your wrist as it pounds against my fingertips

> and I'd know you'd want me as much as I want you.

Holy fucking shit.

Jessie's fingers couldn't type a response quickly enough.

> **I want you.**

> **My hands up your arms,**

> **along your shoulders,**

> **caressing your collarbone.**

> I'd swipe my tongue up your neck, tasting your skin's saltiness and sweetness.

Heart pounding, Jessie felt her pulse throb between her legs, felt herself clench as she read his litany of messages. Her mouth went dry, and she licked her lips, her fingers flying over her screen in response.

> And I wouldn't be able to resist pressing my lips to yours.

> Swiping my tongue inside to taste you.

Three little dots appeared immediately, and a moment later, a string of messages pinged one after another.

> Your cotton candy lips would be so soft.

> The minute I felt them I'd imagine them,

> on the rest of me,

> everywhere…

Jessie jumped in with her own fantasy move, desperate to show him the images in her own mind.

> I'd kiss my way down your chest.

But Hank seemed to have other ideas as his messages popped through one after another.

> I'd thread my fingers through your hair.

> Guide your mouth back to mine.

> Not done with those lips, baby.

Baby.

Oh, damn. Jessie didn't think this situation could be hotter, but it just went from sultry to blazing.

———

Hank wasn't there - in fact, Jessie didn't have a goddamn clue where he was - but she felt him. She felt the gentle tug on her scalp where he'd pull her hair to direct her attention. She felt his big, warm hands cupping her cheek, bringing her mouth back to his. Jessie's brain couldn't concentrate enough to dwell on the bond that stretched between them, even though they remained virtual strangers, because his messages kept rolling in, one after the other.

> I'd make sure your chest was bare to me,

> and my hands would cup your tits.

Jessie's hand slid up beneath the hem of her sweatshirt, her fingertips ghosting along her stomach until they grazed the bottom of her right breast. With her right hand, she typed a reply, soaring high on his attentions and feeling loose-lipped.

> **You'd think they're too small.**

Again, his reply was instantaneous.

> No,

> I know they're the perfect size.

Perfect.

Groaning with her rising desire, Jessie circled her nipple, felt it constrict and peak in a way that left her body covered in gooseflesh.

> I'd move my hands down until I could cup the heat of you.

"Oh my God," Jessie stammered aloud, her breath hitching.

> Are you touching yourself, Jessie?

> YES!

> Good.

> I'd find you slick and wanting.

> So warm and moist as my fingers slide inside…

"Oh my God," Jessie repeated, this time her voice little more than a whimper. Every action he wrote sent her soaring higher. She was ascending in a flash, her heartbeat untamed and savage against the cage of her ribs.

Hank's narrative prompted her actions, their minds connected and his words playing out in her mind and in her body like a shared vision.

> Do I feel good?

The softness of his question caused Jessie's thudding heart to falter, sent her heavy breathing off rhythm. Only the truth… that's what Hank had said the night before. Jessie knew she would give him nothing less than her complete self, her whole truth.

> So good.

> Need more, baby.

Hank didn't hold back.

> I'd make sure you were ready for me,

> then rub my cock along your cunt.

Jessie moaned as her hands slid down her stomach, past her belly button.

> Then I'd press inside.

> and slide home…

Holy shit!

Her fingers slid lower, following every tantalizing

detail of Hank's seduction.

> You'd be so hot and tight.

> I'd barely be able to stand it,

> but you'd take all of me.

> You'd fit me like a glove.

Ah, fuck!

> You'd be so pretty with my cock buried in you.

Jessie's fingers circled her bud in a frantic pace, her hand sliding lower to gather the slick dripping from her center.

Somehow, her right sent a message, but three letters on repeat were all she could manage…

> OMG!

* * *

But Jessie couldn't possibly be bothered with writing anything else because she was skyrocketing, hurtling through the atmosphere at light speed, on the edge of the universe with nothing but an entire galaxy of stars bathing her in their light.

When she opened her eyes, Jessie stared at her bedroom ceiling, her breath coming in ragged pants. She didn't know how long she lay there, chest heaving, when her phone pinged.

> Did you just come for me?

Jessie blinked, staring at her phone screen. She licked her lips and forced herself to take a deep breath, then typed her reply.

> **Yes!**

> **Did you for me?**

Hank's replies come gushing in quick succession again.

> Fuck yeah baby!

> Just coated my stomach,

> like a goddamn teenager.

Maybe it was post-orgasmic bliss making her loopy, but Jessie couldn't contain the snort of amusement that escaped her.

> **I can't believe we just did that.**

> Fucking amazing!

> Now go to sleep, pretty girl!

Disappointed filled Jessie. She was about to ask why they needed to end their chat when she glanced over and saw the time. It was already after eleven o'clock; they'd been at it much longer than she realized. With a yawn, she unwillingly agreed.

> **Okay.**

> **This was unbelievable.**

> **Thank you, Hank!**

It was already getting late, and with her body sated, it was easy for Jessie to follow Hank's gentle command. She got herself ready for bed and did as she was told. A few minutes later, she typed Hank a *goodnight*, then curled up beneath her sheets. Her phone vibrated with one last message.

> I'll be here when you wake up, baby girl.

> You will never be alone.

CHAPTER SIX

Derek stopped at Lexie, the one and only decent coffee shop, on the way to work. It was Friday, he would get to spend the day with Jessie, and Hank would get to spend the evening with her. He was giddy as a fucking schoolboy.

He'd sent Jessie a message first-thing upon waking, as promised, and had already gotten a good morning back from her along with a sleepy-faced selfie, presumably from her bed. Jessie's hair had fanned around her head atop her pale pink sheets, an angel with a chestnut halo. Last night's activities did nothing to stave off his morning wood, and the minute Derek laid his eyes on the intimate picture Jessie sent, he'd had no choice but to jump into a tepid shower and take care of business.

There was no way he'd make it through work otherwise and, frankly, it was questionable if he would even after jerking off in the show.

As he left the coffee shop with a to-go cup in each hand, a shiver of anxiety rippling through him. Derek knew, somewhere shoved down deep, that he was engaging in the most dangerous of games. He was going to hell for what he was doing, and with each day that passed without revealing the truth, Derek's chances of righting the situation with Jessie slipped through his grasp.

Derek was losing control. That made him jittery. And that fear led to him to hating himself for what he was doing just a little. And the hate left him wanting to sabotage this entire thing - wanting to give up on any hope of happiness - the hope of ever convincing Jessie to see him not as a colleague but the man he was and could be he. If he dwelled on the sensations too long, Derek was tempted to give up and simply bury himself in his own dark insecurities.

Jesus, he was a goddamn rollercoaster of emotions.

Get it together, Jansen, he chided himself as he stepped off the elevator into the office lobby, his hands warm from carrying the cups even though the temperature had dropped significantly overnight and the skies now threatened snow.

He tugged off his gray beanie and tossed it onto the floor of his cubicle, glancing next door, relieved to see he'd beaten Jessie to the office. After sliding off his messenger bag, Derek strode into her cube and left the latte on her desk, right in front of her keyboard. He borrowed one of her permanent markers and wrote on her cup - not her name like the big chains did, but some-thing else.

Derek smiled at his handiwork and escaped back to his side of the cubicle, clearing her work area just about two minutes before he heard the elevator ding. Seconds later, the distinct smell of sweet jasmine and… Jesus, he didn't know what it was... followed. As usual, he could scent Jessie from across a room; she smelled like sunshine, light, and just sheer fucking happiness.

"Morning, Derek," Jessie chirped as she walked by the entrance of his cube to get to her own. Carefully facing forward to keep his expression from her, Derek felt his smile tug into a full grin when she must have noticed what awaited her at her desk. "Oh, what's this?" he heard her ask aloud to no one in particular.

And then an amused cackle. He could tell by its tenor that the laugh came from deep in her inside, and it made Derek solemnly swear he would spend the rest of his life giving her reasons to make that sound every damn day if she'd let him.

A moment later, Jessie's head peaked above the top of their shared cubicle wall, obviously standing on her tiptoes as she raised a brow at him in question. "I suppose it's you I should be thanking for this," Jessie paused and dramatically looked at the words labeled in careful print on the coffee cup she held raised above her head, "'not swill.'"

Derek schooled his expression and glanced at her, catching the mirth in her eyes. He gave a barely perceptible dip of his chin in acknowledgment. "Perhaps."

"Oh, Jansen, you're a terrible liar," Jessie chuckled.

He clamped his jaw and his nostrils gave the tiniest twitch as warning bells started ringing in brain again. Here's your chance, they clamored, abort-abort-abort!

Derek felt heat creep up the back of his neck along his hairline, his pulse hammering in his throat at what he knew he needed to do. He opened his mouth to speak, his brows furrowing in contrition, when suddenly Jessie's face disappeared from above the cube wall.

"I got to hit the lab to get the printer warmed up. See you!" He heard her call cheerfully from somewhere on her side of the partition.

His window of opportunity passed like a speeding bullet.

Derek exhaled deeply, simultaneously disappointed in himself and thoroughly relieved that he hadn't had to give up the ruse just yet. Knowing Jessie was out of her cube and busy in the lab, he snatched his phone and send her a message on the app, something that would keep her thinking about him throughout the day and hopefully set the tone for what he hoped would be another thrilling evening of... well, Derek didn't know what the hell to call it.

Did it still count as sexting? What he and Jessie shared felt a lot deeper than that. To Derek, their virtual...

exploration... felt a lot like baring more than skin or fantasy. It felt like walking in a dream and losing his footing, only to find he was falling deeper into a rabbit hole - a wonderland of possibility - a dream he didn't want to ever wake from.

Falling, Derek thought to himself.

It seemed to him he'd done the falling for Jessie months ago. But before, he'd fallen alone with no voice to ask for her hand. Now, because of this thing with Hank, Derek was falling all over again. But this time around, his muscular arms didn't hesitate to reach for hers, and together with Jessie as his beacon and his backbone, Derek felt like he just might bring his imaginary wonderland to life.

He opened his phone and selected an image he'd saved the night before, along with a few other favorites he'd instantly known he'd wanted to share with Jessie. He attached a picture, this one another black and white, a zoomed in photo of a man's hand grabbing a fistful of a woman's tank top, his knuckles brushing the outside of one of her breasts. The woman's hand wrapped around his wrist as if to hold him near.

No faces, no identity, just pure desire. Sheer possession.

But beyond that, it was the way the woman's hand gripped the man's wrist... the mutual need in the image so obvious and thick Derek could taste it on the back of his tongue. The man's body language said you're mine and the woman's answer in turn screamed never let me go. If that wasn't a fucking flawless projection of everything he desperately wanted with Jessie, nothing was.

Quickly, Derek shoved his phone back into his bag - he couldn't risk any alerts popping up on his screen, especially if Jessie was around. Then he opened up his work email and got the rest of his day started, but it took every fiber of his being to hold off from checking his phone until right before lunchtime.

When he finally did, hiding in plain sight as best as he could by hunching his hulking frame over his phone and letting his shaggy hair fall around his face in a curtain, he prayed Jessie wouldn't be back to her cubicle for a few more minutes.

When he unlocked his screen, he broke into a grin. She'd replied.

> My friend says sexy pictures are like love letters.

Love letters.

Derek huffed a breath through his nose at the word, his pulse spiking. Jessie couldn't really mean love, could she? She likely meant the word in its broadest sense - the images serving as a way to convey attraction, desire, maybe affection. But love?

Sure as shit, Derek knew how he felt about Jessie, and he definitely knew how Hank was feeling about Jessie… but did that mean Jessie was feeling some of those same, deeper stirrings, too? And if she was, who exactly were those feelings for?

> Your friend is right.

Derek hoped his simple acknowledgment wouldn't scare Jessie away, or leave her feeling alone in her thoughts. Because her friend was right: despite their sexual content, each image he'd shared was a depiction of his heart and soul, of his deepest desires, of his pure and aching want.

Again, Derek shoved his phone away and took a deep breath, willing his body to behave. It was almost time for him to grab some lunch, then he had just a couple of meetings left before he could finish up some design work and hit the gym. If tonight would be anything like the last, he needed to release some tension big time before getting home.

* * *

It was a couple hours after he ate a quick lunch - just a hot dog from the street vendor today, since Jessie had still been busy working - when Derek's office line rang, the caller ID reading 'Lab.'

"Derek Jansen," he stated as he brought the receiver to his ear.

"Hey, it's me." Jessie's voice sent a little shiver down his spine. Derek wasn't sure if they'd ever actually spoken on the phone before. They usually talked only in person, or sent infrequent text messages mostly about work schedules or what they wanted to eat for lunch. He wanted to record her voice, to press the phone against his ear, to somehow keep the melody of it close for when he'd be left to only typed words later…

Clearing his throat, Derek focused on the phone call, hoping Jessie would blame his overt distraction on his usual aloof detachment and nothing else. "What's up?"

"Come down here. I think I have a mold ready for you to look at."

Derek hurriedly headed down to the lab. When he walked in, Jessie was hunched over one of their firm's less expensive 3D printers, the denim covered apple of her ass on full display. *Jeans Fridays* never looked so good.

The door closed with a swoosh behind him, and Jessie glanced over her shoulder, her eyes bright with excitement. "Did you bring it?" she asked.

"Right here," Derek answered, holding up a circuit board that needed to fit in the redesigned chassis and giving a little wave with it.

"Okay," Jessie announced, standing back to make room for Derek next to her at the lab table, rubbing her palms together in anticipation, "moment of truth."

Derek's lips twitched in the tiniest of smiles. She was so damn cute. He couldn't think of another engineer in their entire company who got as much joy and excitement over their work. Jessie was one of a kind, especially in the engineering world filled with a disproportionate amount of socially awkward techies. Like him.

When he slid the board inside the chassis, he was met with no resistance. Derek flipped the locking mechanism closed and felt the board snap into place. Beside him,

Jessie hissed out a celebratory 'yes!' as Derek marveled at the precision of her work.

"It fits like a glove," he praised.

Jessie sucked in a breath, an audible gasp filling the space between them. Derek felt the shift in the room as he sensed her body tense where she stood beside him. His eyes flicked to his right, and he watched as her neck and cheeks flooded with color. Only then did Derek realize the words that just came out of his mouth.

Shit. Shit, fuck!

This was it. The game was over. She'd know - she'd have to know, now that his big mouth just uttered the same words he'd used the night in the middle of getting her off during their chat.

You'd fit me like a glove...

Derek's own face felt flushed. How could he be so stupid? He opened his mouth, the truth ready to spill from his tongue like water through a burst pipe when Jessie pasted a smile on her face and gave him a chipper "Thanks!"

He swallowed thickly, his esophagus constricting around what felt like a tennis ball in his throat. Derek couldn't speak at all. He just stood there, unlatching the plastic mold and retrieving the circuit board within.

"Well, I'll work on a metal alloy version next. I should have it done early next week," Jessie stated, her voice returned to normal as she jotted in her notebook.

Derek nodded, swallowing once more and willing his voice to sound normal. "Sounds good. Thanks," he added before giving her an awkward wave and turning to exit the lab.

As he opened the door to the hallway, Derek stopped and looked over his shoulder.

"Jessie?" He waited for her to look up from her notes and meet his gaze. He gave her a rare, soft smile. "Good job."

* * *

When Derek got home from his daily routine at the gym, he followed the same formula as the evening prior: he put his phone on the charger, took a long shower, made himself drink a giant glass of water along with a scarfed-down sandwich. Then he sat down on his bed to wait. But tonight, he didn't have to wait long.

As he checked the app for messages, he tamped down a surge of butterflies as soon as he saw he already had one from Jessie waiting for him. He took one last swig of his water as he thumbed open the notification, and doing both at the same time was a stupid choice. A death wish. Literally. Because Derek was choking, having sucked in a surprised gulp of air at the same time he meant to swallow, shocked by the image on his screen.

Jessie had sent another selfie. But unlike the sweet one she'd shared in the early morning, this one lit his desire like a fucking Christmas tree.

It was zoomed in just to show her chest, nude but completely covered by the strategic placement of her arm across her breasts - just the hint of their soft globes peaking above and below the band of her arm, as if the photo had been taken from above while she lay down.

She captioned the photo with, Can I have more pictures of you?

"Fuck."

The single word escaped him like a prayer, and a benediction it was. Derek would kneel at her feet for the rest of his life, worship her soul if given the chance.

> Hey pretty girl!

> That's some pic you sent.

Jessie's reply was spontaneous.

> **It's entirely unfair I haven't seen your face.**

> **What if I'm ugly?**

Time idled for a moment as Derek waited for a response to his question. In that span of sluggish seconds, Derek's brain immediately started bundling together a heap of potential statements to correct the horrible trajectory he'd just put their conversation on. He did not want to discuss his appearance - besides the fact Jessie might make a mental picture of Hank that looked similarly to himself, his face, full of strange angles and distinct features, was the one topic guaranteed to put Derek in a foul mood.

But not your body.

The thought came out of nowhere, sending a jolt of confidence deep into his belly. He furrowed his brow, surprised at the realization that, yes, he was proud of the hard work he put into his physique. Derek knew he would likely be attractive at least from the neck down.

Jessie's reply finally pinged his phone.

> **You could never be ugly.**

> **Not to me.**

"Damn," Derek sighed, in awe of everything about this woman.

With two sentences, Jessie had just made him feel like a king in a castle, awash with confidence and warm pride. He bit his lip, pondering how he could give Jessie what she asked for without jeopardizing his identity. He wanted to give her something in return, and if she asked for more pictures of him? *Well, he'd find a way. Derek needed just a couple more days to make sure Jessie knew what he was made of, and then he'd confess.* In the meantime, he could work with it...

The perfect idea smacked him upside the head.

> I'll send you another photo soon.

> **I'd like that, Hank.**

> **I have something for you when you do.**

Derek's brows lifted. "Do you now?" he murmured as he tapped his screen, eagerness speeding his pulse.

> Be right back...

Derek stripped off the shirt he'd put on after his shower and headed back into his bathroom. He needed to be strategic about how he cropped it, but he was pretty sure he could manipulate a picture of his chest in the mirror without giving away anything too revealing of his identity.

After a quick snap and a couple of edits, a picture of Hank's chest filled the screen of his phone. Derek sent it off through the app, his drumbeat heart thumping away. He hoped she liked what she saw because it certainly wasn't something that Derek would ever have had the chance to display... A broad, nearly hairless chest and firm, curved pecs - a result of both genetics and hard work. Massive shoulders anchoring smooth, sculpted biceps, a thick trunk of a chest leading to a definitive "v" above his waistline - all courtesy of hours in the gym.

> **Are you kidding me???**

Derek huffed a laugh through his nose at her message.

> Hmm…

> Should I be?

> **That's just… you're huge.**

> **Wow!**

He couldn't help but smirk over her word choice. Derek turned it back over to Jessie.

> Now I guess it's your turn to entertain me.

He watched the little dots appearing on his screen, wondering if Jessie would dare to send another photo of herself tonight. Derek wasn't prepared for what she sent instead.

> **So remember we talked about pictures being like love letters.**

There was that word again. Love. Derek sucked in a breath and replied.

> Yes.

> I was thinking about that and I wrote something for you.

> A real letter.

And then she attached another photo, but it wasn't of herself. It was of a note in her own writing, on a blank notebook page like the one he'd seen her use at work on multiple occasions. In fact, she'd had the notebook with her in the lab earlier that very day.

Dear Hank,

This may seem strange to you, being so old-fashioned. But there's so much. I'm feeling, and I needed to use my words to get my jumbled thoughts together. I'm a technical person. I like the certainty of math and measurements, equations and theorems. I'm not used to letting my emotions control me, or frankly, feeling so out of control. With you these last few days, a part of me I never cared to know has grown stronger - there's a strange desire in me, but it doesn't scare me anymore.

It's come alive. Because of you.

You've been the teacher I never knew I needed. You've shown me that my place as a vibrant, sensual woman doesn't have to be the same place I hold in my career... that I don't have to be in control all the time... that I can give my trust and be rewarded with passion and kindness and fulfillment.

I know we've only just "met" but I feel changed. I feel this powerful bond between us, and I just know there's a reason we've found each other.

I want to meet you for real.

To see your face. Touch your skin. Hold your head and say thank you.

Thank you for what you have taught me about myself in these brief hours.

Yours,
Jessie

Derek finished her missive, his eyes burning hot, his jaw clenched tight as his own emotions warred within him. How could he feel so elated and culpable at the same time? How could her words together be the gift he never thought he'd received and a dreaded reminder of the wicked punishment he knew he deserved?

When Jessie learned the truth, none of her words would hold true. Derek knew it, sure as the stars in the sky.

CHAPTER SEVEN

> H ank...

"Shit!" Derek hissed, realizing he'd been lost in pensiveness and he'd not given Jessie any sign of how deeply her penned words had moved him.

> I'm here.

> **Don't have anything to say.**

> Pretty girl...

> You got me on my heels.

> **Not as much as you desire?**

Derek shook his head at her question, marveling at how Jessie could even think of such a thing. He needed her to know what she meant to him. Derek needed it, and so did Hank. Because right now, the lines between the real man and the created one were blurred. Suddenly, he recalled how much Jessie had liked the poetry line he'd sent the day before. He quickly typed a reply and dropped his phone on his bed as he jogged into his living room to find the book he was looking for.

> I could never get enough of you.

———

A moment later, a book of Neruda's poems in hand, he typed out one of his favorite passages.

Derek finished the last line and waited. A full minute passed, his heart jack-hammering his ribs, his pulse spiking, a sheen of sweat on his brow.

> I think I'm going to cry…

> **No tears,**

> **But I know.**

> **Neruda gets to me, too.**

> It's perfect.

> **You're perfect.**

> How can I repay you?

Derek's chest expanded exponentially with his breath. His ribcage, still bare from when he took the picture, had no option but to spread its breadth to accommodate his ballooning heart. His cheeks twitched in a pleadingly soft smile.

> **Hmm…**

> **Take off your pants, Hank.**

Wait. What?

Derek blinked down at the phone in his right hand, his eyes widening in surprise. Another ten seconds passed, and he just stared, his mind trying to keep his racing thoughts under control. Could she mean to…

> **Are they off?**

"Shit!" He hissed again, dropping his phone on the mattress and scrambling to strip down in one swipe. He flopped back down on his bed, eager and panting, as he retrieved his phone.

> Yes, they're off.

> **I wish I was there.**

> **So I could take you in my hand.**

> **Feel your soft cock's foreskin.**

"God," Derek breathed, his voice quivering as much as his left hand was as it tentatively stroked along his semi-hard length.

> **I'd look up from where I kneeled,**

> **And watch you get hard for me.**

> **Your eyes locked on mine.**

Derek closed his eyes, picturing Jessie on her knees, the muscles in his abdomen clenching. He forced his eyes open and managed a one-word reply.

> Yeah!

> **My tongue would find the top of your cock,**

> **and I'd lick the pre-cum from its tip.**

"Sweet Christ," Derek hissed.

> **And then I'd take you in my mouth,**

> **every inch,**

> **and take you all the way to back of my throat.**

His eyes closed, Derek's palm worked his solid length,

changing his grip to tug, his blood running feverishly beneath his skin as he climbed wickedly fast, oxygen sapped from his lungs.

> **Make yourself come for me, Hank."**

> **Let me swallow your cum and suck you dry.**

"Holy fuck!" Derek wailed, his hand now working a frenetic pace, his hips thrusting into his grip, his pulse clobbering his arteries with an unrestrained fury. "I'm going to come," he chanted to no one, his balls tensing and his cock swelling as he felt the last semblance of control slip.

He couldn't manage a real word on his phone so he just tapped whatever nonsense he could before the wave took him, a violent arc cresting higher and higher, until the white ropes of his release painted his bare chest in rhythmic spurts like whitewater crashing on the shore.

* * *

When the blackness faded into a pinpoint and Derek's eyesight returned, he reached for his cell phone, gasping for air, his head lolling from side to side on his pillow in a post-orgasmic stupor. "Holy shit, holy shit, holy shit," he panted, sucking in air with every repetition.

On his screen, he saw his last attempt at a message to Jessie: > mmm.

And her reply, simply ellipses and a question mark.

> I've never come so hard in my entire fucking life.

Jessie's answer took a moment to appear, the three little dots traveling in waves as she presumably replied.

> **So it felt good?**

> More than good.

> I think I'm dead.

Derek barely had an ounce of energy left, but he wouldn't leave without satisfying Jessie in return.

> I wish I could swap kisses with you.

> **Why can't you?**

> Let's meet IRL.

Derek's heartbeat skipped. The warning lights in his brain flashed bright yellow: *Danger!*

> **Soon.**

> Let me take care of you now.

> No, it's all right.

> **That was my gift to you.**

> **Part of my 'love letter'.**

* * *

Derek bit his lip and tilted his chin to stare down at the spend splashed across his skin. The guilt threatening to swallow him whole, but the joy he felt in knowing he was finally getting through to Jessie - finally showing her the man he was inside grumpy facade, his insecurity projected... the man he could be - buoyed him. But the guilt sat upon his shoulder, not letting him fully enjoy this revelation, because the reckoning would come. Sooner or later.

Derek sighed, temporarily stuck in this purgatory.

But Jessie deserved to know she was his angel, maybe his one saving grace, and he'd be damned if he failed her after what she'd just offered him.

> I think it's the best gift I've ever gotten.

> both your words and… this.

You, Derek thought to himself, just you.

> **Good.**

> **Now goodnight, Hank.**

Jessie followed her words with a heart, and then as quickly as the icon appeared on his screen, the green indicator next to her name vanished as she went offline.

Saturday morning

The morning broke into a sheet of blinding white. Jessie slipped from her sheets and padded over to her bedroom window, taking in the wonderland on the other side of the glass. The snow that had threatened the day before it started after she'd gotten home from work. Jessie was thankful she didn't have to deal with her commute - albeit a short one - in the wet mess three floors below.

She yawned and stretched, and as she did her mind immediately wandered to the night before… she'd purposely ended her chat with Hank quickly, knowing if she lingered on the app, they'd get right back into something physical. And though Jessie wanted it - and badly, by the empty ache still lingering like a shadow deep in her abdomen - she wanted something else more.

Something more than a physical release… something she'd gotten hints of every single time they'd connected online. She wanted something real, and Jessie was thinking what she had with him could be it…

Jessie wanted Hank to be real. Flesh and blood; skin and bone; body and soul.

She sighed and sank back onto her bed, sliding her back against the headboard and tucking up her knees. She took her phone from the nightstand and, heart tapping a staccato beat, opened up Fish.

Delight flooded her veins, warm and syrupy, as she saw a message waiting for her from just an hour earlier. Hank must have sent it as soon as he woke.

> Good morning, sexy!

> Starting my day with a shower.

> And wishing for this.

His words were capped off with yet another black-and-white photo, this one simply of a man and a woman sharing a soft embrace, their faces mostly obscured as they tucked tenderly into the crooks of each other's necks, standing beneath the spray of a shower head. The photo was laziness and longing, comfort and compassion, desire and dedication.

It was everything Jessie could ever have hoped for.

Her lips curved into a gentle smile, her pulse pounding thickly beneath her hot skin, her breath shallow.

Jessie did an image search of her own, flipping through one black-and-white photo after another until she found exactly what she was looking for. The picture was of a woman, obviously nude but artfully left with the focus on the foreground near her feet rather than the rest of her body left mostly in shadow, reclining on a bed, her body language an explicit invitation.

> Still in bed.

> Wish you were here.

She sent her message and the artsy photo with a mostly contentful sigh.

* * *

There was just… this unsettled part of her that niggled at her brain, making her feel anxious and uncertain. Jessie replayed the events of the last few days, trying to figure out the roiling in her belly and the clawing at the back of her mind that didn't seem to want to let her enjoy whatever was happening between her and Hank in peace.

Her fingers tapped Paige's name, asking if her friend was game to grab breakfast. Jessie needed to talk her feelings through, and there was no one better than Paige for hearing her out and then telling it like it was. Paige, though kind as the day was long, didn't mince her words. Jessie knew her best friend's brand of honesty was exactly what the doctor ordered.

* * *

An hour later, the two ladies sat at their favorite

neighborhood diner, deep mugs of coffee steaming on the formica table between them.

"So you gave your online boy-toy a virtual BJ," Paige said with a grin. "Nice!" she cheered, holding up her right palm for a high five.

Jessie rolled her eyes and lifted her hand slowly, doing her best to subdue the grin tugging at her lips. Heat flared along her chest and cheeks as she darted her eyes at the diners surrounding them, hissing a half-hearted "Shhh!"

Paige chuckled, the sound a low, amused rumble. "Well, it sounds to me like you're having a great time with this dude. You're getting each other's rocks off, he quotes poetry and calls you pretty… honestly, he sounds too good to be true." Paige quirked an accusatory brow, then shrugged. "But other than that he's maybe, possibly, a bit too perfect, what's the problem here? It's not like you're marrying the guy."

The words hit Jessie like a freight train. It took her a moment to realize she'd stopped breathing, her breath locked tight in her lungs, her pulse pounding, rocking her in her stillness.

Paige's eyes went wide, several emotions flashing through them in quick succession: surprise, disbelief, concern, and finally, sympathy. Her friend slid her back against the vinyl booth, rolling her shoulders back, her smile soft and empathetic.

"And there's the problem," she stated, her voice kind, full of a patient resolve Jessie could never repay her for.

Sucking in a deep lungful of air, Jessie blinked back

the tears burning her eyes but lost the fight as she felt one fat droplet slip from her lid and down her right cheek. She gave her friend a petrified nod.

"Jessie, honey," Paige began, then stopped, shaking her head as she continued, "are you sure you're not just… lonely?"

Jessie nodded, biting her cheeks to keep a sob from escaping. Not here, not in the diner.

Get it together, girl.

She sniffed and wiped at her cheek before clearing her throat. When she answered her friend's question, her voice was thick with emotion. "I've always been lonely," she admitted. "But this is… different." Paige slid her hands around her coffee mug and waited in silence for Jessie to go on. "I think I have genuine feelings for him. Like, I can't stop thinking about him."

Jessie squeezed her balled-up paper napkin in her palm, schooling her voice as she confessed the most damning of her dishonorable thoughts. "And the worst part about all of it is, when I close my eyes and picture Hank and I… together, doing things…" Jessie paused, swallowing the walnut of guilt weighing on her throat, "it's Derek's face I see," she admitted in a shaky whisper. "It's Derek's voice I hear when I read his words."

Paige leaned forward, her shoulders hunched, her dark brows knitting together. "Oh, sweetie," she sighed. "Tell him."

A fresh wave of tears surged, Jessie's throat getting

tighter yet again with the pressure of her own guilt and confusion. "Tell who?" she gasped in a quiet sob.

"Both of them."

* * *

Pelting snow badgered Jessie the entire walk home from the diner - heavy, wet flakes stuck to her lashes and cheeks, and soaked through her pink wool hat by the time she'd walked only the first of the three-block distance. It was the Saturday before Christmas, but the storm seemed to mute the normal hustle and bustle of the streets, forcing people to slow their pace, hunker down... maybe enjoy more of the what the holiday season was truly all about.

Jessie wasn't feeling she was doing a wonderful job of living in the holiday spirit of giving, gratitude, or grace lately. In fact, she felt downright selfish; needy for having had to pour her heart and soul out to Paige not once, but twice just this week! She felt downright resentful of the fact that she would spend the holiday alone... again. Paige had invited her to the family festivities, but Jessie just wasn't feeling chipper enough to deal with her giant and boisterous crew this year.

And living with grace? Haha. That was a joke.

Jessie had once read that living with grace meant embracing a conscious awareness of our feelings of being safe, loved, and blessed to be alive.

Derek, despite his surly nature, somehow always made

Jessie feel protected. On the other hand, Hank had made her feel loved, and with the way her body reacted to his words and imagery, for once in her life, Jessie felt blessed and truly alive.

But now she was a jumble of conflicting emotions, yearning for Derek, for something she suspected would always be out of reach… and frightened to move forward with Hank, afraid of making him real, afraid of the possibility that he wasn't at all the man she believed him to be.

* * *

She trudged up the three flights of stairs to her apartment and locked the door behind her, stripping out of her sopping wet layers. Jessie sank into her couch and kicked up her feet, gripping her cell phone like a lifeline.

First, she scrolled her contacts and stopped at Derek Jansen. They rarely texted outside of work, but if she waited until she same him Monday, she'd surely lose her nerve.

> Hi. Any big Christmas Eve plans? Want to leave work early and grab a drink with me at the pub?

It surprised her to see the three little dots appear on her screen right away; Derek must have had his phone in hand to see her message so quickly.

> No plans at all.

> I'm free.

Jessie sucked in a lungful of air and let it out slowly.

Okay, one down.

Next, she opened up *Fish*. She'd missed a reply from Hank while at the diner. He must have liked the photo she'd sent of the woman's figure on the bed, laying back in invitation. His message in response to her *wish you were here* simply read, *you surely will know.*

Biting her lip, Jessie typed two lines, her hand trembling.

> Meet me at Lexie's tomorrow at one.
> I think I've fallen for you.

CHAPTER EIGHT

erek's sweaty palms gripped his phone, adrenaline coursing through his veins as he stared down at the screen in abject horror.

"What… in the actual the hell?" he bellowed, not giving a shit if the neighbor on the other side of the ridiculously thin apartment walls heard him.

Within a single minute, Derek had swung from elation over Jessie's invitation for drinks to complete and absolute terror at the message Hank had just received. His rage boiled beneath the surface, his heart pounding, and surges of wild anger sparked, making him feel as though if he just willed it so he could channel lightning from his fingertips.

Derek stood in his living room, his empty hand a tight fist at his waist, his legs spread in a wide stance as he stood breathing harshly, hovering over his couch as if it were the enemy. He stomped his foot like a petulant child and roared an angry growl. "Fuck!"

Was it possible to be jealous of himself? Because he sure as hell was.

She's falling for Hank? Great. Exactly what you wanted, asshole.

Wrong!

The bitter taste of bile crept up Derek's throat, his stomach in knots. "Fuck," he repeated. This time the single syllable escaped on little more than a gasped whisper.

"Okay, get it together, Jansen," Derek muttered as he slid his left hand through his hair to brush it off his fore-head, gripping the raven strands and tugging until he felt a searing pain on his scalp. Finally, all of his energy felt spent, seeped through him like a sieve, and he collapsed down onto his old, worn couch, his folded knees awkward in front of him.

"Why are you doing this?" he asked aloud. As Derek heard his strained voice, he wondered if he asked that question of an imaginary Jessie or of himself.

With a sigh as deep as a chasm, Derek swiped his screen to return to the dating app. Damn Fish. Why the hell had he ever let himself do this? He wished he could go back in time to the beginning of the week when he'd had that genius idea and make it die in a fire.

Time travel not being an option, Derek shook his head as he typed his reply. The game was over… and Hank's time was up. He messaged Jessie back, being as truthful as he could be. He'd never be able to chat with her as Hank Johnson tonight; not after what she'd confided in him… not with the way he - Derek - felt about her. It would be more wrong than anything he'd already done. And he'd done a lot of wrong.

> Have a conflict tonight.

> I'm sorry we can't chat.

> But I'll be there.

Quickly, he logged off the app and made himself focus on his other predicament.

Jessie wanted to have drinks with Derek. Okay, no big deal. They were friends… sort of. She probably had nothing better to and just wanted some company. Who else would she ask, anyway?

Derek returned to the text conversation between him and Jessie. He read over his reply. No plans at all. Sounds like fun. He sounded like a fucking bucket of laughs. No wonder he was perpetually alone. He squeezed the bridge of his nose and screwed his eyes shut. He could do better than that, couldn't he? Jessie deserved better, for certain.

He typed one more line.

> See you soon!

If nothing else, it was honest.

* * *

By noon, Derek thought he might be having a cardiac arrest. His heart was a vicious drumbeat, his pulse a rapid thrumming, his blood sprinting through his veins. His arrhythmic heart, the tightness in his lungs and chest, and the faint feeling every time he stood left him desperate for comfort. For someone to hold him and hear him and steer him in the right direction.

So he sloshed through the snow-covered sidewalk and took the subway to Penn Station, then hopped on the 1:45 train to Laurelton. By 2:15, the train was coming to a stop. The Lyft Derek had ordered waited for him to take him the six minutes' drive. The nearly hour-long trip was totally worth it, Derek thought, as he rang the doorbell of the sprawling manse.

The door whipped open a moment later, and a small woman with salt-and-pepper hair pulled back in an elegant chignon stared up at him, her dark eyes knowing and her lips pressed into a thin line.

"Derek…" she began, her tone suspicious, "what did you do?"

"Hi, Mom."

"Hi, son," she replied, a resigned grin tugging at her lips. "Well? Come on in," she ordered, swinging the door open wide. "I'll make you a sandwich."

Fifteen minutes later, Derek had filled his mother in on the whole Jessie debacle, leaving out the most saucy parts, of course. But Paula Lewis-Jansen was entirely too astute not to put two and two together. She hadn't made her living as a successful lobbyist without having enough cunning wit and an obscene amount of emotional intelligence that allowed her to seemingly make deals out of thin air. No, he didn't have to say he'd been messing around with Jessie as Hank, taking advantage of his position of anonymity and putting her in a position of questionable consent, threatening his own ethics.

The unimpressed lift of Paula's single brow told him everything. Oh, she knew, all right.

"Well, Derek, you've made quite a mess for yourself, haven't you?" she sighed, exasperated.

Derek sat quietly stoic, his hands hanging limply in his lap. There at the kitchen table, in the seat that was always his directly to his mother's right, Derek felt like a teenager being chastised for failing a school assignment all over again. He swallowed hard around the ridge in his throat.

"Do you think there's any way I can fix it?" he asked, his gaze firm on the oaken pattern of the table.

"Do you think there is a way?"

God, he hated that. He hated the way she'd always turn his questions right back onto him. Like she was an oracle, but refused to help without making him figure everything out first. Couldn't she - for just once in his goddamn life - tell him the right answer?

Derek clenched his jaw and felt his nostrils flare in frustration. He crossed his thick arms over his barrel chest like a petulant child. Paula just waited, watching him in expectant silence.

Finally, Derek huffed an answer. "Obviously, I have to tell her the truth."

"About?" Paula prompted.

"Everything," Derek muttered, his eyes still locked firmly on the dining table's surface. "And I probably need to just," he paused, swallowing thickly again, "give her time."

Paula breathed deeply, then nodded once. "Those are both good things. I just don't know if they'll be enough." She gave him a sad smile. "But I'll be rooting for you, honey."

That did not satisfy Derek. No - no way. He came all the way out here to think and formulate a plan and this was… it was horseshit.

"Come on, Mother… there's got to be something else I can do to show her." He shoved the chair back from the table, his hand tugging at his shaggy hair again, his agitation rising. He started pacing the kitchen floor, his long legs crossing the distance in three strides. "I mean, I'm him! He's me! Both of us are fucking in love with her. What more could she want?" he cried.

Paula stood and leveled him with a single look. "Sit your ass right back down, Derek Jansen," she commanded.

Derek sat, while Paula remained standing, her petite figure a monolith above him. He watched her from beneath heavy brows, his eyes up even as his chin tilted to his chest in admonishment.

"You lied. You're in the wrong; not Jessie. So you best be thinking of every way you can come clean with her, and frankly, even then, she may refuse you. And you better prepare yourself for that, young man."

"Every possible…" Derek trailed off. "What, you think I need to come up with some… grand gesture?" he questioned, his voice cracking with emotion on the last word. "I should stand outside her apartment in the street with a boombox in my arms, blasting our song?" he spat, his anger rising like the tide.

Paula slid her fists to her hips, the only sign of her own risen ire. "Maybe a grand gesture wouldn't be such a bad idea, kid."

Hours later

Derek slept for shit.

He tossed and turned all night long, anxiety a pit in his stomach, acid coiling and slithering in his belly like a snake.

He hit the shower, hit the gym. Even after a massive weight lifting session followed by a brutally paced run, Derek felt like a live wire. He wished he could take that unbridled energy and divert it somehow, channel it away in order to stabilize his emotions, to ground himself in any way he could. But no engineering cheats or creative design could save Derek now.

Once he got home, Derek showered, languishing beneath the spray. He longed for the days before he'd ever invented Hank. How he wished the only thing he'd have to confess today was an unrequited crush.

At a quarter to one, Derek tossed on his jacket and his gray wool beanie, then locked his apartment door behind him. It was still fucking snowing. The sidewalk was a mess of white, slick with icy parts from too many pairs of feet tamping it down. He approached the end of the block and watched the entrance to Lexie at the corner, looking for Jessie. In all the commotion and upheaval of yesterday's messaging mayhem, Derek hadn't really processed the fact that Jessie had chosen his - Derek's - regular coffee shop for her and Hank's meeting place.

His stomach soured again. This whole thing was a mess. And it was no one's fault but his.

Derek yanked open the shop's door, the force of his overbearing pull causing the welcome bell above to slice through the cold winter air with a macabre jingle.

Jessie.

There she was, sitting at a corner table in the back, her body facing the door. The discordant bell startled her, her shoulders flying back at attention. Jessie's gaze met his, moving from confused surprise to pleasure, then to worry.

Derek stood stock still in the doorway, the glass sliding closed behind him to brush him forward into the shop as if the binding force of the universe simply willed it so.

"Derek!" Jessie gasped, looking up at him as he slowly stalked toward her table. "What are you doing here?" she asked, her voice quivering, her eyes darting frantically behind his bulking frame toward the entrance.

"May I sit?" Derek asked, motioning toward the chair across from Jessie's bistro table.

A deep crease formed between Jessie's brows. Derek could see the panic in her hazel eyes. "Yes, of course, but—"

"It's okay, Jessie," he conceded, guilt lacing his words.

"No, it's just… I'm supposed to be meeting someone and I wouldn't want," she stopped, cleared her throat, "I wouldn't want you to get the wrong idea…"

"Jessie." Her name, soft and determined on his lips, brokered no argument. Derek's eyes held hers, his expression painfully in check, his breath coming in shallow spasms.

"Yes?" she breathed, eyes wide and wet, like a part of her knew that whatever happened next, it would change everything.

"It's me."

Jessie blinked her honeycomb eyes at him, not fully comprehending what Derek was confessing, but somehow connecting to that strange bond they'd discovered over their intimate chats, tapping into it intuitively.

Her breath hitched. Her cheeks flushed pink.

The actual words were unnecessary now - smart girl had already figured it all out - but Derek had to say it all the same.

"I'm him. I'm Hank Johnson."

CHAPTER NINE

For endless seconds, Jessie didn't move. She couldn't; her body was revolting.

Every joint, every muscle, every cell hung halted in a nightmare fugue. Her lungs burned and fought for breath as if she'd been submerged, her lips finally parting as she gasped and heaved in a quivering gulp of air. Her entire body trembled as her cheeks and chest flamed red, her ire and utter embarrassment seeping through her pores.

And yet... she couldn't tear her eyes away from Derek's. Jessie was locked in the prison of his searing gaze, the whites of his eyes raw and bloodshot, his dark eyes brimming with tears beneath heavy, worrisome brows.

Jessie blinked, trying to snap out of her agony, her breathing coming in rapid gasps, the hot hair of her breath puffing down onto her shaking hands. Her stomach cramped, then she felt her throat constrict at the same time as a bitter saliva gathered at the base of her tongue.

"I think I'm going to be sick," she cried, shooting up from the table and darting to the shop's back corridor.

She slammed the restroom door shut and gathered her hair behind her head just in time. Her diaphragm spasmed repeatedly, squeezing out her meager breakfast and the few sips of coffee she'd had while waiting for Hank…

Derek.

Derek was Hank.

Jessie sank to her knees on the tile floor, unable to keep herself upright any longer. The surge of emotion flooded her, weakening her knees and slacking all of her muscles, turning her into a rag doll as she wailed aside the cold porcelain, shoving her palm over her dirty mouth to mute her anguish.

Too many feelings to count warred within her. Jessie was angry, betrayed, hurt beyond recognition. Ashamed. Inexplicably guilty. Somewhere among the turmoil and outrage, Jessie even felt some sick justification, as if there was now a reason her subconscious had kept jumbling Hank and Derek together all along. And lastly there was a small part of her - a part she wanted to deny but couldn't - where a tiny, puzzling sense of relief rushed, only a trickle among a torrent.

Jessie reached up to flush and pushed herself up on weakening legs. Her whole body shuddered and swayed, unstable as a newborn colt. She gripped the sides of the sink with either hand, rooting herself, before splashing cold tap water on her face. It was no use; her skin was mottled with red blotches, her mascara smudged beneath her lashes.

She sniffed deeply, swiping at her sloppy nose. Jessie stared at her disastrous reflection. "I have to get out of here…"

A swell of adrenaline spiked her bloodstream. She needed to get out of this bathroom and escape the shop without Derek seeing her. Jessie couldn't let him see her like this, wouldn't allow him this intimacy, too, on top of all he'd stolen under the guise of Hank.

She turned the knob and peeked out into the tiny hallway. She'd partially expected Derek to be right there, hovering on the other side of the door, waiting in ambush. But the shadowed hall was empty, save a couple of cardboard boxes waiting to be broken down. To her right, the dimly lit hall opened up into the shop, bright whitewashed light seeping in through the street-facing windows. To her left, Jessie spied a red exit sign above the alley door.

She shoved her hat over her head, and with one last sniffle, she scampered left, pushing open the big metal door and emerging alone into the bitter cold.

* * *

Jessie heard the shrill doorbell ring repeatedly on the

other side of Paige's apartment door, as her shaking pointer finger pressed the button repeatedly.

"Jesus Christ. What?" Paige bellowed, her voice distorted and metallic over the intercom.

"Paige?" Jessie croaked.

"Jessie? What the hell…? Come up, come up."

The lobby door unlocked with an angry buzz, and Jessie stepped inside. The heat of the small space was such a drastic difference from the cold and wet outside. She felt it smack in her face. Stomping the snow from her boots, Jessie trudged up the stairs, finding Paige standing with her hip holding her apartment door open, wearing a face creased with worry.

"What's going on?" Paige asked as Jessie approached. She took one look at her friend, and a fresh wave of tears spilled onto Jessie's cheeks. Paige sucked in a breath and held her arms out in a "v", ready to envelop Jessie. "Oh, honey," she murmured as Jessie landed in her embrace.

The two women slipped inside the apartment, and within moments Jessie was cradling a cup of hot tea with honey, sharing her news with Paige.

Paige stared at Jessie, her jaw dropping open. "Are you fucking kidding me?" she asked, enunciating each word.

"I wish," Jessie huffed, grabbing a tissue from the coffee table for her nose.

Paige's eyes narrowed. "And you just left him there… just snuck out the back door without a word?"

"Well…," Jessie hedged, "yeah!"

"Jessie, honey, I know you're mad," Jessie shot a

warning glance at her friend, just knowing there was about to be an unwelcome 'but' somewhere in Paige's next statement, "and you have every right to be, but-"

"And there it is," Jessie mumbled.

"But," Paige continued in her kindergarten teacher's voice, talking over her friend, "this does not resolve more your conundrum."

Jessie blinked, her brain unable to process whatever it was Paige was trying to tell her. Paige pressed on. "You've had feelings for Derek for months. You fell - hard, I might add - for Hank in a matter of days. If they're one and same, don't you think maybe it's... a sign?"

"A sign of what?"

"You know," Paige waved her hand in the air between them, "like a sign that you're... meant for each other. Or something."

"That's preposterous," Jessie replied, but there was no fire left in her. Her response only a ragged whisper.

Paige leaned forward and ducked her chin, bringing her line of sight directly in front of Jessie's. "Is it really? Because that's how you keep winning, my friend. Not fighting what you hate, but saving what you love." Paige reached out for Jessie's hand and squeezed her in solidarity. "Do you love him? Is what you have - or could have with Derek - worth saving?"

"I... I don't know."

Paige was quiet as she sat beside her friend. Jessie's breath had finally come in a slower, more controlled rhythm, her eyes drying as she settled into the aftermath of her fateful rendezvous.

"Listen," Paige ventured, breaking the precarious silence, "why don't you just stay here for the rest of the day? Hell," she added, giving Jessie a playful shove, "borrow some stuff and play hooky tomorrow, too."

Jessie's shoulders sagged. "Ugh, I wish I could… but I have lots of work to do before we close," she protested weakly.

A single dark brow arched in question as Paige scoffed, "You think it's really going to be a busy day on Christmas Eve, Jessie? It's ridiculous they don't just give it to you as a holiday."

"That's true," Jessie agreed, releasing a deep sigh. She dipped her chin and cupped her forehead with her palm. "Oh, shit. Work… I have to see him at work, Paige!" Jessie lamented, her voice muffled by the scarf still bundled beneath her neck.

"I know, sweetie," Paige cajoled, rubbing Jessie's back. "One thing at a time."

* * *

Jessie gave up pretending she would go home and make it into work the next day, after all. It took little effort for Paige's influence to reign, and so by ten o'clock the next morning, Jessie stretched on Paige's couch, dressed in a spare set of her friend's flannel PJ's and tucked beneath a Sherpa blanket. Her lap was littered with used tissues, the full box of Kleenex wedged beside her on the couch as she watched her second Hallmark Christmas movie of the morning.

She'd not slept well, and before Paige had left to go run and deliver some gifts to her sister's apartment a few blocks over, her friend had encouraged Jessie to finish this movie and then try to take a nap. Jessie had agreed, but she knew as she snuffled at the film protagonist's heartbreak over a dumb miscommunication, there would be no rest for her.

Her situation was just as bad as these contrived, manipulative, mushy holiday movies the hopeless romantic in her couldn't help but adore.

In the movies, there was always some grand gesture. There was some way that one of the main characters, who you just knew were destined to be together, did something to make up for all the little white lies. Jessie's tears flowed hot on her cheeks, her nose red and somehow both stuffed and runny, because with the hurt, anger, and embarrassment she felt, Jessie didn't even know how she'd ever even go back to working in the same space as Derek, not to mention considering anything more.

It was all just too much for Jessie's overwrought brain to process.

Beside her, Jessie's phone pinged, and she actually welcomed the distraction from the goings on of the movie. She swiped her screen and her heart skipped a beat when she saw the Fish alert. Indignation tore through her like a savage wind, and though her first reaction was to immediately delete the message without reading it, the preview of what Hank - Derek - had written showed on her screen and, of course, her stupid eyeballs read it.

> When you said you thought you were going to be sick, I didn't think you were really ill. You okay?

Ugh, she wished he would shut his stupid, beautiful face. She was not ready to chat with him like he was some old chum. She didn't know if she'd ever be ready to speak to the man again, and here was checking in on her like a good pal?

Well, he had another thing coming.

Jessie's fingers tapped away on her screen, her pulse pounding heavy in her temples.

> **I'm deleting this account.**

She hit send and quickly deactivated her profile. And then, with the fever-pitch of her heated blood coursing through her veins, Jessie decided—you know what? She'd had enough wallowing in her own misery. She'd had enough of feeling impotent and out of control here on Paige's couch like an invalid.

Well, Jessie knew she was far from debilitated, and she'd be damned if she let anyone - not even stupid Derek Jansen, impact her career or her reputation. Jessie tossed the blanket off her legs, sending it whipping into the air to land on top of Paige's bookshelf.

She was mad. And she was going home, taking a shower, and fucking going to work.

***

By noon the next day, Jessie walked with determined strides into her cube, purposely avoiding looking over at Derek's. But although his back faced her, she realized he somehow detected her presence, because from the corner of her eyes she saw Derek scramble back from his desk and nearly trip over himself to stand, his large body unfolding in a jumble of limbs.

He stood stock-still and wide-eyed, staring over the top of their shared wall, just watching her. She dropped her bag beside her desk chair as her eyes caught a coffee cup from Lexie sitting beside her keyboard.

Jessie's heart tightened, the unwelcome memories of the day before rushing in like high tide. Slowly, she reached for it, her fingers wrapping around the cup, long-gone cold to the touch. He must have had it waiting for her this morning.

Jessie clenched her jaw and lifted the cup, then spun a half-turn before dropping it unceremoniously into the wastebasket with a loud thunk. She brushed her palms together as if in good riddance before she took a seat at her desk and wiggled her mouse. Her eyes locked straight ahead and, most certainly, not trying to catch Derek's reaction in her periphery. She popped in her ear buds, but didn't bother playing any music. She wasn't really in the mood, she just wanted to send the message loud and clear that she had nothing to say to him.

By one o'clock, Jessie was reconsidering. Actually, she

had a lot she wanted to say to Derek. She felt her blood pressure skyrocketing; her heart felt like she'd ingested about five Red Bulls. She felt her pulse in her throat and her hands shook as she failed time and time again to direct the mouse on her screen to place a design exactly where she wanted it in her schematic layout.

Her office phone rang, startling her like a gunshot. "This is Jessie," she answered.

"Hey, Morrison," Terrence's voice, warm like tobacco, came over the line. "Listen, we need you in the conference room. Our project's run into a little snag."

Jessie's heart sank. She wasn't sure she could handle more bad news today. But she told Terrence she'd be right down and stood slowly, fixing her skirt. She took a deep breath and grabbed her notepad, steeling her nerves to come face to face with Derek as if she were facing a tribunal.

———

Jessie headed down the hall and took a seat at the conference table, avoiding Derek's gaze. But she felt it - oh, she felt it like the heat of a thousand suns - her cheeks pinking despite her efforts to remain aloof and professional.

"So," Terrence began, gesturing to the small group of four gathered in the room, "our customer sent some new specifications that don't really work with our current design." Jessie heard annoyed grumbles from the rest of the team as she watched Terrence, his face morphing into a remorseful grimace. "And I know it's Christmas, but we're going to have to redesign the circuit board and the chassis one more time, and quick. We have the holiday tomorrow, but we'll have to get it done by Friday or we'll risk meeting our production milestone. We'll also need new software designed before we can integrate," Terrence added, flicking his gaze toward the two software engineers on code.

"Jessie, Derek," Terrence said, directing his attention back to the two of them, "can you two talk offline about how to expedite all of this? And we'll need to re-do a new 3D model by the week's end, too."

"Yup," Derek assented with a nod, glancing at Jessie quickly before backing down at the table.

Jessie chirped a clipped "Sure" before turning to face Derek, her expression completely blank. "Jansen, meet me in the lab." She stood and stormed out of the conference room, leaving a gust of wind in her wake.

Before the door whooshed closed behind her, Jessie heard Terrence's bewildered voice mutter, "What was that all about?"

I'll tell him what it's all about , Jessie thought, anger making her see nothing but red as she strode to the empty lab. There were maybe fifteen whole employees at work, with it being the holiday, and the place felt like a ghost town.

A ghost town thoroughly haunted by the specter of Derek Jansen-slash-Hank Johnson.

Jessie heard him enter the lab behind her and shut the door.

"Jessie—"

She spun around, her feet rooted hips' distance apart as if she needed to withstand a hurricane force just having the courage to face him.

"How dare you?" she seethed. "'Nothing but the truth,' Derek?" She shook her head, her voice deep and trembling. "Or should I call you Hank? You fucking liar."

Derek's lips twitched, his jaw ticked, his eyes widened and blinked once. But he stood there, saying nothing, his Adam's apple bobbing in his throat as he swallowed. Jessie watched as remorse filled his gaze, his broad shoulders curving in on himself, his large body sinking in defeat.

"Say something!" Jessie wailed.

Fight me! Fight for me.

Slowly, Derek shook his head. His mouth moved to form words, but nothing came.

Finally, he swallowed thickly and said, "I can't, Jessie." Derek shook his head again, anguish rolling off him in waves so thick Jessie could barely breathe. "Because every word you said is true." He tilted his chin up in guilty acceptance. "I am a monster. And I lied. But everything Hank shared?" Jessie watched Derek force down another swallow, watched his eye twitch again. "That was all me. And it was all true."

Jessie closed her eyes, her heart clenching with a pain so deep it cut… cut straight through the earth and split it open between where they stood, threatening to swallow her in its gaping maw.

She heard the rustle of his clothes as he took a step toward her, and Jessie's eyes popped open in silent warning. Derek's hand shook as he lifted it from where it hung limp at his hip, reaching toward her tentatively.

"Jessie," he whispered, voice shaking with emotion, "give me a second chance." Jessie watched the determination solidify in his gaze, his chin trembling and then clamping down as he spoke through his teeth one last, pleading word. "Please."

Jessie couldn't help it; the tears just streamed down her cheeks, her eyes leaking like a sieve. She'd already been barely keeping it together all day, waffling between utter depression and the fiery flames of violent outrage. But this… watching him now, the sincerity in his eyes, the pain and resolve in his face as he kept his molten eyes on hers… Jessie was now pretty sure this entire ordeal had just gone and cleaved her heart in two.

Through a curtain of tears, Jessie released a sad puff of breath, her lids shuttering her from his gaze for just a moment. She felt a fresh wave of sorrow leaving fiery trails on her skin, from her cheeks straight to her chin. Reluctantly, she opened her eyes once again, finding her voice, hoarse as it was.

"Don't do this, Derek," she pleaded.

The moment the words left Jessie's mouth, Derek's arm dropped back down to his side, limp with defeat.

With an almost imperceptible nod, he spoke. "You're right."

He rolled his shoulders back and rose to his full height, the space in the lab suddenly compressing with the breadth of his frame. Derek continued, the stoic exterior Jessie had become so familiar with over the last two years sliding back into place. "I'll email you a proposed timeline for the recent design changes," he began, the deep timbre of his voice quiet and controlled. "You shouldn't need me for more than the revised circuit board, and I'll leave it with Terrence," he stated, his gaze suddenly distant. "I'll leave it with Terrence so you don't have to... well."

Derek pressed his lips into a flat line in some attempt at a warped smile. "I'm sorry, Jessie."

He nodded once, as if in affirmation of whatever thought might have just crossed his mind. "Merry Christmas," he clipped. Then he turned and, without another glance, scurried out of the lab.

The whole time they'd spoken, Jessie had wanted to shut him out, to hurt him the way he'd hurt her... to force him to leave her in peace. But as she stood there alone, there was no peace. Only heartache, and the solitary surprising thought that niggled her mind: please come back to me.

CHAPTER TEN

Alone in the lab, Jessie got her face under control before shuffling back out to her cubicle. By the time she got there, Derek's cubicle was empty, his messenger bag and his little banker's lamp switched off - a sure sign he was gone. A deep ache bloomed in her chest at the sight.

In a fog, Jessie rolled out of her desk chair and sank into it, eyes swollen and scratchy, her gaze unfocused. She knew getting any work done the rest of the afternoon was a joke. Between the general holiday fever on the rise throughout the office and her disastrous last twenty-four hours, Jessie thought perhaps she should just go home… again.

On second thought, she stuck around for a while more. She could go back to the design issue she was dealing with before Terrence had called, or maybe make some notes about alternative designs that would meet the specs for the redesigned circuit board so she could be ready to be productive for Be -

No , she corrected herself, just for when she returned after Christmas.

Tucking into her work, Jessie attempted to shove the memories of everything that had happened that morning into the far recesses of her mind. Her rational brain knew she would gain nothing by replaying the scene at the coffee shop... the scene in the lab... repeatedly. But the part of her that was truly just a glutton for punishment couldn't seem to stop the images from running on repeat in her mind.

It's me. I'm Hank Johnson.

I'm a monster.

Please...

Jessie's stomach rumbled with an angry growl. She realized she had eaten nothing all morning at Paige's and in her rush to get to the office and confront Derek, she'd skipped lunch. Now it was after two o'clock, her adrenaline was settling, and she was famished. Her hunger pains benumbed as notification for her work email popped onto the corner of her screen. Jessie's eyes immediately zeroed in on the sender's name: Jansen, Derek.

Her heart stuttered and sputtered, unclear whether this news brought relief of more worry. Jessie blinked slowly as she remembered Derek had said he'd email her a timeline for their urgent redesign... the battering wings in her belly subsided as she realized the message could be nothing more than that.

Deciding to get it over with and to start dealing professionally with Derek as just another coworker for the sake of her career, Jessie switched to her mail client and clicked on Derek's subjectless email.

It wasn't a timeline.

The first line of the message's body was one word: Please.

All Jessie could picture was the way Derek's face looked in the lab ninety minutes earlier... the way his normally self-controlled facade had been destroyed, the raw edges of his emotions revolving like a kaleidoscope on his face, morphing from one broken expression to the next.

Beneath that single word, he'd embedded a link to an audio file, and the additional instruction staging "Press play."

Her first instinct was to delete the damn message. He couldn't send her personal emails at work, anyway.

But Jessie could only see that single word slipping from his full, trembling lips... hear that single word as it was whispered to her, pleading and desperate. She could only see his hand reaching for hers, asking with every cell in its makeup to join him... to make things right between them.

"Damn it," Jessie muttered. There was no way she could delete the message; no matter how angry she was, her heart just couldn't turn off like that. Not yet.

Not when the thing that crushed her the most was the fact that, despite her sorrow and all that had gone to shit over the last day, Jessie still held a candle for Derek. And she'd sure as hell never get over the intense feelings Hank had born in her.

Yes, the hurt independent woman she was fought tooth and nail to deny those two facts, wanted to pretend they meant nothing. But that would be a lie.

And Jessie was done lying to herself.

She pressed play.

* * *

After she'd checked the email from Derek, getting any further work done had been a lost cause. The audio file had been a link to a song, and its words kept assaulting her, making concentration on anything else but the song's lyrics she knew without a doubt Derek had handpicked.

Jessie had packed her laptop and said goodbye to the few people who'd held out until mid-afternoon on Christmas Eve and had headed home. The song had consumed her walk, playing in memory on a loop, the words flitting in and out of her mind in snippets, like road signs along the highway.

"And as I sat with the echoes of lies that I told…"

Yes, he'd definitely told lies, Jessie joylessly acknowledged as she trudged through the still-falling snow, deep in thought, her hands shoved into the pockets of her coat and her head tucked against the wet and the wind. But Derek had insisted that everything he'd shared under the guise of Hank had been the truth.

What was she to make of that? Hadn't she created a profile on Fish for a similar reason? For a way, to make a mask that could shield her, protect her, embolden her?

The skies darkened quickly. The storm's cloud cover deeply shrouded the sun, and daylight was already scarce, with the solstice having just passed. Everything around Jessie was gray…

Ain't that the truth of it, she thought wryly. Sometimes, even engineers have to admit it's hard to make the world fit into black and white, good and evil, right and wrong.

Jessie's boots, heavy with snow, clopped up the stairs to her apartment. She bit her lip, the chapped and wind burned skin rough against the tip of her tongue, as more of the song's lyrics glided through her mind.

"Well, everything has changed, and now it's only you that matters… I will find any way to your wild heart."

The words replayed in her memory once more as she reached her apartment door, heartbeat faltering and her eyes slipping shut from the intense rush of emotion that flooded her. Jessie lay her head against the cool wood of her door, her hand resting on the knob as her body claimed support from the onslaught. The tears started again, hot and flowing unbidden.

With Herculean effort, Jessie unlocked her door through the haze of her crying eyes. She stepped inside and meandered past her kitchen despite the hunger gnawing at her belly and headed straight for the comfort of her bedroom. Having been at Paige's the night before, Jessie was immediately met with the memories of when she'd last been in her bed… her thoughts possessed by Hank and the prospect of finally meeting him in the flesh.

Little had she known, she'd already met "Hank"… she'd already been drawn to him, had already fantasized about him when she'd fantasized about Derek. Jessie had already imagined his full lips against hers, more times than she could count. Had imagined Derek's big, muscular arms holding her, making her feel safe and sound.

Jessie sank down to sit at the foot of her bed, her eyes unfocused as the memory of what Hank's- Derek's - bare chest looked like from the picture he'd shared. Jessie had known he was fit, but she'd did not know what was going on beneath those button-downs and modest vests. A shiver slipped down her spine and the fine hairs on her arms prickled, gooseflesh rising.

She tried to keep her hand from reaching for her purse.

Tried really hard not to fish around in her bag for her cell phone. Told herself not to do it, not to open Fish. Not to re-activate her profile.

But she didn't listen.

Jessie's pulse quickened as she hastily marked herself as invisible on the app, ensuring no one could see her activity. Curiosity gripped her, and she dug her top teeth into the flesh of her bottom lip, feeling naughty and depraved for treating Derek like a piece of meat as she scrolled back through her message history with Hank, searching for the photo.

The cropped selfie of him shirtless.

Whoa.

It was hard to reconcile that she was seeing Derek, the unflappable engineer whose tough exterior she'd barely broken through.

Jessie's eyes skimmed over the words he'd written her in their chat, the memories battering her like storm waves on the shore - relentless, wild, unstoppable. She looked at each black-and-white photo Derek had sent as his alter ego, her drumbeat heart pumping hot, greedy blood through her veins. And then her breath escaped her in a mesmerized puff, her body reacting to the memory that crossed her mind with a deep shiver.

Paige had said the pictures were love letters… Jessie had told this to Hank, and he'd agreed. Did that… could it mean that he - Derek - loved her?

"Oh my God," Jessie gasped, her heart clenching in the cage of her ribs, her eyes brimming once again.

Just then, the dot next to Hank's name turned green. Could Derek be looking for her? Somehow, Jessie knew in her gut he was. That silvery thread that connected them told her he was online, lying in wait for her.

Maybe he was ready to fight for her, for them.

Was it enough? Did she dare to start this with him? Her mind swirled with questions without simple answers. All Jessie knew was that she ached and longed and missed... even while she still seethed over what Derek had done.

Her hand shook as she opened their chat. Half of her mind shouted at her to drop her phone and desist this ridiculous behavior immediately. But she couldn't ignore the memory of Paige's voice asking her if she didn't think this series of absurd events could've been a sign.

You win not by fighting what you hate, but by saving what you love.

Paige had asked if what she could have with Derek was worth saving. She closed her eyes, her breath coming in rapid pants, her chest heaving with nerves and jumbled emotions.

"God help me," Jessie whispered, as she tapped out a single missive.

> **I'm so angry with you right now.**

A reply pinged her phone, instantaneous. Jessie recognized his words as the lyrics from the song he'd sent on constant replay in her mind for hours.

> It's only you that matters.

> I will find any way to your wild heart.

She whimpered aloud; the tears flowing freely, her head throbbing and aching with confusion. She wanted this - craved it like a junkie - and yet she needed him to understand how deeply his dishonesty had hurt her. Needed Derek to know her trust in him, someone she'd always held close to her heart despite the walls he'd constantly erected, was seriously damaged.

But goddamn, she was tired of fighting her feelings.

Tired of burying them. Sick of lying in wait for Derek to realize she'd been there all along, probing at his tough exterior, her engineer's mind exploring his structure and composition, assessing his shell for weak spots.

Because he had realized it. And maybe it took this farce for him to wake up - for them both to wake up - but Jessie felt… different. Changed.

A series of messages lit up her screen like fireworks.

> I'm so sorry for what I did, Jessie.

> but the words are true…

> I wanted you any way I could get you,

> I was blinded by it.

> It was a stupid, crazy move,

> probably the stupidest fucking idea a man could have,

> but I had to try.

Oh…

His words - honest and bare of all pretense - were too much for Jessie to bear. Her heart swelled at them, but her mind was still muddled. And more than anything, she was afraid. This strange desire that had awoken with Hank now bloomed inside her soul, making her feel things she couldn't explain, making her deal with things her meticulous, organized mind couldn't easily sort and label.

Jessie curled into a ball on top of her comforter and let the tears flow. She was confused and still angry, hurt and yet part of her was soaring. As she quietly cried amidst her chaotic emotions, Jessie couldn't help but wonder if maybe this sensation of slipping down a steep slope, not sure if she wanted to catch herself or not, was why it was called falling in love.

The thought jerked her upright.

She licked her dry, chapped lips and sniffled as she reached for her phone. It was her turn to share a line from the song, because there was nothing that could be closer to the truth.

> **Now everything has changed,**

> **and I can't tell what matters.**

Then, braver than Jessie could ever recall being, she added her own words.

> **I think I miss you.**

A moment later, Derek's response appeared.

> Derek? Or Hank?

Jessie swiped the tears from her cheeks, her brow furrowing in thought.

> **Just you.**

Quickly, before she could admit to anything else in her jumbled state, Jessie exited out of the app. She pressed her palm to her chest and felt the pounding of her heart. Her eyes were puffy and sore from the endless bouts of tears she'd shed over the last day, her body spent and exhausted from the emotional upheaval.

And yet, she felt… hope.

She closed her eyes and, almost immediately, Jessie fell into a deep, dreamless sleep, her cell phone clutched in her hand like a lifeline.

CHAPTER ELEVEN

Derek spent most of the night awake, staring at the patterns on his bedroom ceiling made by the shifting holiday lights on the street below. He'd begged out of going to his mom's for Christmas Eve dinner, having shared with her the reason for his lousy mood.

"What will you do now?" Paula had inquired, her voice full of sympathy.

"Honestly?" Derek had replied, releasing his breath in a long, thoughtful sigh. "I think I better figure out a grand fucking gesture."

And so he'd spent the night with his arms crossed behind his head, resting his eyes occasionally but never once really letting his thoughts drift away from the task at hand. Jessie had messaged that she missed him... There was no way he was going to let a statement like that go by without drastic action, not when he was fighting for his salvation.

———

Christmas morning dawned in shades of peach and pink, the hint of a blue sky miraculous after almost two straight days of snow. The world outside glowed brightly, the snow reflecting daybreak. The soft, warm colors outside reminded Derek of Jessie's skin, always golden and sun-kissed, even in the winter. He was so far gone for her. It was ridiculous.

Derek looked at his phone for the hundredth time, eager to re-read the last message she'd sent him, desperate to prove to himself yet again that she'd really written it - that it was there, in little pixilated words on his screen - and not just his wishful thinking.

Just you.

The words gave Derek a sense of determination, the tiniest sliver of faith that he could turn this disastrous ship around… that he could make things right between him and Jessie.

Just you.

That's what he desperately wanted to communicate to her - to prove to her there was no one else who occupied his thoughts, no one else who made him burn the way she did. Who made him make foolhardy mistakes and asinine decisions? Derek couldn't see anything but Jessie. Even in the goddamn sunrise, he saw her. Only and ever her.

Derek sat up, eyes wide despite his lack of rest. An idea had crossed his mind, and he suddenly know exactly what he needed to do.

It was entirely too early, and he was sure Jessie wasn't yet awake, but he scrambled out of bed and grabbed the same poetry book off his shelf that he'd used the other night. Derek flipped through it, trying to find the line he was looking for.

"Here we go," he spoke to himself as his gaze landed on the right sonnet, skimming to find the line he remembered.

Derek tapped on his screen and bypassed Fish. On his phone, he scrolled through his messages to the last one he'd gotten from Jessie, when she'd invited him for the drinks they never got to have.

He was done wearing Hank's mask; this message was coming directly from him.

> "Your wide eyes are the only light I know from extinguished constellations."

Only you, Derek thought once more as he hit send. He put his phone on the charger before heading to grab a shower and get dressed. It was time to go.

* * *

Regardless of the sun finally making its presence known, the snowstorm had ushered in a nasty front, leaving bitter cold air in its wake. Derek wore four layers in the sub-zero temperatures, his fingertips going numb even inside his black leather gloves. The snow was blinding in the morning sunshine, and he squinted even from behind his Ray-Bans.

He wondered how long it would be before Jessie woke. Derek stripped off a glove, gripping a leather fingertip between his teeth and pulling. He shoved the glove in one pocket, then pulled his cell phone out from the other. He checked the time and realized the next step of his plan was due.

Opening up his chat window with Jessie, he saw his message was still marked as delivered, which led him to believe she was still asleep. After all, it was only seven a.m. on Christmas morning, and Derek couldn't fault her for remaining wrapped up in a warm bed. He attached an image he'd found earlier in the morning, the next step in *Operation: Redemption.*

The picture was yet another black and white, this one cropped tightly around the profile of two faces in silhouette, the man's lips hovering above the woman's neck, her lips lingering just millimeters away from his collarbone. The image made the couple look like puzzle pieces, perfectly cut to fit one another, dark curves and angles sliding into white space, making the unified picture resemble yin and yang. Darkness and light. Two parts of a whole.

Derek typed out the words he'd prepared before he hit send:

> I'll wait as long as you need.

> As long as it takes.

> Because you'll always be worth it.

> Please call me when you wake up.

He wondered if he'd survive - literally if she didn't call.

* * *

Derek didn't have to wait long to find out. About ten minutes later, his pocket vibrated as his phone rang, startling the hell out of him.

"Shit," he hissed, juggling the phone in his hand as he used his teeth to strip off his glove once again, afraid his frozen fingers would bobble it and send it falling into the snowdrifts at his feet. Finally, on the fifth ring, Derek swiped to answer the call, his anxious voice deep with lack of sleep. "Jessie?" he breathed.

He heard a sniffle on the other side of the line. "Hey," she croaked.

"Thanks, um," Derek paused, releasing a slow breath to get his racing heart under control, "thank you for calling me."

"Yeah," she breathed. "I guess we have some things to talk about."

Behind his sunglasses, Derek's brows lifted in relief. "Do we?"

Jessie was quiet for a moment. When she spoke, Derek could tell by the clipped tone of her voice and the careful pronunciation of Jessie's words that he'd already fucked this up.

"I assumed that's why you wanted me to call."

Squeezing his eyes shut and shaking his head at his botched words, he quickly clarified, "No, no, that's not what I meant. I…" he forced a swallow down his thick throat, "I was just relieved. That you would… that you would be willing to talk with me."

After a beat, Jessie replied, ever the pragmatist he knew. "Oh. Well, we have some sorting to do, don't we?"

Derek wanted to sort everything - to put every last piece of their crazy puzzle in place - so he could finally earn Jessie's affection. And he'd been standing out in the cold for the last forty-five minutes, begging for the chance. There was no way he was giving up now.

"Yes," he stammered, "we do."

She was quiet for another beat. Then Jessie spoke again. This time, her voice was timid, so unlike what Derek was used to with her. "I really liked the song, Derek." Another beat. "Thank you."

"I meant every word, Jessie," Derek professed, his voice quivering with the shivers wracking his body from the cold. "The song, the ones I messaged you, the ones I said as Hank… all of them."

"Derek," Jessie said in a rush of words, her courage coming through loud and clear, "do you… do you have genuine feelings for me? For me, you've known these past two years?"

He closed his eyes and pictured Jessie's smiling face. Pictured her cajoling him at work, the way her grin was almost contagious, even to an asshole like him. Pictured her joy and pride when she made a design come to life flawlessly at the office. Pictured her that summer night on the harbor cruise, sitting beside him at the bar, making him feel like maybe he'd just discovered the meaning of life.

"Yes," he breathed.

She groaned. "I wish you were here in person," she blurted. "I just want to… scream at you and smack your stupid barrel chest for what you've done." Jessie released a deep sigh. "And then maybe finally just… touch you."

This was it. It was time.

"Jessie," Derek urged, "look out your window."

He heard rustling, then looked up just in time to see the blinds on Jessie's window snap upward, her surprised face coming into view.

She was brighter than the sun.

"Derek…" she began, breathless, "what are you doing out there? It's freezing!"

"No shit," he laughed. "But I've been waiting for you."

"There? In the snow?" she questioned, her voice twisting in concern.

"Yeah," Derek nodded, still looking at her three floors up. "Right here."

Jessie darted away from the window, and Derek heard a strange muffled sound. "Jessie?" he asked, "Hello?"

He got no reply, and panic flooded his iced limbs. "Shit, shit, shit," he hissed, hiking his bag onto his shoulder and looking around like a lost puppy. Had he just lost all chances and fucked this up even worse than before? Had his gamble failed?

Movement to his right caught his eye, and Derek turned to see Jessie in her building doorway. She was disheveled, still in yesterday's clothes, her hair a mess, her feet tucked into unlaced snow boots, her chest heaving with her breath.

She'd never looked more beautiful.

He stood up to his full height and shuffled his feet to face her completely, his fate squarely in her hands. They stared at one another; her glinting into the bright light of day, raising her hand to shield the eastern sun from her eyes, him stock-still and solemn as he watched her, awaiting judgment.

"Come inside, Derek."

* * *

After following Jessie up three flights of stairs in silence, she opened the door for him and ushered him into her apartment. The rush of warmth battered him, and Derek quaked with relief from the bitterness outside. He could barely feel his toes.

"I'll get you some tea or something," Jessie muttered as she turned and headed toward her tidy kitchen, avoiding eye contact with him.

"No," he called, his voice more commanding than he'd intended. It seemed to stop Jessie dead in her tracks.

She glanced over her shoulder at him, eyes wide and questioning, face flushed.

"No?"

"I mean, wait," he said, sliding his bag off his shoulder and holding it in front of him in a weak offering. "I have something here. For us."

Jessie furrowed her brow as she turned and strolled back to where Derek stood. He unbuckled his messenger bag and withdrew a tall insulated thermos. "Coffee," he said, holding it out toward her.

She stood in front of him, her mouth fighting the hint of a puzzled smile. "You've had hot coffee with you the whole time," she said, her words a statement and not a question, as if she was clarifying her understanding.

"Yes," he admitted, his eyes wide and unblinking.

"But you didn't drink it?"

He shook his head. "No." Swallowed thickly. "I was waiting for you."

Jessie took a half step closer. "And what if I hadn't invited you in?"

Derek paused, considering. "Then I'd still be waiting."

Jessie's tongue darted out and swiped at her rosebud lips. Her gaze drifted from his eyes to his lips and back up again, and Derek was dying inside, desperate to know what she was thinking. "Give me a minute," she blurted before dashing down the hallway and disappearing into her bedroom.

Alone in her living room, Derek shoved his discarded boots beside hers before heading toward her couch.

Gingerly, he sat on the edge of the cushion, not sure what was happening. He placed the thermos on the coffee table and slipped a blue cloth covered book out of his bag and set it down beside the thermos.

He glanced around the small space and noticed was how bright it was, peaches and yellows accenting her neutral furniture, the walls the palest shade of pink. It was tidy and sweet, just like Jessie.

Derek heard running water and looked quizzically toward the hallway. He hung his head in his hands as he stared at the book he'd placed on the table. It was his copy of Neruda's poetry, the one he'd had since the elective in college he'd been required to take had introduced him to the poet, turning the class into an unexpected favorite for a guy neck-deep in an engineering discipline.

Derek just hoped the words he'd inscribed on the front cover conveyed all he felt in his heart. If standing outside of her apartment in the cold, committed to delivering this to Jessie, wasn't a grand gesture revealing the deepest desires of his heart, Derek didn't know what was.

He flipped open the cover and read over the note he'd painstakingly printed early that morning.

Dearest Jessie,

Let's move away from the mistakes of our past. We'll kill them, if we have to. Because there's no future for me without you, no peace without your kind heart, no light without your smile.

These poet's words do speak for me, but I swear I'll never hide behind another's words again. You deserve my truth - today and always.

I know you fear being hurt and being alone again, but I promise to stand by your side, if only you'll let me.

Please don't be afraid. I feel it, too.

Yours,
Derek

* * *

Derek didn't know how long he sat in Jessie's living room, over thinking and second guessing himself. But suddenly, her light floral scent overwhelmed his senses. A moment later, she appeared, her hand coming to rest on the arm of the couch.

"Hello," Derek marveled as he took in Jessie's damp hair curling at her shoulders, the freckles smattered across her nose, her face clean.

"Hello," she whispered.

"Will you sit with me for a second?" he asked.

Jessie shrugged, licking her lips. "Okay."

She sat, and Jessie wasn't nearly close enough for Derek's tastes, but he supposed it was a start. After all, he'd be lucky if she ever let him touch her the way he longed to after the stunt he'd pulled. His only hope lay in his sincere offerings. With that thought and a silent prayer in mind, Derek took the book from the table and held it out to her.

"This is for you," he murmured, his eyes never leaving hers.

Jessie looked down at the book as he placed it in her hand. "Neruda's poetry?" she whispered, her finger tracing the embossed title on the cover.

Derek used his pointer finger to flick the front cover up, revealing his neat block print on the inner page. Jessie's eyes flicked to his, looking at him through her lashes for a long moment before her gaze turned back to the book. She was quiet as she presumably read his inscription before finally lifting her chin to meet his eyes once more.

"I..." she started, her nose turning pink and her watery eyes darting around the room, "I don't know what to say," she admitted, her voice thick with emotion.

"I'm really sorry, Jessie," Derek lamented, his heart pounding with the need for her to know just how desperate he was for a second chance. "For everything."

Jessie sniffled and blinked her tears away. She shifted the book to her left hand, then slowly overturned her right to rest on her knee, palm up. She held it aloft for a moment, then looked directly at Derek and whispered, "I know."

Derek's heart skipped a beat, wondering if she was really offering her hand, offering her acceptance. All he could think about was the first picture she'd sent him on Fish, the one with her hand outstretched, stuck in cyber-space. But not this. This was real - this was Jessie, flesh and bone. Derek slowly lifted his hand until it hovered above hers, their gazes never breaking hold of each other. Tentatively, he let his pointer finger slide against the tip of hers.

Electricity jolted through him at the touch, and he flicked his finger back, dragging his hand away. "Thank you," he said with a nod, his lungs filling with a hopeful breath.

Jessie's breath stammered, too, before she released a puff of air, her hands gripping the book in her lap with white knuckles.

She cleared her throat. "What do you have, there?" Jessie asked, pointing with her chin toward the thermos on the table, the intense moment they'd just shared fading to a slow simmer.

Derek blinked up at her. "Do you have any mugs?"

Her lips twitched at the absurdity of the question. Of course, she had mugs. She rolled her eyes at him good-naturedly, the simple exchange between them reminiscent of... before.

Derek watched Jessie retreat toward her cozy kitchen, her legs clad in soft buffalo-check flannel, a black thermal t-shirt stretched snugly across her strong shoulders and elegant back. She retrieved two mugs from a wooden mug tree on her counter and pivoted back toward him, settling down on the couch beside him. Derek unscrewed the thermos and poured some creamy coffee, still steaming hot, into a mug, before sliding it over toward Jessie. He poured a second for himself, then re-screwed the lid.

"Thank you, " she whispered, staring down at the

mug as she slipped her palm around the warm porcelain. Carefully, she raised the mug to her lips and took a tentative sip. Her brows lifted as the taste hit her tongue and as soon as she swallowed, her hazel eyes met his. "Mmm," she murmured before quirking a brow at him. "Don't you take yours black?"

Derek took a sip from his mug, relishing the heat as it slid down his throat, warming him from the inside out. "I do," he admitted, "but you don't." She held her mug and stared at him, her eyes softening in appreciation. "You take yours with cream and entirely too much sugar," Derek added, a glint of mirth in his own dark gaze. "Almost makes the junk you drink tolerable."

Jessie's lips twitched, the little creases on the outside of her hazel eyes crinkling in what Derek hoped was amusement. "Well," she paused, taking another sip, "this is definitely… not swill. "

Derek chuckled, sliding his own paw of a hand against his mug, seeking its warmth. "Not swill, no," he agreed. "It's imported organic Colombian," he stated, his mouth fighting a smug smile.

Jessie set her mug down on the coffee table, shaking her head ruefully. "You really are a coffee snob."

Derek's eyes followed the motion of his arm as he set his mug down beside hers, then lifted his chin to catch her gaze from beneath his lashes. He stared at her beautiful face, wary and trusting all at once before declaring in a deep, soft rumble, "I have exquisite taste."

Jessie blinked as a serious flush climbed her cheeks.

"Derek," she exhaled, her eyes sliding closed for a moment before flitting back open, "you say these things and…" she trailed off.

Derek swallowed. He canted a dark brow. "And?"

"And," Jessie began, tucking her bottom lip beneath the edge of her teeth. The tip of her tongue peeked out once again before she released her lips and continued. "They make me weak."

Derek shook his head vehemently. "You could never be weak, Jessie. You're as strong as they come."

Color bloomed on the apples of her cheeks yet again. "And what about you?" she asked, her voice thick with something Derek couldn't quite identify. "You're strong," Jessie said, her eyes raking over his chest, "I've seen your picture."

Derek's breath came quickly, the skin on his forearms breaking into gooseflesh beneath his shirt. "On the outside, yes. But inside…," he swallowed, locking his eyes on her honeyed gaze. "I'm molten. I burn for you."

Jessie's eyes fluttered shut as a puff of warm breath escaped her, ghosting over Derek's face. She blinked her eyes open and shot her hand out to clutch the shirt at his chest. "Oh my God," she gasped, yanking him toward her. "Get over here."

His mouth crashed into hers, two galaxies colliding. Her lips were soft and pliant, her tongue swiping along the seam of Derek's lips. He opened to her, surrendering to Jessie's soul. His tongue slipped into the heat of her mouth, tasting the sweet coffee on her tongue, moaning at the luscious taste of her .

Her grip on his shirt loosened, and Derek could feel the heat of her palm where it lay against his chest. He slipped one hand behind Jessie's back, his fingertips tracing over the notches of her spine, while his other hand closed atop hers, pressing her palm directly against his drumbeat heart.

Slowly, Jessie pulled back, her mouth hovering an inch from his. "Is this okay?" she sighed.

Derek inched back further, angling his face so he could see her better. His jaw worked soundlessly, his gaze fixed firmly on Jessie's questioning eyes. "Jessie," he breathed, tilting his head so his forehead rested against hers, "this is more than okay."

The hand not pressed against his chest slid up along his ribcage and over his neck until she cupped his cheek. "Take me to bed?"

Derek gripped her hips and went in for a quick kiss, his teeth nipping her full bottom lip as he retreated. Then he yanked her forward unceremoniously, wedging his hulking arms underneath her thighs and hoisting as he stood. Instinctively, Jessie's long legs wrapped around either side of his waist, holding herself tight to him as he meandered down the hallway, making slow progress as his lips continued to seek hers.

He fumbled at a closet door and Jessie shook her head, mumbling next one between wet, panting kisses. Derek shuffled through another doorway and kept walking until he felt Jessie's mattress against his knees. Jessie must have realized they'd reached her destination because she slid down the length of his chest and planted her feet on the bed, her breasts landing right in his face because of the height she now had over him.

Without hesitation, Jessie whipped her thermal off and tossed it to the floor, revealing a solid black cotton bra beneath. Derek whimpered, his eyes locked on the soft, freckled flesh before him. Gazing up at her from beneath his heavy brows, Derek swallowed and summoned all the strength inside to make his mouth form actual words.

"Jessie," he panted, "tell me what you want here, because before we get too far…" he swallowed densely. "I need to know what you want."

Jessie raked her fingers through his hair, brushing the unruly locks off of his forehead. "I want you, Derek," she said, her lip forming a half smile as her cheeks flushed with color once again. "I've always wanted you ."

Her words were a benediction, bathing him in warm relief. Derek blinked, unsure how this moment could possibly be real. It was all he'd hoped for.

He ghosted his fingertips over her ribs and watched her flesh react to his touch, her eyes turning from honey to rich, dark whiskey, the fine hairs on her arms standing on end, her nipples tightening behind the cotton of her bra. His hands hovered at the clasp at her back, snaking one long finger beneath the bra's band.

"I will not want to stop," he admitted, his voice a low rumble.

"I won't want you to stop," Jessie whispered, shaking her head.

Derek quirked a brow at her, his head still tipped up to meet her eyes. "Protection?"

Jessie's shoulders slumped. "Shit," she hissed, "no."

Derek's eyes fluttered closed. "Me either," he muttered. "I wasn't expecting-"

"No, no," Jessie agreed, giving his firm chest an understanding squeeze. "I understand." She huffed, her expression doing little to hide the warring inside of her. "Maybe you could just..." she paused, face flushing bright red, "pull out?"

She was goddamn adorable, standing before him half naked but embarrassed by her words. Derek huffed a short laugh, then brushed the stubble of his cheek along Jessie's jaw line. "Jessie," he began, drawing out the syllable, "as much as it pains me to say it, you know that's not a good idea."

"Oh, God, I know," she groaned, pressing her breasts closer to his face, her body seeking his mouth. "Just... just do it, Derek. Please," she begged.

Derek was a powerful man. He could bench press over three hundred pounds. He'd completed two marathons and many half-marathons. But there was no way in hell he was strong enough to deny Jessie not this. Not now.

"Shhh, baby," he crooned into her neck, "I got you."

"Derek," she murmured, yanking on the shoulder of his shirt, "take this off."

He complied, grabbing the back of his shirt collar and yanking it over his head in one sweep. Jessie was shuffling out of her flannel pants, her fingers hooking into the elastic waistband of her black cotton underwear.

"Wait," Derek panted, reaching his hand out to still her wrist, "let me."

Jessie nodded, and Derek watched her throat bob as she swallowed. Oh, Sweet Jesus, her throat… Derek felt his balls tighten, felt the prickling deep in his abdomen as his cock hardened further. With absolute control, Derek replaced her hands with his and slid the material down over the soft flare of her hips until gravity took over, sending her panties to her ankles. Jessie quickly kicked them off as a shudder sent her body trembling.

Derek returned his hands to the band of her bra, unhooking the material with a flick of his wrist. Jessie extended her arms, helping him to slide the garment off of her limbs to join the quickly growing pile on the carpeted floor.

Jessie's naked breasts bobbed in front of Derek's eyes, the dusky pink flesh of her nipples pulled taut, pebbled and hard, asking for satisfaction. Without another moment, Derek's mouth darted forward and snaked his hot tongue over her warm, smooth flesh, tasting the sweet jasmine of her skin. They moaned at the same time, the relief of the touch and of being touched more than either could bear.

While Derek fondled one breast and suckled the other, alternating between grazing his teeth on the tender skin and laving at it with the flat of his tongue, he felt Jessie's hands slide between his skin and the material of his jeans, popping his button and lowering the zipper. With a couple of forceful shoves, his pants were sinking to his knees, and Derek used one hand to hastily shove them off his feet, sending them to the pile, too.

"That's better," Jessie murmured, the backs of her knuckles skimming along his boxer briefs, skirting and teasing the length of him.

"Fuck, Jessie," Derek choked out, swiftly moving his hands from her breasts to cup her face, tilting it down to meet his gaze directly. "I want you on my face."

"Oh…" Jessie breathed, nodding, her pupils blown wide. She stepped back and sank down onto her bed, making room for Derek as he followed suit. Derek crawled up to the pillows and flopped onto his back before reaching his hand out to her, soft, cautious and wanting.

"Jessie," he breathed, "come here, beautiful."

Jessie practically scrambled up his chest, her wet heat dragging over Derek's briefs, making him hiss in pleasure. He caught her hips and guided her forward until the apex of her thighs hovered over his face, then slowly pushed her down until a strip of neat, coarse hair met his lips. He pressed his nose into her mons as the tip of his tongue snaked out to tease around her slit. Jessie was slick, practically soaked, her desire sweet and tangy all at once. Derek hummed in approval before running the flat of his tongue from her opening to her clit, lapping at her juices.

"Oh, fuck," Jessie trembled above him, her thighs already shaking as Derek held her steady.

He continued to work her, firming his tongue and sliding it inside, backing out and teasing her entrance, gathering her arousal and sliding up to circle her clit. He teased and sucked, fucked her with his tongue and scraped his scruff against her sensitive nub until Jessie hovered above him, her hands white-knuckled as she gripped her headboard, her head tipped back in wild abandonment.

Derek hummed his approval again, the vibrations against her center making Jessie hiss with pleasure as she rocked her pelvis in time to his licks and thrusts. When he skimmed his right hand up her left thigh and slid his thumb right into the heat of her as he grasped her clit between his lips and sucked, Jessie bucked once and went completely still, a quiet, keening wail the only sound save Derek's rapid breathing.

"Oh my God," she gasped, her head hanging heavy on her neck, her eyes hooded and shiny with desire. "Jesus Christ, Derek," she panted, pushing her hips backward until she straddled his chest, her lithe legs squeezing him, her still quivering cunt dampening his skin.

"Good?" Derek murmured, his eyes meeting hers.

Her lashes fluttered closed, her chest rising with a deep breath. "So good."

When she opened her eyes, Derek quirked a brow. "More?"

In answer, Jessie dragged her hands along his ribcage, then planted her palms on his chest for leverage to scoot down further, dragging her damp heat over his belly until she brushed up against the spongy tip of him, his pre-cum sticking to her own slick flesh with a viscous, magnetic pull.

"More," she said, breathless, wriggling her hips to slip the tip of his cock inside her.

Derek grabbed the base of his cock, hard and throbbing with need in his grip, holding himself prone as Jessie continued to inch down his length. It was slow-going—the best torture - as she rocked her hips and lifted and lowered herself, making agonizingly slow progress.

"You're doing so good, baby," Derek marveled, squeezing the swell of her hips, "taking all of me so well."

A rush of arousal slicked down his length, his words having the desired effect on Jessie as she watched him, eyes still glazed and hooded, her jaw hanging loose as she continued to work her hips in tiny rocking motions. Derek dragged his right thumb across her abdomen and down until it landed on Jessie's clit, rubbing small, soft circles around the bundle of nerves. With a soft mewling sound, followed by an animalistic grunt, Jessie sank all the way down, her thighs atop his and his cock buried to the hilt.

"Jesus fuck!" Derek gasped, sliding both hands back to

Jessie's hips and forcing her still, desperate to gather himself for a moment. "Don't move an inch or I'm going to come," he croaked. Jessie froze, her breathing coming in short pants, her abdomen twitching with shivers of pleasure.

"Oh, God," she moaned, closing her eyes, "so full."

"Jessie," Derek whined, his eyes rolling into the back of his head, "I swear to God…"

"Sorry, sorry," she soothed, doing her best to stay still. "It's just… so good."

Derek counted down from ten as slowly as humanly possible, biting down on the inside of his cheek and focusing on his breath. By the time he got to one, he felt like he could move. There's no way he'd last long, but by God he was going to make it good.

"Okay," he whispered, nodding. "You can move, now, baby."

"Mmm," Jessie hummed, tucking her bottom lip under her teeth as she rode him in a slow, rocking rhythm.

"That's it, pretty girl," Derek cooed, "so good." Jessie picked up the pace, her thighs lifting and lowering at a rapid clip, her palms still braced on his chest as she worked herself over him. Derek slipped his thumb back to her clit and pressed, giving her a little more sensation as she shook again, her thighs slamming down on his with every downstroke.

"Oh, God," she whined, "that's it, yeah- right there." She curled her fingers, her blunt nails digging into his pecs as she whimpered her last words, "I'm going to come, Derek, going to come -" right before her pussy clenched down on him, her walls fluttering along the thick length of his cock, her hips rocking as she rode him to completion.

When her body finally stopped quivering around him, she sagged bonelessly, her chest flush with his and her hair falling in a curtain on his neck. Derek remained still inside her, his cock harder than steel, his balls aching with the need to come so fucking bad. He pressed a kiss to the top of her head, the brown strands like silk on his lips.

He slid his arms around her back and held her tight against him, so close he could feel her heart pound a staccato rhythm against his chest. "Shhh, it's okay baby," he soothed, feeling her as she lay limp and wrecked, panting above him. "I'm just going to..." he left the statement unfinished as he started slowly lifting a hip to gently turn them to their sides, keeping her body flush to his and his cock buried in her.

After another quiet moment, Jessie's lids fluttered open as they faced each other side to side. "Back to Earth?" Derek teased, his voice a low rumble. Jessie's liquid honey eyes locked on his as she nodded. "Ready for more?" he rumbled, and Jessie nodded again, her top teeth digging into her plush bottom lip once again.

With that, Derek rolled over completely, fitting himself in the cradle of her hips, his cock deep inside her heat. He started with a slow piston, a low, guttural growl escaping his lips every time he sunk to the hilt, a gasping breath every time he slid out of her warmth. But it wasn't long before nature took over and he was moving with mechanical speed - a raging bull, a man on fire, a man in love - as he gave one last, blinding thrust before fighting every cell in his body to pull out. Gripping himself in his hand, Derek held his cock in a vicious grip and pumped three times before coming all over Jessie's tits in multiple spurts, the thick, white ropes of spend painting her flesh.

"Holy shit," Jessie breathed, glancing down at her chest and then back up at him.

Derek lifted his head, the rest of his energy going to keeping himself propped on his single arm so he wouldn't crush Jessie beneath him, and took in his handiwork. A half smile tugged at his lips as he exhaled, spent, a lewd pride swelling in his lungs as he stared at his come painting Jessie's skin. "There's my pretty girl."

Jessie shivered and gasped, her eyes rolling to the ceiling. "That was so hot," she panted.

A second later, her attention was back on him, and Derek lifted his chin to press a sweet kiss on her lips. He dipped his head down again to look at the mess he'd made, then looked up at her from beneath his brows, a mischievous grin forming. "Wow," he said with a chuckle, before Jessie joined him with a giggle of her own.

"Be right back," he said, pushing away and walking bare-ass naked to Jessie's bathroom before returning with a warm, damp washcloth to clean her skin.

"Thanks," she murmured, pulling him down to lie beside her. Jessie slipped a leg over his chest and wrapped her arms around him like a tree trunk, pressing and molding her body to his like two pieces of a puzzle sliding into place.

Derek wrapped his arm around her back and closed his eyes, his pounding heart finally settling.

He lay there, soaking in a deep contentment that extended well beyond his sated body - an unexpected epiphany striking him. His whole damn life, Derek had struggled with his ungainly size, his loping stride, his goofy gait. He'd spent his youth and early adulthood downplaying the prominent features which always plagued his confidence.

But right now? In this moment, with Jessie tucked to him like a key in its lock, Derek knew exactly what his body was made for.

CHAPTER TWELVE

One year later

Jessie sat across from Paige at their new favorite bar, this one a hipster gastro pub with amazing revival cocktails in the heart of Jessie's new neighborhood. Paige sipped a drink mixed with vodka, peach, ginger, lemon and blueberry. Jessie took a sip of her hot-pepper infused drink.

"Oh my goodness," Paige chuckled, taking another sip, "this is some fruity magic."

Jessie swallowed and wagged her tongue, waving her hand in front of it jokingly. "And mine is spicy!" she exclaimed, her eyes watering. "They're not kidding with those Hellfire Bitters."

Paige cocked her head and grinned. "We are so pretentious right now, aren't we?"

Grinning, Jessie looked down at their drinks and the hipster decor and giggled. "We are," she said with a nod. She lifted her glass again in salute. "But, hey, it's Christmas!"

"That it is," Paige agreed, pinching her straw and sucking down the last of her cocktail. "Speaking of..." she began, waggling her brows, "aren't the two of you hosting Derek's mom for Christmas Eve tomorrow night? Nervous?"

Shaking her head, Jessie smiled softly. "Not really," she admitted. "It's not like it's the first time I'm meeting Paula or anything."

To the contrary, Derek had introduced Jessie to his mother several months earlier, shortly after they'd finally finally - gotten together. The first time, they'd taken the train out to Laurelton for a Sunday afternoon visit and dinner. By their second visit for Mother's Day brunch, Jessie had known for the first time in forever that she, too, had someone to call mom .

"True," Paige agreed. "But it's different when it's your place and you're cooking and stuff."

Jessie grimaced. Paige was all too aware that Jessie wasn't a natural in the kitchen. Her phone buzzed in her pocket and Jessie pulled it out, giving a sheepish grin to Paige as she glanced down at it and typed a quick reply. "Sorry," she mumbled.

"Jessie Morrison," Paige chided in a sing-song voice, "are you sexting right now?"

Jessie's head snapped up. "What?" she gasped, her

face flushing from more than the alcohol in her cocktail. "No, of course not."

"You sure about that, Morrison?" Paige pressed. "Because that's the third time you've answered a text on your phone in the last twenty minutes."

"I—" Jessie scrambled to find an appropriate response. "Okay, yes," she rolled her eyes. "I'm texting with Derek," Jessie admitted sulkily.

With a grin, Paige pointed her finger at her friend. I think the word you're looking for is sexting," she corrected. "Don't deny it, you dirty thing."

"Ugh," Jessie groaned, "I'm sorry, Paige, you deserve my full attention—"

"No, no!" Paige giggled, "I'm just dying to know why you're sexting when you're going to see each other in like," she looked down at her phone to check the time, "less than an hour."

Jessie shrugged, taking a sip of her cocktail to stall. "You know... to, uh, build the anticipation?" she squeaked.

"Of course, it must also remind you of the humble beginnings of your epic love affair," Paige added with a teasing grin.

Oh Lord, did it.

Jessie tried to quash the butterflies in her stomach at the thought of what she'd just texted with Derek, but Paige saw right through her. In the year they'd been together, she and Derek had played out every fantasy, every erotic photo they found that piqued their interest.

And they found that the remnant personas of 'A.A.Bev' and 'Hank Johnson' sometimes gave them the perfect excuse to push some boundaries.

Like now, for instance, Jessie mused as she shoved her phone back into her purse, trying to forget about the image of a man's hand grasping a woman's head - tender and possessive, raw and vulnerable all at once - as she kneeled before him, swallowing him. Jessie vowed not to pick her phone back up until she and Paige were heading out.

Jessie took a deep breath and tried to quell her blush. Smiling, she gave Paige an enigmatic "Yep," before making a face at her friend's suggestive comment and adding, "And that's all you're going to get out of me, missy."

"Ha!" Paige cackled before reaching her hand across the table. "Jessie, in all seriousness, though… I'm glad you're happy." Paige cocked her head to the side, inquisitive. "Do you… do you think he could be the one?"

Jessie's smile bloomed from ear to ear. "I know he is."

"Ooh," Paige gushed, her eyes going wide. "Do we hear the sound of wedding bells? Should I shop for a Maid of Honor dress with the New Year's sales?"

Shaking her head, Jessie chuckled lightly. "Nah," she demurred, "Derek and I agreed we don't want anything like that. Just something simple. Quiet. We don't need fanfare. Just… me and him, a justice of the peace, and a vow."

"Ugh," Paige groaned, pulling her hand back to cup

her chin in her hand, "you two are so sweet you make me want to puke."

* * *

Christmas Eve dinner went off without a hitch. Between her and Derek, they'd successfully made roast beef with a gorgonzola cream sauce, parmesan mashed potatoes, and roasted cherry tomatoes.

Paula had oohed and ahhed, not only over their delicious meal topped off by a caramel bread pudding, but over their darling new apartment. "Darling" was the polite way of addressing their minuscule square footage, their second bedroom so small it was little more than a closet. But they had two bathrooms, access to a beautiful rooftop garden, and a prime historic location in Williamsburg with a ten-minute walk to their office.

It was perfect.

Derek slid the last plate into the dishwasher and grinned at Jessie. "All done," he announced.

"Want a prize?" Jessie asked, one eyebrow cocked and a sly grin on her face.

Watching her in silence for a moment, Derek's expression softened, his dark eyes alight from within as he trailed his gaze from her lips to her chest and back again. "You know I do," he nearly growled, desire thick in his voice.

Jessie dropped the dish towel she'd been using on the granite counter and turned from her place beside Derek to face him, squeezing herself in between his massive body and the sink. She tipped her head back, a half smile on her face, as she stroked her fingers through the shaggy hair at the nape of his neck.

Derek's eyes slipped closed, a contented moan of pleasure escaping his lips as Jessie caressed him. "Mmmm. Feels good," he murmured. After a few more moments, Derek sighed and opened his eyes, then cupped Jessie's hand in his before sliding it down to clasp it in front of his chest. "I have something for you."

Her wide eyes lighting with joy, Jessie's lips broke into an effervescent smile. "You do?"

Derek chuckled. "It's Christmas. 'Course I do."

"That's true," Jessie agreed, her eyes still glaring, "but tomorrow's Christmas. Not today."

"Same difference," Derek said with a shrug, teasing her.

"Well, I have something for you, too," Jessie admitted, lacing her fingers with his where their hands remained clasped at Derek's chest.

He arched a dark brow at her. "You want to go first?"

Jessie's cheeks flushed, her lashes fluttering as she shook her head. "No. You go."

Nodding, Derek pressed a kiss onto Jessie's forehead. "Okay. Come on." He turned on his heel and used their clasped hands to guide Jessie out into the living room. He led them toward the gas fireplace and their small tabletop Christmas tree situated beside it.

He bent down to switch on the gas for the fireplace, and on his way back up, Derek clocked the back of his head on the exposed brick mantle. "Oh, mother fu—" he cursed, cutting himself off by biting down on his lip and pressing his hand to his skull. "That hurts like a bitch!" he hissed. "I think I might have broken something," he whined, squeezing his eyes shut.

It's not that Jessie didn't have sympathy for her boyfriend; she was sure brick didn't feel good colliding with one's skull. But what the hell could Derek possibly think he'd broken? She couldn't help the little puff of laughter that escaped her as she reached for Derek's face, steadying him with her hands on his cheeks and making him hold her gaze.

"Oh, Derek," Jessie snorted, "there's no way you broke anything. Your head's hard like a bull's." She rubbed her thumbs in soothing circles along his forehead. "See?"

"Ugh, it really hurts," Derek muttered, squinting one eye. "Do you think I'm concussed?"

This time, the laughter peeled out of Jessie, completely uncontrolled. "No, you big lug!" She pulled him further downward and close to her, pressing his cheek against the soft pillows of her breasts and squeezing him into a tight bear hug. "There, there," she soothed, teasing him with the fact that she was comforting him on her bosom. "Doesn't that feel better?"

Derek was quiet for a moment before replying. "Yeah," he sighed, "it does."

"Mmm," Jessie murmured in contented agreement. "That's my Ferdinand, off smelling roses and not paying attention to what he's doing..." she chided, her hand running across the broad plane of his shoulders.

"You're the only flower I smell, pretty girl," Derek replied, his voice muffled by her curves.

Jessie hitched in a breath. "You know what it does to me when you call me that."

Slowly, Derek peeled himself off of Jessie and stood to his full height. Looking down at her with a knowing half-smile, he replied, "I know. What do you think I say it?"

Jessie clucked her tongue and swatted playfully at Derek's bicep. "You mean you only say it for ulterior reasons? It's not true?"

"Babe," Derek huffed a breath out through his nose, incredulous, "you're beyond beautiful." He waited to catch her hazel eyes with his. "You're... stunning... breathtaking." He kissed the tip of her nose, his lips plush and warm. "Miraculous. Luminous."

Her eyes softened, a sheen of warm affection flooding her expression. "The things you say to me..." Jessie sighed.

Derek cupped her cheeks in his hands, tilting her head just so as he spoke to her in hushed tones. "You make me feel brave enough to say anything... brave enough to put my heart in your hands." Jessie watched his Adam's apple bob as he swallowed, his brows creasing in concentration as if he searched her eyes for a hidden message. After a brief hesitation, he released her face and folded his large body in half until he was kneeling before her, his head reaching her waist. "Brave enough to lay my life at your feet," he declared, his voice a deep rumble she could feel in her belly.

Jessie swallowed hard as she watched Derek's giant hand reach out to grasp an ornament from a back branch of their little tree. His hand emerged from the greenery with a looped red ribbon tied to a metallic circle dangling from his fingertips, the ribbon and charm swaying and catching the multi-colored tree lights.

It wasn't until Derek untied the ribbon's bow and held out his open palm that Jessie realized it was a ring. A white-gold ring with a small sapphire framed by two diamond baguettes. Derek shifted, bringing one knee up as the other remained kneeling.

"If you're not too busy the day after Christmas," Derek rasped, "how does a trip to the courthouse sound?"

Jessie's knees went weak, and quickly she sank down to join him on the floor, her heart beating frantically in the cage of her chest, her eyes burning with unshed tears. This was all she'd ever wanted, more than she could have ever hoped for. Her hands shook as she grasped his wrists, needing his strength to keep her upright.

Her eyes fluttered closed, a single tear slipping down her left cheek. "Is this really happening right now?" she whispered, voice shaking, afraid it was all but a dream.

Jessie felt Derek's warm hand on her cheek, his thumb

gently swiping the tear away in a broad stroke. Her dampened lashes fluttered open to see Derek's face right before hers, his brows lifted and his lips fighting a smile. "Before you cry, could you maybe give me an answer?"

Biting down on her lip and fighting her own goofy grin, Jessie replied, "Can you repeat the question?"

His lips twitched as he gazed at her, his palm still cupping her cheek. "I asked if you would go to the courthouse. With me." Derek's grin faded for a moment, his expression suddenly intense and sincere, his dark eyes searching hers. "I'm asking if you'll marry me, Jessie."

The words made her stomach flip, made her eyes go fuzzy and her heart skip a beat. She felt elated, as if she was levitating, no longer bound by gravity, floating some-where among the stars. With a soft smile, she made words come out of her dazed mouth. "I don't know, Jansen," she said, her throat thick with emotion. "I'd say it sounds like forever."

Derek's jaw clenched and his eyes came alive with a gleeful mirth. "Is that a yes, Morrison?"

Jessie grinned. "You won't be able to call me that much longer, because that's a hard yes."

Derek slipped the elegant ring into place on Jessie's left hand, his barrel-sized arms snaking around her to pull her knees flush against his and wrap her in a tight hug. He buried his nose in the crook of her neck, breathing in her sweet scent. "You make me so happy."

She brushed her teary eyes against the soft cotton

covering his shoulder, her face pulled into a smile so wide her cheeks ached. "You make me so happy."

They lingered there for a moment, locked in each other's embrace, before Jessie spoke again. "I want to give you your present now."

Slowly, Derek pulled away and sat back on his heels. "Okay."

"Go to our bedroom," Jessie commanded softly.

Derek quirked a brow. "Okay… alone?"

She smiled and said, "I'll be right behind you."

Doing as she asked, Derek stood and walked toward their bedroom, turning his head to glance over his shoulder at her every few steps. Jessie smiled and nodded. As soon as he disappeared into their room, she reached over and switched off the fireplace gas… enjoying the fire would have to wait until tomorrow. She flicked off the lights as she moved through the apartment, but left the lights in their bedroom on full as she entered to find him sitting at the foot of their bed, looking a little lost and wary.

Jessie moved to stand in front of him, pressing his knees open wider so she could wedge herself between them. She licked her lips and started with the top button of her black silky blouse, slipping loose each mother-of-pearl fastening as her hands descended. Derek watched her every move, his own eyes growing wide when she shoved the panels of her top open to reveal a crimson satin push-up bra, the front clasp adorned with a festive rhinestone.

"What's this?" Derek asked, rubbing one finger beneath the right strap of her bra, his voice thick with desire.

"This," Jessie paused as she pushed her black leggings over the flare of her hips and shimmied them down and off her ankles, "is your gift." She stood in matching panties, the deep red satin a glorious contrast against the toned, golden skin of her abdomen.

Derek grinned, his eyes lighting up like a kid in a candy store. He reached both hands out, fingers bent and ready to palm the globes of her breasts, when Jessie caught his hands with hers. "Uh-uh-uh," she tutted. "Not yet, Jansen."

He lifted his brows in question, but slipped his hands back to his lap, looking at her full of intrigue.

"Stand up," Jessie commanded once again, her voice gentle but firm. Derek did as he was told, and Jessie quickly moved to take his place at the foot of the bed. When he was positioned standing directly in front of her, her nimble fingers popped the button of his jeans and pushed them and his boxers straight down in one go. His cock, already half hard, bounced free in front of her face. Jessie watched as she wrapped her right hand around his shaft and felt saliva pool at the back of her tongue. For as long as she lived, she'd never get over the perfection of him - thick and long, velvety to the touch, a blunt head purling with desire as she gripped him.

Without hesitation, her tongue swiped at his slit, tasting the slightly bitter saltiness. As her tongue came in contact with him, Jessie felt Derek jerk and swell in her hand, a deep groan escaping him. "Jesus, baby."

Looking up at him from beneath her dark lashes, Jessie opened her mouth and slid his entire manhood inside, swirling around his tip, curling her tongue to feel every swelling ridge. She used the hand that wasn't holding the base of his cock in place to reach for one of his hands, dragging it from where it hung limp at his side to the back of her head, telling him without words what she wanted from him.

What she was offering him.

What she was gifting him.

Derek whined as he threaded his fingers through Jessie's silky mane, grabbing a fistful as he started to gently thrust his now rock-hard cock inside her mouth. Jessie closed her eyes and forced herself to relax, loosening enough to feel his head at the back of her throat with every push of his hips. Little whimpers slipped from his lips with every press into the wet heat of her mouth, and Jessie couldn't help but open her eyes wide to glance up and try to get a glimpse of his blissed face. Derek's head hung loose from his neck, chin tipped forward without the strength or gumption to hold himself upright. His eyes were glazed over, completely wrecked, as he watched his cock slide in and out of her mouth.

Jessie felt wanton. Used for his pleasure. Completely fucking powerful.

She felt Derek twitch, heard his breathing hitch as he whined - this large, mighty man mewling like a kitten. She slid off of him, releasing him with a soft pop, and Derek hissed, his eyes blown wide in shock and needful desire.

Jessie was panting, too, trying to get air back in her lungs as she said, "Take off your shirt."

Derek scrambled to do so, like his arms couldn't move fast enough. In seconds, he had his shirt wadded and tossed on the floor, his wide, smooth chest bare and on full display. Jessie stood, meeting him toe-to-toe. She kept her eyes locked on his as she unclasped her bra, then slipped her wet panties down her thighs. Sitting back down, Jessie scooted backward on their bed, bending her knees as she extended her hand, beckoning him wordlessly.

Derek complied, placing one knee at the foot and crawling his way up the mattress to her. Jessie guided his hands to her breasts, finally letting him cup and massage the soft flesh, her nipples pulling taut at his touch. She moaned quietly as she reached between them to once again grasp his length in her hand before guiding him to her wet and aching center.

Derek's cock - big enough that it often required a little maneuvering to get him fully seated within her - slid right home as Jessie lifted her hips and shoved against him, soaking and slick with desire.

"Fuck!" Derek gasped as he settled between her legs, the muscles of his impressive ass flexing as he strained to sink even deeper. "Fuck," he repeated, his voice trembling.

Jessie slid her hand over the curve of his rear and

pressed, encouraging a rhythm as she circled her hips. Derek's lips found the column of her neck, his tongue taking long swipes and little nibbles on the sensitive skin, his breath hot as he panted in her ear.

There's nothing in the world that will ever be as good as this , Jessie thought as she lay prone beneath his weight, trapped in the best possible prison. As she felt the head of his cock drag along her inner walls, the practiced angle of his thrusts hitting her in a magical place.

"Right there," she whispered. "Don't stop. Oh God," she moaned, "don't ever stop."

He mewled again, little grunts escaping along with his heavy exhales. Beneath her palms, she felt the dip of his glutes with every deep thrust, his cock nudging her womb.

"I want you to come in me, Derek," she huffed, her eyes glazing over as the pressure continued to build, the fluttering deep in her gut spreading to her limbs like a warm glow. "Fill me up with your cum baby," she gasped at the first fluttering of her cunt.

Hearing her dirty words made Derek practically growl. The rumble in his chest so deep its vibration sent Jessie teetering fully over the edge, her muscles clamping and quivering all around his thickness. "Oh God," Derek grunted. "I can feel you, baby. Feel you coming for me." He continued to thrust shallowly as Jessie rode out her orgasm, keeping her on the wave for an impossibly long time. "That's it, come all over my cock," his hoarse voice whispered. Then, a deep groan as he gave one last forceful thrust before stilling, then swelling and spurting inside her, hot and throbbing.

———

Jessie moaned as the last aftershocks of her pleasure passed, her palms sweaty against Derek's ass, her chest and forehead covered in a light sheen of perspiration. Derek's face rested at the notch of her collarbone and she could feel the dampness on his forehead and hair, too.

Even sweaty and with his sticky spend already leaking out of her, Jessie couldn't tolerate the idea of getting up to shower. She felt too good, her limbs jelly and her heart pumping bliss through her body, completely high on him. As if he could read her mind, Derek sighed and pressed a wet, open-mouthed kiss to Jessie's neck. "Stay here, baby," he murmured as he pulled out of her, leaving Jessie feeling suddenly empty and cold; incomplete.

A moment later, Derek was back with a warm cloth. "You take such good care of me," she murmured with a smile as she took the cloth from him and swiped at her chest, then between her legs. She folded it and tossed it over to the hamper.

Derek chuckled. "Nice shot," he said, yanking their bedding down and pulling her against him.

"I'm full of hidden talents," Jessie replied sleepily, coming to rest her body flush against him, his bicep and chest her pillow.

"Don't I know it," Derek agreed smugly as he

wrapped his arm around her, pulling her ever closer, his palm cupping the back of her head as if she were precious cargo. It made Jessie's heart flutter, made her eyes burn, made her lips yearn to smile.

Jessie closed her eyes, sighing with contentment, as she remembered the thing she'd read so long ago, the words about living with the genuine spirit of the season: giving, gratitude, and grace.

She slid her left hand along Derek's ribs and looked down with sleepy eyes at the dainty ring on her finger. In forty-eight hours, she'd officially give him her heart, and he'd give her his name.

She was grateful for every moment with Derek, even the rough ones that led them here, to now, to this moment.

With Derek, Jessie felt God's grace; in Derek's arms, she felt cherished... safe. Protected and loved.

She squeezed her thighs over his chest, tucking herself even more tightly against him, their flesh nearly one. "I love you, Derek."

Sleepily, Derek replied, "Love you, too."

Jessie sighed, ready to end the day in his arms, ready to start the next day by his side. Ready to repeat it every day for the rest of their lives. Nearly asleep, Jessie felt Derek's nose brushing along her mouth, the words he spoke a soft murmur along the shell of her ear.

"If you're lonesome, wake me."

LUCA

CHAPTER THIRTEEN

octor Luca Michaelson hears his pager going off nonstop.

"We have a twelve-car pileup, about fifteen minutes out! Multiple traumas, so we need all hands on deck!" Luca hears from out in the hospital's hallway.

Luca groans; Holly's voice ringing in his ears a bit too loudly. It looks like it's going to be one of those nights and he's definitely too tired.

Once the surgeon's fully up, feeling a bit groggy, Luca hops off the bottom bunk and grapples for his pager in the dark.

Before he can even touch the floor, the door opens and in comes angry-looking Nurse Amber.

"Michaelson, we've been paging you for the last ten minutes! Get your ass to ER now!"

Not a second later, she's gone, probably off to scream at the other group.

There are many things that Luca enjoys about his job, and Amber's yelling isn't one of them - especially when she's in one of her moods in the wee-hours of the morning. Luca hated being on the receiving end of her tirade.

Two minutes later, Luca is up, running out of the door and down the hall to the ER. His white coat billowing behind him as he hurries.

* * *

Being the highest ranked trauma center in the state, Mornington Hospital's ER is constantly busy. Car crashes are an everyday occurrence, along with other traumas that never seem to conclude. The ways people injure themselves is astounding.

Luca reached the ambulance loading dock and is immediately handed a surgical gown and a pair of rubber gloves. Nurse Amber scoffs when she sees his rumpled scrubs and bedhead.

"Nice nap?"

Luca rolls his eyes and smirks. "Perfect, actually. Four surgeries in a day will tire you out, not that you would know."

Amber's facial expression turned sour as she turns away huffing. Luca sees Thomas and Holly trying to hide their laughter.

Contrary to this situation, Luca actually gets along with his coworkers. Thomas, who's inside with him, is the most hilarious pediatric surgeon at the hospital. Holly, who usually keeps to herself, is good at dishing out orders in any stressful situation. Luca definitely hands it to her; she's one of the best trauma surgeons he's met.

Despite Amber's tough character, she can be nice sometimes. She has a drive for competitiveness, something she and Luca share in common. Amber was used to being called the best at everything but was in for a wakeup call when she began working with Luca. In actuality, they're a lot more alike than Luca would care to admit. This makes good entertainment when they're battling over the number of surgeries they performed per day.

Just when Luca is tuning back to Thomas instructing Holly about the details of their incoming trauma victims, someone stumbles through the doors and skids to stop of the ambulance bay.

"Hey! Did I miss the party?"

Luca groans seeing Damien grinning while putting on a pair of gloves. He opens his mouth to tell him off before the doors open once again, interrupting.

"Now is not the time for jokes, Dr. Brady."

Subconsciously, everyone straightens up and turns their attention towards Chief Mackwood. She's flanked by both Dr. Armstrong and Dr. Taggart. The expressions on their faces are serious.

* * *

The group are in their final year of residency and haven't been Dr. Mackwood's interns for some time now. Still, they tend to worship the ground she walks on. The novelty of being mentored by one of the best heart surgeons in the country always brought thrills.

A siren blaring close by snaps Holly back to attention. Her expression shifts as she puts on her game face for telling everyone of the situation they will have on their hands.

"Multiple in critical, and a high number of head injuries."

They're in for a long night.

———

The first ambulance comes screeching to a halt and everyone rushes forward. The next few minutes are a blur of shouted orders and gurneys being wheeled through the ER with moaning patients. Luca follows Thomas into a trauma room to help assess a young girl with a nasty gash on the side of her head.

Luca takes out his flashlight to shine it into the young girl's eyes as Thomas tends to her other injuries. "Hi sweetie, my name is Dr. Michaelson, can you could tell me your name?"

The girl tries to moan out her name but it's obvious she's not conscious enough to articulate well. "Okay, I know it hurts. It's just very important that you try and follow my finger." He waves it in front of her face and is happy to see she can follow the movement perfectly with her half-lidded eyes.

Before Luca can speak, Thomas pipes up, "She's

stable for now. I'll take her up for a head CT and page you if she needs surgery. Go help the others."

Luca nods and dashes out and back into the ambulance bay. The last ambulance has just pulled up and Amber is helping the EMTs unload the gurney. He saunters over as vitals are listed.

Luca begins pulling the gurney as Amber spots him and grabs ahold of the end of it. "This patient is mine, I was here first," she growls and Luca sighs.

"There are signs of mild cardiac distress and this patient obviously has a massive head injury, so if you don't mind, this one is mine."

Amber was about to say something when someone clears their throat from behind. The person in question jumps down from the back of the ambulance and Luca freezes.

The woman is young and looks close to Luca's age. Her hair is brunette with curls near the back of her neck. Her eyes are brown and are framed by black-titanium frames. Luca sees there's a large amount of blood on her shirt around the area where it's rolled up. This woman's attractive in a nerdy way. Luca's breath hitches as he watches her twirl her hair nervously.

"If you wouldn't mind, I'd like to assist?"

Luca is so dumbfounded by how cute the woman before him is, that he doesn't realize he's being spoken to. At his look, the woman giggles and twirls her hair again as she starts to push the gurney into the ER, while Luca and Amber trail behind her.

"I was driving to work when I came across the accident. I'm also a trauma surgeon."

It's been too long since Luca has spoken and Amber is starting to look at him out of the corner of her eye. "This isn't normal," she wonders. "Luca Michaelson does not get turned on around women in the ER and is speechless over this one he met not two minutes ago."

Luca comes back to himself when he sees the nurses lifting the patient onto the table while the female trauma surgeon puts on a pair of gloves and gown. His eyes drift over to the patient seeing him trached with a straw. This is Luca's first time seeing this.

"You trached him? With a straw?" The brunette looks up from her assessment of the patient's throat and smiles as her face turns reddish.

"He was going to die. I had no other choice."

Luca shakes his head and smiles as he begins his assessment of the patient's head. Just as he's about to open his mouth to flirt with the trauma surgeon, Amber's pager buzzes.

She reads the page and chuckles. "Holly needs an extra pair of hands in the OR, preferably another trauma surgeon with more experience. You up for it doctor?"

The brunette looks up and smiles. "I'm Dr. Winstead. And I'd love to help if you guys don't mind."

"Come with me." Amber drags Dr. Winstead off and down the hallway while Luca is left alone with the patient. Luca makes sure the patient is stable and sends him off for a CT before seeking out Dr. Winstead to ask for her first name. Maybe she'll want to go for a drink later.

"Michaelson! There's a stopped heart in OR five!"

Luca huffs and glances toward the hallway Amber and Dr. Winstead just went down before turning and running towards OR five.

He hopes the brunette's patient surgery lasts as long as his.

CHAPTER FOURTEEN

S everal hours later, Luca is dragging along as he comes out of the OR; his scrub cap hanging loosely from his hand.

The surgery had not gone well. Amidst complication after complication, the patient's heart had survived, but would possibly have repercussions on his everyday health.

Luca turned the corner to find his coworkers sitting around the nurse's station exhausted. Damien was snoring with his head in his arms and Holly was slumped against the wall. Even Amber looked ready to sleep for about a week. The only one who looked awake was Thomas, and he was going over charts smiling.

Luca doesn't know why Thomas is always in a good mood.

Amber perked up at the sight of Thomas and grins. "You just missed the cute trauma surgeon."

Luca straightened up at the mention of Dr. Winstead

realizing whom Amber's referring to. He groans sagging in his chair. If Luca could, he'd bang his head against the desk nonstop.

Damien groggily looks around. "What'd I miss?"

Amber starts giggling. "Michaelson here has a crush on the trauma surgeon that trached the patient with a straw."

Holly sits up at thinking of the brunette who helped her earlier in the OR.

"Come on man, can't you go a week without wanting to get into some nurse's panties?" Damien says as he rubs his goatee.

Luca rolls his eyes. "First of all," he starts. "I don't have a crush on anyone. Aren't we on the clock here?" Then he turns to Damien, "And I can't help it if the ladies are constantly around willing to have some fun."

Everyone yells, "Oooooooo!"

Luca smiles and stands up. "Anyway, my shift is officially over. See you all tomorrow bright and early."

Luca walks out of the hallway to a chorus of intakes' groans.

CHAPTER FIFTEEN

Luca Michaelson has a problem.

He doesn't commit after hookups, learning in medical school when his first fling, Alice Walker told him they were free to see anyone, at the beginning of their rendezvous. However, Luca had at first perceived them as the perfect couple. Since then, Luca has never settled down. It's easier that way. Just sex is nice and it's better that he chose a career where it's hard to get emotionally involved.

It's been a week since the night of the twelve-car pileup and Luca is still thinking about Dr. Winstead. No matter what he does, he cannot get her out of his head. Luca, when he sees a patient's family member trailing the gurney with blood-spattered clothes, pictures Dr. Winstead's clothes that night, too. Then, he'll see someone sipping from a straw and think about how the brunette trached a patient with one. And if Luca sees a woman with black-rimmed glasses, all he can think about is the brunette's eyes and her nerdy look.

Luca begins to believe he's going mad.

He's been at the bar across the street from the hospital more times in the past week than he's been in the last year. Every night ends the same: he goes, he gets drunk, he starts looking for a hookup, and then he leaves because he starts thinking about Dr. Winstead.

The surgeon can't stop imagining running his hands down Dr. Winstead's curvy figure.

"Luca!"

A shout startles him from his daydream, making him spill his charts on the floor in the process. He glares at Damien as the plastic surgeon laughs and walks by. Luca is a mess and it's been like this all week. To him, it's Dr. Winstead's fault. Dr. Winstead, who he was only in the presence of for five minutes, and spoke all of six words to.

As Luca hastily picking up his charts, he sees Holly crouch down and begins to help. "So," she starts, "you ready for the merger with the hospital down the road?"

Luca groans. "Not really," he blurts. "We don't need any more traffic around here. Especially when Amber is running things. It wouldn't surprise me if I had to clip an aneurysm of hers by the end of the week."

Holly chuckles as they stand back up and she hands him the rest of his charts. Her eyebrows scrunch as she debates on what to say to Luca next. "About that surgeon from last week?"

"Seriously, you're still on that? Yeah, she looked good,

that's it. No biggie," Luca huffs and turns before Holly can figure out the trauma surgeon is all he's been thinking about all week.

* * *

The remainder of the day moves slowly. Luca has back-to-back surgeries up until five in the evening. When he finally leaves the OR, he finds the hallways in utter chaos. Most of the faces Luca has never seen before, and he realizes it's because the employees from the hospital down the road have begun to arrive.

Thomas whizzes past him; his bloodied shoes leaving a trail behind. When he sees Luca, he pauses looking at him crazily. "Michaelson, trauma needs you in OR one stat!" Thomas yells before dashing off.

Luca sighs before taking off running. Looks like yet another long night is in store for all.

———

Luca reaches the OR and immediately begins the scrubbing process. He vaguely makes out someone gowning a surgeon in the OR in front of him, but the woman doesn't look like Holly.

When he finishes scrubbing, he rushes to the door and goes in. "You paged?" Luca asks as a surgical nurse helps him put his gown on.

"Yeah, I've got a patient with a bad spinal injury and could use a consult before I go in to repair it."

Luca whips his head around at the voice and

promptly loses his mind. It's Dr. Winstead standing in front of him once again.

He knows why she's here. There was talk that she worked for the hospital down the road. Now with the merger, she'll be working at Mornington with Luca.

Luca takes a moment to inhale before smiling at the trauma surgeon. He walks forward to see the x-rays. Dr. Winstead smiles, almost as if she's nervous. "The patient fell out of a second-story window and it doesn't look too good at the moment."

She hands the x-rays to Luca as the nurses and anesthesiologist prep the patient to go under. Luca observes the scans and lets out a low whistle. "Yeah, this is bad. We're going to need to go in and do a spinal repair right away."

Dr. Winstead lets out a sigh, disappointed at the patient's prognosis. "Well, you can take it from here. This is above my usual patient level," she replies as she begins to discard her gown and gloves. Quickly, Luca makes a decision.

"Wait!"

Dr. Winstead is startled and looks up. Luca clears his throat as his face beams. "Please stay. I mean, if you're not busy, please observe, even help." Luca giggles and comes back to himself. "You can watch the magician perform his magic," Luca wiggles his fingers towards Dr. Winstead.

Dr. Winstead nods looking embarrassed before she wrings her hands nervously and gestures for Luca to begin. Luca grins and then goes about preparing for the surgery.

———

"So," he starts, drawing out the end of the word, "what's your name?"

Dr. Winstead laughs a little while raising her eyebrow. "Hmm, Dr. Winstead?" she says it like it's a question.

Luca shakes his head. "I mean your first name. As nice as it's been to call you Dr. Winstead in my head all week, I'd like to know your first name."

The brunette sputters and becomes flustered at the fact that Luca is thinking about her.

"Bethany," she says quietly blushing. Luca wonders if her reactions spread to her bosom. He finds himself imagining pulling up Bethany's shirt and finding out for himself.

Luca shakes the thought out his head. "Scalpel," he says and is handed the instrument by one of the attending nurses. He smirks as he cuts into his patient. "Bethany, it's nice to meet you. I'm Dr. Luca Michaelson."

"I know," Bethany replies quickly, and then her eyes widen as she backtracks. "I mean, I heard—from your coworkers. Last week, I asked the other trauma surgeon for your name. Not for any reason, I mean, I just forgot to ask you myself before I left and it seemed impolite. You know?" Bethany takes a deep breath and shakes her head.

"And I'm going to stop rambling and embarrassing myself any further."

Luca chuckles and wasn't the only one appreciating the moment. "I don't mind. I actually find it cute." He sends another smirk Bethany's way as he continues to work on his patient. The more Luca flirts, the more open Bethany becomes. It's fun to watch.

"Cute? Well, thanks," Bethany says, almost like she had to force herself to say it.

———

They continue to talk for the next half hour and Luca even brings up the straw trach. Bethany blushes under the praise and brushes off Luca's compliments. Luca sees that anytime Bethany's complimented, she says they aren't true and brushes them off causing him to quickly counter.

Soon enough, Bethany gets paged for a consultation down in the ER. She looks disappointed she has to leave and walks toward the exit slowly.

"Hey, Bethany?"

"Yes?"

Luca smiles and pauses for a second. "Want to go out for coffee or something like that? Let's say tomorrow?"

Bethany smiles and nods. "I'm off at six. I'll wait around for you to finish your shift."

"Great. See you then, Beth."

Bethany's face reddens at the nickname.

CHAPTER SIXTEEN

"*Damn it, damn it, damn it!*"

It's half past six the next day and Luca's in a bit of trouble in the OR.

Holly has her hands in the patient's open chest cavity as Luca frantically thinks about what to do next.

This surgery had been rocky from the start. The patient crashed three times before he was even put on the operating table and was currently cardiac-arresting for the fourth time. To any surgeon other than Luca, the patient would have been a lost cause, but Holly and Luca were not going down without a fight.

Truth be told, Holly was Luca's favorite to assist in surgeries. Her skills and quickness were incomparable. She was as dedicated to her patients like him, and together they made one hell of a team.

It was another ten minutes before Holly gave a low sigh and slowly retracted her bloodied hands from the patient's chest as the heart monitor continued to flatline. Her voice was grim when she called, "Time of death: 6:34."

Luca ripped off his gloves and scrub cap. "Damn it," says Luca as he quickly wrestles out of his surgical gown.

"Luca?" Holly calls as he washes his arms in the scrub sink.

He sighs. "I know this patient was a lost cause, but it doesn't make losing him any easier." Holly nods as Luca frantically scrubs his hands and arms in the sink. "And I was supposed to meet Bethany half an hour ago. Now, she's probably going to hate me. This was our first date or at least attempt at one."

"Luca, please stop!"

He pauses and looks down finding his arms looking red. The scrubber falls into the sink as he groans. "Look, I'm sure she'll understand. She's a surgeon too, so she knows what it's like. I'll take it from here, inform the family, and you hurry up. Don't worry. I got this."

Luca wipes his forehead and Holly smiles like that's all he needed to hear.

———

Ten minutes later, Luca's running down towards the main entrance to find Bethany leaning against the wall, tapping away at her phone. She's dressed in a grey cardigan and fitted jeans, with her thick-rimmed glasses sliding off her nose. She looks so relaxed, and Luca just wants to skip coffee, lay down next to her and fall asleep.

Luca makes his way towards her while excuses are already popping up in his head. When Bethany looks up, she sees Luca in front of her, babbling nervously. "I'm so sorry. I got caught up in surgery and thought I'd be finished early. The shit was a pain in the ass and unfortunately, we couldn't end up saving him—"

"Luca, it's okay! Are you okay?" Bethany looks at him in concern, but her eyes are twinkling. "I understand. Surgeon here, remember?" She points to herself with an eyebrow raised.

"Yeah, I'll be fine." Luca lets out a breath he wasn't even aware he was holding. He's never been so concerned with reassuring someone like this before. It's foreign and makes him feel slightly uneasy but grateful at the same time.

Bethany hesitated before asking her next question. "You said you lost the patient?" Luca nods. "Well, would you like to ditch the coffee and come over to my place? You need some cheering up to do."

Observing Luca's shocked facial expression, Bethany blushes to realize what it sounds like she's offering. "I meant, you could come over and we could order a pizza and watch Netflix or something. I know when I lose a patient I always just want to stay in and avoid people for that evening. Not that I didn't want to have coffee with you! You know what I mean—"

Luca cuts her off by grabbing her hand and Bethany's

mouth snaps shut. Luca smiles as he squeezes her soft hand. "Pizza sounds good," Luca says gesturing for Bethany to lead the way.

———

Luca has no idea what he's doing.

The word 'date' isn't really in his vocabulary. Sure, he's taken a girl out for a drink or two before ultimately taking them back to his apartment, but they hardly counted as dates. His one-night-stands were always like ghosts that come at night and go in the morning. Luca made sure they understood his 'casual-hookup' stance.

Besides, Luca has never felt the urge to look for something more. While most he knows outside of work are settling down by getting married and having children, Luca doesn't see the point especially being twenty-nine at the door knocking on thirty. His appearance deceives many as if he's in his early twenties. Luca intends to use that to his advantage as much as possible.

It's not like being a surgeon offers him much leeway anyway. Even if Luca wanted to date, he works about seventy hours a week, so it's not like he even has the time. The only potential candidates in his dating pool that would understand would come from a similar medical background. And there's no way he'd ever think about dating any of his coworkers.

Bethany is his coworker now though. And Luca doesn't understand how he's only known this woman for two short days and already feels more for her than any of the women in his life.

———————

They're lounging on Bethany's sofa, binge-watching a trashy reality show. An empty pizza box sits on the coffee table along with two half-empty beer cans and Bethany's rambling on about the most complicated surgery she's ever had to perform while Luca can't stop staring.

His chest feels light and there's this feeling he's having. Every time Bethany smiles, his heart trips over itself before going in overdrive. The heat radiating off of Bethany's side is driving Luca crazy, and all he wants to do is move over until there's no space left between. Bethany's thigh has been pressing all along him all evening. There's a tingling sensation in Luca's fingers, almost as if he's aching to reach out and twine his fingers with Bethany's. He has his suspicions on what's happening, but would rather not examine it too closely.

"And then, get this, just as we're closing up, the patient flatlines again and—"

Luca laughs awkwardly realizing Bethany wasn't joking about her patient. Though, it was as if Luca had just joined the conversation.

Bethany stops abruptly and looks at him. "Is there something wrong?" Luca stops laughing and shakes his head. He doesn't want to let Bethany know he's currently having a panicking attack.

Bethany worries for a second before moving closer. Her side is now a body of heat, pressed tightly against Luca's. She holds his hand to calm him down. Without saying another word, she focuses back on the TV and resumes watching.

Maybe it's a date.

———

Surprisingly, the night ends with Bethany walking Luca to the door.

They had just topped off the evening trading surgery horror stories and getting to know one another. Luca had flirted with Bethany the entire night, her eventually warming up and flirting back was just as aggressively. It was the first time Luca had ever spent a night with a woman he was attracted to and didn't at least end up making out with her. Truth be told, it was the most fun he had had in months.

Now, Bethany is leaning against the opening of her apartment door, the gold numbers of 303 glintings in the low hallway light. Luca is hesitant to leave and doesn't want the night to end. He's scared that once he's alone, he'll go back to his old ways.

"So," Luca says as he shoves his hands in his pockets.

The right side of Bethany's mouth pulls up a bit. "So —" she repeats back, drawing out the end of the word. She takes a small breath before beginning, "We could do this—"

"Let me take you out to dinner," Luca blurts out without a second thought. He doesn't know why he even said it; he's never actually gone on a dinner date with a woman before.

"Sounds perfect." Her smile graces her features.

A second later, Bethany moves over and plants a small kiss on Luca's cheek. It happened so fast that Luca isn't even sure if he imagined it or not.

There's a wicked gleam in Bethany's eye as she backs into her apartment and holds the door. "See you later, Dr. Michaelson." She quickly shuts it and Luca is left standing out in the hallway dumfounded.

A shiver runs through his body as he goes over Bethany's tone of voice when calling him by his professional name. He finds that he likes it quite a bit.

Luca smiles and turns to walk down the corridor.

Nobody has to know if there's a slight skip in his step until he reaches the street.

CHAPTER SEVENTEEN

Luca and Bethany have texed each other at all hours.

Bethany is usually the one to text first since she enjoys taking the earlier shifts at the hospital.

"Good morning!"

"How are you this cheerful so early in the morning?"

"I've been in surgery since 5 am."

"Why are you talking to me then? Go rest."

"Ok, but I have coffee waiting for you. Would you rather I drink it?"

"You're a godsend! Be there in 15."

Luca, more often than not, attempts to send dirty texts during his lunch break if they aren't working on the same shift.

"What are you wearing?"

"I'm not doing this with you. I have on my scrubs and a white jacket. Nothing new to report, LOL."

"Oh come on, Beth."

"Whining will get you nowhere."

"You're no fun."

A large portion of their text conversations also consists of complaining about their current patients.

"This mother of four is an absolute pain in the ass. I've had to explain a thoracotomy at least five times already."

"Yikes. I have an inoperable tumor and the patient refuses to accept my prognosis."

"Please kill me. My patient is refusing treatment even though they're going to die."

"Just had to clean up puke for almost a half an hour."

Luca doesn't care when his friends tease him for always being glued to his phone.

———

A week later finds Luca sitting behind the nurse's station and drowning in charts. The slap of more paperwork snaps him out of his thoughts. He looks up to find Damien leaning against the station with a cocky grin. Luca sighs, his headache is already coming on.

"So—" Damien starts as he opens one of his charts, "Did you sleep with the new trauma surgeon yet?" The guy even wiggles his eyebrows.

Luca doesn't want Damien to know he and Beth haven't slept together yet. Over the past week, they've gone out a few times but Beth acts nervously whenever Luca suggests they move onto more fun activities at home. Bethany laughs and tries to change the subject as quickly as possible.

Luca doesn't know what he's doing wrong, and frankly, he's going insane from not having been laid in a while. Bethany and her perfection are killing him.

The silence stretches on for a few seconds as Luca tries to avoid answering the question. When he doesn't reply, Damien raises his eyebrows. "No way dude, you didn't—"

Damien's comment is cut off by an array of shouts and footsteps pounding in from the ambulance bay. A second later, Holly is seen pushing a gurney rushing down the hallway. Bethany is straddling a patient that's unconscious and is doing chest compressions as the patient's pushed straight to the operating room. Her white coat is covered with blood and her glasses are down to the end of her nose.

"He's crashing! We need to get to OR, stat! We need cardio!"

The whole scene is over in less than a minute. The image of Bethany straddling the patient, her thighs framing their thin frame, is replaying inside Luca's head. He wants to run his hands through her hair, maybe hold it from behind. *Maybe Bethany has a kink for that?* Luca sees Beth as shy in person and kinky when turned up.

"Man, you are so whipped!"

Luca hears Damien close to his ear. "I'm not whipped," he grumbles as he starts shuffling through the charts. "We're not going out."

Damien smiles. "I cannot believe you two haven't slept together yet. How does it feel to be the one working so hard to get laid, dude?"

The pen in Luca's hand makes a sizable indent in the chart from how hard he's gripping it. Damien doesn't notice his shift in mood and continues to go in. "Seriously. Even lame man Thomas is getting some from that new badass ortho surgeon Becky."

Luca is saved by his pager going off. He smiles and waves the object in Damien's face. "Sorry. I've got a craniotomy coming in. Have fun with your rhinoplasties buddy!"

CHAPTER EIGHTEEN

Luca hasn't been laid in a month, which is something he hasn't had to endure since high school. He was new in this town and even he had women at the bar across the street who gushed over him. Lately, he's gotten cold feet to even take one of them home if offered a chance mainly because of Bethany's face keeps flashing in his mind.

Two hours later, Luca is exhausted headed to the on-call room. His last surgery had left him drained and he still has about five hours left on his shift.

When he opens the door, light floods into the shadowed room and illuminates the bunk on the far wall. Luca's throat goes dry when he sees Bethany sit up squinting against the light.

"Oh. I didn't know you were in here." Luca goes to close the door when Bethany yawns. She lays back down, her scrubs wrinkling further as she gets comfortable again. Smiling at Luca, she pats the open space next to her as an invitation.

Not one to turn down an opportunity, Luca slides in. They're laying on their backs, shoulder to shoulder, and Luca can't get enough of the heat radiating off of Bethany's body.

For a few minutes, the sound of their breaths and Luca's racing heart could be heard in the silent room.

"How was your day?"

Luca almost laughs.

Bethany chuckles and starts rambling on about her multiple surgeries and traumas. Luca can't help but stare as she gestures wildly with her hands and recounts every little detail. Bethany's eyes are twinkling as she explains a complicated operation she had to endure with Holly.

Luca's so captivated by Bethany's tale that he doesn't realize what he's doing; his hands tangle into Bethany's hair and he's tugging her forward to press his lips against hers.

Luca feels Bethany gasp. Suddenly, her hands wrapped around Luca's neck and pulling him closer. The kiss turns frantic quickly.

They stay like that; trading kisses for what feels like minutes, hours and years. Luca can't tell, but he doesn't ever want to stop.

All too fast Bethany pulls away. Luca's vision blurs for a minute and then he refocuses in on Bethany looking at him. "What was that for?" Bethany sounds breathless and shocked.

"You're cute when you ramble," Luca grins watching Bethany blush. "Honestly? I've wanted to do that since I saw you jump out of that ambulance."

Bethany yanks Luca back in. This time, there's nothing gentle about their kissing. Bethany bites at Luca's lips, almost enough to be painful. Luca's tongue quickly becomes well accustomed to Bethany's as his hands roam all down her back.

Before Luca knows it, Bethany has him pinned to the bed, her thighs straddling his waist. Luca's mind flashes to the scene from earlier with Bethany giving chest compressions to the patient below her. He chuckles but is cut off as a tongue laves its way over the side of his neck. Seconds later, Bethany's teeth are nipping and sucking their way to his collarbone. Luca doesn't think he's ever been this turned on.

"I've wanted—" Bethany kisses against the underside of Luca's jaw, "to do this—" then a kiss to his Adam's apple, "for weeks," she finishes with a kiss to his collarbone. Luca moans when Bethany gazes into his eyes. He feels the intensity going straight to his groin.

"Then why haven't you said anything?"

Bethany just shrugs and suddenly looks shy again. "I wasn't sure if you wanted this."

Luca laughs and flips Bethany over so he's the one on top of her. "Are you kidding me?" He grabs Bethany's wrists and pins them above her head. "I took you out! I even had to endure Damien telling me how 'whipped' I am over you," he punctuates each word with a kiss down Bethany's neck.

Bethany giggles and leans up to capture Luca's lips again. They kiss for a few more minutes and Luca's just beginning to trail his hands down Bethany's body before she protests and rolls out from under him.

"No, I'm not having sex with you in a break room, Mr. Michaelson."

"Oh come on," his whine is raspy. "I've been a good boy for far too long. Now it's about time for me to do something bad."

Bethany laughs and rolls her eyes. Just as she's about to ponder the thought, her pager goes off. It's her cue so she gets up, gathers herself and walks towards the door. "See you later, Dr. Luca."

Luca silently wills his manhood to go back down.

———

Two days later and they still haven't done *anything*.

Luca is convinced that Bethany is doing this to drive him crazy.

Maybe she's conspiring with Holly. The two trauma surgeons have become close and formed a team of sorts. When they're not performing surgeries together, Holly is joining them at their lunch table or butting into their conversations. She seems to take great joy in Luca's frustration and Luca doesn't find it amusing.

They're all sitting around a table in the hospital cafeteria and Bethany is telling the story of her first solo surgery. Luca's hand slowly inches its way up to Bethany's thigh. Bethany is so absorbed in spinning the tale for Holly that she isn't even aware of what Luca is doing.

Luca grumbles and tightens his grip.

Bethany startles a little and looks in his direction. Luca smiles innocently and playfully blows a kiss without Holly noticing. Holly sighs and gets up when she feels her pager going off.

Luca comes over and sits next to her wanting to kiss but Bethany slowly pulls away. "Luca," she rebukes. "We're at work."

Luca smiles while his hand wanders a little higher on Bethany's thigh and brushes against the clit area. This time, her breath hitches and her bottom lip slips in between her teeth. Luca finds the sight amazing. "So?" he breathes into Bethany's ear.

Bethany shakes herself out of her stupor and pulls back to look at Luca again. Her expressions shifts and she glances around before dropping her voice to almost a whisper. "We can't do this here. You should come over tonight."

"Hmm, so you're inviting me to your place for what reason?"

"Do you want me to spoil the surprise?"

Luca can't do anything but swallow and shake his head. At that, Bethany smiles and entwines her fingers with Luca's hand. She stands and pulls Luca towards the exit, all the while keeping a firm grip on his hand. "Come on, let's go watch that cardiac procedure Amber was rambling about earlier."

———

For the next hour, Luca is paying close attention to Bethany's hand resting nicely in his. He can't help but think that their hands fit pretty well together.

Luca sees that Bethany is a tease.

Every few minutes, the brunette trauma surgeon leans over to whisper something in Luca's ear and all the neurosurgeon can focus on is her warm breath ghosting over the shell of his ear. Bethany's thumb is rubbing patterns into Luca's hand, and he doesn't think he can remember one second of the surgery Amber is performing.

Their shifts are finally over and Bethany is trying to open the door to her apartment but is failing quite spectacularly with Luca's arms wrapped around her from behind as she's being sucked on the neck.

There's a dangerous feeling spreading throughout his body as he strokes his hand through Bethany's hair. He's never felt like this; this pure adoration is completely foreign. Yet, Bethany still doesn't cave into his wishes and after an hour of foreplay and dinner, Dr. Michaelson is once again out the door.

———

It's been going on a month now and Luca is wondering where he and Beth are going in this relationship. They never had a deep conversation, but Luca is sure it's not just a fling. Yet, he often wonders, *"Are we serious? Or just friends with limited benefits?"* Luca isn't sleeping with anyone and he's almost sure Bethany isn't either. They spend every minute if they're not in the operating room with each other.

For the first time, Luca finds himself wanting to settle down. He would like to show Bethany off to his family. It would be nice if he could come home to her, eat dinner and spend the night.

Surprisingly one day, Luca is willing to ask his co-worker, Thomas for advice. For once in life, he didn't want to fuck this up.

The moment he does, he's in an empty hospital hallway being grilled by Damien and Amber, while Thomas' sitting off to the side.

"Is she good in bed?"

"Have you scored yet dude?"

"Sickos, if you don't mind, I came here to talk to Thomas, not to be interrogated."

Amber puts her hand over her mouth, while Damien looks like he's going to continue pressing.

Thomas sees what's about to happen and comes to the rescue. "What's up, Luca?"

Luca slumps back against the wall and scrubs a hand across his face. "I don't know what to do about the nurse."

"Who, Bethany?"

"Yeah, who else would I be talking about?"

"My bad, dude. What's up?"

"I like her and have never felt like this over a girl before. I'm almost thirty and I feel like if I don't do something soon then—"

Amber hears Luca and comes over to put her hands on his shoulders. Luca didn't even realize he was hyperventilating. "Calm down."

"Have you gone on a date with her?"

Luca nods.

"Okay. Have you done other things?"

Luca nods again.

Damien yells. "Okay Mr. I-don't-do-girlfriends, she's your girlfriend. What's the problem?"

"She's not my girlfriend!" Luca yells, flinging his arms out. "Sure, we've slept together and gone on some dates, but she's not my girlfriend!"

Thomas' eyes go wide as Bethany comes out of a room nearby and just stands there. Her demeanor spells disappointment and Luca's stomach drops to his feet.

"Damn, she heard me!" is all he thinks at the moment

"Is that all I am to you?" Bethany's voice is low and cracking. "Just some fuck? A toy to have fun with?" A bitter laugh escapes her mouth as she reaches for her glasses.

Luca can barely breathe. "Bethany, listen—"

"No!" The word is so sharp Luca stumbles back. "I don't want to hear it! Whatever this was, which I had the wrong idea about, is over."

Luca reaches out for Bethany's hand and she backs

up. "Don't touch me! You liar!" She dashes off with tears streaming down her cheeks.

"No, Beth," Luca mumbles as he backs up until his back hits the wall and buries his face in his hands. He can't hear Amber, Damien Thomas calling his name.

None of it matters. Bethany's gone and it's his fault.

CHAPTER TWENTY

A week passes and Luca avoids the on-call room at all costs. He tries to schedule his shifts so they don't coincide with Bethany's and tries to avoid all conversations outside of work.

Amber has had it with his moping and has tried to convince Luca to talk to Bethany. Every time she does, she receives the same response: "She asked me not to talk to her, so I'm respecting her wishes. I don't need her."

Luca misses the warmth of Bethany's palm in his and her quiet laughter that she always tried to muffle into his neck. He misses the kisses Bethany would press to on side of his neck for their dinner dates. He even misses the 'no sex in the on-call room' rule because it meant she respected herself.

So, Luca goes through the motions. He goes to work, performs his duties, saves lives, and tries not to get in anyone's way, especially Bethany's. More often than not, he ends up at night at the bar across the street after work before calling an Uber to take him home. He hates being home alone. Bethany's silence is closing in and suffocating him.

Luca's bed feels hard and cold, devoid of the warmth and sweat that usually occupied the sheets when he dreamt about Bethany. The mattress seems far too large; an empty space adding to the feeling of remorse.

He's never been so wrecked over someone, not even his cat when it had run away.

———

Back in the OR the next morning, Luca's reeling from his thoughts. He shakes his head and tries to refocus on the patient lying on the operating table. The lights are too bright and his hands are too unsteady.

"Dr. Michaelson?" Thomas calls Luca in his professional doctor's voice. Luca looks up to find him peering over his mask, his scalpel frozen in midair. "You okay?"

Luca clears his throat and rolls his shoulders backward. There's a pop as his neck cracks, soreness from his sleepless nights. "I'm fine." Thomas looks skeptical but doesn't press on.

———

There's an entourage awaiting Luca when he finishes scrubbing at the end of the operation. Amber is at the head of the nursing station with a scowl on her face. Damien looks as if he's trying to pretend he doesn't want to be there and Holly is a little further back and looks like she was forced to tag along.

"This needs to end right now, Michaelson," Amber emphasizes every word intently.

"I don't know what you're talking about, Amber."

"You need to go talk to your sweetheart!" Damien bursts out. Everyone turns to him, shocked for his bluntness. "Look, it's not like you to be so torn up about a girl, man. I hate to admit but you've been looking like a lost puppy for the last week." Luca is shocked at Damien, never having seen him so serious. "Also, for all of our benefit, your moping has been fucking depressing."

Luca was just about to walk away until he hears someone clearing their throat. It's Holly coming forward.

"Please talk to her, okay?" Holly looks at Luca concerned. "The woman's a mess, acting like she doesn't care. For the last week, Bethany can barely look anyone in the eye. Every time she sees you she gets hopeful but is disappointed when she sees you're still avoiding her."

Luca clenches his fists and looks at all of his coworkers. "Thanks for all of your concerns, but I'd rather you didn't butt into my business."

A feeling of disappointment is heavy in the air as he walks away.

———

A new evening and Luca sighs for the third time in the past twenty minutes as he gazes down at a patient's chart. He's reread the same sentence over ten times, but the words just can't seem to stop blurring.

He's currently at the nursing station in the ER, a place where Bethany rarely comes down. It's become Luca's new hiding spot.

It's been a slow night. A few cooking accidents that ended in a trip to the ER and a few car accidents. But nothing out of the usual.

That's until a new patient stumbles through the doors.

The man is bloody. It's unclear whether it is his own, but there doesn't seem to be any running blood or open wounds. The man is tall and lanky, shaking like a leaf that will be blown away any minute. His eyes are dark and bloodshot red and he looks in a daze. Luca was about to stand up when he heard a voice nearby.

"Sir? Are you alright?"

Luca gets out of his chair quickly seeing Bethany standing in front of the stranger with both arms outstretched. "Sir, do you need any help?"

Then in slow motion, almost as if the man's snapping out of a daze, his head jerks up and eyes gazing on Bethany's. A split-second later, the man is charging in her direction causing Bethany to slam against the wall. The impact sent some triage kits to the ground.

The man's grip on Bethany tightens as he slams her up against the wall for a second time. Then, Bethany grabs for his arms but she's too slow. He tosses her to the ground and kicks her in the stomach. A second later, the crazy man's pinning Bethany down on the ground with his hands going for her throat.

The whimper slipping out of Bethany's mouth is what sends Luca into action. He sees red and nothing else matters except for his girlfriend.

He jumped on the deranged man, "Get off of her!" and manages to grab the guy around the waist and pull him off her.

A minute later, hospital security came to the ER and Luca hands the crazy man off while pushing him away. Luca's hands flit over Bethany's groaning figure on the floor. His heart is racing.

"Bethany," his voice cracks as a few tears run down his cheeks. "Bethany, can you hear me?" A pained moan is the only answer he gets. From Luca's position on the floor, Luca yells to the hospital staff crowded behind him, "We need to get her into trauma! Move it, people!"

―――――――

At his order, everyone snaps into motion. The next few minutes whiz by as the group works as a team to get Bethany into the trauma room and onto the table. She's hooked up to a heart monitor and her vitals are taken.

All Luca can see is the blood staining Bethany's coat and bruises blossoming sickly across her cheek. He's too shaken to check if the blood is Bethany's or the crazed madman's. It doesn't matter. All that matters is that Bethany is in pain.

Minutes later, Holly rushes inside. Her gaze flits to Luca before her eyes stiffened and she's grabbing him by the hand. He's being dragged out of the door as there is panic as more doctors and surgeons arrive.

Bethany is hurt and they're taking him away. They're forcing him out and that's not right. Luca has to be there! His surgeon needs him now more than ever.

"Holly, stop! I need to be with her!" Luca is trying to pull away from her arms around him but suddenly, he feels so powerless. "Bethany needs me! Stop! Let me go! Holly!" Luca sees the head of hospital security, Officer Frank come and grab him from behind, leading him away from the scene.

Luca sits with his hands over his face as the man tries to calm him down. Officer Frank attempts to explain to Luca that Holly needs to go back and can't focus with Luca in the room.

"If anything fucking happens to her, it's on you all," Luca yells.

It really doesn't matter. None of Officer Frank's words matter to Luca at this very moment.

Luca is in an empty trauma room while Thomas is standing guard at the door trying to distract him and it isn't working.

"I'm sure she's fine!" Thomas smiles. "Holly should be here any minute now—"

As if summoned by some hidden freak of nature, Holly walks through the door with a clipboard. She looks exhausted, but there's not a sign of the look they always had when the doctors deliver bad news to the families.

Holly cuts right to the chase. "Bethany's fine." Her words caused Luca to let out an exhale; an invisible weight of gravity being lifted off his shoulders. "She's got some minor scrapes and bruising, along with some nasty internal bruising to her abdomen. Her head cat scan showed no major issues, but she does have a concussion. We're going to keep her for a day or two for observation." Holly pauses as if she was debating her next set of words.

"Bethany's very lucky you were there, Dr. Michaelson. That crazy guy would have killed her if it wasn't for your help."

Instead of asking to run off to Bethany's bedside as Thomas and Holly believes Luca will do, he sighs in relief and then turns to go rest in the on-call room.

———

Just because Bethany got hurt and Luca saved her life doesn't mean she doesn't want to see him. Luca wants nothing more than to make Bethany happy but still, he stays away.

A week later and he still hasn't seen her. He's taken his avoidance to another level, ducking into empty rooms and supply closets whenever he sees the brunette trauma surgeon coming his way. She appears to have recovered quickly, with only a few scrapes and bruises still visible.

But Bethany seems to be moodier than ever. On more than one occasion, Luca saw the trauma surgeon snapping at Holly and his other colleagues.

It's late on a Friday night and Luca is walking down the hallways of the ICU with no real place to go in mind. Just when Luca's thoughts are wandering off to a certain trauma surgeon *again*, his pager goes off.

It's from trauma in OR three. Luca assumes it's Holly and huffs before taking off down the opposite end of the hallway.

When he comes inside the operating room masked, he

finds the hospital staff is already cleaning up from an operation.

And Bethany is standing in the room's center as the only doctor on sight.

Luca does everything to keep his composure though his heart is racing faster than ever. "You paged?" He prays his voice doesn't crack.

Bethany crosses her arms and slightly grins. "Yes, I did." She chuckles but stops abruptly. "Since this seems to be the only way I'll be able to talk to you."

Luca tries to conceal his facial expression but fails when he sees Bethany's eyes harden.

"Doctor, listen—"

A burst of laughter comes from the trauma surgeon. "No! You do not get to avoid me for close to three weeks and then try and talk your way out of this! You're going to listen to me now whether you like it or not."

Luca steps back and raises his hands to show his peace. Bethany sighs before taking her scrub cap off and clutching it in her hands. "I wanted to thank you, for saving my life," her eyes are fixed on the ground. "I could have died that night. So, you know, I'm grateful for your assistance. Thanks."

Luca opens his mouth to speak but Bethany holds up a finger halting him. "I need you to tell me," she pauses for a second before looking straight into Luca's eyes while her gaze is piercing his soul. "I need you to tell me what you were saying that night with Damien, Amber, and Thoms," she demands, with no room for excuses.

Luca sighs and slumps back against the wall. "Bethany, I like you and all—"

He doesn't get far before he's being interrupted again. "I more than like you!" Bethany's words ripped Luca's heart out, causing his hands to thrust forward. "Damn it!" he curses and starts pacing back and forth.

The urge to tell her what he meant is stronger than ever. Bethany cares for him, probably more than Luca feels for her. Their relationship has been on pause over a huge misunderstanding. With Luca never feeling this way over a woman, damn it if he's not going to let this go now.

"You mean—" Lucas sighs and steels himself by walking forward a few steps. "You mean the world to me." Bethany's shocked look urges him on. "That night, I was trying to get advice from Thomas and ask about what to do next about us. Then I lied when Damien and Amber kept pressing me. I'm sorry." he gestures. "Still, we never once had a conversation about *what* we want in this relationship."

Bethany crosses her arms again. "Wasn't it obvious? Did I think you would want me for more than a quick fuck? Maybe. Luca, I heard about your other rendezvous and I'm not that kind of girl, you know. From the beginning, you never once said where we're going with this-"

"I didn't want you to hear that! Most of that nonsense isn't true." Luca's tone grows desperate not wanting to let Bethany continue to doubt him. "I never brought it up and was waiting for the right time to have a conversation about it."

Bethany still looks wary causing Luca to step forward and grab for one of her hands. The warmth of Bethany's palm in his is almost enough to stop him in his tracks but he has to reassure her. "You're the first person I've ever considered being in a relationship with. I'm almost thirty and have never felt for a person the way I feel about you. I don't know how to express that but with you, I'm willing to find out."

Bethany's mouth is hanging open in shock, her eyes twinkling with hope. She still hasn't let go of Luca's hand. "Bethany, you're the most wonderful person I've met, inside and out. You always put your patients' needs before your own, even when you don't need to. Don't ever doubt that you're the perfect soul for me."

Her grip tightens before speaking. "You're meaning to tell me that this was just a huge misunderstanding? That all you meant by that was that you needed to ask me first?"

Luca just nods as a lump suddenly forms in his throat at the wide smile Bethany shoots his way. A second passes before Bethany's fingers are twining into Luca's curly hair and he's being tugged forward.

Their lips slam together, weeks of desperation pouring out between them. Luca moans obscenely into Bethany's mouth as his tongue runs along her teeth. As Bethany sucks at Luca's bottom lip, he slips his hands to her ass and squeezes. The laugh he receives is lost in the moment.

They remain like this for minutes. The quietness of a

weekday night in the OR. There is nothing else to disturb them as they wrapped around each other like a blanket.

Luca pulls away slightly. "So," he whispers. "Be my fiance?" he grins and Bethany can do nothing but chuckle pulling Luca in for another deep long kiss.

CHAPTER TWENTY-TWO

The next morning finds Luca hugging Bethany as the couple walks towards the nurse's station.

Thomas and Holly are resting behind the counter, the first of the two looking far too merry for the early hour. Amber is furiously writing in a chart, and all three of them seem to be disregarding Damien, who is gesturing wildly with a cocky smile on his face, no doubt spinning one of his unbelievable tales to one of nursing assistants.

Luca squeezes Bethany's hand as she nervously pushes her thick-rimmed glasses up her nose. It's amazing to see how comfortable the trauma surgeon can be and then turn immediately shy around others.

"Your attention everyone," Luca says after clearing his throat. The four surgeons look up at him, their eyes zeroing in on their clasped hands. "I would like to introduce you to someone," Luca says with a flourish as he tugs Bethany forward slightly. She's already blushing this early in the morning.

Amber's face shows confusion. "Luca, we already know—"

Luca interrupts her with an eye roll and his fingers tighten minutely around Bethany's. "Everyone, meet Bethany," he smirks quickly before continuing. "My fiance."

Bethany puts her hand over her mouth in shock. Luca hears Amber and Holly cheering and Thomas clapping. He can even hear Damien letting out a sigh of relief with a 'thank god' muttered.

Bethany continues smiling as she leans forward to give Luca a small peck. As she goes to pull away, Luca snakes a hand into her dark hair and opens his mouth. Bethany gasps in pleasure as they kiss, not giving a damn if they have an audience.

As they continue kissing, Luca can hear everyone's pagers go off. The four other surgeons scoff and laugh as they run off down the hall, leaving the two lovebirds alone.

Bethany sighs and rests her forehead against Luca's. "I think they will need us," she says as she goes to reach for his pager. Luca stops her by grabbing her face and rubbing her cheeks.

"They can wait a few minutes," he says into the stillness between their lips. Bethany smiles as they bask in comfortable silence. "Hey, Beth?" Bethany hums and Luca takes a deep breath. "I love you."

Bethany looks a bit in shock and then her expression changes into one of total peace. "I love you too." They're already at the word 'love' and Luca doesn't have a problem with it. He knows what he feels for Bethany is a once-in-a-lifetime thing. He's sure they'll get married soon.

"Winstead! Michaelson! We need you in the ER!"

With that, Bethany gives Luca another quick peck before she's being pulled down the hallway, both of their game faces are on.

And they will be alright.

AL

PROLOGUE

Numb—the only word that can describe Detective Cynthia Jones. She's been sitting in the lobby of the precinct for hours senseless, unaware of how long.

"We'll take care of it. We're on it. We'll get to the bottom of this," Captain Rowland says escorting Cynthia to his patrol car. "We'll find those responsible. Let's get you home."

Just like that, her partner, Kenneth Miller was killed returning home from his shift earlier in the day. Flags were lowered at half staff around the city and the Mayor and Police Chief vowed to find his killers. With Kenneth's sudden departure, there wasn't even a sign to hold onto for a God's sake.

Cynthia's vision blurs; the Vogue magazines on her table are swimming around. This wasn't supposed to happen. She was so close, having the perfect partner on the force and was finally in love. Kenneth and Cynthia dated for close to six months after meeting on the force. He had proposed to her just two weeks ago, only to have him ripped away.

Cynthia curls up on the couch, drifting until someone knocks.

CHAPTER TWENTY-THREE

Six Weeks Ago

It's hard to remember a time Cynthia hasn't seen her former lover and partner, Detective Kenneth Miller go over his paycheck's deductions from his desk in the corner. This is Detective Cynthia Jones' first day back at work and she was called down to the coroner's office. As she walks down the hall, no one looks up at her. Kenneth's death is fresh in everyone's mind. The moment she reaches the door, the coroner yells "Poison!"

"That's it?" Cynthia looks on folding her arms. "You could have called me?"

"Despite having the latest technology in this room, I still prefer to meet face-to-face." The coroner looks at his papers and hands them to Cynthia. "We found thallium sulfate on the victim."

"What's that?"

"It's a tasteless, odorless, colorless liquid. The symptoms often mask as other symptoms and are almost impossible to detect."

"Are we talking about the jogger from the park? I thought you said he died from heart failure."

"That was my initial prognosis, Detective. Once, I got the body on my good old-fashioned table here, I found a bit more than what I was expecting."

"Sounds like you're fond of your work?"

"Yes, indeed."

Officer Al Sanchez walks in and snatches the report from her. "Give me that back," Cynthia said pinching him.

"You already read it."

Cynthia snatches it back, "Thank you, Officer."

"How are you doing, Detective? It's good to see you."

"I'm better. I needed the time off. Thanks."

Cynthia smiles at coroner's handwriting. "This is some old-fashioned scribbling." She gives the papers back. "So. I guess the question is - who wanted this guy dead?"

"That's up your alley, Detective," Officer Al said.

"Of course, smart ass—Al. Let's go. I need to talk to Samuel's wife."

"After you, Ma'am."

"Tea, Detective?" Mrs. Janson said wiping her tears.

"No, thank you," Cynthia replies looking at the photos on the mantel.

"You, Officer?"

"No, thanks, ma'am," Al said flipping through his notes. Mrs. Janson puts the kettle on the table and goes inside the kitchen. Al turns to Cynthia, "I wouldn't if I were you."

"Wouldn't what?" Al looks toward the kitchen.

"Never mind. Hey, those photos on the mantle don't have Samuel in them."

"I didn't notice. I'm only an officer."

"Just stop it. Changing subjects, why don't you have some tea then?" Cynthia said. "Scared?"

"Better to live than die."

Cynthia pinches Al. "You're such a mess."

"One life to live."

"Funny! This is coming from the man who talks bad about my favorite soap opera," Cynthia said moving closer to Al.

"I said I'd be more careful, remember? Almost got killed the last time I took charge."

"I'm glad. Would you have knocked the cup out of my hands if I were to take a sip?"

"I would have if I thought it was poisoned," Al said staring into Cynthia's eyes. "Remember, I've been put in charge to protect you, Detective."

Mrs. Janson returns just as Cynthia ponders her response. She looks at Al as the wife of the late Samuel Janson speaks.

———

Andrew, an employee at Samuel Janson's coffee shop in town, grasps his stomach and collapses while Cynthia and Al are interviewing him. *That could have been me*, she thinks, watching him wither on the floor. She's down next to Al holding Andrew.

"Oh my god!" says the clerk.

"Hurry, ma'am. Get me some cold water," Cynthia said.

"Dispatch—We have a thirty-three. Tell the boys to bring Prussian Blue for poisoning. Hurry, we're at—" Al looks up seeing the girl run for the phone.

"Yes, sir. They're five minutes away. Over and out—"

Andrew groans, "I feel... like I'm on fire."

"Can you tell me what you ate or drank in the last 24 hours?" Cynthia said.

"I had—" Andrew squirms.

Al pats Andrew. "Hang in there, buddy. Help's on the way."

———

Cynthia watches as Al talk with the paramedics. She comes up and flashes her ID while they're loading Andrew into the ambulance. "Thank God, you were here to save us, Big Al," Cynthia said as the ambulance pulls off.

"That's what I do."

"Our suspect knows we're on his trail."

"I believe so, Detective."

———

Nothing is ever that easy. The Investigative Unit went over every inch of the coffee shop but found no traces of thallium sulfate. Cynthia's team had spent hours going over the security footage, resulting in no new leads.

"So, I'm back to square one?" Cynthia's eyelids are beginning to feel like they're sticking to her eyeballs. "Time for a break." She turns to Al, who's been on patrol making sure no one except authorized staff enters. "I've looked over these case files for the fifth time today and still zilch," Cynthia said putting them inside her briefcase. "Boys, let's wrap this up in five."

"Ok, Ma'am."

"Big Al, let's go get something to eat and—?"

"And what?" He said glancing up at the clock.

Cynthia's tone was awkward. "Oh, I'm sorry for intruding. Maybe you have a date or two—"

"No, ma'am." Al touches her forearm. "I don't." She stares at him and Al said, "Unless you count my partner, Barry in. He's at home waiting for me to get off. He usually makes dinner for us."

Cynthia smiles, aware of Al's hand still resting on her arm while she clicks on her laptop. She should move, and let it drop, but she doesn't want it to move. The memory of Al's eyes earlier and promise to protect her has her mystified. Just as Cynthia starts to daydream, she lifts her hand to move the mouse on her laptop. Al's hand moves back. "I guess I'm in a threesome if Barry comes along."

"Oh my God! You have such a dirty mind. Barry's a home body. He's not coming."

"Don't mind me."

Cynthia shuts down her computer and Al gets up. "Let me give Barry a call and tell him I'll be late."

Cynthia sighs and folds her hands. "Now, who sounds like they're in a relationship?"

"No, he's just my roommate."

"Right—buddy."

Cynthia realizes that her thumb had been stroking where her wedding band used to be.

Al comes back into the room. "We're good."

"Great! Do you like pizza?"

———

Turns out Al doesn't like pizza, at least not the kind Cynthia was thinking of; quick slices on-the-go. He suggests a bistro named Janson's in town, with some of the best pasta Al claims he had tasted on this side of the Atlantic.

The place is more intimate than Cynthia expects; candlelights and couples lingering over glasses of wine. The place is nearly empty despite being dinner hour. Glancing over the menu, it's more pricey than Cynthia expected. "Maybe we should just get a couple of hot dogs and take them back to the station."

"Oh, come on," Al said looking over the menu. "If we did so, we'd waste hours in traffic."

"Well, unless your salary is three times more than a detective's, I think I'm going to have to order the—" Cynthia purposely picks the cheapest thing, "pasta e Fagioli."

"So cheap," Al said. "You must think I brought you here to spend all of your money. I'm here for a reason."

"What reason, Mr. Al?"

Al cuts his eyes toward a waiter a few tables over, pouring wine for a couple more interested in each other than their meal.

"The waiter? He's probably a college student working part-time. What do you think?"

"Why are you asking?"

Al shakes his head. "Never mind. Look at the manager over there near the kitchen."

"Whoa... did Samuel... rise from the dead?"

"Maybe." Al giggles. "The waiter is Samuel Janson's cousin, Bill. I had my boys look into Samuel and found them all here."

Cynthia closes the menu seeing the cover. *Janson's*. "I can't believe I didn't notice."

"I think someone wasn't happy in the family business."

"Maybe," Cynthia said. "Have you eaten here before?"

"No. But Barry told me the food is 'to die for.' Let us hope he doesn't mean that literally."

The waiter starts walking toward them and Cynthia said, "Put the files away, Al. Hurry!" She pulls up her menu and pretends to read it.

"Actually, I want him to see these."

"Oh my God! No—"

"How are you folks doing this fine evening?" The waiter took out his pen. "Is this your first time at Janson's, sir?"

"It is, actually. I think I'll have some pasta but what do you recommend?" Al opens his menu beside the folder, marked with Samuel's name. "Or maybe I'll go with something with seafood in it? "

Cynthia watches Bill Janson out of the corner of her eye. His eyes widen when he sees the file and his hands are shaking. "Our baked ziti is some of the best in Manhattan, you can't go wrong there." He takes a step backward and glances back as if looking for an escape.

"I'm not sure what I want." Cynthia pulls out her badge and places it on the table. "Maybe we can talk about your best dishes back at the station."

Janson breaks and runs directly for the kitchen causing the patrons in the restaurant to yell. Cynthia pulls out her gun and her cell phone out at the same time, tossing the latter to Al. "Call for backup!"

Cynthia enters the kitchen yelling, "Freeze!" The kitchen staff is in shock as they come out one by one. Janson overturns a tureen and a cart and Cynthia fires off a warning shot. "Don't make this any worse, Mr. Janson!" Finding himself cornered, Bill grabs a knife from the rack and brandishes it.

"Drop it, Mr. Janson. It'll be a lot easier for you if you just come with me."

"Why?" He slashes with the knife and lunges. "You've already decided I'm guilty."

Cynthia's sure he's guilty now but she's not going to be his judge or jury. She takes another step closer. "You can tell your side of the story at the station. We are good listeners."

Bill slashes again, and Cynthia moves backward. Her back hits the edge of a counter, and that gives Bill just enough room to slash at her hand. She moves it just in time but the gun goes flying and skitters under a stove. Cynthia stumbles trying to grab something - a pot, a pan, a tray - anything that will block him. Her hands close around something and it's heavy enough. She grabs it and hits Bill. "Fuck!"

The back door bursts open, and Al comes charging in. "No, Al—" Cynthia yells looking for her gun. Al tackles Janson to the floor but Janson still has the knife.

"Al! He's armed—"

Janson plunges at Al and Al twists out of the way, but not enough. The knife cuts through Al's coat and Bill loses the knife. As Al subdues Bill, Cynthia manages to kick the knife away. Bill's hands are now behind his back and he's handcuffed.

Cynthia is by Al's side. "Are you okay?" She yanks off

her jacket and presses it against the wound now starting to stain his maroon waistcoat. Cynthia wanted to ask why Al didn't just wait for the damn backup, but she knows she owes him her life.

"It's not as bad as it looks." Al's blood is soaking through her jacket. "Cynthia, if I die, I—"

"Shh," she said. "No one's dying today." Not on my watch. Hang in there. The paramedics are on their way."

Cynthia presses harder, comforting Al until they arrive. She holds Al's hand as the paramedics work on him.

———

At the hospital, Cynthia stands by his side with his roommate, Barry.

"I'm so glad you made it through surgery in one piece," Cynthia said.

"I told you I'm here to protect you."

"Hey, Al. You're going to get yourself killed over a woman."

"For this one, I might."

"Stop it, Al. You're making me blush."

They chat for a bit and days later when Al's well enough, Cynthia doesn't ask him yet about what he was going to tell her.

CHAPTER TWENTY-FOUR

Cynthia doesn't really hear it at first, she's detached from awareness barely feeling the covers above her. Someone's knocking.

Go away. Leave me alone. I'm enjoying this nothingness.

But someone knocks again. "Cynthia?" The voice slams her back to reality.

Her heart pounds, as the room's springs back to clarity. Still, she feels locked in the prison of her nothingness.

"Cynthia, please open the door. It's Al."

———

Three Weeks Ago

Cynthia's back at work and somehow it feels worse than the weeks Al was in the hospital. Not because she couldn't see him every day - she could, but because she couldn't work with him since he was assigned to desk duty.

She's lost track of the number of times she turned to Al to ask what he was going to say only to find Detectives Dustin and Liam or the Coroner Dr. Wesley interrupting. *She'll ask Big Al whenever she gets time.*

Cynthia sends Barry messages asking if Al is well enough to lead her detail again and Barry asks but Al tells him Captain Rowland hasn't given him the okay. The day Al is sent back as Cynthia's detail, he texts, "I'll meet you there."

"And—"Cynthia texts.

"I'll be there in twenty minutes."

"I guess," she texts back.

———

They're standing over the latest victim - an old woman who's sitting peacefully in front of her television. Al and Cynthia cover their noses at the stench of the corpse. Through his scarf, Cynthia says, walking around the armchair, "Our victim here could have passed away from anything. But do you see the ruddiness of her cheeks?

"Yes, I see them."

"Well, normally, the body after several days would turn blue. Call Dustin in here to check the kitchen."

"Yes, ma'am."

"There's no carbon monoxide here. All of the appliances run on electric," Dustin said. "I will get the guys to do a full inspection once you guys are finished." Dustin tilts his head at Cynthia gesturing she's ready to leave with Al.

"Ok, Dustin. Thanks, I'll take Mr. Sanchez with me to go pay a visit to one of her relatives."

"Detective, I'd like to ask for your permission to go back to the station."

"I already texted Rowland. She won't be needing you."

"Yes, ma'am—" Al puts his scarf back over his nose.

"I need you to give me a ride? I took a taxi over here."

"No, problem."

———

Cynthia watches Al as they head for his patrol car. He seems healthy. What's going on with him then?

"I'm doing better," Al said as when Cynthia asks him. He's looking sideways as he drives. "Do you remember anything about that night?"

"Just a little. They put me to sleep in the ambulance. I'm just glad Janson didn't poke me in the heart."

"I'm glad, too. You were so fussy at the hospital. I thought they would keep you sedated."

"I was?"

"Yes, you were, Big Al."

Then there was a long silence.

Cynthia had stopped talking.

If she meets Al's eyes, she will kiss him. Al had saved her life again and Cynthia knew she owed him.

"I'm sorry," Al says after they've been on the road a while.

"What are you talking about, Al?" Cynthia sees Al's eyes on her, but she keeps hers on the road.

"I'm glad you were there—"

Her eyes break from the road. "I had to—" she says, turning her attention back. "It was a close call."

"Yes, it feels weird when one has suffered a loss one."

Even as Cynthia nods, she's reminded of his words before the ambulance came. "Al…"

"Yes, Detective?"

"Before, when you thought you were dying…"

"I nearly did."

Cynthia senses Al's trying to change topics. "What were you trying to tell me?"

"Ah." Al's gaze falls toward his hands. "I wanted… to tell you not to worry. That I would see you again."

"If you died, you'd see me again?" Cynthia laughed. "Where in heaven?"

"Maybe so or hell." Al reflects on what to say next. "You know my head wasn't on straight after losing all that blood. I just hoped to see you again."

"Okay, Al." Cynthia says under her breath, "I see I'm not going to get your confession today."

"What did you say?"

"Nothing, Big Al."

Cynthia has heard her share of deathbed confessions

and getting the truth out of Al was going to be hard. "Well, I'm glad you're okay. Thanks for saving my life again."

"What are partners for?" Al shrugs and concentrates back on the road.

———

The autopsy on the old woman had come back. It wasn't what Dustin or Cynthia expected. The woman actually died from carbon monoxide despite not having gas appliances in her apartment. "This is a murder, then," Cynthia said balancing her phone on one ear as she types the victim's information into her laptop. "Penelope O'Shea. There's not much on her: never been in trouble, married for thirty years before her husband died of a heart attack. No children, no significant assets, not even a car. "I can't imagine why anyone would want to kill an old woman as sweet as this lady."

"There's always a reason," Dustin says on the other line. "This was premeditated."

"Probably." Cynthia grabs her things. "Time to interview the neighbors. Do you want to come along?"

"I'm on my way." When Cynthia reaches her car, she realizes she hasn't called Al to accompany her. She texts him before starting the engine.

———

A moving van is out in front of the building when they arrive. Cynthia sees a woman looking onward while movers come in and out of the building. "Excuse me, ma'am. May we talk to you for a second? This is Detective Dustin Holiday and I'm Detective Cynthia Cowens."

The woman frowns. "I'm Natalie Gaines. Is there something wrong?"

Cynthia looks at Dustin. "Did you know Penelope O'Shea, the old woman who died in this building?"

"Mrs. O'Shea?" The woman glances toward the third-floor window. "I saw her around, walking to the bodega on the corner in the mornings, doing things around the apartment building, but I didn't know her personally. Really sad that she passed away. Guess it was the old woman's time."

"Well, we are not convinced that it was yet," Dustin said. "We're here to investigate her murder."

"Murder? Oh, God!" The woman put her hands over her mouth. "Here? The crime rate's the lowest it's been in years."

"Well, murder can happen anywhere, no matter how safe the neighborhood is, Ma'am," Cynthia said writing something on her notepad. "Do you recall anyone being close to Mrs. O'Shea?"

The woman thinks. "Ah—maybe Mr. Pak on the second floor? I saw them working on the rooftop garden together every start of spring." Her voice lowers. "I always thought they'd be perfect for each other, both widowed, around the same age…"

Cynthia's face blushes, thinking of Al. Do people talk about Cynthia and Al this way around the precinct? "She avoids looking at Al, but the woman gives Cynthia a cue about the hunk next to her. "Well, the two also used to play cards up there, when the weather was nice." The woman glances toward the roof. "It's really beautiful up there."

"Thank you, Ms. Gaines," Cynthia said after getting her details. "We might be in touch." Cynthia and Dustin head into the building, leaving Al outside to monitor the movers.

"This neighborhood is being gentrified. The shop on the corner Ms. Gaines is referring to is closer to a breakfast diner than a bodega," Dustin said as they stop in front of the first door on the second floor. No one comes to any one of the doors, no matter how loud they knock. "Perhaps Mr. Pak's already moved?"

"I think Ms. Gaines would have known that. She seemed to know a lot about both Mrs. O'Shea and Mr. Pak despite her claim of 'not really knowing' them personally."

Cynthia begins to walk toward the stairs. "I'll try again. Go see if you can find someone on the third floor who knows them?" She pulls out her phone as she descends the stairs.

"Ok."

After a few minutes of searching, Dustin comes through with a name - Ned Hamilton - and a number. Cynthia calls while standing in front of a door. Whatever the reason, Ned doesn't pick up and Cynthia leaves a message. Ms. Gaines is on the first floor with the movers, who are finishing up.

"Al?" Cynthia calls down the stairwell. "Did anyone come in here?"

There's no answer.

"Al!" she yells. Is it really that hard to hear down there? Maybe he's busy speaking with someone.

Cynthia jogs downstairs, feeling something is wrong. Where is Al—the man who could get himself into trouble at a moment's notice.

Al's not in the hallway and looking around yields nothing. The sinking feeling doubles as Cynthia looks outside and doesn't see him on post. She goes back inside, stopping at every door to listen—still no Al. Suddenly, Cynthia remembers the rooftop garden. Maybe, he's up there.

"Dustin, come to the second floor. I can't find Al. I'm going up to check on Ned Hamilton."

"I'm coming—" His voice is faint on the line.

Cynthia then calls Ned's number. He doesn't pick up but Cynthia traces a phone ringing to an apartment on the second floor. "Hello?" She said banging on the door. "Mr. Hamilton? Are you in there?" The ringing continues, but Ned doesn't pick up. What is that smell?

Cynthia waits for Dustin to come down and then he kicks in the door. They see a middle-aged man on the floor. As they step inside, they're overwhelmed by the gas.

They cough, stumbling back out into the hallway. "I'm going back in, Dusty."

"Wait."

Cynthia covers her face and goes back inside. Dustin joins her and opens the windows, and then shuts off the stove. Meanwhile, Cynthia bends over to check Mr. Hamilton. He still has a pulse and is covered in blood from a bash to his head. A lamp is on the floor, broken in pieces. Someone did this, then turned on the gas to finish the job.

They can't stay there for long. Back in the hall, Cynthia calls 911. "We need paramedics now." Dustin goes back inside and pulls Mr. Hamilton out while Cynthia heads to check the other rooms, with her gun drawn.

The bedroom door is open. A man in on the bed with a gas mask over his face. Is this Mr. Hamilton's attacker?

Oh my God! It's Al.

Cynthia gasps and coughs. She goes to the window and opens it then kneels down to check on Al.

He has a pulse and no other signs of trauma. "Al? Al, can you hear me?"

There's no response at first but then he groans and rolls his head toward her "Cynthia?"

"Al, what are you—" Cynthia coughs again struggling to pick him up. She wants to say that Al is too heroic for his own good, acting like he has a death wish sometimes like he's some sort of superhero.

By the time she gets him up, Dustin comes back in

and helps. They hear the sirens approaching. They lay Al down beside Mr. Hamilton, and his eyes flutter toward Ned. "It was him, he—" Al coughs and then says, "Handcuffs."

Dustin handcuffs the still-unconscious Mr. Hamilton, asking Al, "Did you knock him out?"

"I—" He coughs again. He levers himself up with a groan to a sitting position, one hand rubbing at his temples. "Call Barry, tell him Procedure Three."

"What?" Cynthia shouts. "Procedure Three? The paramedics are right outside, Al, and they're taking you."

"Carbon monoxide—" He wobbles,"...can cause brain—" He sighs. "Can't work if—" Al slumps over groaning.

"Al!"

Dustin runs out to the hallway. "Up here, on the second floor!"

"Call Barry—" Al murmurs, and then there are several incoherent words. Cynthia leans in, to try to catch whatever Al's trying to say. "Need Barry now—don't worry—my Cynthia." He stops talking and she feels his lips brush her cheek.

Al passed out, but the paramedics are there, asking Cynthia questions as they take Barry and Ned downstairs. She calls Barry during the ambulance ride.

"Procedure Three, Al said. What's that?" Cynthia said.

"Ok. What hospital are you going to?"

"New York-Presbyterian."

"Ok, I'm on my way. I'll call backup. Thanks, Cynthia."

"What's Procedure—"

The phone hangs up. Cynthia doesn't even get an explanation. She stares at the phone, trying to hold on to the memory of Al's lips on her as if it will keep him alive.

CHAPTER TWENTY-FIVE

The voice is distinct. Cynthia feels her mind playing tricks on her but it's a voice she desperately needs to hear again?

It doesn't matter. She finds herself walking across the hardwood floor as if in a dream, her fingers curling around the doorknob, and turning.

Cynthia regains her conscious in enough time to stop herself. This is madness.

In the past several months, she's learned to accept things that once seemed insane in stride. It was part of the rollercoaster ride of getting to know Officer Al Sanchez. She came to embrace it, the excitement of not knowing what awaited her day to day, making each new case an adventure.

But this? Hearing Al's voice on the other side of the door - a voice silenced forever - is beyond madness.

Cynthia closes her eyes for a moment, takes a deep breath, and then pulls aside the door curtain to look.

Three Weeks Ago

She heads for the hospital as soon as possible the next morning, after staying with Al until she could barely stay up. His partner, Officer Barry put several bills into her hand, told her to get a taxi, go home and rest. Cynthia's thoughts are filled with images of shootings, drownings, car wrecks, stabbings and gas leaks. Every scene ends with Al Sanchez trying to tell her something - something important - and then he's gone before he can get the words out. She stares at the wall long before the first rays of sunrise across the windowpane.

Al had been sedated in the ambulance and then later in the hospital bed. As he lay there with an oxygen mask over his face, the doctor had tried being hopeful about his condition. Sanchez hadn't been exposed as much to the carbon monoxide as their murder suspect, Ned Hamilton, he told Cynthia. Hamilton had suffered severe brain damage from the gas - not head trauma, apparently, Al had hit him in just the right spot. Cynthia could fathom what was in the doctor's eyes when he was trying to soften the hard truths. He told her that Al could lose his memory. At any rate, when Al Sanchez wakes up - the doctor told her he couldn't say if Al would be able to work again.

———

A week goes by and it becomes routine that Cynthia checks in at reception at 7 AM and right as she gets off the elevator, there's Barry already there, carrying two paper cups of coffee. "Cynthia!" Glancing at the cups, he says, "Here."

"You drink. I've had enough coffee for the week." She looks at Barry hoping for good news. "Is he awake?

The usual answer is no but today there's something different.

"Yes, Barry's up."

"When?"

"A couple hours ago. The first thing he did was ask for you," Barry says, nudging her. "I was a bit afraid."

"How... how is he?"

"Oh, you know Big Al. He'll bounce back." Barry jerks his head toward Al's room. "Come on, he'll be happy to see you - I was gonna make him wait to call you until after breakfast."

Cynthia walked into the room, not sure what she'll find. "Cynthia! You didn't have to come so early." Al closes his book and places it beside his half-eaten breakfast.

She looks at Barry amazed at Barry's quick recovery.

"Are you kidding me?" Cynthia comes over to the side of the bed, placing her hand in Al's. "Of course, I was coming back right away. But Al, we've got to keep you out of the hospital."

"I agree," he says, while Barry adds, "Amen!"

Cynthia's a bit taken aback, they're both so chipper. "Has the doctor been by to see you?"

"Someone came by about a half-hour ago," Barry says, busying himself with moving a chair for her to sit in. He removes a towel from it. "They're saying it was a miracle that I survived."

"I know, Al."

"I'll undergo an MRI later this morning, and should be ready to go home soon." Al squeezes her hand. "I'm sorry that I keep putting you through all this."

"And after you promised!" Cynthia teases, not letting go. Her thumb traces little circles on his as if to make sure he's going to stay right here. "I'd say don't do that again, but I know you."

"Perhaps I shouldn't make those promises," Al says.

"Maybe."

———

Perhaps, he should go back to life in the Coroner's Office. After all, he's not a detective but was trained with the best. Cynthia should rely on Dustin more and Al less. She'd do it if it meant Al would stop putting himself in danger. But Cynthia had missed him, even more, when he was recovering from that stab wound, but she doesn't know if she can go through this again.

They've been quiet for several minutes. Barry slipped out, sensing that the lovebirds need this time alone. Cynthia won't let go of Al's hand pinpointing the moment Al had gone from mere colleague to friend. Now, he's become someone she cannot imagine life without.

———

Cynthia backs away from the revelation as her guilt begins flooding her. It has been only a year since she lost Kenneth. She knows that this is too soon, even though her body doesn't seem to agree. She gives Al's hand a light parting squeeze and then reaches for the chart hanging from the edge of the bed. Glancing at it, she asks, "So they've given you a clean bill of health?" She smiles at the words at the bottom: The patient is expected to make a full recovery. She puts it back and something catches her eye at the last moment. "Wait... 'Alvareo' Sanchez?"

"What?"

She points to the name on the chart. "It says right here, 'Alvareo Sanchez.'"

Al's mouth opens. "How odd! I'll have Barry take care of it."

She hopes that's all it is - that they got his name wrong. What else could they have gotten wrong? His condition? "Maybe you should get a second opinion after you leave."

"I'm sure it's only a mistake" He stares at Cynthia. "If it would ease your mind, I will."

"Al… what does 'Procedure Three' mean?"

Al turns pale as he opens his mouth. But just then, a nurse comes in, bustling past Cynthia to go beside Al. "Finished with that?" she asks, pointing to the tray. "Not hungry, I see."

"I'm not big on breakfast."

The nurse chuckles. "You and half this floor. Well, you can get something you like better later." She holds up a finger to him. "But after you're gone, Mr. Sanchez. No more unscheduled strolls through the hospital."

"What?" Cynthia said looking at Al. This guy can't stop his shenanigans even here?

"Oh, yeah, we caught this one wandering the halls in the middle of the night, out of his hospital gown, with his coat on," The nurse said pointing at Al. "You've got an MRI in a few minutes. Stay put." She grabs heads out of the room, almost bumping into Barry coming the other way.

"I found a coffee shop with those bagels you like, Al."

"Did you know Mister Al went wandering last night?"

"What?" Barry shakes his head. "Did you sneak out when I was asleep?"

A weird look passes between them. "Yes, I did. I couldn't sleep and now I feel much better."

"Al!" Barry and Cynthia say together.

"Why not? I'm feeling better. No headache, my pain, and my head is on straight. I didn't feel like watching TV out of fear I'd wake you."

"Just because you studied medicine doesn't mean you can diagnose yourself!"

"Yeah… Mr. Alvareo," Cynthia said.

"Cynthia saw a mistake on the chart," Al says, sharing that odd look with Barry again. "She's sharp, even this early in the morning."

"Huh, well, we're getting you out of here the second that MRI is finished," Barry said. "They can't get anything right." Barry turns to Cynthia. "You should come and have lunch with us at my place."

"Well, I…"

"Come on," Barry says.

Cynthia looks over at Al. She's been avoiding getting close to anyone because the last time she did, she lost that person. The closer she gets to Al, the more she's almost lost him. Every sign points to turning in the other direction. But something about Al keeps drawing her in.

"Alright!"

The men smile and Cynthia says, "I'm cooking."

———

After just a quick call to Dustin and Rowland, she finds herself sitting beside Al in the back of a taxi. Barry had insisted on sitting up front. Once they're on the road, she nudges Al. "You sure you're feeling all right?"

"The doctors said I was fit to go home, didn't they?" His eyes stay on the passing buildings.

"Al, tell me the truth."

He turns toward her, then, taking her hand in his. "Alright, here is the complete and honest truth. I've never felt better than I do right now."

"Fine, Al, I believe you." Cynthia laughed it off. "You don't have to say it like that."

"Almost there, lovebirds!"

Cynthia smiles while Al caresses her hand.

———

"I can get out whatever you need," Barry said.

"Just let me have a look, and I'll let you know." She looks inside the cabinets and refrigerator. "Looks like you have everything I need."

Barry leaves out of the kitchen. "I'll leave you be. Think I'll go down to the shop and see if I can't scare up some customers." Cynthia is left with Al, at the table, with a book in his hand.

"I'll be fine here," she tells him. "Go rest and watch some TV."

"I'm fine here, too. I often sit here and read while Barry cooks." He turns a page.

Cynthia takes a bottle of olive oil from the pantry. "Is Barry the usual cook around here?"

Al closes the book. "I dabble sometimes... but Barry is the man."

"So you have a system here?" Cynthia fills a pot with water and adds salt and oil before turning the burner up to medium-high. "I guess you guys have been living here for years?"

"About five. Barry is like family."

"Maybe he is."

"Most of the time, we are but we have our issues sometimes."

"Oh?" Cynthia takes a mixing bowl from a cabinet and puts ground beef inside.

"Barry brought home the wrong tea again," Barry said after opening a cabinet.

"Well, that's family."

Cynthia and Al laugh enjoying this moment without a murder case hanging over them. She starts placing the meatballs into a skillet. "I can't imagine the two of you doing anything worse than bickering over who gets the obituary first."

"You'd be surprised. Once, Barry and I fought and our neighbor called the police on us."

Cynthia drops a meatball. "You, two—what was the argument about?"

"Well, it—" Al doesn't want to tell Cynthia everything. "Just a disagreement over some life decisions."

"I see." Cynthia puts the pasta into the boiling water thinking Al was not ready to open up to her.

Cynthia turns the meatballs and then sets down the

spatula. "Everything looks good, smells good but—" She pauses. "Damn it!"

"What?"

"There's supposed to be garlic in the meatballs. Maybe I can put it in the sauce instead." Cynthia glances around the countertops, opening some of the cupboards.

Al gets close to her. "Let me." Without waiting for Cynthia to move out of the way, he reaches into a cabinet just above her head. His body is only inches away and she's enchanted by the smell of his cologne. His unshaven scruff on his cheeks and chin is so close Cynthia could run her fingers down it by simply lifting her hand. Her eyes are drawn to his long-lashed eyes and lips... She finds herself trapped, not being able to make her muscles obey.

Al pulls down a couple of garlic bulbs. "Here they are." He senses how close they are and how it would take so little movement to close the distance.

They hover there, not moving, not speaking, barely breathing. He seems just as loath to move as she. The moment extends so long that Cynthia knows she has to move, to get out of the way or she will get in trouble.

It's Al who moves, his lips come down on hers, asking for consent. Cynthia pauses before conceding in. Al's lips move slowly waiting for her to take the lead. When she doesn't deepen, Al pulls back to look at her. His head tilts slightly, a non-verbal request for permission to kiss her again. As he waits, his eyes drift down to hers, as if he's hungry for more.

Cynthia pulls Al in. This time there is nothing gentle,

there is no question of whether she's ready for this. She's been in denial for so long.

Al's hands encircle her, one climbing up to tangle in her hair and the other coming up to grip her shirt. His fingers brush her just below where Kenneth's ring hangs. That brief thought flits away as he presses her into the counter, one leg nudging between hers. The closeness, the sensation of it, makes her body thrum. Cynthia's insensate to anything but the pressure.

It's so strong that she almost doesn't respond to the bubbling sound of the pot boiling over. Al pulls away just as the flames leap from the pan.

"Oh my God!"

Al lunges forward to twist the burners to off, and the smoke alarm goes off. Cynthia covers her ears while Al snatches an oven mitt and covers the skillet and the pot. Cynthia sees flames licking up the side of Al's sleeve. "Al!" He steps back and pats out the fire with a kitchen towel.

There's shouting and the couple knows who is doing it. "What the hell have you done to my kitchen!?"

Cynthia looks at Al, he looks back, smokes in the air around them while the alarm is still blaring.

"Sorry, Barry."

"You know what—I don't even wanna know. I should have cooked myself. Get out of my kitchen!"

Al and Cynthia go in the living room, banned from entering the kitchen and just stares at each other. She's not sure who starts laughing first, but soon they both are.

The moment has passed, and Barry, Cynthia, and Al don't mention it for the rest of the day.

Cynthia gets a text while eating, "Looks like we have another dead one, Al."

CHAPTER TWENTY-SIX

Al stands there, shivering from the morning chill, his eyes are bloodshot.

"Al, is that you?"

Cynthia unlocks the door.

"Al…"

It's really him, somehow, in the flesh. "Cynthia," he says, his voice breaks on the single syllable. "I—"

"How?" Her voice breaks. "I saw you—"

"It's—" he smiles. "It's a long story." He gestures inside her apartment. "May I?"

———

A Week Ago

Liam's voice is the first she hears as she enters the Coroner's Office. "Seems to be pretty cut and dry?"

She stays back, to listen to whatever Liam has to say but doesn't enter. Liam's bent over the deceased; one Oscar Warren, a doctor from the Upper East Side. Meanwhile, Al is back on duty and is by the door, looking on with his sweetheart.

"I mean, the bullet was shot at close range. Looks like a nine millimeter," Liam said. "I'd say a right-handed shooter based on the angle of entry, between five and six feet in height, and an amateur." He stops, waiting for comments. But when Cynthia remains silent, he says, "I mean, you're the Investigator in charge here. Wanna come closer?"

"I'm just taking it in," Cynthia cuts him off. "You're correct so far. Go on. I'm listening."

"Glock 19, Generation Four," Liam adds. "One of the most sought after handguns in the black market." Al looks on smiling while checking out Cynthia's rear end.

Cynthia closes her eyes thinking more about Al than the deceased. It's been two weeks since the kiss in the kitchen, and neither one of them has wanted to bring up the subject.

She takes a deep breath and steps fully into the room. "What have you got for me?"

"Detective Jones!" Al says, turning. The subtle shift to using her last name instead of her first is a first.

"Officer Sanchez." Cynthia steps past Al. "Liam, you said something about a Glock 19?"

"Yes." Liam points to the bullet wound with his scalpel.

"Alright, so we have a murder," Cynthia says. "So?"

"It might be a crime of passion rather than a robbery."

"Was anything stolen?"

"Nothing."

"Well, when the report comes in—" Cynthia pauses while looking back at Al.

A memory of Al, shirtless in pain pops up. She's daydreaming while Liam is talking to her. Will she ever see Al again like this?

"Detective Jones?" Liam waves. "Are you here with me?"

Cynthia blinks and turns around from Al. "Yes, yes." She puts her hand on her head. "Just wondering about the victim. Dr. Warren wasn't married, right?"

"Maybe he was a 'playa.'" Al says from the door. "Maybe he never bought into the idea of settling down."

"Maybe," Cynthia says. Detective Dustin comes into the room with Dr. Warren's credit card records.

"Thanks, Dustin."

"Al might be right. Most crimes of passion don't always stem from love gone sour. It could have been revenge... fear…disappoint."

"We'd better get going." Cynthia pulls Dustin. "Dustin and I will look into Warren and see what we can dig up. Thanks, Al for the tip."

"Certainly," Al said not reacting to her Cynthia's non-invite.

———

The longer Cynthia spends in Al's presence, the more questions come up. "I'll let you know if we need you for this one, Al."

"As you were."

Al nods and waves goodbye.

The farther Cynthia gets from the Coroner's Office, the quicker her steps are. Just as she's reaching the doors, her cell phone buzzes. She stops but closes her eyes when she sees the name, Barry.

Can you come 'round to dinner tonight?

It's the fourth time he's invited her over since she almost set fire to his kitchen. Knowing how close he and Al are, she's sure Barry knows something, and now he wants to make up. Cynthia's ignored the texts but this time, she texted back.

"Not tonight, Barry. I just got a new case. Maybe some other time?"

"Ok. Don't be a stranger."

She pockets her phone and reaches for the door to push it open.

"Detective Jones?"

She turns around. It's Liam, jogging. "What, Liam? What is it now?"

"Oh, no," he says, bending over and breathing. "I'm glad I caught you. I thought I was going to have to chase you all the way to your car."

"I do have a phone, you know."

"Yeah, I know but I think it's better to talk about in person." Then he lowers his voice. "And away from your partner.'"

"What's going on?" Cynthia looks at Dustin. "Hey Dee, give us a minute. Matter of fact, I'll meet you at the squad car."

"Ok."

"I just wanted to ask... is there something going on with you and Sanchez?" Liam said.

Cynthia opens her mouth to try to deny it when he goes on, "I mean, just a couple weeks ago, you two were hitting it off."

"Liam, this is not the time."

"Okay, sorry."

"There's nothing to be. "

"Well, Sanchez is happy, everyone around the precinct is as well."

"I'm wondering why are you saying this—" Cynthia glances to make sure Al doesn't come out and see them.

"You saw how Al was checking you out back there?"

"Yes. And—" she said, "Nothing is wrong with us."

"There is but you, two are acting like there isn't."

"Al has been going through a lot. I have too with all these crazy murders. That's all, Liam."

"Maybe—I wish you both just make love and call it a day."

"You're such a mess! I have to go. Bye!"

Once Cynthia in the driver's seat, she slumps forward, resting her head on the steering wheel.

"What's wrong, C?" Dustin said.

"I got a headache."

"Want me to drive?"

"No, just give me a minute."

———

"You were right about checking Mr. Warren's credit card records," Dustin says on the drive out. "Seems like he stayed at the Ritz Carlton and the Berring Park at least twice a week. Someone in the staff probably recognizes him."

"I hope so. It's too bad that no one seems to know what Warren did during his time off."

"Some people live in a cave," Dustin says. "I mean, you know I can't help talking about my wife and kids, but someone like Captain Rowland? As old as she is, I don't even know if she's married."

"She doesn't wear a ring, but that doesn't mean anything." Cynthia thinks of the ring on the chain around her neck and image of Al kissing her.

"Even Al. I mean, you see him all the time. Does he ever spend time with anyone outside of that jerk room-mate of his?

Cynthia looks out the window as Dustin keeps his eyes on the road. "As far as I know, Al's not seeing anyone."

Dustin laughs. "Sanchez's a bit of an oddball - maybe there's no one who will put up with him."

Cynthia feels offended but doesn't speak. Dustin sees the look on her face and apologizes. "I'm sorry, Cynthia, I know you two are——"

"Well, Al's a work in progress."

———

The hotel staff is pretty helpful telling Cynthia and Dustin that Warren was a good tipper and friendly. At the Ritz Carlton, he was seen regularly with a woman.

"Dr. Warren rarely came in with the same person twice," the receptionist says at the Berring Park, leaning in to whisper. "He was a big playboy."

"Never with the same woman, huh?" Cynthia said.

"Rarely. There were a few I saw more than once - a younger Asian girl, an older woman, and a middle-aged man in a suit. Dr. Warren didn't have a preference."

Dustin leans on the counter. "And they always checked-in?"

"Not always. Sometimes, Dr. Warren had drinks at the bar with the person he brought in, and left."

As they're walking away from reception, Dustin sighs. "That's gonna be a lot of footage to go through. You're thinking what I'm thinking?"

"Let's focus on the woman from the Ritz Carlton."

"Exactly." He glances behind him as they're exiting the front doors. "Bet Al would have nailed down the suspects before the receptionist finished her sentence." Dustin clears his throat before asking, "You wanna call him in on this one?"

"Think we can't handle this on our own?"

"No, that's not what I'm saying, I just, you know... wondered why Al isn't on detail with us."

"He's working his way back up." Cynthia tries to keep her voice low. "Maybe Captain doesn't believe he's fully healthy."

Dustin doesn't answer back until they get back to the car. "Cynthia, you'd tell me if there were something wrong, right?"

"There isn't anything wrong - other than a case that needs to be solved."

———

They spend the day tracking down their mystery lady and did so right before the dinner hour. "Andrea Villiers?" Cynthia says, knocking on the door. "Police. We need to ask you a few questions."

Ms. Villiers answers, wearing in a black cocktail dress, slipping on her heels. "Can I help you?"

"Ms. Villiers, we're looking into the death of Oscar Warren. What was your relationship with the deceased?"

Ms. Villiers puts her hand over her mouth. "Death? Oscar's dead?" She steps back. "But we were going out this evening—"

"At the Ritz Carlton?"

"Yes," Ms. Villiers said.

Cynthia holds out her hand and Ms. Villiers takes it. "Would you like to sit down?"

Ms. Villiers nods and the two of them go over to the couch. "When... did Oscar die? How?"

"He was shot to death sometime last night, between 2 and 3AM," Cynthia said. "Were you seeing each other?"

"Oh my God!" Ms. Villiers puts her hand on her head. "Yes, he was my boyfriend."

"Were you serious?"

"I thought we were. We saw each other a few times a week. Sometimes he would come over here, sometimes we'd go out to the Ritz Carlton, or just take a drive."

While Cynthia is talking with Ms. Villiers, Dustin is walking around the apartment, observing anything unusual.

Ms. Villiers trembles and Cynthia takes a blanket off the couch and places it around Ms. Villiers's shoulders. "Can I get you some water?"

"Yes, please."

Cynthia pours water, and out of the corner of her eye, she sees Dustin opening and closing drawers, looking for evidence. She then hands her the glass, and Ms. Villiers takes a sip.

Dustin fishes out a Glock 19 from a drawer between two gloved fingers. "Ms. Villiers, does this belong to you?"

Ms. Villiers turns. "Yes, my father gave it to me as a present. He told me I should have it because of the crime in the city." Then she seems to realize why Dustin is asking. "But I didn't kill Oscar!"

"You won't mind if we run ballistics on it." Dustin bags it. "Where were you last night between 2 and 3AM?"

"In-in bed, like I usually am." Her hands tremble, the water in the glass sloshes.

"You have anyone who can verify your whereabouts at that time?"

"That won't be necessary. I know Ms. Villiers."

"Al, what are you doing here?" Ms. Villiers says.

Everyone turns to see Al at the doorway. He steps inside, nodding to Cynthia and Dustin. "How did Al know we were here? Dusty—" Cynthia murmurs.

"Ms. Villiers's gun could have been used for the crime but is she the shooter? Remember the murderer was right-handed."

Cynthia looks at Ms. Villiers's hands, cradling the glass, right hand over left.

"In fact, we went to school together." Al continues, "I'm sure she's not responsible." Al walks up to Dustin and holds out his hand.

"I'll call Ballistics down here."

———

Within thirty minutes, Dustin has verified the gun wasn't the murder weapon. Ms. Villiers said she hasn't had anyone over since Oscar came by last weekend. Cynthia watches as Al and Dustin assure her that she'll be protected. With a light touch on Ms. Villiers's arm, Cynthia stands, taking her phone from her pocket. She points to it, and then out the door into the hallway. Dustin nods, but Al doesn't seem to notice.

When Cynthia's out in the hallway, she sighs, "I'll let you boys handle the rest."

"Need a ride, C?"

"I'll take a taxi back."

She steps outside to wave a taxi down when someone says, "Detective? Detective!"

A taxi pulls up.

"Cynthia!" Al says, appearing beside her. "Please, let me drive you back."

"Wesley Heights," she tells the taxi driver before turning back to Al. "I'm Detective now? What do you want?"

"Let me apologize. Dustin had asked me to come down just in case—"

"Well, here you are. Thank you once again. You're not dead at least. Now, I'm going to go home."

Al stops her putting his hand on her arm. "Cynthia…"

"The meter's running."

"Then let me hop in with you."

She pauses, looking down at his hand on her arm, its warmth and pressure reminding her of why she's needed a break from him. Then Cynthia looks up. There's a yearning there, stronger than she's ever seen. Despite that, she knows that if she tells him to go, he will. She opens her mouth to say that and while doing so, her eye catches a figure walking toward Villiers's apartment building. Al's eyes follow hers. "It's that guy a suspect?"

Cynthia walks up to the taxi driver, tossing a twenty dollar bill in his lap. "Sorry, it looks like I'm staying."

———

Unholstering her gun and placing it in her coat pocket, the two walk back toward the building. Cynthia calls Dustin but it goes to voicemail. "Hey, Dustin," she says at the tone, "A man just entered the building, about 5'8", black hair, think he might be after Ms. Villiers."

"That's Tim Rust," Al whispers. "From the Berring Park Hotel. I know him. We went to school together, too."

"God, Al! You went to school with everyone today."

"That weasel, Tim Rust, was a criminal in third grade. I head him off before he gets to Ms. Villiers's if that's where he's headed."

"No, Al. Let me handle this."

"I'm here to protect and serve."

"Cut the bullshit, Al. You're going to get yourself killed." Cynthia radios in the precinct. "Possible murder suspect, Tim Rust, on the loose. Be advised. Present location - Ms. Villiers' apartment.

"Over and out, we're heading to your location now, Detective."

Al follows and at the stairs, Mr. Rust notices them behind him and smiles. Cynthia smiles back, threading her arm through Al's looking like a couple on the way home. Her other hand stays in her pocket, fingers curled around the trigger.

They let Mr. Rust get a little farther ahead to allay his suspicions. He leaves the stairwell to go to Ms. Villiers's floor and pulls a set of keys as he walks. Cynthia looks toward Ms. Villiers's door. Where is Dustin? Still inside the apartment with Ms. Villiers?

Mr. Rust turns his head to look behind him again. Cynthia pretends to be in her own little world, squeezing Al's arm and leaning in to whisper in his ear giggling. "Act natural."

Al turns to whisper in her ear as well. But Mr. Rust panics, swiveling toward them and pulls out a gun. "Get back!"

Cynthia and Al draw their guns. "Tim Rust? Police! Drop your weapon!"

"No, you drop your fucking weapon," Mr. Rust says shaking. "I'm gonna get away… or else."

Cynthia takes steps toward him, hoping to calm him down. "Just lower your weapon, Mr. Rust. All we want to do is ask you a few questions."

"He was mine," Tim murmurs, twitching on the handle of the gun.

The door to Ms. Villiers's opens, startling Mr. Rust. His gun goes off and the bullet goes wildly off to the right. Then he turns to point at the door.

Bang!

Rust drops to the ground, and his gun falls out of reach.

Cynthia risks looking behind her as she approaches Mr. Rust. She expects to see Al lying bleeding on the floor, considering his track record. But he's securing the scene calling in backup.

What she sees in the doorway is not Dustin, but Ms. Villiers. A curl of smoke rises from the end of the barrel held rock steady in her hands. Then she crumples to her knees, lowering her weapon.

Dustin comes running from the back of the apartment, huffing. He pries the weapon from Ms. Villiers. "All clear."

"How did you get that weapon, ma'am? I took it from you earlier," Dustin says.

"I have two; the one you have and another in the front, just in case."

"Are there more guns in the house?"

"No, sir."

Cynthia squats beside Tim. He's dead, a clean shot through the heart. Before she can call for Al, he's with her on the other side of Tim. "I think Mr. Rust matches our profile for the murder," Dustin says picking up another Glock 19 that fell feet away from Tim.

———

Al and Cynthia ride in silence. It doesn't seem to matter if Al is included or excluded - she can't protect him. He's going to get himself into trouble no matter what. So she has a choice. And she'd rather have him by her side, where she can keep an eye on him. Cynthia glances over at Al, at the way the passing lights are reflecting off his face.

"So—" Cynthia says, "we can't put this talk off much longer."

"I'm sorry," he says, eyes flinching away. "I shouldn't have kept you waiting."

"You're sorry?"

"Yes." Al studies his hands as if he's afraid to look at her. "I believe I was - how did Barry put it? - 'freaked out.' It's just been so long since I have been in something like this."

"So, there have been others," Cynthia says, "Like Iona. And then there's all the... equipment... in your basement."

"Just a gym rat. That's all." Al licks his lips before continuing, then finally turns back. "I needed to be sure this is what I wanted."

"And—" Cynthia licks hers. "Is it?"

He takes one of her hands in his, and her palms are sweaty. "I do if you do."

The fear of losing Al, just like she lost Kenneth, keeps latching onto her soul and whipping her around before she can take that final step but today is different. "I want it."

Cynthia comes forward, her hands skim over Al's police jacket to grasp the lapels. She pulls him closer, not worried about what the taxi driver will think - he's seen much worse in his career than two adults making out in the back seat. She wants to do much worse, to make up for the two weeks of dithering that seems silly now. But it will have to wait.

Her hands slide below his jacket, her fingers playing across his back to touch as much as him as she can. His fingers are drawing designs across her blouse, up into her hair, with more kisses.

Al's touch is starting a fire, fanning sparks to flames - welcome ones, unlike the fire in his kitchen. She shifts in the seat, bringing one leg up and over his to half-sit in his lap, never breaking the kiss. Al groans saying, "Cynthia," before beginning a trail of kisses down her neck.

Cynthia closes her eyes and relaxes her tongue inside his mouth. She groans and shifts, grinding on him. She can feel his cock against her; planted, bulging almost erupting.

The car slows down and the driver clears his throat. "We're here, ma'am."

"Sorry!"

Cynthia climbs from Al's lap, pulling her purse from the floor to pay. She glances at Al, his police jacket is riding up exposing his white shirt. "Let me pay."

"No, I got it," She pays and the couple gets out.

"Do you want to come inside? Have a cup of coffee?

Maybe continue where we left off?" Al says as he opens her door.

"The latter sounds better," Al rubs her as he speaks, "I think we have much to discuss."

Cynthia can't get the money out fast enough to pay the driver.

A l is there, asking for permission to enter. It is like he's a vampire. Cynthia nods and takes a step forward, to feel Al, to see if he's real.

She's drawn to him, like a magnet - and her touch turns into a hug. He's warm, definitely real. She gives into the craze, pulling him in tighter.

"Oh, Cynthia," he says playing with her hair, "the last thing I wanted to do was cause you pain."

Al then releases. He touches her cheeks and runs down the tracks of tears. "I should have told you," he says. "Long before this ever happened."

"What are you saying, Al?" Cynthia can't break the spell.

"How I knew what my ending would be."

Last Night

It's Dustin's that wakes her. "Cynthia? Cynthia, are you okay?" "Hurry with the paramedics. We may have casualties."

Her vision starts to clear. She nods but stops herself and shakes it 'no.'

"What happened?"

"There was a blast." Dustin squats beside Cynthia who reaches down and life one of the pieces of shrapnel. There is no sign of Al."

"Oh my God! Look at Barry. Where's Al?"

Cynthia whips her head toward the living room to see paramedics bending over Barry's body. His eyes are closed and he's shaking.

"They're working on him," Dustin says. "He's alive - looks like he got hit in the head pretty badly. Cynthia, you're bleeding. What the hell happened?"

She closes her eyes for a moment. "There was a package delivered. When Al put it in the chair, we heard a hissing sound. Al grabbed it and ran. That's all I remember. Where's Al?"

"It looks like you were targeted—we can't find him," Dustin says.

"Where is he? He can't be just gone."

"I don't know."

Dustin pats her on the shoulder. "We'll find him." He holds out his hand to help her up. "You're hurt. We need to get you to the hospital."

"No, I can't leave without Al." Cynthia pulls herself up, using the arm of the sofa as leverage. "Al, Al—"

"Cynthia, we have to go".

She feels his hands on her shoulders. "Dustin, don't let IU touch anything."

"Ok. They won't until you go through it first. We have to go now."

Lowering her hand, she turns to face him. "Dustin, where's Al? I need to find out where he is?"

"We'll find him. I know."

Cynthia concedes.

"Don't touch anything. Bring every last envelope to the fucking precinct!"

———

Instead of going to the hospital, Cynthia heads to the precinct with Dustin. Boxes are brought in one by one piling up on her desk. She feels that Al had left a secret - and she cannot permit anyone else to see them. Although Cynthia can't explain it, her gut feeling is that Al's secret and his disappearance are connected.

After her hasty repacking, whatever system Al had is in shambles. A journal from the 1800s mixed with newspaper clippings from the 50s. Underneath photos and drawings without any date at all and notes in Al's handwriting. There are many references to death; different types, covering over a hundred years. Some horrific, some mundane. Al has always considered himself a student of death; she had no idea how far it went. Still, these leads were farfetched.

"Detective Jones." Captain Rowland's voice startles her.

Cynthia looks up, pushing her hair behind her ears. "Yes, Captain?"

Rowland pauses. Cynthia hadn't cared what she looked like after the blast. What are a few cuts when Al's missing?

"Go home."

"But Captain, Al is—"

"I know. Detective Dustin filled me in. The FBI was called in to assist. They're doing everything they can. Al will be found, Detective."

"No, I can't just give up like this. He's my—"

"Detective, you look like hell and can't do your work in this state." Cynthia steps forward. "It's midnight. Go home, get some sleep. We have this covered."

"Captain—"

"Do I have to give an order?"

Cynthia shakes her head and places everything back in the box. Rowland watches her, waiting until she's left the precinct. Though Cynthia doesn't turn around, she feels a uniformed officer watching her until she gets into a squad car and it pulls off.

She replays the night's events… until someone knocks on her door at 3 AM.

"Detective, we've found Al," An officer said.

"Where is he?"

"He was burnt badly and didn't make it."

"Where was the body found?"

"A few feet from the fire escape. He almost made it."

RYAN

CHAPTER TWENTY-EIGHT

"Ryan! Can you start closing up, please?" calls his mother from the washroom, her voice nearly drowned out by the whirring of the dishwasher. Ryan wipes his hands on the tea towel tucked into his apron, leaving streaks of turquoise royal icing on the fraying cotton and heads towards the door.

He adjusts his chef's cap as he steps onto the shop floor, noting the time on the register reads 5:25 pm, just five minutes until closing. In front of a busy display of ribbons, candles and decorations, is a woman in her thirties with dark curly hair styled into loose curls over her shoulders. She has on a forest green, knee-length dress, with a black jacket, and a pair of black and white Adidas trainers. In one hand is a black laptop bag, and on her opposite shoulder is what Ryan recognizes as a Louie Vuitton handbag.

The woman reaches out to slip a large number one

candle off its hook, adjusting her laptop bag, and holding it in the same hand. She fingers the variety of spools carefully, feeling the weight and texture of the ribbons, considering what she wants. Once the woman decides on a yellow and white checkered one she turns, only to freeze in surprise at the sight of Ryan. Their eyes meet, both not expecting to be confronted by such beauty on this quiet Monday afternoon.

"Hi," Ryan says smiling, having quickly straightening himself. "Can I help you with that?"

"Oh, yes," the woman says, looking equally as if she's had to snap herself back to reality. She points down to a ribbon she just decided on. "May I please have a meter of this?"

"Sure," Ryan says, grabbing the scissors from the pot next to the register and walking over to measure and cut the length. He rolls it up before asking if that's all. The woman explains she needs to get a few more things, so Ryan offers to watch the candle and ribbon by the register, as well as her laptop bag. "I'm about to lock the door," Ryan says, pointing to the clock which now reads 5:29. "No one will run off with it, and if I run off with it, at least you know where I work?"

The woman giggles at his lame joke, and it makes Ryan's heart stutter.

The sound reminds Ryan of the clatter of fridge-cold chocolate chips being poured into a bowl of cookie dough; a sound he's loved since childhood when he and his grandmother used to bake together, him standing on a chair at her kitchen counters, wearing an apron. Ryan always used to 'accidentally' tip one or two of the chocolate pieces onto the surface instead of the bowl, and he and his grandmother decided they weren't destined for the cookies and should be eaten there and then. It was a sound of joy and happiness.

But then the woman frowns, "I'm sorry. Am I stopping you from closing up? I can just pay and go." She says it sincerely, though he can tell she is eager to buy more.

"No, no, it's fine," Ryan says smiling, walking towards the door and turning the key in the lock at the bottom - in the most un-menacing way he can, trying to make it clear that she can leave any time and he's not trapping her into his cake shop to have his way with her . . . though his pants tighten just a smidge when he considers it. Ryan clears his throat. "We have plenty of cleaning up to do here, take your time."

"Thanks," she says and places the candle and her bag on the counter before taking a small wicker basket from a stack on the floor and wandering towards the rows of colored fondants. She picks up a packet of grey modeling paste, pausing to read the label 'Miller's Cake Shop' logo on it. "Is this homemade?" the woman asks.

"Yeah," Ryan says. "Pretty much everything in this shop is. All organic, no artificial sweeteners or preservatives."

"That's great," the woman says. "My sister-in-law will love that."

"Are you making a cake for her?"

"Yeah. Well, it's for my niece. She turns one in a week and we're having a party this weekend."

"How lovely," Ryan smiles. "First birthdays are always the best. Well, I'll leave you, got some frosting I need to put in the fridge. Just shout when you're ready or if you need any help."

"Okay, thanks."

Ryan returns to the kitchen and leans against the counter for a minute. Then, he puts the frostings into containers and affixes the appropriate labels before placing them in the fridge. Ryan notes down the temperatures into the logbook, before moving on to check the stocks of butter, eggs, and fruit, deciding whether he needs to put an order in tonight or tomorrow. He tries not to let his mind wander back out onto the shop floor, where the impossibly beautiful woman is currently browsing through the racks of cutters, molds, sprinkles and other decorations.

When he's finished and has wiped down the last of the surfaces, Ryan hears the soft clearing of a throat. He takes off his hat and white apron – now stained from a day of piping mermaid cupcakes and tempering chocolate – and throws them into the corner. The woman smiles waiting for him by the till, carrying a wicker basket full of cake tin, a rolling pin, parchment paper, sprinkles, candles, and ribbons. The woman seems to be buying literally everything she needs to make a birthday cake.

"Can I get a board and a box too?" the woman asks, gesturing to the neatly stacked white ones and silver boards behind him. After selecting the size for her tin, Ryan unpacks the basket onto the counter and offers for her to purchase one of their jute bags to take it all home in.

"I love the branding," the woman says, tracing the shape of their logo where it's been printed onto the bag. "Vibrant colors, and crispy design. Eye-catching. Very simple and effective."

"Thanks," Ryan says. "I designed it."

"You did?"

"Yeah."

"I'm impressed," the woman says, her voice drops a little and her eyes flick up to meet his. He slows his ringing-up of her items, electricity sparking between them for a fraction of a second before she averts her eyes and he clears his throat, trying to dispel the awkwardness.

In an attempt to fill the silence, Ryan asks her about the things she's buying, and she admits to never having made a cake before. He comments that with the amount it's going to cost her she should have asked him to make the cake for her instead.

"Could you?"

"Sorry," Ryan says, scratching behind his ear.

"We're fully booked for wedding season."

The woman hums and explains that's how she ended up in this predicament. After Ryan offers her a questioning glance, she explains. Turns out, a friend of her sister-in-law who was originally supposed to make the cake broke her arm. Too late to order one from the bakery nearby, and with their kitchen being a disaster zone due to renovations, they were left with no other option but to accept her offer to do it. The family friends' eldest brother nor his wife could, as they're flying in from Boston for the weekend, neither can her sister or mother because they're in Europe until Thursday.

The woman rests her elbows on the counter and lowers her head into her hands. "I really don't know why they agreed, or why I even offered. I think no cake would have been a better option!"

"Hey now, I'm sure you can do it," Ryan says. "If you need any tips this week just come on in, I'd be happy to help."

"Thanks."

"Where is your mom and sister traveling in Europe?" Ryan asks, interested, having spent a year of his early twenties backpacking around Europe and trying to gain apprenticeships in bakeries, first in France, then Switzerland, before finding he really couldn't crack the code and ended up in Yorkshire, somehow managing to set up a place at Dolly's Tea Parlor in Brantham.

"They were in France first, but they've been at Wimbledon for a couple of weeks now."

"Cool. For tennis?" Ryan said.

"Not now," the woman said looking at her feet. "My sister was a player before."

"Your sister was playing?" Ryan said. "At Wimbledon?"

"Yeah, Jessica Roth. Have you heard of her?"

"You mean, three-time Grand Slam winner, two-time Olympic medalist, and sweetheart Jessie Roth is your sister?"

"Yeah," she sighs. "She's the one."

"I thought she retired?" Ryan said.

"She and Roger got a wildcard into the mixed doubles," she shrugs.

"Roger...?"

"The Roger," the woman mumbles, looking down at her wallet before retrieving her credit card and holding out for him to take.

Ryan gapes but quickly snaps his mouth shut seeing the woman's look of mild exasperation. He finishes ringing up her items and tries not to grimace at the $75 everything comes to. Glancing up to see that she's looking down in her bag, Ryan turns the display on the register away, so she cannot see the total. "That'll be $50 please."

He thinks for a moment that the woman might be onto him, her eyes narrowing. Ryan takes her credit card and inserts it into the reader, waiting for it to connect.

"Sorry," he says, as the device takes its sweet old time to ask her for her pin number.

"No problem," she says. "These machines are often pains."

"No, I meant, I'm sorry about the thing with your sister. I know what it's like to have an older sibling who everyone has heard of." Ryan shrugs when she looks up. The woman's eyes glance on the logo on the wall behind Ryan, possibly to the framed picture of the replica

Hawks jersey cake he made with 'DALE 22' on the back.

"Oh," she says. "Grayson Miller, he's your brother?"

"Yes."

"I mean—at least we get good tickets?" she says.

"I can get box seats at the Bellevue whenever," Ryan says.

"But no good when they're on the other side of the world and you have a court date?"

"Yeah not much good when they're for a match that finishes at 11pm and you have to be up at 4am to bake," Ryan says.

They look at each other suspended in the moment. "Well," the woman says, as she keys in her pin. "I best be off and let you get on with your evening. Thanks for everything—" She scans his embroidered name on his white chef's jacket—Ryan.

"You're welcome. By the way, what's your name?"

"Trina."

"I'm—"

"Ryan. I know," Trina says pointing to his name tag.

Ryan chuckles while Trina unlocks the shop door letting herself out, and raising her hand goodbye.

Trina nearly falls on her face as she enters the cake shop on her lunch break, a strong wind that's picked up pushes the door open harder than she was ready for and pulling her in. Her black heels slide underneath her.

"Hey there," Ryan says comes out of nowhere, as does his arm, wrapping around her waist. Trina recovers herself quickly and moves away as soon as she can. The ghost of his toned forearm against her sends a shiver up her spine.

"Hello again," he says. An errant curl has fallen onto Ryan's forehead and Trina can't take her eyes off it, doing everything in her power not to lick her lips at the man she spent the rest of yesterday evening trying to get out of her head.

"Hi." Trina's hand comes up to her face to tug a

strand of hair from her lips, which she had coated with lip balm before leaving the office minutes ago. As she tucks the final tendril behind her ear, Trina realizes that the shop is silent and that Ryan's watching her intently.

A car horn sounds outside and Ryan's eyes snap back to reality. "How's your cake coming along?"

"Oh. Not well," Trina huffs, fixing her handbag and removing the lanyard from around her neck, fiddling with the clip.

"Oh no," Ryan says. "What happened?"

Trina shrugs her shoulders and waves her hands. "I have no idea, but what came out of the oven couldn't be called a cake!" Ryan raises his eyebrows. "I think the measurements were off or something? Whatever it was, the whole thing was a waste of time."

Ryan grimaces.

"I remember seeing something I liked yesterday. Can you show me where your cake mix is?" Trina chuckles.

"Of course! Follow me." Ryan waves his hand to follow him to the wooden shelves stacked with multiple brown bags with orange 'Miller's Cake Shop' labels.

"You make this yourself, too?"

"Yeah," Ryan says. "All blended by yours truly. All-natural, all organic. Just add liquid; Hell! you can even make them vegan."

"Wow!" Trina looks over them, her mouth waters as she reads all the flavors. "These all look delicious, I don't know what to choose."

"Would you like to try one?"

"Huh—sure why not," Trina says slurring. "But as long as it's not too much trouble? I don't want to eat anyone's cake."

"No worries."

Ryan heads over to the table in the corner with three spindly chairs arranged around it and Trina follows him. She puts her bag on one of the others and sets her lanyard down. She notices Ryan glance at it, and Trina is glad that she'd made her hair for the day.

"What does the 'T' stand for?" he asks.

"Oh, it's just my name," she says thinking she heard Ryan whisper something under his breath.

"Pardon?" she asks.

Ryan shakes his head. "Nothing, just cake!" He says. "You don't have any allergies, do you?" She shakes her head 'No.' "Great, I'll be back, Trinnie." Ryan dashes off and she can't help but smile hearing his giddiness.

Ryan returns from the kitchen carrying a white cake stand and places it on the table. He takes a seat across from her and Trina switches her attention to it, having spent the time he was gone admiring the interior design of the shop; a pleasant aesthetic of white walls and dark wood, with touches of orange, black, and brass in the furnishings, artwork and light fixings.

"Wow," Trina says, looking at the cake in front of her. It was cut into eight slices, and instead of being one flavor, each was different.

Ryan turns the stand as he points:

"So, this slice is lemon zest and fresh raspberry with raspberry coulis-rippled buttercream.

The second is lemon mousse with lemon buttercream and shavings of white chocolate.

The third is Madagascan vanilla topped with whipped cream and seasonal berries.

The fourth is three-shade vanilla with vanilla buttercream.

The fifth is a dark chocolate chip with orange zest buttercream.

The sixth is red velvet with cream cheese frosting.

The seventh is carrot with orange zest cream cheese frosting.

And the last is a rich and moist chocolate with dark chocolate ganache."

Trina can feel her mouth-watering at the prospect of frosting all of them. She's glad she didn't pick up her usual chicken and avocado wrap on her way here; a little cake won't hurt for lunch, particularly on a week like this, right? She looks back up at him, hoping there's no drool on her shirt.

"Wow," Trina says again. "These look so delicious!"

Ryan passes her a cake fork and a heavy napkin. "Dig in," he says as he turns the cake plate around so the raspberry slice is the one directly in front of her. "I recommend you start with the lightest and then work your way around to the dark chocolate one, I think you can enjoy the textures and flavors better. Oh, and you'll want to cleanse the plate between each." Ryan jumps up and grabs a carafe of water and a couple of glasses from behind the register, causing the table to wobble as he sits in haste. Trina glances in amusement as he turns the cake stand around and lifts the first slice down onto a small plate in the stack he brought over earlier.

Trina digs in, glad to see that he's also holding a fork and is joining her, making her feel a lot less guilty about this extravagance. The flavors explode on her tongue, the hint of lemon pairing perfectly with the tang of the raspberries, the gentle sweetness of buttercream balancing beautifully. Trina could easily devour the whole slice, but she'd never been able to manage the others, so instead, she reaches for the glass of water, takes a sip and then moves onto the next one.

They chat as they eat, each slice different, but just as good as the other. Trina asks him about the shop and when it was started it; Ryan tells her about their original location, and about how much work it took to get it to this one. He shows her some photos on his phone of the renovations they did.

After that, Trina shows him some pictures of Kiara, her youngest niece, for whom she's attempting to make this cake, and Ryan says she's really is one of the cutest kids he's ever seen.

It's easy, talking to Ryan; perhaps easier than Trina's found it to talk to someone in a while, particularly someone she'll admit that she likes. Trina only finds this instant level of comfort with women; which explains why her last long-term relationship. Her most recent flings have been women and Trina doesn't know if she's ever connected with anyone this instantly before.

The ease makes her wonder if he's too good to be true? Whether, in a moment, the other shoe will drop? However, Ryan's casual mention that he's single causes her stomach to flutter; her body's telling her literally to follow her gut and switch off her brain for a second.

Trina is smiling and blushing like a fool now. Ryan is decent enough not to draw attention to it. She's trying to work out how to let him know that she's single too, and most definitely interested - she can't stop herself from licking her lips. The door opens and Ryan turns to see who's entered, the angle perfectly displaying his chiseled jawline and neck muscles.

"Hey, Mom," says Ryan, and now Trina knows the connection, she can clearly see the resemblance. "Any luck with the strawberries?"

"Yes," his mother says putting several punnets of the ruby red fruit on the counter before wandering over to them at the table. "Ollie's Organics just had a delivery and gave me a deal on the price."

"That's great!" Ryan says, turning back to Trina and raising an eyebrow. "Supply-chain issues," he says and Trina nods.

"Which's your favorite, sweetheart?" Ryan's mother says, with the name 'Sarah' embroidered in orange on her chef's jacket.

"Chocolate," Trina gushes. "Though, I think I'll go for the vanilla this time."

"Yes, vanilla is our most popular for weddings, a real crowd-pleaser," says Sarah.

"Oh, no," she says. "I'm not—"

"When are you getting married, dear? We haven't got a lot of slots left this side of Christmas, I hope this one's told you that?" She nudges Ryan.

Trina glances at Ryan and knows the feeling.

"Sorry. I'm not getting married," Trina says. Sarah pucks her lips. "Well, It's just me."

"Oh," Sarah says. "I—"

"Trina's buying some cake mix for this weekend," Ryan says with his eyes fixed on Trina.

"I see," says Sarah, her eyebrows furrows towards her son. She turns to take the strawberries off the counter. "Ryan, could I speak to you in the kitchen for a minute, please? I need to ask you about the supply of caramel."

Ryan's head whips over resembling that of a kid who's been caught with his hand in the cookie jar. "Sure," he says, slowly, as he rises from the table. "I'll—be right back," he says before slipping through the kitchen door.

Trina fiddles with the napkin in her lap, trying, and failing, not to eavesdrop on what's happening in the kitchen, catching snippets here and there.

"It's not a big deal, Mama!"

"That service is for weddings only, Ryan."

"I'm trying to help her out—Mom."

"That costs $50!"

Trina's eyes widen feeling guilty that she has gotten Ryan into trouble. She looks at her watch; seeing she needs to head back to the office soon. Trina starts to tidy the table, brushing the crumbs into her hand and then onto one of the empty plates, stacking their glasses and refolding the napkins. Ryan and Sarah's voices are still echoing through from the kitchen.

"If this is because of some crush of yours, Mr. Ryan—"

Trina trips over the leg of one of the chairs as she hurries to gather her things, hanging her lanyard back around her neck, nearly ripping an earring out in the process. She's deciding whether she's going to stay or flee when Ryan reappears on the shop floor, red-faced and with his hair mussed up.

"Thanks for letting me taste the cakes," Trina says, wringing her hands.

"No problem," Ryan says, perhaps a little too loudly. "Did you want to buy some cake mix?"

"Yeah, why not. I'll take the vanilla, please." Trina decides she's going to go along, ignoring what just happened.

"Here you are," Ryan says, reaching up to the shelf and grabbing one of the bags. "This should be the right amount for your tin."

Trina is impressed that Ryan remembers what size tin she bought yesterday because she certainly doesn't!

He rings her up on the register. "That'll be $7.50."

"What about the cake frosting?"

"Oh no, that's fine, don't worry." Trina hands over a

twenty-dollar bill. She then grabs the bag and hurries towards the door.

"Wait, ma'am!" Ryan calls after her. "You forgot your change."

"Keep it," Trina says stepping over the doormat while heading out.

Ryan is about to start counting the cash in the register when the bell above the door sounds at 5:25 PM for the second time this week. And, for the third time in as many days, he feels his cheeks start to redden and his pulse quickens as he takes in the woman walking through the door.

Today, Trina's business attire is swapped for a pair of checkered yoga tights with splotches of maroon and pink, a sports bra, and a white vest top. She has her hair up into a bun and is carrying a yoga mat and an Adidas sports bag along with her handbag and laptop bag.

Ryan has to work very hard not to let his mouth drop when he sees she looks stressed.

"Trinnie, hey," Ryan says. "Everything ok?"

"The cake sank."

"Sank?"

"It has this huge dip in the middle." She says. "I think my oven is broken."

"Oh gosh," Ryan says. "Do you need some more cake mix? I can go grab you some on the house."

"No, no, I can't," Trina says, placing her hand on top of his on the counter, to stop him from leaving. It felt like it was to stop Ryan from breathing more like. It takes her a couple of seconds to realize what she's done and she quickly moves it. "I don't have time to make another cake this week, I'm teaching a class tonight and tomorrow. Oh god, when am I going to do this right?"

Ryan tries not to get distracted by the sight of her back and shoulder muscles. He wants to get lost in her, but Ryan does his best to distract her, to find out a little more about this woman who intrigues him so much.

"What are you teaching?"

"Oh, me—" Trina stutters. "Tonight, I'm having a barre class in a studio uptown, then tomorrow is my weekly elderly fitness session I do at a local retirement home."

"In a retirement home?" Ryan says. "That's amazing. Which one?"

"Red Oaks up on Chambry Street."

"You're kidding?" he says.

"Do you know it?"

"Yeah, we donate cakes and pastries to them for their coffee mornings on Wednesdays."

"Sometimes, I went to those as well before class."

"That's crazy?" Ryan says. "That we both have been there but never met? Do you know Devin?"

Trina chuckles. "Oh yeah. I know Devin!"

She smiles seemingly much calmer now. He watches her reach out to turn the charity tub around so that Trina can read which organization it supports - a local women's shelter.

"And a barre class? Is that a ballet thing?" Ryan asks, intrigued, noticing the definition in Trina's legs and the shape of her bottom. He tries not to stare for too long, but he can't help to do so.

"It's based on ballet, but it's more of a fitness class; strength training, cardio, and flexibility," Trina explains. Ryan nods along. "We use resistance bands and dumb-bells, but mostly it's bodyweight stuff. This class has become quite popular in the city now, and the studio I work for is all female-owned, which is pretty cool too."

"That's interesting," Ryan says. "Can men join?"

"Of course!" Trina says. "Why, do you want to come?"

"It sounds like an intense workout." The thought of lifting any weights around Trina sounds appalling. He's spent most of the day frosting three hundred chocolate cupcakes with strawberry buttercream and his hands and wrists are aching.

"For sure," Trina says. "I can't stand the gym. I see you are fit. Do you work out regularly?"

"I rarely have the time so I end up doing stuff in the house and at buddy's place on the weekends." Ryan gestures to the shop around him and Trina nods. "I do pushups in the mornings regularly."

"Oh, me too," Trina smiles.

Ryan nods. "But aside from that, I normally unpack the delivery guy's van three times a week and play a bit of football when I can. My aunt and cousins own a field, so sometimes I'll help out there during the summer."

"Ah, so there's more than one family business you're involved with?"

"Baking and football, that's what us Dales do."

"That's really lovely," Trina says, glancing away. She checks the time on the fitness tracker.

"So I have a solution for your cake woes," Ryan says. "How about I defrost one of our 'emergency cakes' for you to come and collect tomorrow? It's fresh. What do you think?"

"No, I couldn't…" Trina says, but Ryan interrupts her. "It's not a problem. I have plenty in there that I made to restock for the busy season."

"Are you sure?" Trina says. Ryan knows she's being polite and offering him the out, but he declines and nods.

"Thank you," Trina exhales, grabbing his upper arm. "Thank you so much." Then, she leans over the counter to give Ryan a quick kiss on the cheek. Ryan clears his throat and she pulls away with a shy little smirk.

A car horn outside startles them and Trina blushes before dashing off. Ryan stands behind the register caught up in the moment, already dreading seeing her for perhaps the final time tomorrow.

CHAPTER THIRTY-ONE

Ryan hurried his mother out of the back of the shop and into her car when the bell chimes. "I'll make sure everything is ready for tomorrow. We have a delivery I need to check on before closing."

"Ok and make sure you check the temperatures on the refrigerators before you leave."

"Yes, Mom."

Sarah pulls off and Ryan dashes back inside to the kitchen and onto the shop floor, smiling when he sees Trina waiting at the door. Her laptop bag in one hand and a small Adidas sports bag in the other. Her hair is now in a ponytail.

"Hi Trina," Ryan says, trying to remain cool and collected. "Come on back." He cocks his head towards the doorway and Trina nods following him into the kitchen.

Stainless-steel benches shine brightly under the strip lights, as do the fronts of the industrial-sized ovens and the row of mixers. To the right, are racks housing every size of cake tin from two-inch dessert rings to 20" squares.

Ryan pulls out a plastic stool from under the island in the middle. The thick marble countertop is cool to the touch and perfect for chocolate and pastry work. Ryan watches enchanted as Trina glides her hand over the polished stone, her finger tracing one of his favorite swirls in the right-hand corner.

Ryan passes Trina an orange apron then instructs her about making the cake leveled, filled, stacked and crumb coated. He answers her questions about flavors and techniques, about where he trained and why.

Trina sneaks a taste of everything Ryan has put into the cake; the raspberry coulis he swirls into the buttercream spread between each layer. Each is faintly flavored with grated lemon zest to bring out the zing in the raspberries that Ryan pulls apart and studs into the pink and white milky way adorning the champagne-colored sponge.

He pinches off a small ball of fondant from the kilogram block he's kneading, making it pliable through the heat of his hands, and gives it to Trina to taste as well. Trina's delighted as she chews on the taster; Ryan's fondant has never had a complaint. Ryan then adds a faint drop of lemon extract to the dough, to offset the sweetness and complement the cake he has so stacked and kneads the fondant further to fully bring out the flavor.

Ryan then dusts the end strip of the marble counter with a small layer of cornstarch - when she asks why he uses it instead of powdered sugar he explains how it's easier to dust off the excess and doesn't dry out the fondant nor mess with the flavor balance. He begins to roll out the fondant, turning the disk between each roll so that it doesn't stick, ensuring an even thickness throughout, and ending with a near-perfect circle ready to be transferred onto the cake.

"Shall we put her name on the cake?" Ryan asks afterward, wandering towards the shelf with the bins filled with cutters and molds.

"Yeah, that would be great," says Trina, moving to join him. He grabs the tin of alphabet cutters and notices that she is reaching up on her tiptoes to get the bin labeled 'Flowers and Butterflies'. He stretches over her to get it.

"And do you want me to make a little animal or something to go on top? To give it a little more dimension and height?"

"That sounds good," Trina says. "Do you have time for that?"

Ryan glances over to the clock - black metal with the numbers and 'Miller' cut out of it - and sees that it's only a quarter past six. "Yeah, I have time. What animal do you think she'd like?"

"Well, Henry and Luna have had a bit of a thing with elephants, so maybe one of those?"

"Great, I love making elephants!" He moves over to the other shelves with the fondant and modeling paste. "So we'll need grey for the elephant. How about this light blue and this egg yolk yellow for the letters and details? We should put some flowers and butterflies around the edge."

"That sounds perfect," Trina says. "They've tried not to be overly pink and girly with her so I know they'll love that."

"I totally get that. I swear, I cringe every time someone comes in and wants to order a gender reveal cake." Ryan rubs at the back of his neck, "I mean, people are perfectly entitled to do whatever they like, but boy equals blue and girl equals pink is so stereotypical before a kid is even born."

"I agree."

They make their way back to the counter and Ryan sets Trina up rolling out some smaller pieces of the colored fondant between two bits of dowel to ensure even thickness and teaches her the easiest way to use the plunger cutters to get clean edges on the letters, butterflies, and daisies. He sets to work on the elephant, stopping as quiet curses and grunts come from Trina, whose talents very clearly lie elsewhere.

"You doing okay there?"

"I really am useless at this," says Trina, dropping the

cutter back onto the counter and squishing the droopy daisy back into a small ball.

"Here," Ryan steps over and sets her up with a new piece of fondant that hasn't been overworked to the point of cracking. "You need to keep it moving so it doesn't stick to the surface." He holds the rolling pin out, but she hesitates in taking it.

"Show me," Trina says smiling. Ryan knows she's flirting, and he goes with it, stepping closer and slightly to the side so he's right behind her. He reaches his arms around hers and Trina takes the rolling pin, but he holds on too, whispering instructions into her ear. Ryan sees her head tilted slightly to the side. His lips are close to her neck and she smells so good that he just wants to latch on there.

Then, Trina's phone rings at the other end of the counter causing them to back away from each other. They have been moving the rolling pin back and forth for a few moments without it having any effect, and the fondant was already at the right thickness. Ryan steps back as she moves from the circle, and Trina tucks a strand of hair behind her ear as she reaches for her phone. But then she pauses, her hand still outstretched, and her mouth drops when she sees the cake.

"Oh my god, this is amazing!" Trina says, delighted, turning back to him.

"Thanks," Ryan says, rubbing at the back of his neck and smiling as he watches her lean down to inspect the paste elephant more closely, her hands quivering as if eager to touch it but knowing she shouldn't. Trina smiles as she checks her phone and then comes back over and they continue their lesson in cutting out the letters and shapes, though the tension has dissipated a little.

———

Twenty minutes later, the cake is finished and they take a step back to survey their work. Trina claps and does a little jump for joy. "This is gorgeous, Ryan, thank you so much!" Before he can brush off her compliment, Trina throws her arms around him, which she pulls away from before he has a chance to savor it. He moves the cake to the turntable on the side bench and Trina follows him, pulling her phone from her pocket, then begins to snap photos of it.

Whilst Trina does this, Ryan sets to work cleaning up the slab, brushing off the corn starch from the counter before filling a bucket that once held a kilo of green dragées with warm soapy water, and wiping it down before drying it off. Once it's dry, Ryan cleans it once more, crouching down so the counter is at eye level and he can inspect for any signs that he was here after his mother cleaned it a couple of hours ago. Once he's done, he throws his apron into the pile of laundry in the corner by his backpack.

Ryan passes Trina the box and she slides the cake into it as he stacks up the items they've used and put them back. The punnet of raspberries tips over as he opens the fridge, the ruby jewels tumbling silently to the floor. He puts the container of frosting and the rind-less lemons onto the nearest shelf before shutting the door and bending down to pick them up. Once Ryan's down on his knees, he finds himself face to face with Trina, who is already picking up the berries.

"You don't have to," Ryan says, as he scoops a couple, his fingertips are smeared.

"It's fine, don't worry about it," she says, as she reaches for one that rolled a little further away. Ryan watches Trina from the corner of his eye, marveling at how beautiful she looks, with that orange apron on.

Trina hisses suddenly and stands, dropping several of the raspberries as she grabs her calf. Ryan reaches out for her, his hand steadying her leg, her free one coming to rest on his shoulder for support.

"Sorry," she grits out. "Cramps." She rubs her calf, leaving streaks of juice across her skin.

"It'll be okay," Ryan says, aware of how close to her he's kneeling, his hand on the back of her knee.

Trina feels it twitch because suddenly her eyes are on his and she's looking down at him. At first, she seems surprised, and Ryan gulps. But then her gaze becomes charged by something else entirely. Without thinking, Ryan comes upwards and presses his mouth to hers.

Trina's lips taste like raspberries and sugar, a flavor so familiar to him. Ryan runs his tongue along the seam of her lips, their tongues tangling, sighing into the kiss as their hands begin to wander and they shuffle closer together. Their bodies are radiating heat despite the cool temperature inside.

Ryan tugs the tie at the back of Trina's apron and once it's undone, it falls, breaking their kiss for the briefest time to remove it. She huffs before recapturing his lips again.

He creeps his hands towards her buttocks and sinks his fingertips into the flesh, marveling at her impressive muscles squeezing at its firmness.

Trina sighs and she presses closer, one hand running up into his hair as the other fists the front of his chef's jacket. For once the heavy cotton that's so comfortable to wear, feels hot.

"Take it off," Ryan husks out, pulling away from her and pulling open the popper fastening at the neck. Trina's eyes raise and her mouth twitches. Trina darts forwards like a cat swiping at its prey and rips open the rest of the poppers, leaving his jacket hanging open and revealing the sleeveless black shirt he wears beneath. She pulls at that too and he steps forward to reach for her again, their hands roaming contrasting paths across the other's body; hers under his shirt and up across his abs, his traveling down from her waist to the hem of her skirt.

Their lips meet again, almost feral now as they devour each other; more teeth than caressing tongues. Ryan starts to walk them back towards the counter, hands moving further up and under her skirt until they're on her ass again, which is barely covered by her lacy panties that he'd quite like to rip off now. He moves his index finger lightly across her center, Trina's breathing hitches and she lets out a gasp. "Ohhh, oh!" The sound makes Ryan's erection nearly pierce his boxers open.

Trina pants as Ryan lifts her up on the counter. She encircles her legs around him, her mouth opens feeling his erection at her center against her. She grips his hair tighter, her fingers scratch his scalp most seductively and Ryan nearly comes.

"Do you know that I fell in love with you the moment you walked in?"

The second the words fell from his lips, Ryan was worried he'd said the wrong thing. Trina smiles. "I did too. Now hurry and fuck me before your mother comes," Trina says.

Ryan giggles as they pull off their clothes and get into position.

CHAPTER THIRTY-TWO

I t's been crazy in the shop all day; people coming in placing orders, deliveries, and lots of questions. Ryan hasn't had a moment to sit down, and even had to call in his cousin at lunchtime, alongside with the delivery driver. Despite the frantic nature of the day, it hasn't skipped Ryan's mind that Trina hasn't come in. He's barely had a second to keep an eye out for her, but he's well aware that the cake is still waiting in the fridge for her.

The shop finally quiets down around five o'clock, giving Ryan and his mother a moment to catch their breaths and prep for for the orders coming in tomorrow. With a minute to go until half-past five, Ryan wanders towards the door ready to lock it, mind whirring about how he's going to get the cake to Trina now, when, suddenly, there's the sound of heels clicking on the concrete skids to a halt at the door, looking flustered.

Trina startles when she sees Ryan, clearly not expecting him to have his face pressed up against the glass. She smiles as he moves to open the door.

"I'm so sorry—I'm late," Trina says. "My boss stopped by my desk and I couldn't slip away."

"Don't worry," Ryan says, nearly reaching out to put his hand on her arm. "Let me grab your cake, I'll be two seconds."

Ryan darts into the kitchen, completely ignoring his mother's questions as he grabs the box from the fridge. He doesn't know what he's going to say to her and is praying she'll be in too much of a rush to get home to stay behind to interrogate him.

Trina looks nervous as he reappears with the cake, biting at her bottom lip, though she smiles when she sees him.

"Here you go," Ryan says, placing the cake into her arms. Trina looks so uncomfortable, he kind of wants to snatch the cake back and give her a hug instead.

"Hang on," Trina says, looking around for somewhere to put the cake down "I need to pay you."

"No. Please," Ryan raises his hands. "It's on the house."

"But—" Trina starts.

"Please, this is the least I can do to try and make your life easy."

"Are you sure? This is cutting into your profits, Ryan."

"I am more than sure," he says. "It's my pleasure."

"Thank you," she whispers.

"It really is my pleasure," Ryan repeats again, stepping a little closer. Trina too moves forwards and looks up at him through her dark lashes, meeting his eyes and holding his gaze. Several moments pass and neither of them blinks as if they're daring each other to look away. She exhales and bites her lip and he licks his in response.

The sound of Ryan's ringtone — it's his brother calling -interrupts their moment. He curses in his head and mumbles an apology as he answers, though he hardly listens to Grayson as Trina smiles and ducks her head as she turns towards the door. Ryan grabs a business card from next to the register and runs over to her, holding up a finger. Tucking his phone, he takes a pen from his jacket pocket and scrawls his cell number onto it.

Trina's fingers are tentative as she takes the card from him. Ryan covers the microphone. "In case you need help, later? Or, you know, next time you need a cake?" Trina smiles, her cheeks redden. She mouths 'thank you' and nods as he opens the door for her to exit.

"Ryan? Are you listening to me?" Grayson's voice cuts through the ringing in his ears and, in a bit of a daze, Ryan can continue the conversation - about their cousin's Shawn's upcoming tenth wedding anniversary - whilst he finishes cleaning before he closes the shop.

———

Trina nearly drops her phone when it vibrates just seconds after she texts Ryan late that evening. She thought he'd be asleep, and wishes she hadn't.

"Ryan, I'm so sorry for waking you. I need your help," Trina texted.

"I'm up. Let's talk." Ryan replied back.

"Okay," Trina responds, her fingers slipping so that her phone's autocorrect has to come to her rescue.

The phone's ringtone goes on for a few seconds, and Trina takes a deep breath.

"Hi," Trina says.

"Hi, Trina. What's up?" Ryan asks so gently that she wants to burst into tears.

"I don't know why I thought I could do this. This cake thing has been a nightmare from the beginning," Trina says.

"Hey, relax," he says. "Now tell me what's happened and I'll see if I can help."

Trina begins telling Ryan about how she started rolling out the fondant, only for her to have not used enough powdered sugar on the surface, so it got stuck. She had rolled it again and used more - she looks around the kitchen and winces at sugar everywhere - but the fondant began tearing and became grainy. Her box of powdered sugar - which has been in her cupboard for far too long - must have dampened.

Ryan hums as Trina explains how she tried to put the powdered sugar on the cake, hoping to disguise it, but then hadn't rolled it out large enough to cover the surface.

When she tried to peel it off, she had taken most of the cake away.

"I swear to God, Ryan, I could have dropped it on the floor and it would look better than it does now. It's a total mess." A tear trickles down her face.

"One second." Ryan's quiet for a few seconds and Trina's worried feeling guilty that she's ruined the cake he so kindly gave her. "You still there?"

"I'm here. I'm so sorry," Trina says.

"I'll make another cake for you tomorrow."

"What? No, Ryan, you can't—"

"No, Trina. It's fine, I can put something together in an hour or so."

"I can't let you do that."

"Trina," Ryan says. "What's your job?"

"Oh, why?" Trina was puzzled. "I'm a partner at a law firm."

"Ok," Ryan says. "Wow, that's great." Trina senses Ryan got a little side-tracked. "So, you wouldn't ask me to negotiate or stand up in court or whatever, would you?"

"No. Why?"

"Because this I can do for you, Trina. We're professionals and know how important it is to be on time?"

"If you say so but this—"

"Trina, I want to do this for you."

"Oh—well, if you say so," she says. "I guess I can't convince you otherwise."

"There's just one favor I need to ask of you," Ryan says.

"Okay, whatever."

"Don't tell my mother." Trina attempts to smother her chuckle with a cough. "I know, I know, I'm thirty-two and co-owner of the shop, but she'll kill me if she finds out I've been in there after closing!"

"No, Ryan, you can't do this. It's going to cause a problem between you and your mother. Really, I can go to buy one at the supermarket and get some cupcakes to go along with it."

"Those are not fresh, and probably been sitting there for over a week!" Ryan says. "If it would make you feel better, why don't you come and help me?"

Trina pauses for a moment. Then surprises herself by saying she really wouldn't mind.

"Ok, I'll see you tomorrow?"

In Trina's mind, she pictures him stuffing his hands in his pockets. "Yeah, I'll be there," Trina says. "How's 5:25? I'll be off around then."

"Sounds great," Ryan says. "Bye, Trinnie."

"Bye," Trina replies.

Trina dumps the fondant in the trash, laughing as she cleans up the mess she managed to make.

ZOE

CHAPTER THIRTY-THREE

At 1600, the alarm on Zoe's phone started to buzz and jingle, ending the nap that would carry her through the first night of three in a row. Zoe stretched out on her soft feather bed, fingertips grazing the touch screen and silencing the annoying alert while a lazy yawn. Wiping the sleep from her eyes, she swung her bare legs over the edge of the mattress. Zoe rolled and shrugged her slender shoulders, sitting on the side of the bed and sliding the weight of her cozy down comforter from her lithe frame. With a natural and unpracticed grace, she treaded softly into the master bath. Going back to work after being off for a stretch was always so bittersweet, she reveled in her time off but always looked forward to catching up on the latest with her friends at work. Silver Bay General Hospital was like an information superhighway, always drama. While Zoe did not partake in gossip, she was not above listening to it… she was human after all.

'Oh!' Zoe blurted, glancing in the mirror briefly before the steam from the shower began to cloud the glass. Despite her days off and the sleep she thought she had caught up on, she still spotted to her disappointment the slightest trace of darkness under her blue eyes. The nightshift was taking its toll but she absolutely adored the nurses and patient care techs on the overnight. For the past 6 years, Zoe gave her life as an RN in the Surgical/Trauma Intensive Care Unit at SBGH. Of the four critical care areas, the SICU was by far the largest. Ever since graduating from nursing school, Zoe knew she wanted to be where the action was. As a new grad, Zoe knew she'd start in a medical-surgical unit, where she would hone her nursing skills and work her way into the trauma unit. Though Zoe craved the adrenaline, she stayed at bay as a staff nurse in tertiary care until a dreaded meeting with her old supervisor, Nurse Herron.

Nurse Herron was a battle-ax, plain and simple. The younger nurses in the unit called her 'old school', because of her stark white uniform with the nurse cap that looked as though it belonged in the Smithsonian rather than the modern world. The uniform never displayed a wrinkle and Herron wore it proudly. "Zoe, dear… you are ready." Zoe smiled, stealing herself back to the present while idly washing with a pink loofah that was foaming her favorite lemon and lavender Bath & Body Works soap. After toweling off, she slipped on a white cotton sports bra and matching bikini before dressing in her 'hospital blues'. The ciel-blue scrubs were provided by the hospital for certain units only, which included the ICUs and the OR... areas that were most contaminated. While they didn't have the most flattering appearance, they were laundered and sterilized daily.

Not one to wear makeup at work, Zoe gently sponged on a touch of concealer and coated her long lashes with mascara. With precision, she finished off her look with her favorite lip balm and pressed her lips firmly together. It was unusually warm out for October and Zoe opted out of blow-drying her long, damp copper tresses. After a quick comb through, she wove the strands into a low fish-tail braid which she draped over her shoulder after securing the ends with an elastic band. As she tucked a few loose pieces behind her ear, her gaze dropped to her phone which buzzed on the sink.

"Hey, girl. It's my turn to stop at Starbucks. Venti Pumpkin Spice again?"

Zoe's lips curled into a small lopsided grin as her slender digits typed effortlessly across the screen, sending the thumbs up emoji back to her best friend and coworker Amber. Almost instantly, another text buzzed in.

"Don't forget, it's Halloween... and as if the gods wanted to punish us further, the moon is full. It's going to be an absolute nightmare. I hope you packed your big-girl panties."

"Fuck."

In the past 6 years, Zoe had never sworn so much in

her life, it surprised even herself at times as she punctuated her vernacular with cuss words. Frequent exposure to trauma changes people and she was no different, experiencing tragedies more so than miracles. They say "Silver Bay is a dangerous place", this fact only made more evident by the hospital capacity being at or exceeding a hundred percent, always. Her eyes narrowed as she stared at the date on the screen, *October 31st… Halloween. Amber was right.* Peeping again, Zoe nodded to her reflection and popped the phone into her front-chest pocket.

Always prepared, dinner was already packed in her lunch bag and waiting on the top shelf of her fridge. Next to it, a large therm0 of cold water. Zoe grabbed both and tucked them into a large-flowered tote that she used only for work and zipped it up, scanning the kitchen for any other items that may have strayed. A creature of habit, Zoe flipped on the light over the kitchen sink and activated the alarm panel, securing the two-bedroom townhouse and snapping up her keys on her way out the door. After locking the deadbolt from the outside, she kneeled down on her small stoop next to the stairs where her jack-o-lantern sat. Using the stem, Zoe gingerly removed the top and turned on the LED light inside which illuminated the pumpkin face. 'Carving pumpkins is not my forte' she said to herself, replacing the lid and skipping down the steps to head towards her white GMC Yukon.

Honestly, the Yukon was too big for her. However, once Zoe had started in the medical field, her father Lou Walker, had insisted she buy a vehicle that was not only safe but would be reliable in all types of weather. Being considered essential personnel meant that reporting to work was not optional, even in times of crisis. The dead could walk the earth and the medical staff would still be expected for assuming shift. The Yukon would easily sweep the dead from the streets Zoe thought, chuckling to herself. Still, the truck was huge for a single woman, but comfortable.

———

Zoe hardly hit traffic working on the off-shift, heading in and out of the heart of Silver Bay opposite of the commuting flow. The Yukon rolled into the parking complex and followed the ramps to the roof, where employees parked. Typically, Zoe tried parking in the same spot, next to the elevator and under the halo of a garage light. As hoped, her spot was open and beside it, a shiny silver BMW x5 idled quietly Amber's SUV. Amber waved, grinning and waving a coffee in each hand; her light brown curls were pulled up into a messy bun atop her head, gently bouncing with her giddiness. 'Well, she seems to be well-caffeinated already.'

With both engines off, Zoe and Amber climbed from their seats and met at the elevator.

"Here you go." Amber handed the piping hot cup to Zoe.

"Oh, thank you! What—"

Zoe had pressed the button for the elevator and was

abruptly interrupted when the familiar sound of sirens screamed. The two young nurses looked at each other, eyebrows raising. 'It's already begun.' As the sirens grew closer, Zoe and Amber stepped to the edge of the garage, ignoring the arriving elevator. A med-flight ambulance was speeding towards the ER, close behind a parade of Silver Bay police cruisers followed, their blue lights flashing and strobing in sync with the ambulances red ones. Without looking away, Zoe asked, "What do you think it is?"

CHAPTER THIRTY-FOUR

Before appearing on the unit, Zoe and Amber ducked into the ladies locker room to switch into their work clogs. When the pair arrived in the SICU, their nurse supervisor, Katharine was conducting an impromptu staff meeting. Katharine was a woman in her own category, much like her previous manager Nurse Herron, but more fearless. She was her staff's most supportive champion, always doing right by her nurses. She handled conflict with poise but wasn't certainly one to cross, especially if you were a surgeon abusing power in her unit. Physically, she was even more imposing, the statuesque blond woman was stacked in all the right places. She kept her icy blonde tresses short in a no-nonsense style, accented by tailored pants suits… never wearing a skirt. Angular features and high cheekbones combined with her frame gave Katharine a fierce high-fashion, editorial look, striking without any cosmetic influence. As if she wasn't perfect enough, Katharine was also very skilled in critical care and thought nothing of changing into scrubs and helping out on the unit, working alongside her staff.

Zoe felt fortunate, as she watched her leader command the attention of the room. She had been 'groomed' into the nurse she was today by Herron and Katharine. When Zoe was deemed 'ready' by nurse Herron, Zoe left her old unit as a one who was bright, motivated, and easy to teach. However, despite Zoe's maturity for twenty-six, she was shy and meek, one could even argue she was a pushover and easy to manipulate. In six years, with the aid of Katharine and the SICUs seasoned nurses, Zoe began to develop confidence and wielded it effortlessly in simple and complex situations alike. With patient care always at the forefront, Zoe earned the respect of both her peers and surgeons. 'Zoe, focus', she told herself. It was then she saw Katharine holding up a bright red pager, 'the trauma beeper.'

"Alright everyone, as we all know… it's Halloween." Katharine's confident voice paused and nurses and care techs nodded, whispering among themselves. "I have brought in extra staff to assist us with the expected onslaught that we will probably come in. Per the hospital board, all staff who are in direct patient care over the next week and picks up overtime will be given bonuses at the end of next month." There was a soft chatter of excitement, however, the veteran staff looked at one another worried. The hospital was not feeling generous; they expected complete and utter chaos.

Almost as if it were timed, there was a sudden deafening thunder. Everyone fell silent, eyes wide and shining. The only sounds heard were the soft beeps of monitors, medication pumps, ventilators, and life-support machines. Katharine swiftly sidestepped to the charge nurse station's computer and brought up the hospital's news feed. Everyone followed quickly behind her.

"BREAKING NEWS" flashed across the monitor and everyone gathered. There was live footage of an industrial area of Silver Bay, where warehouses, factories, and mills littered the seaport and its scattered piers… completely engulfed in flames, whipping and licking the air, consuming everything in its wake. Zoe's mouth gaped open and she looked over at Amber, who was gasping in disbelief. The SICU staff was completely floored, the silence finally breaking as a pretty brunette by the name of Josie spoke up. "We are going to have a lot of burns to manage tonight. Get ready."

Katharine shook her head slowly, face remaining glued still stuck on the screen. In a voice that seemed far away, paling in comparison to her demeanor just moments before. "No…" Adding even more quietly, "We won't. Fires like that take everything with it."

The realization washed across the group; everyone in that area would likely be burned alive. Zoe felt her mouth go dry as her skin began to prickle. She tried unsuccessfully to swallow her stomach back down from her throat, soft fingertips brushing and covering her lips. She felt Amber rest her head softly on her shoulder, the fingers of her free hand intertwining with that of her friend's.

Suddenly, the phone rang and the trauma beeper screeched to life. Some jumped while others remained lost still in thought. Josie answered the phone. "Hello? Yes. Understood. OR Seven with ETA of four hours. Multi-trauma. K9 Police officer… wait, what do you mean the dog won't leave?" Josie raised her eyebrows as Zoe watched her furiously scribbling down details of the incoming admission.

Josie continued, "This is ICU. We can handle it. What? What do you mean they're staying down here? We are barely going to have enough room to accommodate patients let alone a troop of cops and a dog!"

Katharine snatched the phone from an exasperated Josie and simply said, "Bring the damn dog."

Katharine hung up the phone and glanced at Josie, while she understood the plea of her trusted head nurse, arguing with the admissions department, it would get them nowhere. Josie quickly regained her composure, passing out the assignment for the night. Non-critical patients had been moved out of the SICU in preparation for things to come, so there were a lot of empty rooms. They would fill quickly tonight and everyone standing there now, would be a different person come the morning.

Josie swept a dark curl from her forehead with the back of her hand while dark chocolate eyes lifted under a thick curtain of ebony lashes, fixating on Zoe and watching her thoughtfully.

"Hey Red?" Zoe immediately lifted her stare to meet Josie's. "This one is yours. A decorated K9 police officer with multi-trauma, ETA is four hours. The dog is with him; a black Rhodesian Ridgeback by the name of Rudy. There'll be a large police presence for his and our protection."

Zoe nodded, making mental note of the details as they spilled from the lips of her head nurse. "Amber will be your secondary, it sounds like you will need it. I will call respiratory for a ventilator, touch base with pharmacy… your big boy is over 6'6 and his weight-based meds will require additional concentration to keep him sedated and comfortable. Additionally, you'll need a bed extender."

Compliantly, Zoe nodded again, it would be a lie if she tried to deny her apprehension but this was her purpose. Amber was already on the phone with supply, looking for a bed extender while the other nurses scattered to their rooms to begin their shifts. Katharine who had suddenly disappeared, reappeared dressed in scrubs. She looked apprehensively at Josie, who was juggling between the phone and the pager. They exchanged worried, close-lipped smiles and nodded to one another.

The pager screamed, again and again, everything was

coming to life and the unit bustled with activity. Like a well-oiled machine, the staff worked with a fervor, anticipating the needs of what the shift would bring. Silver Bay tonight would have their hands full.

464

T he SICU was the largest ICU in Silver Bay General Hospital and was also the most recent to get renovated. The twenty-four room section was modernized with the latest technology. The shift had only been a few hours in and the 24-bed unit was nearly full. Besides, there had been 3 codes so far, one of which where the patient survived. Zoe watched as two morgue carts wheeled past her assigned room while she and Amber continued setting up. Room 24 was quite big at the end of the hall. Getting the report of the patient and list of several officers and a dog arriving, Zoe, in fact, hoped it would be large enough. Slowly, she turned to watch Amber who was setting up some suction canisters. "Hey!"

"Hmm?" Amber turned and eyed her friend who had paused. Zoe took her to the open glass slider and pulled back the privacy curtain. They were almost toe to toe, when Zoe inched close to Amber's ear, whispering.

"Don't you think it's strange. It's Halloween. In past years, we've seen first-hand rival gangs in Cyprus Row come in here in the dozens."

"So?"

"So… Cyprus Row is such a dump. Anyway, I was thinking about the explosion we saw earlier by the seaport. I wonder if it was caused by fireworks or a terrorist attack."

Amber was nodding as she listened, almost thinking Zoe was going mad. "Girl, if you don't stop thinking about that. We already had 9-11. We don't need another one. Girl, we got work to do."

"I don't know just seems weird." Zoe licked her lips and took a deep breath. "The ambulance we saw when we were coming in was driving from that aread… then, within a half-hour, the entire area is gone, Amber. We might be under attack."

"Does seem a bit odd since you put it that way but don't worry. We'll make it."

Zoe opened the curtain, glancing out to the rest of the unit. In the far corner, one of the patient care techs, Shauna was having a very deep discussion with Dr. Eric Salinger, a 4th-year surgical resident. To say that Zoe disliked the pair would be an understatement. Shauna was a petite hottie, with mousy fair ash brown hair that was always halfway pulled up. She was ok but not stunning. Zoe always saw her look as though she had taken a huge bite out of a shit-sandwich. Shauna did not get along well with the others either, her poor work ethic and attitude towards everyone including the patients made her an unpopular choice when the nurses needed assistance. The fact that she kept company with Eric did not bode well either. Zoe crinkled her nose as Amber peeked over her shoulder. "Speaking of weird. Look at those two," Amber added.

"Right? They give me the creeps, even more so when they are together like this."

Eric looked okay would be handsome if he wasn't always smiling. That constant grin spoke as if he knew the exact date and time in which the world would end. He paraded around the hospital as if he was already a resident physician, being bossy to nurses and others. His behavior knew no bounds. Eric and Katharine had gone a few rounds before after he had been rude to one of her staff. Days later, he offered the nurse an half-hearted apology that was demanded only by his superiors. According to the other surgical residents, Eric was a butcher in the OR. He preferred patients to be under as little anesthesia as possible, arguing that patients had better responses when awake than not. The anesthesia team was not fooled however, openly and abashedly scolding Eric in front of his peers whenever the topic would come up. Recently, the surgeons and anesthesiologists had grown tired of his antics and his OR privileges were temporarily revoked. Eric was ordered to do research until the hospital board of directors stepped in.

The nurses were glad he was confined to a desk in the hospital's library. Yet, here he was... talking to Shauna, nearly nose to nose and her giggling indicated there was something going on.

The moment was broken as the sound of a bed being wheeled down the main hall was heard; it was moving fast and there was quite a bit of commotion as several voices loudly tried to speak over one another. The bed, with the length extender that Amber had so nicely found, came briskly around the corner. Anesthesia was at the head, one gloved hand pushing as the other squeezed an Ambu bag, providing the intubated patient with oxygen and mechanical breaths, not of the patients own making. On either side of him, two techs kept pace, each one wheeling an IV pole that had several pumps and channels infusing medications. With so many infusions running, the flashing lights on each of the channels reminded Zoe of a Christmas tree. On either side of the bed, two residents and two attending surgeons pushed, remaining was Dr. Lake, who was the director of the SICU... steering at the foot.

A kind and gentle natured man, Katharine and her nurses enjoyed working with Dr. Lake, who despite his advanced age was as sharp as a tack. Patients and their relatives also loved him; his calm and supportive bedside manner was unparalleled. Though he was the director,

Dr. Lake was an expert anesthesiologist and intensivist. One week out of the month, he took his turn in the rotation of the SICUs intensivists, to which there were three others, and performed rounds and fulfilled a week-long on-call schedule. His truest passion, besides patient care, was teaching the residents who rotated. Each resident would be completely under Lake's spell as he talked and taught; frequently scribbling notes and answering questions he would quiz them on.

Zoe was relieved when she saw that Lake was on this week. Amber swiftly unhinged the glass as Zoe grasped the foot of the bed, helping guide the heavy bed. At that moment, her eyes went wide as saucers… she was looking at quite possibly the largest man she had ever seen in her life. Unexpectedly, a cold wet nose touched her fingers and she directed her wide-eyed stare to the furry jet-black mass at the foot of the bed. Glassy brown almond-shaped, intelligent eyes watched her intently. His ears triangular and erect, swiveling in response to new noises, taking in rapidly changing surroundings. Besides that, the dog Rudy was perfectly still, like a statue. The behavior from the K9 surprised her, but Zoe didn't really know what to expect. Having never seen a Rhodesian Ridgeback before, she had quickly cruised the internet for a quick reference. Though she had read its physical description, it paled in comparison to the proud looking animal that was laying in front of her. It was large, maybe 80lbs squarely built and well-muscled, despite this… it was not bulky but rather compact, agile-looking.

"Zoe?" Dr. Lake yelled, her head snapping immediately to face him, as the bed was locked into position in Room 24. "Are you taking our friend here?"

"Yes, Doctor."

Anesthesia stopped squeezing the Ambu bag momentarily to connect the ventilator to the patients breathing tube. Other nurses, including Katharine, swarmed into the room, helping to settle the new admission. None of them spoke but went about the task at hand without any direction, like bees in a honeycomb that instinctively knew what must be done. The in-room monitor came alive, displaying numerous numbers and tracings which indicated the man's vital signs. Zoe agreed to take the report from Anesthesia then, satisfied at the moment with his stable condition. Katharine was at the head of the bed, making a list of all the infusions that were running, dose and volume, confirming also that each channel was programmed with the correct documented weight. Amber took note of all of the man's invasive lines. He had a radial arterial line in his right wrist which showed second-by-second blood pressure, in a red waveform displayed on the monitor just under his EKG reading which was green. The man had a triple lumen MAC line above his left collarbone… instead of having peripheral IVs. This special IV was centralized in the patient's body, directing the medication infusions to his heart via his superior vena cava. This particular one had a way of measuring his cardiac output, the yellow waveform on the monitor belonged to this PA line. "Urinary catheter?"

Amber chimed out, another nurse answering affirmatively while taking account of the amount of urine in the bag. Josie who appeared opposite of Amber squatted down and called out, "Chest tube to suction!" as a soft bubbling noise is heard.

Amber moved towards the patient's head and was about to document the placement of the breathing tube, when she did a sudden double-take of his face, gasping inaudibly. The left side of his face and neck was a devastating burned and scarred. His mangled skin was a jigsaw as it twists and craters, around his left eye and Amber wondered if the man's vision is intact. At his jaw, the skin here is especially thin and superficial, it wouldn't take much to expose the bone of his mandible. Her assessment continues, finding he is without a left eyebrow and where his ear should be, is a gnarled stump.

Zoe finishes her scribbled report in a shorthand that only she can comprehend and look to her team. The OR techs begin to file out and Anesthesia heads to the desk to write a transfer note. As she passes Lake, he squeezes her shoulder gently. "I'll write you some orders, dear. In the meantime, blood pressure with a MAP >65, heart rate 60-100 and SpO2 should be >96%. They say ventilating him has been problematic… more than likely due to his size. They put him way under. The officer shall rest tonight and tomorrow, we will wean him off slowly."

Silently acknowledging, Zoe steps up to where Amber is and is also taken aback by the sight. However, it was not the scars Zoe noticed first, and not knowing what possessed her at that moment, her fingers grazed the forehead of the sedated officer and softly brushed slickened black strands of hair that stuck to his face away. Turning her hand, so that the underside was against his skin, her knuckle just ghosting over his right, heavy brow and down his defined cheek. His jaw was prominent and masculine, the slight stubble that grew there tickled her skin. Withdrawing her hand, gaze fixated still on his face, Zoe let out a breath she wasn't even aware that she was holding in. She realized then that she was alone with Officer Sam Dalton, the other nurses had left to settle another admit rolling through. Amber went to tend to a phone call at the desk. Rudy softly thumped his tail against the blankets, making his presence known, in case she had forgotten. Zoe hadn't, she was very much aware of all the work that needed to be done."

Zoe purposefully moved quietly to his right side, leaning to whisper in his ear… just enough over the bubbling chest tube, beeping monitor, click of infusion channels and whirring of the ventilator.

"I'm Zoe—" Drawing a deep breath, "And we will spend this night and the next, and the one after, together."

CHAPTER THIRTY-SIX

Zoe grabbed a basin and supplies, moving with speed, there was much to be done. Once she was satisfied with Officer Dalton's vital signs, initial assessment and confirmation of having back up medication infusions in the waiting, she began peeling back the hospital bedding which was heavy with saturated blood from the OR and tossed them into an open hamper. Her blue eyes assessed the massive man before her, only covered now in a hospital gown which was rumpled and soiled. With towels and bath blankets stacked beside her, Zoe began to unsnap the shoulder of the sleeves… her gloved fingers fumbling, as if she was a first-year CNA again as if she had never given a bed bath before. Biting down on her bottom lip, she whispered to herself, "Get it together, Zoe!" As Officer Dalton's bare chest came into view, she felt the heat rising to her cheeks, flooding the pale skin there. He was an absolutely beautiful and massive specimen, and though he lay comfortably in this sedated state, his muscled physique remained impressively hard and defined… as if he was carved from stone in the very likeness of a god. His expansive chest, dappled with dark hair rose and fell in compliance with the ventilator. The right side of his thoracic cage suffered some sort of crushing injury, causing several ribs to break, which in turn punctured and downed his right lung. To help with the re-expansion of the lung, a chest tube was placed and bubbled quietly as Zoe stood and admired the handsome man in front of her, almost in a daze. Voices outside her room brought her back, one was Amber, who was arguing with two men, though Zoe did not seem to recognize. "Zoe!" Amber called out.

Zoe turned to look towards the curtain and could see the heels of Amber's clogs as if she was blocking the door.

"There are two very annoying officers here to see your patient. I told them you were busy right now and they would have to wait."

She heard them again teasing Amber, their boots nearing her clogs.

"Annoying but terribly good looking, eh?" One officer said.

Zoe raised her brows and draped a towel over Dalton's chest, his lap still covered by the bottom half of his hospital gown. Making sure he was adequately covered; Zoe scooted to the door and poked her head out the edge of the curtain and over Amber's shoulder.

"For god's sake, there are some good lookin' nurses here!"

Both officers exchanged a grin before looking back at the brunette and redhead before them. The shorter of the two men ran his index finger and thumb along with his dark goatee before offering a sly but sincere smile, almost speaking directly to Amber.

"I'm Officer Adrian Blumenthal… and this here is Officer Hank Lowell." Nodding his head towards the larger man, who like Zoe, was a redhead. Hank's icy blue stare looked then to Zoe, his thumbs resting gently atop the silver buckle of his belt. "How is our boy?"

Zoe slipped out fully from behind the curtain, finding herself under the imposing stare of what she assumed were close friends of Officer Dalton's. With ease, she folded her hands, having had discarded her gloves before coming to the door and looked at them intently, exuding sudden confidence. "Officer Dalton has suffered many injuries and while I cannot give you specifics right now, what I can tell you is that he is resting comfortably. He is on a ventilator. Once I am done with giving him a bath —" Zoe felt the heat on her cheeks flare again. "I'll let both of you come in and see him." The look of relief upon their faces quickly changed to amusement.

"Where do we sign up for baths?"

Zoe and Amber looked at one another and then shook their heads. Amber hid her lips behind her hand, for fear that even the tiniest of giggles would slip out. Seriously, Zoe folded her arms across her chest. "It would be helpful if you two could call Officer Dalton's family and tell them what has happened and that he's here at SBGH."

"Well, to be honest… Sam doesn't really have any family," Officer Adrian explained.

"How about a wife?" Zoe added. Another soft blush betrayed her intent.

"No!" Hank added, eyeing Zoe's cheeks suspiciously before grinning.

"Girlfriend?" The question passed Zoe's lips before she could even catch it.

"No, lucky for you." Adrian chuckled before giving the blushing redhead a wink.

"Oh! You wicked, wicked man!" Amber giggled melodiously, gently swatting at Officer Blumenthal and then at Hank, whose attention had been directed back to the nurses' station. Hank was staring unabashedly at the statuesque Katharine who busied herself with the phone that wouldn't stop ringing. Zoe excused herself and stepped back into her room, hearing Amber wheeling chairs over for Officers Adrian and Hank. As she returned to the bedside, Zoe glanced to the foot of the bed, where Rudy laid. The dog lazily looked back at her, his head resting on his front paws, body, and tail curled into the remaining space. "Good boy."

* * *

While refilling the basin with warm water, Zoe snatched up several washcloths and a bottle of surgical soap and then wheeled everything over via bedside table.

Removing the towel from Officer Dalton's chest, she admired his masculine form, only briefly this time and began working. Gently, she washed the ruined left side of his face first, inspecting the twisting mass of scars which appeared old, as they were healed. The mangled flesh shone as the soapy washcloth removed grime and dried blood. There were no facial fractures but there were the beginnings of bruising. She dipped the washcloth again and tended to the right side of his face, handsome and rugged. She noted a small laceration above his thick dark brow and cleaned it with new gauze, dabbing ointment on it after. Taking the flashlight from beside the basin, Zoe tenderly opened each one of his eyes and flashed the light into his pupils. The officer's eyes were dark grey; the color of storm clouds racing over an angry sea. The pupils briskly constricted to the light, which was the reaction Zoe was expecting, thankfully he was not found to have any head injuries. At that moment, Zoe found herself hoping that maybe tomorrow the distant and glassy stare those stormy grey eyes had now would be replaced with vision, seeing her upon his wake. She shook her head then, repeatedly and silently scolding herself with how unprofessional she was being. This was her patient and she was his nurse.

Moving to the head of the bed, another refreshed water basin in the bin, she stood looking down as him and purposefully started pushing his dark black hair back from his forehead. Noting some glass pieces, she double gloved and picked out the larger pieces by hand and then with a small black comb, cleaned out the rest. As she started to lather his hair with shampoo, she imagined how he wears it when at work… or even at home, a smile tugging at the corners of her lips as she pictured him sporting a low ponytail at the nape of his thick neck. Though she did not think of him to rock a man bun, she twisted his freshly clean and damp hair into a bun atop his head so it would not get in the way of lines or equipment. Idly, she wondered then what it would feel like to run her fingers through his hair under different circumstances. 'Oh, my God, just stop,' she pleaded.

Zoe then moved to continue with the bath. With fresh washcloths, she soaped up his shoulders and chest, avoiding the chest-tube dressing in which she would change to her liking afterward. It would be a lie to say Zoe didn't enjoy giving Officer Dalton this bed bath, and though this type of care was something Zoe gave all her patients, she felt guilty about letting her mind wander while Officer Dalton was in such a critical state. Feeling foolish, she took a deep breath as the washcloth ran down his stomach, over each and every individual abdominal, soaking the trail of soft black fuzz that continued reaching his pubic area, disappearing from sight under his gown. 'He's not even flexing… he is just so yummy- Zoe!'

His lower half still needed to be washed and Zoe felt another wave of heat rush to her face and her stomach filling with butterflies? Pursing her lips together, Zoe let her gaze move to his still-covered lap but as her thoughts began to drift, there was a soft knock and Katharine appeared. "I saw that your curtain was still closed, Zoe. I thought perhaps you needed some help." Relief overcame Zoe, while she remained outwardly professional, she was thankful Katharine's assistance would keep her laser-focused. Rudy alerted to the newcomer lifted his head and swiveled his triangular ears. Katharine smiled at the dog who softly thumped his tail a couple times before settling his chin on his paws.

"I figured we could finish the bath and then ask the officers outside how to get my new friend here off the bed, so we can change the sheets."

"Good idea," said Katherine.

Zoe spread a fresh towel over Officer Dalton's lap before pulling the hospital gown completely away. Katharine at the moment did not seem none the wiser, gloving up and taking a washcloth into her fingers, wringing out the excess soapy water. Shifting the towel to expose the officer's thigh, Katharine carefully began to wash his left leg. "What a shame this happened, Officer Blumenthal and Lowell both say adamantly how dedicated of an officer he is. Dependable, honest, strong. How much he loves his K9…"

Katharine studied his face with admiration, and what may have even been a pity. Zoe was standing watching, and Katharine moved to her side to do the other leg. Similar to the injury to the right side of his chest, his femur had been broken and hip dislocated, both re-set and repaired in the OR. While his orthopedic injuries would be painful and likely require physical therapy, but it was his internal injuries that worried Zoe. Officer Dalton suffered a grade IV liver laceration which caused him to lose a lot of blood. He was present with unstable and unpredictable shock-like symptoms. While in the OR, the surgical team transfused him with units of blood, while searching for the source of the bleeding.

As Katharine re-dressed his hip dressing, she eyed Zoe curiously, wondering why she hadn't yet completed urinary catheter care, after seeing the towel still on Officer Dalton's lap. In Zoe's hesitation, Katharine found her answer and she demurely hid the tiniest, innocent smile. Unaware, Zoe put on another pair of gloves on and reached for another washcloth. Not wanting to place herself in a negative light in the presence of her supervisor, Zoe delicately moved the towel and wasn't prepared for what was underneath.

———

It is said that nurses see more men private parts than the ladies of the night who reside on the street of silk. Though Zoe had certainly seen her share, Officer Dalton's was truly exceptional. Zoe's gaze widened, with her dry lips parting… she couldn't be sure, but did she just gasped? Doing her best to avoid any eye contact with Katharine, Zoe moved the washcloth to Officer Dalton's impressive manhood. Though not erect, its length was partway down his muscular thighs. However, it was his girth though that started to make Zoe sweat. Her fingertips were unable to touch one another as she wrapped her slender digits around his thick, veined stick. With the most delicate touches, Zoe maneuvered the washcloth around the head and the rubber catheter. 'Your boss is literally standing a few feet away, get it together you creep,' Zoe thought.

Katharine was now placing new heart-monitor leads on Officer Dalton's chest in attempts to move things along, ending Zoe's palpable tension. With luck, they had found an extra-large hospital gown which would accommodate the Officer's hulking frame. Zoe was pleased, Officer Dalton was squeaky clean with new bandages, besides his obvious injuries and breathing tube, he looked okay. Zoe watched the officer as Katharine left to ask Officers Blumenthal and Lowell about Rudy. When she returned, the redhead was swift on her heels whipping the curtain closed behind her. "Move. You are in our way!"

Josie was sassing the two officers at the door, getting them to move as Amber followed inside.

"Ok. See that K9's harness?" The nurses looked over to the counter where Rudy's harness sat and Zoe looked back to Katharine curiously for more direction. "Right now, it is off... meaning Rudy is off-duty. We have to put it back on him."

"That seems easy." Zoe took the black and olive green nylon heavy harness with military-grade buckles and a few Velcro patches. One read: "I am the Rudy". Rudy suddenly sat up from the bed in full attention. His deep brown stare was hyperfocused on Zoe as she approached him with the harness in hand. He was even more impressive from this angle… angular, lean and athletic. The way he sat perfectly still was almost disarming. Carefully, Zoe began slipping the harness over Rudy head and ears, smoothing straps down and around his chest. Rudy was patient as Zoe worked the harness like a rubrics cube. Finally, Rudy was "dressed" and he leaped from the bed with a graceful agility Zoe, nor the other nurses had ever seen from a dog.

"What a good boy," Amber cooed, reaching for him. The dog who just moments ago was lying upon the bed, thumping his tail to the delight of the ladies was in work-mode. Rudy ignored her advances and silently inched to the closed curtain, in the path of the doorway.

The nurses busied themselves helping Zoe roll her patient from one side of the bed to the other so that all of the soiled sheets could be replaced with fresh new ones. Before leaving, they also cleaned the room; the soiled linen went into the hamper, blood was wiped from the floor and bed rails, all unused linen was folded neatly and placed into the cabinets. All evidence of the chaotic scene it had been when Officer Dalton first arrived was now cleared. Zoe thanked her co-workers gratefully and dimmed the recessed lighting which shone over Officer Dalton's resting body. She smiled and washed her hands before stepping to Rudy in the doorway, ruffling his thick fur behind his ears.

"Officer Blumenthal, Officer Lowell… you can come in now."

CHAPTER THIRTY-SEVEN

The two officers stepped past Rudy, the dog didn't move or react, even as they scratched his head on their way coming by. They looked serious; Hank with his mouth slightly agape and Adrian with his lips pressed into a hard line. The color drained from their faces as they took in the sight of their fallen comrade, Officer Sam Dalton. Despite his injuries, both men noted how well-kempt and clean Dalton appeared. He was scrubbed pink, his shoulder-length black hair freshly washed and piled onto the top of his head. The laceration above his right eye was bandaged.

Adrian was the first to come to his bedside, extra careful not to kick over the bubbling chest tube chamber on the floor. Hank followed but stood facing Adrian. Zoe stood quietly at the foot of the bed, allowing them to take in everything. Of the two, Zoe though Hank was more receptive than Officer Blumenthal. Hank's pale icy-blue eyes welled ever so slightly with salted tears… threatening to roll down his cheek if they filled anymore. One of his hands rested on the bedrail while the other one softly grasped Sam's forearm. "We are here for you, brother. Adrian and me, Hank. And Rudy, too." Adrian looked at Hank as he spoke, then back to Sam who looked so tired, he could have been sleeping. Without taking his eyes off him, Adrian finally spoke, "He looks better."

Zoe smiled as Adrian faced her.

"So, you wash all of him? Like, everything?" Like two teenage boys, the two officers began to snicker. Zoe gave them a curt nod before Adrian continued, "Well, he is not going to like that one bit. Could have bought him dinner first before checking out the goods."

Zoe wanted to laugh, but her professionalism overtook her. "Alright, you two rascals, out. I have things to do." Hank and Adrian exchanged grins again.

"Just wanted to brighten the mood, that's all."

The officers left and Zoe whipped the curtain shut and moved to the equipment cart pulling out blood tubes and other phlebotomy pieces. She then took the blood from one of the lines and wistfully examined Officer Dalton's face. "I will happily buy you dinner when you make it out of here if you like." Placing the vials of blood into a bag and disposing of her gloves, Zoe left the room.

———

Adrian and Hank were almost too large for the chairs Amber had given them, but neither cared for their friend was alive. Adrian was not bashful as he watched Amber scurry around the unit, her passion for work, especially on this night, was appealing for the hardworking, blue-collared man. Despite being so busy, Amber was sensitive to Officer Blumenthal's harden stare… men staring at her was not a new thing for the bubbly brunette with bouncing curls. Amber stepped purposefully with an extra swing, her slender hips taunting Adrian as she darted across the unit. Adrian's lips tugged into a slight one-sided smile as his neck craned to examine the way Amber's curved backside looked as she bent over the desk, answering the phone. "Would you look at that?" Hank stopped talking, realizing Adrian hadn't heard literally anything he said. Hank grunted in response, mildly annoyed. "Think I got a chance, buddy?"

"No. The only thing she would ever let a man like you lick would be the bottoms of those purple clogs."

"I would gladly lick those… before I…"

Both officers straightened up and become quiet as Zoe emerged from the room with a biohazard bag tucked up under her arm as she washed her hands.

"One thing I do know, brother… he is going to like that one."

"Agreed. He is so lucky."

Both officers chuckled. Adrian resuming his stalking of Amber as Hank, significantly less obvious, almost shy glanced in the direction of the beautiful blonde, "the leader" of the nurses he assumed.

———

Zoe found an unused portable workstation and unplugged it from the wall and headed towards the nurses' station where Amber was standing. "He staring you know… like you are a delicious meal." Zoe remarked softly, amused.

"Oh darling, I know. I am that delicious." Amber shot a sideways-glance at Zoe and winked. "How long do you think before I have his balls tucked neatly into my back pocket?" Zoe giggled and in unison, the two nurses challenged the officers, with stares of their own. Caught off-guard, Adrian nearly lost his seat in the rolling chair which caused Hank to roar. Zoe and Amber burst into laughter, even Katharine who was passing through with an armful of supplies was harmless by the laugh of Officer Lowell. Her lips pursed and the smile that formed then revealed her, freezing the wide-eyed Hank.

"Zoe!" Josie chided. "Your labs came back and 24's H&H is low. I paged Lake for you." No sooner had Josie ended, the phone rang again and Dr. Lake was on the other end saying he had ordered blood for Officer Dalton and he should be transfused as soon as the units were ready. Taking a moment, Zoe sipped on her cup of coffee and picked up the phone on the first ring when rang again. Hanging up, Zoe put down her cup and headed over to Shauna, who was sitting idly at the desk, playing with her phone.

"Shauna, would you please go to the blood bank and pick up the blood for Room 24,?"

Pretending she hadn't heard the request, Shauna continued typing and even had the nerve to laugh as if she had read something funny. Zoe squinted; Shawna's antics would not be tolerated tonight. The entire staff was so busy, despite how the hours ticked by and here was Shauna, on her ass, taking up space and converting oxygen into carbon dioxide.

"Shauna!" Zoe snapped. Shawna stopped, tucking the phone into her breast pocket. "Yes?" She pretended in a sickeningly sweet voice. Standing, Shauna invaded Zoe's personal space, though she lacked the height to face her nose to nose. Not affected, Zoe stone-walled the mousy girl whose face puckered and soured into a familiar position. "I need you to get blood from the bank for Room 24, for Officer Dalton."

"You think you are so much better than me," Shawna hissed. "It should be me in your shoes, rich little Zoe Walker with the world at her feet. Too bad all of that money can't buy life for you to get a damn boyfriend." Zoe's eyes narrowed into slits which caused Shauna to smile so wide that it reached her eyes.

"Out of the way!" Amber buzzed, barging her way between the two, shouldering Shauna really hard. Embarrassed, Shauna crossed her slender arms across her less than ample chest, storming off.

"I'll get the blood." Amber was already heading towards the door that would lead her to the main elevators.

———

Zoe was back at Officer Dalton's bedside priming a new line for the blood as Amber appeared with a small cooler of blood. She had heard her coming when Amber teased Adrian and Hank, "Hi fellas", and cooed Rudy, who hadn't moved. Per protocol, both nurses checked the blood to match the units to both the patient and the order Dr. Lake had written. They signed off on the workstation on wheels that Zoe had rolled into the room to document on. Amber watched Zoe hang the blood, then smile at Sam. A romantic at heart, Amber leaned against the wall and cocked her head purposely. "You like him, don't you?" Zoe stood at his side, one of her hands resting softly on his own large hand as she allowed her gaze to sweep once more over him. "Silly, isn't it?" Amber shook her head softly, a soft curly lock of hair escaping her loose messy bun. "No."

"Zoe, don't let anything that useless cunt, Shauna says get to you. You are better than that…" Before she could finish, Zoe interrupted in a way that only a best friend could. "Come stay over; we get off at the same time." Amber's chin nestled on Zoe's shoulder; she hadn't made a sound. "Hmm, since I already packed. I hope you stocked up on Captain Crunch with Crunchberries!"

Amber always had a way of twisting a situation, making light in a time of darkness. Zoe stifled a soft laugh before she nodded and peered back at Amber's large brown eyes.

Zoe and Amber worked on transfusing the reminder of the cooler into Officer Dalton, while Zoe diligently documenting in-between. The extra volume helped Zoe lower Officer Dalton's blood pressure and reduce his heart medications. By 2:30 AM, which also was known as dinnertime, Zoe was even able to turn one medication drip completely off. After repositioning Officer Dalton, Zoe and Amber left the room.

Rudy was gone, as was Hank. "Nature calls." Adrian quipped happily as if reading Zoe's and Amber's thoughts. That wasn't the only thing calling, everyone on the unit was starving and the smell of pizza carried through the unit. Katharine appeared wheeling a metal cart stacked with pizza, the box was familiar… "Pepper's Pizzeria" was the local's favorite in Silver Bay. Suddenly, the salads that Zoe and Amber had prepared no longer seemed appetizing. The nurses and support staff, with the exception of Shauna, gathered around at the nursing station and sat shoulder to shoulder. Zoe and Amber sat next to one another and across the desk from Josie and Katharine. Engrossed in her food, Zoe listened to the chatter of the others. Some discussed their weekend plans while others babbled about their patients and the craziness that had transpired. "We still have five more hours to go!" Everyone moaned.

Zoe turned her attention back to Room 24. Hank was back with Rudy and was filling a bowl full of water for the K9. Rudy refused and went back to his post, which caused Hank to frown. Putting down her crust, Zoe wheeled over in her rolling chair, propelling herself with her long legs. She then undid the buckles to Rudy's harness, allowing the straps to fall as Hank watched. Rudy stepped out and padded to the bowl, lapping up the water with rapidity. Sliding from her seat, Zoe kneeled next to Rudy who saw her after he had his fill. As water dripped from his black muzzle, a large pink tongue lolled out and licked his black-rimmed chops. "Good boy Rudy. You are so cute… Oh, yes you are." Zoe had both hands in his thick fur when Rudy tipped over in a heap, rolling onto his back and exposing his belly. Zoe's laughing attracted Amber from her meal and soon, both girls were on the floor, scratching and fawning over the off-duty officer. Adrian and Hank watched the girls with Rudy. "Some guys just have all the luck," Adrian said playfully. Amber stood then and without a word curled her index finger under the chin of Officer Blumenthal and began scratching his goatee. "Jealous, are we?"

"Very," Adrian answered, his eyes glued to Amber's ass as she tipped his head back effortlessly, staring down at him. A crooked smirk swept across her lips as he shifted uncomfortably in his seat; the crotch of his uniform suddenly forming. Adrian moved his legs so that they were wide enough to be on either side of Amber's, it took every bit of restraint for him not to pull her onto his lap. As a self-proclaimed womanizer, this was new territory for Officer Blumenthal. Adrian wasn't a bad guy, but he was used to the badge-bunnies and one-night stands. Yet, here was Amber... beautiful, confident and commanding, getting the very best of him...publicly. Hank and Zoe watched wide-eyed in complete and utter quietness, even Rudy had stopped his wiggling. Bending at the hip, Amber leaned in placing both of her hands on each side of Adrian's thighs, grasping the chair seat. Fascinated with their closeness, Adrian sucked in a sudden breath as Amber tilted her head forward as if talking to his lap. "Down, boy."

Zoe and Amber were already heading back to the desk when Adrian blinked himself back into reality. Hank slapped him on the shoulder. "I think I'm in love," Adrian sighed and sunk deeper in his seat, tugging at his uniform.

Rudy left behind his fellow officers and padded swiftly to his master's hospital bed, leaping effortlessly between Sam's strategically placed feet, both legs elevated on several pillows so that neither heel would touch the bed. Rudy stared intently at Sam as if he was willing him to wake. When that didn't work, Rudy bumped his nose into Sam's knee and again, slightly harder. Nothing. With a snort, Rudy laid back down, curling his body around himself. Though his eyes closed, his ears remained upright, moving slightly when detecting noise.

———

Morning came, and the night staff was completely exhausted as the day team trickled in one by one. Amber and Zoe waited for their fill-ins, all the while making Hank and Adrian promise to come back tonight. Zoe had explained to them that per Dr. Lake; Sam's vital signs, chest x-ray, and labs looked fine. Zoe explained she would be turning off the paralytic tonight and lifting the sedation for the first time. Both officers were hopeful by the news and promised repeatedly that they would be the ones on duty again tonight. Their morning fill-ins came in the form of Officer Paxton and Officer Ross, both rookies who were cute. Upon seeing Zoe and Amber, both lit up. "Wow…" Jealousy surged instantly through Adrian, giving each rookie and effective slap across the back of the head. "Don't even think about it." He warned. River and Paxton swallowed at one another nervously.

After the report, Zoe went to Officer Dalton's bedside. Rudy opened both eyes and lazily looked at her. The rookies had brought food for Rudy. In a small bowl, meat and chicken captivated Rudy but he looked again at Zoe instead. "I know, boy. It'll be okay… you'll see. Your master will come back. He has to." Rudy coasted out of the bed, not like he had before and stared into the bowl of his favorites. Zoe urged, kneeling beside him and finally, almost begrudging Rudy made work of the bowl. Zoe ran her fingers through his fur as the dog was lonely without his partner. It broke Zoe's heart seeing Rudy appear so lost; he leaned his heavy frame into her side as they sat together on the floor. The Ridgeback was warm, like a little heater and this brought comfort to Zoe who smiled, draping her arm around ot. "Lets' get you dressed for the day." Zoe took the harness and slipped it easily on, buckling each clasp and making sure all the straps were even. As if the harness were magic, Rudy transformed into the dutiful officer at the doorway. Zoe returned to Officer Dalton, and though she knew she shouldn't, she had to graze the backside of her hand down the ruined side of his face. "I will be back tonight, Sam... nothing will keep me away. Until then, rest easy."

Though Officer Paxton and Ross had been warned, they couldn't help but smile like two green boys as Zoe and Amber walked past, arm in arm, their work bags draped over their shoulders. In the locker room, the girls changed. "Zoe, I'm fantasizing about eating Captain Crunch." Zoe laughed as she pulled up her pair of baggy sweatpants.

The girls took the elevator to the top floor of the garage in the chilly autumn morning. "We survived another Halloween." Amber nodded and grinned. Without another word, they climbed into the Yukon and x5 and followed one another to Zoe's house. Though it had a double-car garage, Zoe parked in the driveway.

Amber, who had her own garage door opener pulled her smaller SUV inside, knowing they would take the GMC later. Once inside, Zoe deadbolted the door and put her bag down. Amber was already in the kitchen and had made two huge bowls. "Ah, you naughty girl!" Wiggling her finger at Zoe, both girls erupted with laughter as Amber playfully groped the cereal box, dancing around with it as if it were a long-lost lover. "My dream is to be ass-deep in Captain Crunch one day…" Amber took a huge spoonful and shoveled it into her mouth and Zoe gave her a side-eye glance.

"By the looks of things, your other dream is to be ass-deep in Officer Adrian Blumenthal."

It took a good few minutes for both girls to settle in after breaking out into a fit of hysterics, both red-faced with hot flashes on their cheeks.

Even though the spare room was set up as a guest bedroom, Amber and Zoe always slept together in the master suite. It wasn't unusual for Amber to stay, especially when their work schedules coincided so frequently. No matter how old they got, sleepovers never got old… it was a tradition for them, ever since they were best friends in high school. Zoe crawled under her down comforter and rolled onto her side to face Amber, already tucked in and waiting for Zoe. Nervously, Zoe looked to Amber. "What do you think he will be like, Officer Dalton, when he wakes up?"

"I'm not sure, but if he knows what good for him… he better be nice." Amber shook her fist out in front of her and Zoe smiled. "Especially after you took such good care of him."

Zoe was quiet and Amber knew why.

"Zoe, what are you going to do? Amber started rubbing Zoe's arm.

"I don't know…but let's have some fun."

———

On Zoe's next shift, Officer Dalton had woken up and it was at the most untimely moment.

Zoe was bending over to adjust her shoe when she heard a drowsy gruff voice call out, "nice ass." She spun around to see the giant of a man smiling.

"Thank you," she laughed, and when Dalton smiled back, his whole face lit up.

"I'm Sam," he said simply, extending a hand towards her, and when she took it, he kissed her knuckles gently. "You know how you see and hear things around you even though you're not conscious? I've been waiting to say something to you, Zoe. Thank you for everything. I think Rudy and I owe you more than pizza once I get off this bed."

"I think you do." Zoe could swear that her heart skipped a beat.